PENGUIN BOOKS

FIELDS *of* GOLD

Fiona McIntosh is an internationally bestselling author of novels for adults and children. She co-founded an award-winning travel magazine with her husband, which they ran for fifteen years while raising their twin sons before she became a full-time author. Fiona roams the world researching and drawing inspiration for her novels, and runs a series of highly respected fiction masterclasses. She calls South Australia home.

T0026366

PRAISE FOR FIONA McINTOSH'S BESTSELLERS

'A blockbuster of a book that you
won't want to put down.'
BRYCE COURTENAY

'McIntosh's narrative races across oceans and
dances through ballrooms.'
SUN HERALD

'This book is fast-paced, beautifully haunting and filled
with the excruciating pain of war.'
WEST AUSTRALIAN

'A fine read . . . The moral ambiguity McIntosh
builds into the novel gives it a depth that takes it beyond
a sweeping wartime romantic thriller.'
SUNDAY HERALD SUN

'McIntosh weaves a diverse cast together,
and you gain an appreciation for her depth of research.'
BOOKS+PUBLISHING

'A captivating saga of love, loss, and the
triumph of the human spirit . . . Fiona McIntosh
is an extraordinary storyteller.'
BOOK'D OUT

'A perfect blend of romance, action,
mystery and intrigue by one of our best
known and popular authors.'
NOOSA TODAY

'Sure to appeal to lovers of period romantic
dramas like *Downton Abbey*.'
WOMAN'S DAY

'Written with zest and a talent for
description that draws you into the world
of the novel and its characters.'
THE AGE

'Everything I want in a curl-up-on-the-sofa
read . . . an exquisite story that just bursts from
the pages and leaps into your heart.'
WRITE NOTE REVIEWS

'Meticulously researched and beautifully written,
The Perfumer's Secret solidifies McIntosh's place as
one of Australia's most loved storytellers.'
BOOKTOPIA

'Spellbinding . . . [Stella is] reminiscent of our
favourite literary heroines of the era, only feistier,
sexier and more independent.'
BETTER READING

'Beautiful storytelling, emotional depth and complex
characters captivated me from start to finish.'
WRITE NOTE REVIEWS

'A grand historical love story ideal for
Francophiles and romantics.'
GOODREADS

'A lively tale with a rich assortment of
ingredients . . . a well-crafted read.'
SYDNEY MORNING HERALD

BOOKS BY FIONA MCINTOSH
AVAILABLE FROM PENGUIN RANDOM HOUSE

Fields of Gold
The Lavender Keeper
The French Promise
The Tailor's Girl
Nightingale
The Last Dance
The Perfumer's Secret
The Chocolate Tin
The Tea Gardens
The Pearl Thief
The Diamond Hunter
The Champagne War
The Spy's Wife

In the DCI Jack Hawksworth series:
Bye Bye Baby
Beautiful Death
Mirror Man

FIONA McINTOSH

FIELDS *of* GOLD

PENGUIN BOOKS

PENGUIN BOOKS

UK | USA | Canada | Ireland | Australia
India | New Zealand | South Africa | China

Penguin Books is part of the Penguin Random House group of companies
whose addresses can be found at global.penguinrandomhouse.com.

Penguin
Random House
Australia

First published by Penguin Group (Australia), 2010
This edition published by Penguin Books, 2021

Copyright © Fiona McIntosh, 2010

The moral right of the author has been asserted.

All rights reserved. No part of this publication may be reproduced, published, performed in
public or communicated to the public in any form or by any means without prior written
permission from Penguin Random House Australia Pty Ltd or its authorised licensees.

Cover photography by enciktat/Shutterstock
Cover design by Louisa Maggio © Penguin Random House Australia Pty Ltd
Text design by Tony Palmer © Penguin Random House Australia Pty Ltd
Typeset in Sabon by Post Pre-press Group, Brisbane, Queensland

Printed and bound in Australia by Griffin Press, part of Ovato, an accredited
ISO AS/NZS 14001 Environmental Management Systems printer

 A catalogue record for this
book is available from the
NATIONAL LIBRARY OF AUSTRALIA National Library of Australia

ISBN 978 1 76104 235 5

penguin.com.au

MIX
Paper from
responsible sources
FSC
www.fsc.org FSC® C009448

This book is dedicated with love to my parents, Fred and Monnica Richards, and to the big family, most of us now scattered throughout the world but all of us bound through blood to James and May Patton and Jack and Elizabeth Richards.

PART ONE

PART ONE

I

Despite the biting wind of a Cornish late-autumn morning, Jack Bryant felt the grip of a much deeper chill. It had found its way beneath his heavy jacket, through his second-best shirt and was now crawling up his back as he was roughly shoved into the hut on the rise overlooking the small town of Newlyn.

The hut, once used by Cornish fishermen, was now abandoned. Jack remembered how as a child he'd watched the men work from this same high point. After sighting the approaching shoals of fish they'd bellow through the five-foot-long speaking trumpets. Then the race would be on for the boats to encircle their catch; up to three million pilchards if it were a large shoal. Jack found their work fascinating but then he had always loved the sea. He'd regularly wished he'd been born a fisherman's son – although that was an empty dream. Instead, he made his living off others trawling for tin, deep in the earth. But the tin mines were doomed; even though the Great War had kept its industry busy with supplying tungsten, peace time had delivered the deathblow.

Cornwall had begun bleeding men, the young in particular, as they left their homeland in search of a new life. From Land's End to the Lizard, the rugged coast had once swarmed with men, women and children, even the odd clergyman, who plundered ships in trouble for lucrative spoils. But now Cornwall would be remembered as a land of holes. Above ground reared the granite engine houses that protected the new machinery, which could lower a man to three thousand feet or haul the ore he'd mined back up to the surface with ease. Tall, elegant brick chimneystacks soared into the air, fingers of fire marking the spots where thousands of men worked below sea level, digging deep into the British earth that yielded a meagre livelihood while mine owners grew fat and wealthy on the profits.

Young Jack Bryant didn't suffer the same hardships as his fellow workers, however, for his family was considered wealthy by miners' standards. Which was why it was ludicrous that he found himself here, standing between two thugs, with a debt hanging over his head that could have been so easily avoided.

The sharp, lonely cry of the seagulls wheeling overhead pierced Jack's rambling thoughts and brought him back to the peril of his immediate situation. He blinked to banish the shards of sunlight that were still dancing before his eyes. He was pushed further inside the murky hut by his burly minders, their expressions as unyielding as the granite the hut was built from. And they had grips around his arms to match. But it wasn't their manhandling that frightened him, or their grim silence; he was accustomed to this when Walter Rally came looking for his money. No, the fear came after being pushed into Rally's big black car, when he realised that he wasn't being taken to the bookie's office in Truro, but to this remote, derelict spot high on the hill, just a mile or two from Market Jew Street in Penzance, where he'd been snatched from.

As Jack's vision cleared, a fresh spike of fear gripped him, prompted by the sight of the shivering, near-naked man strapped to an old wooden chair in the middle of the shed. The prisoner's head snapped up at the commotion of Jack's arrival and he immediately began babbling. Jack recognised him but made out none of the words. In truth, all he could hear was his own blood pounding through his ears and a voice that sounded very much like his father's baritone and filled with the same weary disappointment.

'Ah, hello, Jack,' it said, its owner emerging from the shadows.

'Walter, I —'

'Save it, lad,' the man replied. 'I have to tell you, I resent your arrogance. I don't think you give me enough respect.'

'Please, Wal—'

Rally held his hand up in the air. Sir Wally, everyone called him – but not to his face.

'I've got a better idea,' Rally said. 'You Cousin Jacks are a tough lot. I'm old enough to remember when your mob's idea of entertainment was to have stoning matches between rival villages. I once watched a gang from South Crofty mine kill someone's pet dog simply because they wanted to stain their flag with blood so the other village knew what they were in for.'

He walked slowly towards Jack and now he was close enough to touch him. Jack stared at the bookie's lustrous, grey hair, slicked neatly back off the high forehead. He could smell the pomade wafting from Rally's head, its scent mixing with cologne. His father would call Rally a dandy, smelling like a woman. The single dimple in Rally's cheek deepened when he smiled. But there was nothing friendly about Sir Wally when he reached up and lightly slapped Jack's face, his eyes narrowing and lips thinning.

'When verbal cautions don't earn respect, young Jack Bryant, I feel I must appeal to your more basic instincts. You tin boys understand brutality.'

Rally nodded at his men and they let Jack's arms go. He resisted the urge to rub them and the even stronger urge to turn and run. Though he was a born optimist, Jack knew he'd only get as far as the door before someone brought him down.

'I'll get the money for you, Walter,' he said, trying to sound calm.

'Oh, I know you will. I just don't want to have to wait much longer. You're part of a new breed, Jack. You don't understand responsibility – not like your father's generation. They worked hard, paid their rents, took care of their families. Whatever debts they had, they always paid.'

'Perhaps I can —'

Sir Wally smacked Jack's cheek again. Jack's blood began to boil, but he fought it back. 'I'm sorry,' he said, looking down.

'I know you are, boy. And don't get me wrong,' Rally began expansively. 'I like you. You remind me of myself when I was your age. But you're unreliable. You're too reckless with other people's money. I'm sure your father has counselled you on this, eh?'

Jack said nothing.

Walter Rally seemed to appreciate his silence. 'You're being careless with what is not yours. Is it true you've now got two girls up the duff? I hear old man Pearce is after your blood . . . or a wedding ring.' He chuckled to himself. 'Hope she's worth it, Jackie. She's certainly a pretty one. Can't say the same for Vivian Harris.'

Jack's mouth opened and shut again.

'Don't look so surprised. I make it my business to know everything I can about those who owe me money. Now, to be honest with you, I don't mind who you screw . . . but screwing me, *that* I mind.'

'Wally, I don't have it right now but I'll get —'

The bookie ignored him. 'In my experience nothing achieves quite the same clarity of mind and purpose as what I'm about to show you. In fact, I am quietly confident,' Sir Wally said, leaning close, 'that you will go home, take your mother's pearls, or your father's silver hip flask, or whatever you can lay your hands on that amounts to fourteen pounds in value, and you'll pawn it as fast as your two feet will carry you. I suspect we may never do business again. But you will have paid your debt to me and I will have taught you a valuable lesson in life. You've got one week, my lad.'

He turned to the near-naked man. 'Now, sitting here patiently is George. He works the tuck baskets down on the shore. That would account for the terrible smell of pilchards in here.' Wally wrinkled his nose. 'His wife, Gladys, hawks fish around the countryside. And in order for Gladys to have a new black beaver hat and bright-red cloak like her companions, George here likes to have a flutter on the horses . . .'

George began to weep.

'Our Georgie has got himself into a very bad way with debt. Now I'm going to show you what we do to people who don't pay me back.'

George began to gabble again, a mixture of pleading and despair, while at some silent signal from Rally, Jack suddenly found himself back in the grip of one of the minders whose breath smelled of stale beer and tobacco. A mean-looking meat cleaver materialised in the other minder's hands and this set off a fresh series of wails from the prisoner.

Jack wished he could close his eyes but he knew this whole piece of theatre was for his benefit. Sir Wally was hardly going to allow him to miss the show. So Jack Bryant fled in his mind as far away from Cornwall as his imagination would permit. If only he were aboard a ship instead, bound for the goldmines of Africa or the Americas, or the copper districts of Australia, that great continent on the other side of the world. He tried to imagine the sea breeze tousling his hair, money in his pocket and a new life beckoning.

Jack's attention snapped back at George's sudden, high-pitched shriek as the forefinger on his right hand was lopped off with a sickening dull thud of the cleaver. Everyone watched the finger fall uselessly to the damp earth floor. The bile rose in Jack's throat and will alone forced it back down. George had no such control. The bleeding man, ashen-faced and trembling, retched and hot liquid gushed as the butcher neatly sidestepped the mess.

'Ah, George,' Wally said softly, like a close friend. 'Just one more, eh?'

George began to shake his head, crying, begging them to spare him.

'One to teach you a lesson,' Wally explained, 'and another so Jack here fully understands what awaits him if he ignores me.' He looked up at Jack and laughed. 'You won't be winding any miners without fingers on your hands, Bryant. You'll be useless without them . . . not much more than a handsome cripple with just your father's money for company.' Wally turned to his companion. 'Let's get that other finger off – nice and neat at the last knuckle.' George screamed.

'You can go now, Jack. You know what you have to do. And don't call my bluff, eh, lad, or I might have to pay a visit to your mother and her lovely embroidery will stop once and for all.'

Jack burst out of the hut and ran down the hill, leaping over a stone wall and sucking in great gasps of air in a vain effort to calm his nausea. He lost the battle and at the bottom he gave up his morning oats into the bushes.

Although he still trembled, he didn't linger. Wiping his mouth with his sleeve, he pushed back his thick, dark hair and loped across the small boulder-strewn moor, desperate to hit the lowland farms that would lead him into the safety of Penzance town. Images of severed fingers, dying dogs and an angry mob wanting to stone him flashed through his mind as he ran.

Down the pathway, he noticed a great crowd of people gathered on the causeway – Taroveor Road – where the cattle were normally herded before reaching the slaughterhouse. He hated Bread Street, where the abattoir was located, skipping over the gutters that would run with the blood of the dead and dying to reach the Savoy Cinema where he had met many a young woman. In his haste and fear Jack had forgotten that the October harvest festival celebrations were now in full swing.

The fruits of land and sea, being of the earth and life in general, were celebrated now more than ever. People brimmed with happiness that world peace had finally been achieved, but their joy had a bitter aftertaste, because so many lives had been lost to the war.

Jack stood self-consciously at the edge of the crowd, trying to compose himself. His overwhelming dread began to dissipate simply from being among others. People dressed in their holiday best were laughing and talking excitedly. Reassured by the general merriment, Jack felt himself beginning to calm. He cleared his throat of the thick lump that had threatened to choke him earlier and looked around. No one had even noticed his presence.

As he finally entered the throng, grateful for the opportunity to lose himself in the crowd, he noticed that among the honest and hardworking were plenty of strangers – vagrants, as well as hawkers – taking advantage of the festivities. Pickpockets, gypsies, and even witches always seemed to do very well at these events.

He could see that a fortune-teller had already set up a booth alongside a quack doctor, who promised to cure anything from gout to warts. A pair of colourfully dressed stilt-dancers strode down Queen's Street, throwing toffee to the children running alongside them. Jack knew that within hours there would be pole-climbing, bull-baiting, equestrian displays, street walkers and sellers, as well as pigeon-shooting in the fields, and no doubt the usual exhibition of animal freaks – perhaps even a human freak or two.

As the day wore on and the liquor flowed, the conduct of the revellers would likely grow crude and among them would appear the traditional dark stranger, wearing a voluminous black cape, pointed hat, and a leering mask with huge snapping jaws. This curious figure would prance down the streets urged on by a man in woman's clothing, and followed by equally whimsically attired men playing enthusiastically on an assortment of musical instruments. It was an old fertility ritual and most onlookers loved the fearsome dancing figure, but Jack had hated him since childhood. To him, the figure spoke of ill-fate and bad omen rather than fecundity and blessings.

He decided on a drink in town to steady his jangled nerves and made his way to The Turk's Head in Chapel Street, reputedly named in 1233 after the Turks invaded Penzance. Jack had heard the story often enough from Landlord Johns. In its time it had also been a favourite drinking hole for smugglers because of its secret tunnel leading directly to the harbour.

He stepped over the threshold, bending his head as he pushed through the small black door, and felt relief at the comfort of the fuggy warmth of the coal fire and the smell of beer hanging in the air.

'You're early, Bryant,' the landlord commented, wiping a tankard. 'Pint of bitter?'

'Better make it half of mild,' Jack replied, sighing.

The landlord grinned. 'Sounds like you need to keep a clear head.'

'No, just tired of your watered ales and high prices.' Since the start of the Great War, the landlord had been forced by the government to dilute the beers he offered to be almost non-intoxicating.

'That'll be threepence,' the man said, drawing the beer. 'I'm surprised you of all people aren't taking your pleasures.'

Jack didn't take the bait; instead he reached for his mug and retreated towards a table in the corner. It was ironic that The Turk's Head was the quietest spot today. The usual patrons were out enjoying the celebrations. It suited him. He nodded at a pair of old men nearby and slid behind his table.

His mind turned to the pregnancy accusations against him. He couldn't say if they were real – the girls Rally referred to were far from shrinking violets, and as his old granny said often enough, it takes two hands to clap. These were willing partners, one of whom had been chasing Jack for many moons. And while Jack couldn't deny that he had taken a drunken tumble with Helen Pearce, he could reel off the names of several men who'd done the same in the past few weeks.

No, old man Pearce or Harris weren't the problem; Jack's gambling debt was. He swallowed almost half of the contents of his mug in his anger at himself. How could he have allowed this to happen? He thought of poor George's ruined hands, and pain aside, how the crippling would affect his ability to work. Times were tough enough. He hated Rally.

But most of all he hated his father and the relentless look of disappointment he reserved for his only son. Now Jack had given him another excuse to criticise, another reason for an argument, another evening for his mother to spend alone weeping in her room.

Jack slipped out of the pub, only to collide with the local grocery shop owner from St Just, the civil parish to which his village of Pendeen belonged.

'Hello, young Bryant,' the old man exclaimed.

Jack nodded. 'Mr Granger, my apologies.'

'In a hurry, are you?'

Jack sighed, thinking of the long trek ahead. 'Yes, eight miles to walk. Sorry.'

'No harm done, lad, I can give you a lift, if you'd like?'

'Thank you.'

'I could use the company.'

'Here, let me carry that for you,' Jack offered, reaching for the big box in the older man's arms.

'Oh, good lad. This is a birthday gift for Mrs Granger. She hasn't had anything new for so long. I thought I might spoil her this year.'

'A hat?' Jack inquired, happy to keep him talking.

'She's been pining over it.' Granger hurried ahead to his car.

He was one of the few dozen men who owned one of the new and much admired Morris Cowley motor-cars produced out of Oxford.

'Hop in,' Granger said. 'I guess you're used to travelling in one of these.'

Jack dutifully kept the hat box on his knees. 'Not as often as you'd think. My father believes I should earn my way.'

'Oh, your turn will come, young man. And you'll appreciate it all the more. Besides, who else is there for your father to leave it all to?'

Jack shrugged. He was convinced his father would rather donate his money to the church than leave it to his only son.

The ride back was pleasant enough. Lost in his bleak thoughts, Jack was only vaguely aware of the soft blur of the countryside and the drone of Granger's voice.

Familiar landmarks passed by. The inn at Newbridge was still open and he felt the drag on the car of the steep hill out of the village as they steered onto the North Road. Jack's cheeks were stung by the northerly wind as they crested the hill and he registered the small chapel just before the top but he only really became aware of his surroundings as they ran downhill past Carn Kenidjack and its unique sound called him back from his thoughts. Nicknamed the 'hooting carn' it gave a mournful sound as the wind whistled through the narrow gap in its rocks. They drove on towards the lighthouse. Jack could see low lights in the small row of cottages a hundred yards ahead, where the lighthouse men and their families lived and served not just as the Pendeen Watch but also for the Longships and Wolf Rock, off Land's End.

'. . . of Britain. Did you know that?'

'I'm sorry,' Jack said, suddenly realising the car had slowed.

'This is the most westerly town of Britain.'

'I didn't know that.'

'I love it up here by the lighthouse, don't you?'

'Yes. I think in a different life I would have chosen a life at sea.'

'Truly?'

Jack nodded. 'Sailor, fisherman . . . I would've enjoyed either very much.'

'Instead you plumb different depths,' Granger observed.

'Yes, but the boom is long behind us. It was a false industry while the war raged. It will collapse completely now.'

Granger nodded, inhaling the sharp salt air. 'You'll be all right, though, son. Your family is well protected.'

Once again Jack didn't choose to correct him. 'Thank you for the lift home, sir. I can walk from here.'

'Perhaps a pint at St Austell Arms?' Granger said with a genial wink.

'No, straight home, I think. I hope Mrs Granger enjoys her surprise.' He got out of the car to prevent any further protestation.

'Oh, now that we've lost both our sons, who else can I spoil?' Granger looked instantly embarrassed.

Jack was used to this awkwardness when people spoke of the young men who'd given their lives in the war. He didn't even wait for Granger to start spluttering an apology.

'She deserves it,' Jack said, lifting a hand in farewell. Granger mercifully crunched the car into gear and was off again.

Jack pulled his jacket around him against the wind that seemed determined to flay his skin from his bones. Autumn's snap cold – certainly up here on the cliff top – would be followed by the bitter winter months to come. He buried his head deeper into his jacket and prepared to face his father and a chill of a different kind.

2

In the darkness, the two-storey house on the hill was like a huge hunched shadow, brooding quietly, well away from the clump of other shadows that held the good folk of Pendeen. Jack loved the majesty of this house that his father had rebuilt for his young wife and son, extending the once-modest dwelling into a grand house within manicured gardens. Charles Bryant had chosen the granite that was quarried less than a mile away, had helped to carry it laboriously by the cartload and then directed how the massive blocks of greyish-brown stone – some as tall as two feet and six inches deep – were used to form the new façades of the additions. Windows with a score of panes at the front, eight or twelve in the side windows, looked out down the small incline to the village. The slate roof supported no less than four proud chimneys and Jack knew at least three would be gently puffing away this night, for his father hated his mother to be cold. Although at night the house loomed dark and sombre, by day the mortar separating the granite blocks took on an almost luminous quality beneath the sharp sunlight and even the slate lintels above the windows glinted beneath the sun's embrace.

Jack had never forgotten how his father had kissed his mother tenderly when he had carried her over the threshold for the first time. The dream of enclosing his family somewhere safe had left a deep impression on Jack. He hoped their family would never part with this house.

All was quiet as he entered, just the ticking of the clock on the hall mantelpiece a reminder that people were alive within its walls.

An older woman emerged from the parlour as Jack threw his door key onto the sideboard. Mrs Shand originally came from Penryn but these days she found it easier to live with them – there was no one waiting at home for her anyway – although Jack wished his mother had not agreed to this arrangement.

'Hello, Mrs Shand,' he said brightly, ignoring her ever-present look of disapproval. 'Any soup on?'

'Help yourself. I've laid a place for you in the parlour,' she said briskly, her mouth instantly returning to its pinched shape.

'Where's —'

'Mr Bryant senior is not here,' she said, seemingly untroubled by talking over him. 'Mrs Bryant is taking a late supper in the dining room with Mrs Hay, who is marking her first year mourning for her son.'

Jack frowned.

'He died in Ypres.'

Jack knew Ypres was where Mrs Shand's own son had given his life, when the Germans used poison gas for the first time against the Allies. She seemed to lay shame at the feet of every surviving son of Cornwall because they were alive and young Tommy Shand was dead.

'Well, I'll leave the ladies to it, Mrs Shand.'

'But what about your soup?'

'I suppose I'm not really that hungry,' he lied. 'I'm tired, and shall be off to bed now.'

'Goodnight.'

Climbing the stairs silently, wearily, pleased at least that he didn't have to face his father's dour countenance tonight, Jack hesitated on the landing outside his parents' room. He wondered why his father hadn't moved fully into the spare room next door, in keeping with the practices of other wealthy gentlemen. The spare room was called 'Father's room' all the same and its furnishings clung firmly to all things elaborate, dark and Victorian.

Taking a breath, Jack stepped quietly over the threshold of what he considered his mother's room, taking care to miss the floorboard that invariably gave a loud groan. He entered a feminine sanctuary of chintz, prettiness and paleness. Though a polar opposite to Charles Bryant's taste, it didn't seem to trouble him. He treated his wife as gently as one would a tiny bird.

It reassured Jack, during his moments of rage or despair, to know that his parents deeply loved one another and that he would always be a product of that love. Charles gave Elizabeth Bryant whatever she desired, but she was neither spoiled nor demanding. What she most wanted, Jack realised, was an entirely happy home, and that was something Charles couldn't give her – because Jack lived in it.

Jack sighed, hating himself for being such a curse on their lives. Tiptoeing across the beautifully furnished Edwardian chamber, he arrived at his mother's dressing table, lit by a magnificent Tiffany lamp – a recent purchase that attested to Elizabeth's fashionable taste. While some of the much grander houses had enjoyed electricity for a couple of years, the Bryant home was still one of the earliest in the region to be electrified and he couldn't blame her for wanting to take advantage of this new luxury.

Jack knew exactly what to look for. Not pearls, as Rally had suggested, but the beautiful diamond watch his father had presented to Elizabeth before Jack was born. It was a little ostentatious for her taste, he'd heard her remark, but Jack had always admired the platinum casing studded with tiny blazing diamonds. He was fascinated by the notion that something so exquisite was crafted from gems that had once been buried beneath the earth. It appealed to him as a seeker of the treasures that existed far below the world's surface.

Easing open the lid of the engraved silver jewel box, Jack

carefully picked through the pieces until he found the watch. His mother wouldn't miss it for weeks – possibly months – he was sure, for she so rarely wore it, and by then he had every intention of buying back the watch and returning it to its owner, who would be none the wiser for its theft.

He stared at the diamonds winking in the low light and the tiny round face fashioned from a blue shell that looked, in this light, as black as his heart felt. This was it, he decided as he twisted the thread-like leather coil of the wristband around his long fingers; this was the last time he would let them down. From here on, he would work hard and live up to his father's ideals.

Consumed by his promise, Jack did not hear someone ascending the stairs, and if not for the telltale creak, he might have been caught red-handed. Fright gripped him when he heard a foot on the noisy floorboard. He had only a moment to slip the exquisite watch into his pocket and school his features into innocence.

'Jack, dear?' Elizabeth Bryant said.

'Hello, Mother. You look lovely as always,' he said calmly, moving over to kiss her cheek and enjoying the gentle waft of her perfume.

Her hazel eyes twinkled in the soft light. 'Thank you, darling. It's very easy to understand why the girls fall for you, my boy,' she said, cupping his face gently as she accepted his kiss.

'Mrs Hay gone?' he asked.

'Powdering her nose. I thought I heard you come in. You're so much earlier than I expected. Anyway —'

Before she could ask, he jumped in. 'You haven't seen my leather gloves anywhere, have you?' he asked, glancing around. 'I've no idea where I put them but I have no intention of another day like today – my fingers froze!'

She gave a soft laugh, the one he always loved to provoke. 'What on earth made you look in here?'

He grinned. 'Desperation, I think,' he said, more honestly than she could imagine. 'I put a vase of flowers in here yesterday, don't you remember?' he added. Even he could believe the lie. He glanced at the bowl of lilies he had actually opened the door for Mrs Shand to carry in.

'Oh, they're not here, darling, I'm afraid. But the flowers are heavenly, thank you. Jack, you look tired. And that mop of yours could use a good trim – you have the Bryant curse of lustrous hair.'

'But you've always said that's what makes us so handsome.'

'That's true. But I have to criticise now and then or you may think yourself too perfect.'

He grinned. 'And how has your day been?' he asked, noticing some new grey in her hair, which was elegantly swept up behind her head. She'd resisted cutting her hair into a fashionable, finger-waved short bob and he was glad of her restraint. He liked how she wore it, even though it revealed what she worked hard to keep secret – that she was now approaching sixty. She'd had many miscarriages before giving birth to John 'Jack' Bryant in her thirty-seventh year. It was old to be a first-time mother but she had embraced her role with tireless energy.

'Well, your father's gone to Truro and will probably stay overnight now, I think,' she said, looking out into the darkness.

'Oh? What's happening over there?'

'The usual,' she said in a resigned tone, 'business.'

Jack nodded. He knew his father told her little about his work. 'All's well, though?'

'Oh, yes,' she said distractedly, primping her hair in the mirror. Her figure remained enviably trim, so her clothes hung perfectly off her frame. 'Business has never been better.'

Jack looked surprised. 'I'd have thought being a supplier to the mines would have its problems these days.'

'Quite the contrary. He's recently signed a new contract to

supply mines overseas. It's all go in places like India and Africa, can you believe?' She shrugged. 'He has the experience and knowledge, I suppose.'

'No doubt. But still he makes me work like an ordinary labourer,' Jack grumbled.

'Jack, don't, darling. We've been over this so many times. You forget your father had his fair share of hardship when he was your age. He was hammering rock!'

'Suggesting my job is meaningless, I suppose,' he replied.

'That's not what I meant. You've had the benefit of a top edu-cation at the School of Mines, and now you have a very responsible position and you're barely twenty.'

'It still hasn't impressed him. And let's be honest here, I only have the job so young because so many of our men are dead.'

'That may be. But you hold those miners' lives in your hands. They are your responsibility. Don't you forget that!'

Her love and support were unstinting. He was sure she was the key reason his father was able to appear so strong, so solid.

'Mother, there's no future in the mines. Malayan and Bolivian tin is cheap. They pay their miners in silver but they sell their tin for gold. The industry in Cornwall is as dead as the miners littering the fields of France and —'

'Stop!'

'Why? Does talking about the war embarrass you as much as it does Father?'

There it was, the real reason for the anger bubbling up within him. Once again he'd directed it at the person who least deserved his rage.

'Jack,' she said, sounding hurt. 'You volunteered like all our young men. They insisted you remain in Cornwall and keep the mines working.'

'Not everyone sees it that way, especially my own father.'

'He understands. It wasn't up to you. Crofty's tungsten was needed badly for munitions.'

'So how do you explain the white feathers I find left in my work gear so regularly?'

'Oh, Jack.'

He shook his head as though it no longer mattered. 'How much longer do I have to do this?'

'He just wants you to appreciate all that we have; he doesn't want you to take it for granted, or forget your roots. But, Jack, you throw it back in his face. You seem to have a dark streak in you that turns away from all that he's trying to teach you, give you . . .'

'Father only got wealthy because the mining magnates wanted Grandpa's land. That's my inheritance too, Mother. Grandpa said so. I was there . . . I heard him say it!'

'You're right. Grandpa's land took your father out of the mines, for which I'll be forever grateful. But don't forget he's made that money work for us tenfold. Your father is a shrewd business-man and as long as you keep behaving so recklessly, he won't entrust the family's wealth to you.'

'So it's punishment?'

'No, darling. It's education, it's growing up, it's acting respon-sibly. He believes the mines will keep you honestly occupied. I suppose the mines are as unyielding as he can be.'

He said nothing, looked away angrily.

'Jack, I have to return to my guest now. I just wanted to see you before you went to bed. Don't be angry, and don't make me stretch to kiss you. You're far too tall these days.'

He kissed her again gently and she touched his cheek affectionately.

'I wouldn't let your father kiss me with a stubbly chin like that. Now, promise me you'll do as he wishes. You'll be surprised how things might turn out.'

Jack already hated himself enough, with the diamond watch burning a hole in his pocket. He watched his mother glide from the room, knowing he was blessed to have her on side, and yet resenting his situation even more fiercely.

––––––––––

Jack left the house at dawn, still shrugging himself into his thick working jacket in his eagerness to be gone. He had slept fitfully and was only too pleased to get up and head to work. His woollen trousers kept out most of the cold but he could feel winter's threat in the air. He buttoned up his jacket over his favourite flannel shirt and wished once again that he had waited long enough for a couple of breakfast pasties to help warm his hands, if not his belly.

The delicious aroma of the baking pasties followed him from the house. His belly rumbled but he would go hungry today. He couldn't face Mrs Shand's look of disapproval and he'd have to take his chances with the knockers, the tiny mischievous spirits that miners all over Britain believed inhabited the mines. The Cornish were of the opinion they were the spirits of dead miners, who knocked on the walls of the shafts to warn of impending danger. The miners always left behind the last tiny knuckle of their pasties in the mines for the knockers.

He buried his chin into his scarf, feeling the rasp of his stubbly beard catching on its wool, and rounded the hill to walk down into the town, the shapes of the small miners' houses brightening around him. He turned left onto the main street and trudged past the Austell Arms and on towards Geevor, where a steady stream of men were now heading to take over the next shift. Jack ignored everyone, briskly turning down the smaller pathway that would lead him into the Levant mine. Now the blast of the Atlantic Ocean hit him full in the face. The sea was just a dark smudge still but he could taste the salt in the air and across the fields could make out the Levant chimneystacks.

Levant was privately owned and not profitable – not even during the war years. It was still very much a mine of the previous century, with its crooked shafts and poorly equipped dressing floors. His father had told him the mine was to be closed down – that was certainly the expectation as soon as the war ended – but arsenic, a by-product of tin, was needed by other mines and Levant could supply it and so it limped on.

The average wage was pitiful and considering the ten-hour days that turned into fourteen, with the miles walked to and from work, the sickness, the terrible working conditions, Jack wondered how most of the miners survived. His job as an engineer on the surface was much better paid and a walk in the park compared to those men he would lower into the shaft.

The St Just region had narrower lodes than some of Cornwall's other mining areas. This meant the miners worked alone, each beating a metal chisel with a heavy hammer until one hand was tired and then he would swap hands. Elsewhere black powder could be ignited to blast the rock face. The men often worked in the dark. The cramped nature of tin mines and their lack of ventilation meant that even the tallow candle fingers Jack's family supplied to the company weren't useful; only able to burn turned on their sides in the smoky, dusty atmosphere. Most of the miners found it easier to snuff their light and give themselves a fraction more oxygen instead. The six fingers of candles per week they were given – strung around their necks, usually – were theirs to keep, and most took them home for the family.

Jack was grateful for his family's good fortune, which afforded him the opportunity to escape the daily trudge deep below the surface, never knowing whether he'd make it back out at the end of a shift. It wasn't hard to despise himself for his whinging, especially as he enjoyed all the benefits of electricity whenever he wanted to turn on a light or heat some water.

'Hey, Jack,' called a familiar voice.

He turned to see stocky Billy Jenner hurrying to catch up. Billy and Jack, like their fathers before them, had been childhood friends.

'Morning, Billy.'

'I'd heard they'd asked for you at South Crofty,' Billy said, falling into step with Jack's long-legged stride.

Jack smirked. 'My fame stretches before me. I'll stay at Levant for now. Shorter walk.'

'Well, watch your back. Dennis Pearce is after you. His Helen is three months gone, they're saying.'

'Well, whatever "they" say, it wasn't me.'

Billy gave him a look.

'Yes, all right, I was with her – but just once, I swear. She's a tart and you know it.'

'Well, I'd be happy to have a slice of that tart!'

'Even short men have a chance with Helen Pearce.'

Billy punched Jack's arm. 'Who said you're the answer to every woman's dream, Bryant?'

Jack laughed and within moments the young men began to play wrestle. It was exactly what Jack needed to lighten the tension of the previous day. Finally, once Billy submitted, Jack hauled the smaller man to his feet. Their breath steamed in the frigid air.

'Look at the state of me. Do you always have to win?' Billy complained.

'I'm surprised you even ask. Now, will you look at that, Billy? You can't tell where the sea meets the sky. Doesn't it make you want to just sail off into the distance and see what's out there?'

Billy looked out beyond the cliff and shrugged. 'I suppose so.'

Jack sighed. 'I didn't get Helen Pearce pregnant. I took her to see a film one night and I haven't seen her since. I think it's wishful thinking on her part.' He winked at his friend. 'She got me in a weak moment . . .'

'Cocky sod. Well, be warned. Pearce is probably going to be the other engineer on today.'

'I'm not worried about Pearce, and you should be more concerned with the future.'

'Don't start that again, Jack. I'm not going abroad to seek some fortune you think is waiting out there for me.'

'The future for us is in Australia or Asia.'

'Your future's already secured.'

'Don't be so sure.'

'Oh, right. I'll try to remember that when I next see you riding in that motor-car, or —'

'Billy, I'm here, aren't I? I'm in my working clothes, just like you, and I'm walking the mile or more to and from my shift. I earn an honest wage. I'm tired of apologising for my family!'

'All right. Calm down. I didn't mean anything by it. The truth is I just don't want to leave Cornwall. It's my home.'

'Fair enough,' Jack said, bored of himself and his ever-simmering fury. 'Come on, let's not be late. You know how Captain Walter is on a Monday.'

Following a path that was perilously close to the cliff edge, Jack lifted a hand in farewell as Billy began the trek down stone steps to the entrance of the mine, cut into the vertical cliff face, one hundred and fifty feet from the surface where Jack stood. He knew Billy was working deep today, well below the seabed in the richer veins that spread horizontally in myriad tunnels. And he would be lowering Billy and his fellow workers into those hot, airless, dimly lit seams for their eight-hour shift.

Once again Jack told himself to heed his mother's warning. He was one of the lucky ones. And if he put his head down, worked steadily and earned his father's trust, everything could be different by next year. He was determined that today would be the day that changed his life.

3

October 1919

Ned Sinclair's senses were in overdrive. His eyes felt as though they were out on stalks, twisting and turning to take in all the sights at once. His nose twitched at the exotic smells, while his hearing homed in on the lowing oxen and the rumble of trams alongside the car as their driver negotiated the teeming streets of Rangoon.

They were recently arrived off the ship and were making their way to The Strand Hotel, which overlooked the Irrawaddy River. Ned's father, having survived the war, had left their home in North Berwick, Scotland, soon after for the far east. He had now been in Burma almost a year and Ned was longing to see his father again. He had reached many major milestones of youth without his father's support or guidance. It was the same for many lads, of course. Ned's mother, Lorna, had been deeply distressed when her husband had chosen to spend more time away from his family on his return, but she had hidden her feelings well. She told Ned that William was working to give their family a chance at a bright future after all the darkness of the war.

Ned thought his mother was a saint, frankly, as well as being beautiful in a pale, fragile way. He was aware that they looked rather alike – he shared her slender build, neat, symmetrical features and large blue eyes. The golden, floppy hair of his childhood had darkened to the colour of the damp sandcastles he used to build during summer on the beach at Milsey Bay, where his father hailed from. He'd been an only child then; his sister, Arabella, had come along just nine years ago. But they'd left Scotland before her birth, returning briefly for a year before war was declared, and his father had left his family with old friends of his wife's in northern England. Lorna was from York originally and had fallen for the dashing Scot when he'd passed through the city on a temporary teaching position. For the past eleven months, his mother had held a private teaching post in St Albans. With the family so often on the move, and Ned essentially home schooled, all traces of his early Scottish brogue had disappeared and Bella, too, had a clear English accent. Ned felt proud of his Scottish heritage and was all too aware he had lost his father's lovely manner of speaking.

His sister was squirming next to him at this moment.

'Stop, Bella. I can't give you any more room,' he scolded.

His mother gave him a tired look. The journey from Edinburgh via Liverpool to Rangoon aboard the Bibby vessel, *Gloucestershire*, had felt neverending. And right now, even talking seemed to sap one's energy. Ned could smell the leather of the car seats, normally a pleasant aroma but today it mingled with the sour tang of perspiration, cloyingly sweet flowers and the earthy smell of oxen. The air was heavy with moisture and he felt beads of sweat running down his hairline. His back was damp and pressed against the car seat, and his shirt would be drenched. He scratched at the tightness of his collar.

'You're twice her age, Ned; a man now,' his mother said gently. 'Your father's going to be so proud that you're a fully qualified electrician.'

'I'm not sure it's going to do me much good out here,' he commented, without bitterness.

'I know that, darling, but I'm so pleased you agreed to come and keep our family together. We're so nearly there now. Here, give me that hat box, and that should give you a bit more space.'

He duly handed over the box with its precious cargo – his mother's newest bonnet, which she would need to wear daily to protect her milky, flawless complexion from the scorching sun. He hoped she would cope in the heat. She should have bought the topi helmet at Port Said, as one of the other women on board had advised. But their fares had absorbed almost all their savings, and his mother had resisted any temptation when they went ashore to part with the few pounds she had left. After Port Said, the temperature had increased and not even a sea breeze seemed capable of penetrating their modest cabin.

The man who had met them in their father's stead was called Fraser, a tall, gangly Scot; another opportunist, who hoped to make his fortune from rubies found in the famous tract north of Mandalay.

'How long have you known my father, Mr Fraser?' Ned asked, aiming to impress his mother with his conversation, for he could see she was too exhausted to do the polite thing herself.

Fraser grinned, pushed back his reddish hair and wiped his flushed forehead again with his already damp handkerchief. 'We first met in North Africa, where we both did our training. While I'm from Glasgow and he's an Edinburgh boy, we're both sons of Scotland. We watched each other's backs as best we could over the next couple of years and vowed if we didn't come home in a wooden box, we'd seek our fortunes together out here.'

'Are you married, Mr Fraser?' Lorna Sinclair asked, dabbing a dainty embroidered square of linen to her glistening top lip.

'No, Mrs Sinclair. I never did meet the right lassie before the war, but as it happens I have met a bonny girl who visited with her family earlier this year. I've decided to go home and ask her to marry me. Mary's a beauty and heaven knows why but she found something to love in me.' He grinned lopsidedly.

'And how will she feel about returning to the colonies?'

Fraser shrugged. 'I don't think she'll mind if it's not for too long. Mary's keen to start a family, though I doubt she'll want to do so in Rangoon or Mandalay. However, since I was granted this small lease by Burma royalty . . .'

She smiled in understanding but Ned knew his mother too well. He suspected she quietly blamed Fraser's grand ideas for her husband's absence. Lorna Sinclair would not admit it but Ned knew she had been hurt and baffled by her husband's actions in coming to Burma. Now she had an explanation, a focus for that frustration, not that she would air a grievance.

'And how goes my father's mining?' Ned inquired, flicking back the thatch of hair that flopped in his eyes.

'We're approaching the wet season, which is another reason why I've decided to head home.' He laughed at Ned's expression. 'It will get much hotter, and far more humid than this, I'm afraid. And the rains can be deadly. But you'll get used to it.' He sighed. 'I've had some success, I'll admit, and your father's on to a good pit at last, I reckon. His enthusiasm never wanes, Ned. His delay is because he wants to bring his family home a prize.'

'We'll just be glad to see him, Mr Fraser,' Lorna commented. 'To my knowledge my husband was trained to be a teacher, not a prospector or trader.'

'Are we nearly there?' Arabella pleaded, her pale, lightly freckled complexion flushed red from the heat. Her undisguised exasperation reflected the emotion everyone else in the car felt but was trying to hide.

'Nearly, Bella darling,' her mother replied absently, staring out at the wide brown river that snaked alongside them.

'Bill's sparing no expense, Mrs Sinclair. I think you and the children will find The Strand more than agreeable.'

She turned and regarded him coolly. 'I'm sure we will, Mr

Fraser, and thank you again for being good enough to meet us on William's behalf.'

Ned couldn't wait for this journey to end.

The Strand was Rangoon's oldest hotel, having opened at the turn of the new century. It had been built by the Sarkie brothers, who had also opened other famous hotels in Asia including Raffles in Singapore.

Ned smiled at the tall, magnificently attired man in a turban who greeted them at the grand entrance. Even if his mother had asked him to walk another twenty steps further, Ned wasn't sure whether he could have done so. It was nearing midday and the heat was searing. But the lobby yawned dark and inviting, and ceiling fans mercifully stirred the air.

'Ned, hurry Bella along, will you?' his mother urged, and by the time he'd reached for his sister's small, thin hand, the family had been swallowed up into the cool, resplendent surrounds of the building.

Ned took in the teak parquet floors, lofty ceilings and painted wall panels of the reception area. Floral arrangements scented the air and inside people went about their business quietly and efficiently. Ned held back, keeping Bella occupied as his mother, aided by Fraser, organised for their luggage to be sent to their large shared suite. Ned had no idea how long they would be staying, either at the hotel or even in Burma, but he had been so glad to escape a Scottish winter. Yet what he wouldn't have given at this moment to feel the bite of that familiar cold on his overheated skin.

Their friends had done everything to dissuade Ned's mother from making this voyage. Ned recalled the horror tales, from children being impaled and cooked over open coals to snakes stealing babies from sleeping cots. Ned had poured scorn on these later, suggesting that her friends were simply jealous of his adventuring father and the romance of what he proposed for their future.

He was relieved that his mother agreed, assuring her children that William would not put his family in any danger. Once again he deeply wished his father had been there to greet them at the docks – if only for his mother's peace of mind.

He amused Bella by allowing her to stand on his well-scuffed boots. He noticed her leather sandals weren't in much better shape. Her lightweight gingham smocked dress surely made her the coolest of them all. The soft green and white checked fabric ballooned as he walked her around the parquet floors, hushing her giggles. He was still getting used to her short, bobbed haircut. He missed her long, golden ringlets, but Lorna had insisted it would be a more practical style for the tropics.

Ned heard a soft commotion of hushed voices and turned to see his mother fainting in the arms of Mr Fraser, and hotel staff running from everywhere to help.

A European doctor had insisted on offering his services to Lorna Sinclair, who was now semi-conscious in the bedroom, being looked after by Dr Fritz and his wife.

Arabella had been hurried down to the kitchens to help pick out a plate of cakes for afternoon tea. After Ned assured Bella that their mother had simply fainted from the heat, she had happily gone off with the beautiful dark-eyed serving girl who was to escort her.

But the taut faces around him had told Ned all was not well. It was up to the general manager of the hotel to explain.

'Master Sinclair, forgive me for being the bearer of such dreadful news, but your father has been involved in an accident.' The man looked down and cleared his throat. 'I'm afraid, sir, that he is dead.'

The only aspect of that chilling moment Ned recalled was the faint scent of orchids wafting from a massive vase nearby, and he would ever after associate that scent with death.

'Dead?' he echoed, unable to comprehend the word.

The man nodded solemnly. 'Our most sincere condolences.'

Ned realised he must steel himself to hear more, now that his sister was distracted and his mother was being cared for. Doors were closed on the chamber, one of the trio of rooms that formed their suite, leaving him with a handful of sombre-looking men, one of them an ashen-faced Fraser.

The manager straightened, took a breath and adopted a business-like demeanour. 'Mr Sinclair, this is Mr Paul Hannigan, chief of police.'

'You're sure of this information?' Ned demanded, his eyes searching their hollow expressions. It was shocking to be called Mr Sinclair. That was his father's title.

Hannigan nodded. 'It was a landslide of sorts, son. We believe your father slipped down an incline, struck his head and landed face-down and unconscious in a shallow pool in the pit. It appears that he drowned. He was found by some local Burmese miners. The commissioner asked me to convey to you his deep regret at this news.'

Despite the chaos of his mind, Ned's body felt numbed to the point of stillness. He suddenly couldn't even move his lips. His mother and Bella were helpless – they needed his father now more than ever before. He felt a fury at his father rising within him for leaving them all alone and penniless so far from home.

Hannigan took his silence as permission to continue. 'His body will be brought to Rangoon as soon as possible.' He turned to Fraser. 'Sir, as a family friend, I understand you've been asked to postpone your travel plans until the corpse arrives. Is that correct?'

Ned flinched at the word 'corpse'.

'Yes, of course. I'll stay with Mrs Sinclair and the children until Bill . . . and, er, help with arrangements.'

The doctor emerged from Lorna's room and everyone's gaze was drawn to his grave countenance. Ned had liked the brisk little man when he'd first offered his help in the hotel lobby and especially liked how Fritz had talked with him directly, rather than to the older people around him.

'She's quiet now, Edward. I'm afraid I've had to sedate her quite heavily as I fear for her state of mind during these first few hours. The fatigue, the heat and the lack of air, on top of this terrible, terrible news, will conspire to undo her. We need her to be stronger before she faces reality. I hope you understand.'

'I do,' Ned said, automatically. What else could he say? 'Thank you, Doctor.'

'My wife is more than happy to stay with her for the rest of the day. And I will not be far away. I'll check on her regularly.' He pushed his glasses further up his aquiline nose. 'I'm really very sorry, son, about your father. Do you need anything?'

Ned swallowed. He was almost undone by the sympathy in the doctor's kind eyes. 'Doctor Fritz, you've been very good to us,' he began, hearing the tremor in his voice but determined to live up to what was expected of him.

'Please, don't mention it.' Fritz squeezed his shoulder. Ned wished he hadn't. The gentle touch prompted a rush of emotion and he needed to stay composed and strong. 'What about next of kin? Has anyone —'

'There is no one,' Ned interrupted.

Everyone shifted awkwardly. The manager scratched his beard thoughtfully and Fraser began to pace.

'No one?' Fraser repeated, incredulous. 'Your parents have no parents still living, no brothers or sisters?'

Ned shook his head. 'They were both only children and all our grandparents are dead.'

The four men around Ned looked lost for words.

'No need to worry about that now, Mr Sinclair,' Hannigan said, recovering first. 'We must ensure we take care of your good mother and offer all the help we can. I will contact the club the expatriates frequent immediately.'

'Thank you,' Ned said. 'Um, may I see my mother, Dr Fritz?'

'Of course. She's sleeping, but you should,' he said, ushering Ned towards the door.

Ned's movement prompted the men to finally shift from their somewhat stunned positions, each promising to be back later in the day, including the doctor.

'Mr Fraser,' Ned called as the quartet retreated from the suite. 'May I have a word, please?'

'Of course,' Fraser replied, although he looked deeply uncomfortable. 'Ned, I don't know what to say. Your father survived the killing fields of Europe but . . .'

'There is nothing to say,' Ned offered, surprised by his own composure. 'I'm struggling to make it feel real in my mind too. I keep thinking this is all some terrible mistake and that my father's about to breeze in through that door and sweep my mother into his arms. We've been looking forward to this moment of arrival for so long . . .' Ned cleared his throat and took a steadying breath. He had to remain strong for his mother and Bella. 'Mr Fraser, I need to have a private word with you about money.'

Fraser took a step back. 'Ned, I'm sorry but I don't have any more to give you.'

He'd expected this. 'I'm not asking for a loan, Mr Fraser. I'm wondering how much you know about my father's financial situation out here?' He frowned. 'Wait, what do you mean, you don't have any more to give us?'

Fraser ran a hand through his hair, clearly embarrassed. 'I lent your father all the savings I had. You see, his first pit was a bit of a disaster, but he was determined to make a go of it – especially after I got my first taste of success. Until I return to England and reap some profits for the past year, I have no more money myself.'

'You mean my father has made nothing?' Ned asked, panic spreading through him.

'He made debt. That's about all. But, Ned, I don't want that money back. Not now. He always thought success was just around the corner and in truth I agreed with him. No one could foresee this.' Fraser sighed. 'He never got his chance.'

Ned ripped off his jacket and flung it at a chair. He pulled at his collar and tie, feeling short of breath. 'My mother has nothing, Mr Fraser. My father used all our savings. We have – had,' he corrected quickly, 'nothing but my father's prospects.'

Fraser looked as helpless as Ned suddenly felt. 'Perhaps back in England you can —'

Ned ground his jaw with anxiety. 'There is no one back in England for us. There is nothing waiting for us. The war has beggared everyone. This was our one chance to make a new life.'

'Ned, I'm so sorry. Why don't you go and see your mother and I'll send your sister back up? I think you need some time.' He began withdrawing. 'We'll talk again shortly.'

Ned nodded. None of this was Fraser's fault, although Ned wanted to blame him, and knew his mother would.

'I'll show myself out,' Fraser murmured, and his relief to be leaving was palpable.

4

Three days passed. People came and went in a blur of soft placations and apologies but Ned barely registered them. He was focused on containing his own hurt and keeping Bella occupied, yet despite his best efforts she was fretting over her mother's sudden silence, her father's continuing absence and the unhappiness surrounding what was meant to be a joyous family reunion.

The inexorable heat continued to stifle rational thinking, and leeched Ned's resolve to stay strong.

He looked at his sister and felt ashamed at how ragged she suddenly appeared. Even though money was limited, his mother always turned them out well with neat, clean clothes in good repair. But the frock Lorna had painstakingly smocked for Bella's reunion with her father was torn now, and grubby. In fact, Bella definitely needed a wash; whatever she'd been eating in the kitchens with her minder was all over her.

'Let's get a bath drawn for you, Bell,' he had said hours earlier, feigning brightness.

'Mummy normally does it. When's she going to wake up, Ned?'

He hadn't been able to answer her question, but he had persuaded her to play in the grand bath and Mrs Fritz had kindly offered to sit with her and was even brave enough to wash the young girl's hair. Bella had protested immediately, but Mrs Fritz had a wonderfully soothing manner.

Lorna Sinclair seemed unaware of the kindness being shown to her family, from the general manager's magnanimous offer for the trio to remain in the hotel gratis until arrangements could be made for their future, to the doctor's free service, or the meals that quietly arrived in her room and were removed untouched. Ned imagined William Sinclair's body would arrive in Rangoon shortly. Yet nothing had been organised because his mother hadn't spoken a word to anyone since she'd regained consciousness. Fritz had used the term 'hysteria' to describe her catatonic state but all Ned could see in his mother was silent grief – a deep, desperate, dangerous grief.

He tried so hard to talk her round and make her understand that her family needed her, to assure her that they could get through this. He kept up a steady stream of encouragement and suggestions, from him taking over the mining of his father's pit in the north, to cutting their losses and selling whatever they could from their few newly delivered trunks of possessions to earn their passage home. But nothing moved Lorna; she didn't even seem to notice when Ned took her hand or kissed her cheek. For almost six years of Ned's life his father had been absent, and though he wanted to view William in heroic terms – a warrior through the war, a pioneer and adventurer beyond it – it was Lorna who had been his rock. She had bolstered his education outside of school hours, pushing him hard, and he knew that was probably why he was the youngest qualified electrician in Britain.

Lorna looked even more petite than usual in the huge hotel bed. Ned craved the comfort of her touch, the reassurance of her voice, but privately berated himself for those feelings. After all, he was almost eighteen now – he was a man. More importantly, he knew Bella needed her mother. The fact that their mother didn't even turn at the sounds of their voices or react to their affection frightened them both. She seemed utterly lost.

Ned didn't know what to say to the hotelier and the other kind people around them when their generosity was exhausted. And it would be. He had empty pockets and his mother's few pounds would not stretch far. He *had* to find some way to coax Lorna out of this stupor – perhaps shock tactics might work? He planned to get firmer with her in the morning, even if he had to shake some sense into her.

They were sharing interconnecting rooms. That night he lowered himself carefully onto the double bed, exhausted. Arabella was asleep in a selfish sprawl of childish limbs and he breathed a sigh of relief that they'd made it through another day.

Tomorrow would definitely be different, Ned decided as he drifted into sleep. He was the head of the family now, and it was up to him to take charge.

Ned awoke suddenly, startled by a sharp noise. The heat had not abated and his side of the bed was damp, the bottom sheet imprinted with his shape as if he had not moved since his head touched the pillow. But where was Bella? Her absence was worrying and he slipped out of bed and headed for his mother's chamber.

The fan was off and the hot night air was so still it felt as if a heavy blanket were draped around his shoulders. Scotland's most bitter cold didn't contrive to steal one's sanity, but if he spent long enough in this wet, sapping heat, Ned felt he could spin into a sort of angry madness.

The door to his mother's bedroom was ajar and inside he found Bella, curled beneath a loose sheet, fast asleep. Her cheeks were flushed, her lips were full and pink and she looked like an angel, but Ned's relief was dashed instantly by the realisation that his mother was not beside her. When he reluctantly checked the closet, she wasn't there either.

It was baffling. His mother's small watch on the teak side table told him it was just before midnight. He'd been asleep for barely half an hour. How could she have slipped away? The last time he'd seen her, Lorna had been lying on her back staring at the ceiling. In that short time since he'd dozed off, Bella had gone in search of her mother and snuggled in beside her, while Lorna for some curious reason had risen and left the room.

Ned walked into the sitting room. He turned on the ceiling fan to high and the soft whirr was a welcome sound. He opened the shutters, yawning, hoping against hope that a breeze might blow off the river and help clear his thoughts. The sounds of the night hit him first, along with the muddy smell of the brown Irrawaddy, and the pungency of spicy cooking. And, as always, the strongest fragrance of all was from the orchids growing outside the window. His sleepy gaze fell upon the night activity of The Strand, the great street on which the hotel stood. Trams, motor-cars, bicycles, rickshaws and sacred cows jostled for position with the endless stream of people. Horns blew intermittently and the occasional voice singled itself out briefly – a shout, a burst of laughter.

His attention was drawn to a commotion not far from the hotel. Cars had stopped, accounting for the sudden increase in impatient horns being sounded, and a tram had halted. There was a growing crowd of people. He watched the activity for a few moments, frowning because he couldn't make out what was going on, but was interrupted by an urgent knock at the door.

The general manager of the hotel appeared, his countenance so haunted that Ned was instantly filled with an unnamed dread.

'Mr Sinclair,' the manager said, his voice shaking. 'It's your mother, sir. She walked out into the traffic. There was nothing anyone could do.'

5

Jack ignored the white feather he found waiting for him after climbing the steps to the engine room. The building clung precariously to the cliffs and was continually buffeted by fierce Atlantic gales. Outside the miners were arriving, clutching their felt hats and candles, most of them stained with the dark-pink dust that clung to their skin and clothes from previous days down the shafts. Nothing would rid them of the earth's touch. Not until bath night in front of the fire, usually before church, would the reddish hue be cleaned fully from their skin. Their mining clothes never lost it.

He opened the window, inhaled the sharp air; it would be a cold winter, adding insult to the injury of the flu epidemic, which was sweeping through Britain. The 'Spanish flu' had started its death toll in the killing fields on the Western Front. Jack was yet to hear of any cases in Cornwall but it was only a matter of time, and there were rumours that the government authorities were about to start spraying the streets. He was sure Penzance would not escape the killer's touch.

Jack looked down at the accusing feather in his hand, hating what it signified, and let it float off on the breeze, along with his despair, telling himself to empty his mind as he did so.

The truth was, Jack's mind was always empty when he was working and concentrating. His mother was right. Lowering the men for their working day and then returning them to the surface

when their shift ended was an enormous responsibility. Safely raising the ore to the women called Bal Maidens, who worked at the
surface smashing up the ore, was a relentless task and he needed
to remain focused. Control was Jack's key quality when he was
first admitted to the School of Mines. His teachers recognised
that almost immediately, and that his grasp of the mechanics and
machinery of mining in the twentieth century was second to none.
But even more important was his agile mind. Bright, intelligent
youngsters were needed now more than ever and with the industry predicting a gloomy future, Jack was fast-tracked through his
training. The mining magnates needed qualified men to prop up the
mines that had slid into debt and also to man new ventures and pursue fortunes overseas.

His engineering skills were currently in demand winding the
famous Levant 'man engine', which moved scores of men up and
down the main levels of the shaft. Getting to the actual rock face
where they'd be digging was a different matter, of course. The
miners would alight from the man engine and scatter down the
honeycomb of tunnels into the pitch dark, using ladders to reach
the lower levels, where the engine didn't travel.

Mining at Levant was said to reach back two centuries, previously yielding copper before it started producing tin.

It was the gregarious Cornish inventor Richard Trevithick
and his engineering colleagues who had developed the engine that
Jack was in charge of this morning. The men stood on timber rods
and Jack would be lowering some of them down as deep as eighteen hundred feet. Usually, three men worked the three shifts tending
the engine. Today, Jack realised, it would be just two of them and a
longer than normal shift. While he was in no hurry to be home, he
was eager to be rid of the guilty cache in his pocket. His plan was
to pay off Sir Wally as soon as he could and by week's end to have
a serious discussion with his father about the future. He was now

determined to put his head down, to work hard and responsibly, but he was equally determined to finally gain his father's support for his plan to give up his job. There were any number of roles for Jack in the family business but so far his father had refused him any part.

Sometime between leaving home and arriving at the engine house this morning, Jack had made his decision to leave mining behind him. If that did not win satisfaction from Charles Bryant, then he'd also made a pact with himself to escape Cornwall – Britain, if necessary – to seek his fortune elsewhere.

It felt as though a massive burden had been lifted from his shoulders in making this promise to himself. Suddenly, Rally's threat and his father's disappointment drifted away, along with the feather. Now he had a plan for the future.

Jack actually grinned but his mood was soured almost immediately.

'Bryant! I've been looking for you.'

It was Pearce. Jack schooled his features into a neutral expression. He quickly took control of the conversation. This was a tactic he could thank his father for. 'Mr Pearce, you're after the wrong man. I did not make Helen pregnant, no matter what anyone is saying.' He was careful not to directly point the finger at Helen for the accusation. 'I only took her out for the first time about a fortnight ago.' Jack added, taking a defensive stance, opening up his muscled arms to the older man.

'Not according to my Helen. She's three months up the duff!'

'Mr Pearce, I am not the father. I give you my word.'

'That's supposed to be worth something, is it?'

'It's as good as the next man's and I don't give it freely.'

Pearce had advanced, his face as stormy as the ocean crashing against the St Just coastline, his fists clenched, itching to land a blow.

Jack didn't want to fight Pearce, especially not today when his spirits had lifted for the first time in a long time, but he didn't take a step back. While Pearce was hardly a small man, Jack was more than a match.

'Helen says it's yours, so it's yours,' the older man said, poking a sausage-like finger into Jack's chest.

'That's because Helen wants it to be mine, Mr Pearce.'

'You're an arrogant swine, Bryant. And staying true to form, I see. As tall and broad as you are, you're still the coward, shirking your duty. Turn around so I can see that big yellow stripe painted down your back! I don't know what she sees in a cringing sissy like you.'

Jack's fury rose. 'I don't know what she sees in me either, so why don't I give you a list of the men who have given your daughter a poke in the last few months and you can choose one of them instead?'

Pearce's rage spilled over and he took a swing. 'Good-looking, my Helen claims? I'll soon change that, you bastard,' he growled, just as the mine's manager entered the engine room.

Jack never did get the opportunity to respond to Pearce's blow, which missed his jaw but connected with his cheekbone as he tried to dodge the clenched fist. He now sat at the controls of the engine, with a swollen eye, blackening by the minute, and an aching cheek. But it was his pride that hurt the most.

Mercifully the mine manager had only seen Pearce doing the thumping, so Pearce copped all the blame. He was forced to cool his heels and was sent home. His wages were docked and he was told to return for the afternoon shift. Until then, the manager would cover alongside Jack.

As it turned out, the rest of the morning passed uneventfully. Jack lowered the men on Billy's shift as the old crew rose to the surface one at a time without a hitch. Then he'd spent the rest of his hours going through some checks on the main fly-wheel, and getting on with the usual maintenance. It was absorbing work that left him to his own company, which was precisely what he needed.

'Bring the men up for changeover and then you're done. Leave immediately, Bryant. I don't care about the state of your face. I want no continuation of earlier.'

'Right,' Jack said, resisting touching his aching bruises. 'Captain Jenner . . . I, er, I'm sorry about this morning.'

The bell sounded. 'All right, Bryant. No need to explain, son. Right, let's wind them up; they'll be damp and wretched today.'

'Will do,' Jack said, grateful for the release, pulling on his gloves and reaching for the levers.

Jenner left as Pearce arrived to relieve Jack. 'Make no trouble now, Pearce. If I hear or see anything amiss, you'll be out of work for more than just a shift.'

Pearce nodded. 'I've got nothing more to say to Bryant.'

'Keep it that way.'

Jack ignored Pearce's arrival as he began the series of lever motions that would coax the steam engine to wind the wire rope that would raise the dozens of men. He imagined them wiping the sweat from their eyes and wearily stepping from the side platforms known as sollars to their standing rods which would gradually lift them, in ten-foot increments, with each stroke of the engine. It was a slow process.

Jack glanced out of the window, waiting for the first miners to emerge. They'd be dirty, fatigued and wet from the sweat of their toil and the heat of the tunnels. Jack was careful to ensure that each crew had warmed water waiting for them in the concrete bath formed in the floor of the 'dry room' to rinse off. Their clothes would have dried stretched over the huge pipes that sent steam from the boilers to the mine's main engine. The entire huge room would be warm and dry and the miners could take a short rest on the long bench before contemplating their walk home in the freezing gales.

Waiting for the final signal, Jack imagined the sense of relief that Billy and his fellow miners must feel at the end of each shift to look up and see daylight after so many hours in darkness.

Jack heard the bell. Time to work. He began pulling at the levers but he thought he heard an unusual soft groan from the machinery. Frowning, he momentarily wondered whether it was coming from the counterweights or the beams. He paused, hoping to catch the sound again, but he heard nothing more. He re-started the lever process. He envisaged the process as he worked, picturing how the rods would dip and pause as more men clambered aboard. And so it went, his hearing attuned for the bell that sounded the signal to wind again, and then Jack would respond, lifting the miners closer to their families.

He glanced at the dials once more. The engine was working smoothly, achieving four and a half strokes per minute, as it should. That curious sound he'd heard earlier must have been a once-off peculiarity.

Then suddenly – and without any warning – the engine lurched to a faster speed. There was no time to think, only to react.

In a blink Jack became the engine's slave, following precisely what he'd been taught and had practised time and time again until he could do it with his eyes shut. Without even a split second's hesitation, he reversed the engine to shut off the steam. It was absolutely the right procedure, but nothing Jack could do could reverse the fatal problem that had likely been in the making for some time.

He waited just moments – although it felt like an eternity – while the great crown wheel turned three quarters of its normal revolution before it shuddered to a halt as he needed it to. A truly unfamiliar sound of shrieking machinery rent the engine room. This was followed by a terrifying judder as a fatal crack spread devastatingly through unseen metal, ripping through its forging and tearing apart structures until, moments later, the engine lost its load.

Jack sprang back, horrified, as an estimated twenty-four tons of men and machine crumpled, plummeting in a sickening avalanche of timber, metal, rock and flesh.

Jenner burst in, yelling, but Jack hardly registered his words. Pearce was flattened against the window, staring out, uselessly trying to see how many men were still at the surface.

'The engine's gone,' Jack said numbly, in deep disbelief. 'It's gone,' he confirmed, too traumatised to allow himself to picture what was unfolding beneath him.

'Bryant!' Jenner bellowed.

Jack looked up, stunned, his lips bloodless, face as pale as his white shirt, suddenly dripping with sweat despite the cold. 'It's gone, sir,' he repeated.

'Then all hands to the shaft!' the captain roared. 'It's going to be a slaughterhouse down there!'

––––––––––

Beneath the surface, the world had permitted what looked like hell to wake and yawn. Men and boys lay twisted and dying beneath tons of rock, machinery and equipment. Luckier ones had died instantly, smashed on the lower levels or crushed beneath boulders or huge timbers. Still luckier ones had clung to whatever they could and whatever had held long enough to get themselves onto the old-fashioned ladders that were now swinging back and forth, threatening to collapse as well. The majority were consigned to a slow, lonely and agonising death awaiting rescue that came too late, or a new, miserable life – some people without limbs, others having lost sight – in which they were no longer capable of earning and would be forever a burden on their families.

The accident was heard for miles around – as far as the town of St Just – and women began to converge on Levant, running with babies in arms, or infants clinging to their skirts. Their wails penetrated the eerie new silence surrounding the mine, and echoed the shrieks of gulls that seemed to taunt them over the lonely coast.

6

More than a hundred men were unaccounted for when Jack and his fellow rescuers clambered down the ladders in a desperate attempt to recover the injured and dying. The first cheers of relief were heard as around twenty miners answered their urgent calls. Each one was clinging to sollars, rods, or ladders, too terrified to move in the inky darkness for fear of falling or slipping; or too injured to help themselves.

Jack Bryant worked like a man possessed, refusing food, even a sip of water, until the captain ordered him to take a mug of sweet, milky tea. Jack had swallowed it angrily, a wild look in his stormy blue-grey eyes; a mixture of fury and fear. Pearce was making it clear to all who would listen that Jack was directly responsible for the deaths of so many men.

Jack ignored the abuse hurled his way each time he surfaced with another injured victim sprawled across his shoulders. He couldn't worry about his already tattered reputation just now, although he did at one point see his father's thin-lipped, baleful countenance glowering at him from a small hillock near the anxious relatives.

Charles Bryant had arrived with crates of new candles and lanterns to help set up some proper lighting. He was watching now as his grim-faced son arrived with a man battered seemingly beyond recognition.

Jack ignored his father and the people who hurled their anger towards him; his only focus was to continue running up and down the ladders, finding every survivor that he could. He was looking for one man in particular and couldn't rest until he'd been found.

Billy Jenner was alive when Jack discovered him crushed beneath a huge piece of timber at one hundred and ten level, his fluffy golden hair slicked with blood and the deep red of the earth that wanted to claim him. Jack, his heart aching to see his mate so smashed and broken, screamed for assistance, and men arrived quickly at the news that another brave miner had been found alive. Now Jack insisted on carrying Billy himself as gently and tenderly as he could. With silent, helpless tears cutting clean tracks through the grime on his cheeks, Jack begged him to conserve his energy, but Billy continued to jabber in his ear.

'I should have listened to you, Jack. We should've sailed off somewhere together. One of those exotic places with dark-haired, dark-eyed beauties.'

'Hush now, Billy. Save your strength,' Jack urged, forcing his voice to remain strong. Just hours ago they'd been laughing about the future; Jack wasn't sure there would be a future for Billy but he couldn't let on.

But Billy knew, it seemed. 'It hurts, Jack. It hurts everywhere,' he murmured breathlessly. 'Keep me conscious. Don't let me die down here. I want to see the clouds again.'

'You're not going to die. I won't let you. I'm going to get you out and you're going to breathe that fresh Cornish air coming off the sea, all right?'

'All right, Jack. I trust you. You know I love you, don't you, mate?'

'Don't get soppy on me.'

'Needs to be said,' Billy said, struggling to get each word out. 'We're brothers, despite different bloods.'

'And looks.'

Billy wheezed a weary half-laugh.

He sounded so weak, Jack began to panic. 'Don't talk, Billy, just listen and hold on. Your mum and your sisters are there waiting for you. Your dad, too. He's hurt but he'll mend. You'll both mend. You'll fish again together. We all will.'

'It's a long way up,' Billy groaned.

'And I'm taking you there.' Jack gritted his teeth as he struggled to lift Billy's dead weight onto his back. 'Hold onto me, hold tight.'

'I'm not sure —'

'You can! When this is done and you're fit again, we'll kiss the ground of Cornwall goodbye and we'll sail off. We'll go to Australia, Billy! It's hot and dry there. Gold runs out of shallow mines. Gold and even diamonds, they say. Opals and pearls and . . .' He felt his friend slump. 'Billy!'

'Yes,' Billy croaked.

'We're almost there,' Jack lied. 'I can see the sky, Billy, and there's sunlight reaching down already and a cool draught touching my face. The Australian women even have all their teeth!'

Billy tried to laugh but it came out as a groan. 'Jack, I think you'll have to do it for both of us. Goldmining, eh? Go seek a fortune for us both, Jack.'

Billy fell silent then and Jack climbed grimly, relentlessly, his mouth pulled into a snarl of effort, his anxiety increasing with each difficult step until hands reached down and hauled him up the last couple of feet.

He gripped Billy's hand and pulled it against his cheek instinctively, covering it with his own large hand. 'I'll see you soon, mate. We made it. You're on the top now. They're going to take care of you and mend you. All right, Billy?'

'Thanks, Jack,' Billy whispered, his eyes fluttering open to slits and a gentle smile creasing his cracked, bleeding mouth. Jack made no attempt to wipe away the tears.

Billy took his last breath moments later, before his mother even reached him through the crowd. Jack told himself that his friend was simply resting, and fixing Billy's face, now in repose, into his mind, he kissed his friend's head tenderly, then walked away. Jack could hear the screams as he began his next descent but told himself they could be any woman's agony, for far too many sons of Cornwall had suffered today.

He didn't dare pause. Didn't let the thought enter his mind that it was Billy's mother screaming her anguish that her favourite child was dead. No, Jack refused to believe Billy was gone. He told himself to just keep moving; find the men who had been at the mercy of that engine and not rest until he could account for each of them.

Despite his courageous efforts, so many of the men he carried died not long after he'd got them into the embrace of their families. It was as though they'd held on just long enough to feel the fresh air on their skin and to see the faces of those they loved before they succumbed.

And with each man he lost, Jack's heart cracked a little wider and his soul turned darker.

———

Five days later, more than thirty families in the close community of St Just were burying their men; five of them were from Jack's own village, whose atmosphere had turned frigid and still. Funerals were being held all over the surrounding region, while scores of families were grieving over their seriously injured members. Many would be permanent invalids, and while their women were glad they were alive, it meant their father, brother or son couldn't help support the family any longer and destitution beckoned.

One nine-year-old boy had remained conscious on level ninety for almost three days in the blackness, pinned on his belly under the weight of his father's corpse. The traumatised boy was recovered with only minor physical injuries, but he had lost the ability to speak.

Those with broken limbs, bruising, or especially those miners with invisible injuries, felt guilty and never drew attention to their woes. The headaches, nausea, dizziness, even the few cases of what family members believed was insanity were kept quiet. These sounded like trivial repercussions when so many had died.

The shock of that day hung heavy over the streets of St Just, bringing misery and heartbreak at every turn.

Jack had all but lived at the mine since the accident, not wishing to face his own family, and hoping his demons could be held at bay by using every hour God gave him for the rescue effort.

But today Pendeen was gathering to bury one of its own sons. Jack had returned home to bathe properly, shave, and put on his dark suit that now hung from his broad but suddenly hollow frame. His mother was nowhere to be seen and the grandfather clock's loud tick had lost its familiar comfort and instead gave an ominous quality to an already strained atmosphere.

Jack took a deep breath, smoothed his Brylcreemed hair, cleared his throat and knocked on the door of his father's study.

Charles Bryant finally emerged, but despite the sharp cut of his dark suit and his pristine white shirt, he too looked like a broken man. For a moment Jack's hopes flared that somehow from out of this dreadful accident they might unearth a common bond that only miners could share.

'Dad, I —'

'Not now, eh?'

Jack held his tongue, wanting to pummel his father with clenched fists for damning even that fragile opportunity to help one another.

They walked in silence down the hill, their gait almost identical, although Jack stood taller.

'Your mother's gone ahead. She's helping with the arrangements.'

There was nothing to say. Jack noticed that even the birds were still and quiet. Nevertheless, it was a beautiful day; crisply cold, no wind, sharply bright. Billy was to be committed to the ground in the Wesley church and Jack imagined the entire village would turn out to farewell him.

Billy's uncle met them at the church gate. Jack didn't need to guess why; he could see those who had gathered to show their respects were staring at his approach, none of their gazes even vaguely sympathetic. He couldn't see his mother anywhere.

'Jim,' Charles said sombrely, raising his hat.

'Charlie,' the man said, ignoring Jack. 'Er, listen, Charlie,' he began, clearly embarrassed. 'Thanks for coming.'

Bryant nodded as if he was surprised his old friend would mention it.

'Charlie, I'm sorry but I don't think it's a good idea for Jack to be around just now.' He looked down. 'You're welcome, of course, Charlie. This is not . . .' He shrugged, unable to finish.

'Not a witch-hunt?' Bryant demanded. 'How long have we known each other, Jim?'

'Charlie, listen —'

'How long?' Bryant repeated, his deep voice suddenly deeper.

'We go back a long way.'

'We grew up together. We mined together. You helped me wet the head of my son and I did the same for your nephew. And when you needed a loan last year, who did you come to?' Now his voice became quieter – it was the tone Jack dreaded because it meant that his father was really angry. 'We are men of Pendeen, James Jenner. We don't turn on each other.'

Jenner looked pained. 'It's not me, Charlie. And it's not you either. But the timing is bad. Everyone believes your son —'

'My son,' Bryant cut in, his face inches from Jenner's, 'is a professional. He graduated from the School of Mines higher than anyone before him. No doubt you've heard the initial report that Jack acted in accordance with correct procedure. The records will show that this catastrophe was an accident. The metal cracked on the main beam, man! It had nothing to do with the engine, or the winding.'

Jack kept the surprise from his expression, hardly daring to breathe as he glanced at the two men, his father pale with compressed rage.

'Dennis Pearce was there,' Jenner hissed.

Charles poked Jack's chest. 'Ask him what you all want to know.'

'What?' Jenner looked astonished.

'Ask Jack, and be sure you look him in the eye.'

Jenner finally regarded Jack fully, raising his gaze with deep embarrassment, but before he could say anything, Jack saved him the trouble.

He cleared his throat. 'Mr Jenner, on my mother's life, sir, I'm not the one who made Helen pregnant. I took precaution and she knows it.'

Jenner's head snapped up. 'Did you tell Pearce that?' he demanded.

'He didn't really give me a chance.'

'Charlie, there's a lot of pain here. Billy's mum . . . well, she's not going to recover from this.'

'Billy's mother has five sons, John. I have one. And he's done nothing wrong. He's as much a victim of this accident as any of the injured folk. The fact that he stands here whole doesn't mean he isn't grieving as deeply as the next. He was there. He was responsible for the daily safety of those men. The mine's machinery let him down but all of you are determined to smear the blood of thirty men on his hands. It's an absolute bloody disgrace!'

'It goes deeper, Charlie,' Jenner said, looking around as the families began to file into the church quietly. 'The boy didn't go to war and now this. It's —'

His father's voice turned wintry. 'You know he was turned down and why. Billy didn't exactly see action either but I don't see anyone accusing him of being a coward.'

'Let's just go,' Jack said. 'I'll pay my respects to Billy later.'

Jenner looked at Jack with an expression of gratitude mixed with helplessness, but Jack said nothing more.

His father gave Jenner a final glare. 'I won't forget this,' he muttered as he stomped away from the churchyard.

Jack hurried after his father, unsure of what to say, and wondering why they were no longer heading uphill to the house but taking a detour towards the sea.

'Walk with me,' was all Charles Bryant said. Jack held his tongue, confused and excited by his father's unexpected support.

7

When they reached the cliff's edge, his father surprised him again by taking off his coat, which he folded neatly, then placed his hat on top. He spread out his starched white handkerchief and lowered himself onto it, careful to keep his trouser creases sharp. Like all the Bryant men, Charles was tall, and broad across the shoulders, but for the first time, Jack noticed his father had developed a slight rounding of those shoulders. How odd that he had not seen this before or taken account of the new lines etched beneath his eyes. The few silver hairs at Charles's brow had suddenly spread treacherously right across his head, turning him into a far older man than the one Jack saw in his mind. How could he have missed all this?

He joined his father and they sat shoulder to shoulder in the most comfortable silence Jack could recall them sharing.

Looking out to sea was a tonic for him. The water was magically beautiful, changing from a sapphire blue at its depths to a luminous emerald at the sandy shore of the tiny cove, where it broke against the rocks and foamed, glinting in the sunlight.

'I used to come up here as a boy and dream of all the lands beyond Land's End,' his father said, startling Jack out of his quiet reverie. 'I was usually with Jim Jenner, warm pasties in our pocket, and we'd talk about all the gallivanting around the world we were going to do when we grew up.'

Jack found it hard to believe that his sombre father ever enter-tained such colourful, daring dreams. 'How old were you?'

His father sighed, then actually laughed. 'About six, I think, when we first began coming here alone. We decided we might like to be pirates – not the sort that threw grappling hooks on stranded ships near the shore. No, we had lofty ideas of being somehow bet-ter than that.'

'Honourable pirates,' Jack suggested, and this made his father grin wider.

'Yes, honourable. We'd only ambush wealthy merchant ships from Spain or Italy . . . that were coming to invade Cornwall. And we'd make our families rich before we sailed away to exotic ports.'

'Merchant ships that were also invaders!'

'I was only a lad. By the age of eight I was down the mines with my father and uncle. We worked over at South Crofty in those days.'

Jack knew this from his grandfather but he'd never talked about those days with his father. 'What about Levant?'

'We all moved across in 1870 or thereabouts.'

'So, your uncle Jamie died at Levant, did he?'

His father sucked air in as he thought about it. 'Uncle Jamie died at South Crofty in the winter of 1869, two days before Christmas.'

Jack recalled the story though he was hazy on the details. But he knew that after James Bryant died in a mining accident, Charles's father had inherited his brother's small cottage on a nice holding of coastal land.

Charles interrupted Jack's recollections. '"Get your boy out of the mines", Uncle Jamie told Grandpa so often,' he said, staring out to sea. 'But we couldn't afford to. We were tin miners through generations.'

'And then the sale happened,' Jack prompted.

Bryant sighed, staring down at his big hands, no longer battered or bruised; these days his nails were trimmed and buffed regularly at the gentlemen's salon in Camborne. 'Yes, and then the sale happened. I hated how mining beggared folk. As young as I was, I could see that we made men in London rich while our families barely eked out enough to feed ourselves. And in those days there were no rights for miners, no strikes or lobby groups or even the know-how. All we knew was how to mine, and how to toil for twelve-hour days.' His father grimaced. 'And how to die before we saw our fourth decade.'

Jack nodded but said nothing.

'Then along came your mother. Fragile creature she was. I still don't know what possessed her to marry me. She could have done so much better. She'd had an education, your mother, she could have married up.'

'She did, Dad,' Jack said. 'Look at what you've been able to give her.' He couldn't remember the last time he'd addressed his father in this way.

'Well, it was because of her I became so determined to get out of the mines if I could. We were all living in Uncle's cottage by then and while it was better than the draughty, crumbling place my parents were renting, the prospects didn't seem that bright.'

'Until they discovered that reef that went below the cottage.' Jack felt like a child again, asking his elders to retell a story he knew by heart.

'That's right. Your grandfather didn't want to sell it, Jack. I fought with him bitterly. Kept telling him it was my future he was throwing aside, as well as yours. You were about three or four months old at that time.'

'I've never really understood how you convinced him. Grandpa was such an old stick in the mud.'

'I reminded him how Uncle Jamie had asked him to get me out

of the mine. My wheezing was really bad and I think that's probably what pushed him over the edge. The mine made an offer to make his eyes pop. You know he gave it all to me.'

Jack turned to stare at his father's profile, his own reflecting an identical strong jawline. This news was a revelation. 'No, I didn't know that.'

'Grandpa wanted nothing to do with the money. He kept mining. Never told a soul about how much he got and swore the mine to secrecy as well. I got it all. I was twenty-seven. He told me to make something of it. So I did. I left the mine that very day, but you see, mining was in my blood by then. I couldn't let it go completely. I tried to think about how I could still work around the mines. Providing the big companies with their raw materials seemed the best idea. I was the one who negotiated to give the men free candles.'

Jack frowned with surprise. 'Really?'

'I've never forgotten what life's like down the shafts. I never did achieve my real aim, to give the men more light, you could say, but when they did deign to set a taper to one of my candle wicks, it burned true. Stupid buggers still worked in the dark more often than not.'

'That was just one of the businesses you set up, though, I mean —'

'That's true. But everything I've done, including the small money-lending scheme I set up out of Camborne, is designed to help the miners. You see, Jack, I never could let go of my roots.'

He knew suddenly where this was leading. 'I understand.'

'Do you, though? Do you really?'

'You wanted me to stay close to our roots – to appreciate that we come from generations of miners.'

His father's expression relaxed, his forehead smoothing. 'That's it, Jack. We were never smugglers or pirates. We were tin miners. And although I was able to move away from the grime and the grinding poverty, give your mother a good life and you some prospects, mining is in my soul. And I wanted it to be in yours too. I wanted you to be qualified, trained in mining. So that some day you could . . .' His father's word petered out.

Jack's heart leapt. Take over? he wondered. He held his breath.

'But everything changed,' his father continued, that familiar tone of disappointment creeping into his voice. 'You're smart, Jack. Far smarter than any Bryant that's gone before. I wanted you to know about the mining industry so that you could take our firm strongly into this new century, with fresh ideas and the knowledge to back them up. I thought with your engineering skills you might build . . .' He stopped and sighed. 'But then the gambling and drinking, the carousing began . . .'

'I could stop it in a moment!' Jack said, his eagerness spilling over as he grabbed his father's suit sleeve. 'Half my problem is frustration. You were a miner and you were raised a miner's son, but I grew up in a house with a housekeeper and fine furnishings! You sent me to school when everyone else was heading down the shaft. And when I should've been learning the ropes of the family business, you insisted I learn a trade and then packed me off to the mine! You set me up for a fall. If you wanted me to be a miner, we should have stayed in Uncle Jamie's house and never sold it!'

Charles Bryant looked at where his son's hand had bunched the fabric of his jacket. Jack instantly let go, regretting the starburst of creases left behind. 'Are you blaming me for your shortcomings? For all the trouble you find yourself in?'

'I'm blaming you for using me to soothe your own guilt.'

'Guilt?' his father repeated, anger and astonishment mingling.

Jack sensed this confrontation had been coming for years. 'You've never quite come to terms with your new status in life, have you, Dad? You dragged yourself out of the holes in the ground to become a successful businessman. I take my hat off to you, because somehow you've pulled it off without earning the contempt of your fellow miners, or the disdain of the people you do business with.'

'Don't throw big words at me,' his father replied.

'Then perhaps you shouldn't have educated me,' Jack growled, tearing at his necktie and loosening his collar. 'Did you expect me to be happy working as a mine winder all my life when I sleep in starched sheets ironed by our servant and get driven about in a fancy motor? Think about it! Don't make me take a constant beating for your success. You've abandoned me, somehow hoping that by making me work the mines, you've stayed true to the community that raised you. There's no pride in showing off that your only son works the mines. There's only humiliation for me and you're its chief instigator.'

His father's eyes had taken on the grey of the granite cliff they sat upon and Jack knew his own mirrored that colour. They were peas in a pod, just as his mother often said. A single gull floated above them, waiting for the updraft. Jack felt as lonely as the bird looked.

'What would you have had me do?' his father demanded. 'I've provided for you —'

'Yes, but you hate me. I reflect what your money brings.'

His father looked astonished but said nothing for a few moments. Then he stood suddenly and began dusting himself down. 'Don't be ridiculous. I've made you what you are, boy!'

Jack's disappointment cut deep; he'd lost all hope that there could be an open and honest discussion between them. 'And are you proud of what I am, what I've become?'

At this Charles Bryant bent down and began lifting his coat and hat, avoiding Jack's eye. 'What happened at the mine is not your fault.'

'I don't need you to tell me that, although your support back there is something I'll carry with me always.'

Now his father's gaze flashed up to meet his, bright steely sparks igniting within his flinty stare. 'Carry with you? What do you mean?' Jack saw a familiar glimmer of contempt in it.

'I'm going to do what I should have done years ago. I'm leaving.'

'The house?' His father gave a short, harsh laugh. 'You won't last a week on your own, the way you spend your allowance —'

'Not just the house, Dad,' Jack said quietly, a curious calm flowing through him. His gaze was steady and direct. 'I'm leaving Cornwall. And I don't want your allowance.'

'What?' the older man roared. 'Don't be a fool. Your future is —'

'Not here,' Jack finished, his tone resigned. 'It's taken too long. And I'm disappointed in myself for not coming to this realisation faster.'

'But what about the business?' Charles asked.

'What about it?'

'I'm not getting any younger,' his father railed.

'Neither am I.' He sighed.

'What about your mother?'

Jack couldn't believe how clear his mind suddenly appeared. 'She loves us. That won't change. And what else won't change is the fact that you and I clash constantly.'

'Listen, now.'

'No, Dad. I'm not going to listen any longer to your rules and how I must live my life. I'm no saint, I realise that I've let you down and given you no reason to hand me opportunities.' Jack stood and gazed back towards Pendeen town, then he looked down sadly. 'Besides, mud sticks. You've told me that often enough. The people we live amongst have made up their minds about me. I'm the villain. I'm responsible for all the sons who died in France, for all the lives lost and damaged at Levant, and for Helen's bastard child. That's plenty for you to be ashamed about.' He reached into his pocket and pulled out his mother's diamond watch, amazed and grateful that it had not been lost during the chaos of the mine's disaster. 'You'd better add thief to my list of failings. I took this a few days ago.'

His father stood speechless.

Jack told him the whole sordid story before shaking his head helplessly. 'I wanted to pay him off quickly so he wouldn't come after you and Mum.'

'He threatened your mother?' Jack rarely heard such emotion in his father's voice.

Jack told his father everything he could remember. 'I'm sorry, really sorry, about it, Dad.'

Charle's mouth twisted with disdain. 'I'll take care of Sir Walter.'

This reminded Jack of everything that he truly loved about his father: his calm strength, his ability to take command of situations, his refusal to allow anything to threaten his family.

Charles cleared his throat. 'So. Where will you go?'

Jack looked out to sea. 'London, probably. I'll take on a labouring job if I can and earn passage on a ship. I've always wanted to sail somewhere.'

'And then what?'

'I don't know. You made me a miner, Dad. Perhaps Australia? They say there's a new goldrush there. But there are opal and diamond mines too.'

'Australia? That's on the other side of the world! And what the hell do you know about opals or diamonds?'

'I'm a quick learner.' Jack pushed the watch at his father. 'Take it.'

The older man didn't touch it. 'I bought this the year you were born. That blue shell face for my son, diamonds sparkling like my wife.'

'I didn't know you were so sentimental,' Jack replied, bitterness creeping into his tone.

'There's a lot you don't know about me.'

'Put it back in her jewel box for me.'

His father ignored the watch, now in Jack's palm, but withdrew a pale, creamy-coloured envelope from his jacket pocket. 'No. If you're going to leave us, keep it. That way you won't forget us. In the meantime, take this.'

Jack frowned.

'Money. I was taking it to Camborne to pay wages, pay some bills.'

'Then keep to that plan.'

Bryant shook his head. The breeze stiffened and caught Jack's hair, ruffling the black mop his mother had wanted trimmed. He noticed his father's perfectly oiled, equally thick hair, didn't budge. 'I insist you take it.'

Jack stared at the fat envelope. His father slapped it into his hand. It was the closest they'd come to touching each other, their two palms almost clasped but separated by the envelope.

'It feels like too much.' Jack suspected there was a small fortune inside.

'Take it!'

'Why? To ease your conscience?' Jack regretted his words instantly.

Charles shook his head. 'To ease yours.'

They stared at each other, the waves crashing below, several gulls now shrieking above. Jack sensed they both wanted to reach out but the divide – like the Atlantic Ocean that stretched out before them – was too great.

'Are you coming back with me to pick up your things?'

'I don't need things.' He stared at the package. 'I can buy the few bits and pieces I need.'

His father gave a soft sigh and began to shrug himself back into his coat, its deep-red lining reminding Jack of the bloodshed of the previous days. 'Well, you should say goodbye to your mother . . . explain this to her.'

Jack shook his head, too emotional to even feel the bite of the cool breeze. 'I can't.'

'You'll break her heart.'

'I need you to mend it for her, then, Dad. Tell her I love her. Tell her I will come back one day. But I can't face her now – I don't want to take away that memory of her tears and disappointment and loss with me. I'd rather remember her smiling at me as she did the last time I saw her.'

His father didn't reply; Jack was unsure whether his expression reflected anger or deep sorrow.

'I'll write to Mum,' he finally offered. 'I can say more in a letter. I promise I'll write to her.'

'You do that,' his father replied gruffly, his own voice thick with emotion, and finally held out his hand.

Jack stared at it for a second, then he shook it, once, hardly daring to meet his father's eyes before he turned to leave. There was nothing to say and he never looked back.

———————

The following night a group of men paid a call on Walter Rally's office. They'd chosen their moment well, with Rally's minder taking a leak out the back. Neither Big Jock Harrison nor Rally knew what hit them, until Rally regained consciousness slowly and realised he was in a car and blindfolded.

He screamed questions at the men surrounding him. In his blindness he guessed there were four other men travelling with him. But they maintained a frustrating, stony silence despite the fortune he offered to be released.

When the car eventually stopped he was gagged and dragged from the vehicle. He presumed they'd taken him further west and was now sure of it when he felt the whip of the cold around his face, the familiar blast of freezing Atlantic air.

His blindfold was finally ripped free and before him stood men whose faces were blacked out with soot.

'Where the hell is this?' he demanded. 'Levant?'

'Hello, Rally,' said a newcomer, emerging from behind a tower, who wore no disguise.

He thought he recognised the local businessman. 'Bryant? Is that you?' Rally asked, squinting into the dimness. They had only moonlight illuminating them.

'Our apologies, Wally. I sometimes forget us miners are used to seeing in the dark,' his captor said.

Men sniggered nearby.

'What's going on?' Rally's cockney sounded even more foreign on this rugged, desolate coastline. 'You're no miner, Charles Bryant,' he accused, jabbing a finger towards him.

'Ah, now, that's where you're wrong, Rally.'

'What do you want?' Bryant was the least ruffian-like of these men, but he looked suddenly more intimidating than the rest of them. Until now he'd always seemed to hide his build beneath his tailored suits. Now he stood before Rally, dark, brooding, in shirt-sleeves rolled up. He had to be well over six foot, like his stupid son; was that what this was all about? Rally's suspicions were confirmed as Bryant began to explain.

'My son tells me you tried to teach him a lesson the other day,' Bryant replied, his voice even but threatening.

'I simply gave him a short lesson in responsibility. You should be thanking me, Bryant. Your lad's been acting reckless and I thought it timely to remind him of his commitments. I did what you should have done months ago.' He regretted that final barb; had forgotten that he didn't have his meaty minders to protect him and suspected Bryant hadn't gone to this trouble to simply offer a warning. Rally's insides, which had just moments ago felt hard and twisted with fear, now felt as though they'd turned liquid. He'd seen it many times before when he'd had to teach someone a lesson; grown men often wetting themselves – or worse – in fright.

'. . . I'm sure you understand,' Bryant finished.

'What, I . . .' He had no idea what the man had just said. He tried to be reasonable. 'Listen, Bryant, your son owes me money, fair and square. You surely appreciate that a man must pay his dues.'

'Oh, I do. How much does he owe you?'

Rally hadn't expected this. He hesitated, thought about saying twenty pounds but Bryant was surely no fool. He decided to cut his losses and hope to get out of this dangerous situation in one piece. 'Forget it,' he said, pasting on his face the friendliest smile he could, frozen from fear but also the harsh wind. 'He can pay it when he can . . . and even in instalments if he wants.'

'Really?'

'Yeah. That's all right. I promise . . . no skin off my nose. We don't need trouble over this, Bryant.' He looked around and found stony glares from the darkened faces of the sentinels guarding him in a wide arc. 'Let's leave it at that, shall we?'

'You see, I wish I could,' Bryant replied, and Rally felt as though a flock of birds had just found themselves trapped inside his body, fluttering around and bashing against his heart, his lungs. There was suddenly no breath, even though he was sure he was sucking in air. Bryant continued. 'You see, I do agree with you that my son should pay his dues. But in his absence I will cover the debt. Jack can owe me instead.' Rally watched Bryant reach into his pocket and pull out what looked to be a wad of notes. 'Tell me how much he owes you.'

For the first time since he'd arrived at the mine, Rally felt a glimmer of hope. He saw the money, Bryant's thumb poised over it to roll off the pounds. Perhaps he might just leave with only his pride injured. He promised himself that if he got out of here, he would head back to London for a while. He hated the bloody miners! He imagined himself ordering a pint of Courage at The Lamb and Flag in Covent Garden and smiling to himself as he took his first sip. Fuck Jack Bryant! Well, he'd take Bryant senior's money. So long as people paid, Rally assured himself, he would always be reasonable.

'Fourteen pounds is what's owed,' he said clearly, his confidence rising like the cold breath steaming from his mouth.

'Fourteen,' Bryant repeated, peeling off some notes. 'Let's call it fifteen. That will cover the interest on the debt.'

Rally kept his expression even. 'That's fair.'

'I'm a fair man.'

Rally took the money, didn't count it – didn't even look at it – and plunged it into his jacket pocket. 'We'll call that settled, then. We could have done this over a beer, Bryant. No need to —'

'Not really. You see there's the small matter of the threat to my wife for us to deal with. I've covered my son's debt, Rally, and now I'm going to exact the debt you owe me.'

'What?' Rally felt as though all his blood had just drained into his toes. 'I don't understand.'

'Let me spell it out, then. Jack told me everything. I've checked the facts, too. George Thomas won't work for a while, maybe not again. You had particular things to say about the South Crofty miners. I was one of those.' He smiled in the candlelight and it looked deeply sinister, his expression like one you might find on a mask. There was nothing sincere in it. 'I think you're the barbarian, Rally.'

Rally reached for excuses, but nothing came; words failed him, frightened away by the threat in Bryant's dark eyes.

'Look, Charles . . .'

'Don't talk to me as though you know me. If you did, you'd know that my wife is kind and sweet. She is good to everyone. Unlike you, she cares for the community and gives away much of the money that I earn, hides it through anonymous donations to the church, to the various mining charities. My Elizabeth is one of the world's good people and does not deserve the stench of so much as your shadow falling upon her.'

'It was just to frighten him. I didn't mean anything by it, Bryant. I —'

'Oh, but you did. You told Jack you were a man of your word so I have no doubt that you made an open threat to my wife and now I will make you pay for that.'

'What? Wait!' Rally screamed as Bryant nodded to the men. The miners closed in on him.

'This is how it feels, Rally. This is what you pay your animals to do to helpless people, sucked into your gambling houses.'

Rally strained to look over his shoulder as he was dragged away. 'Bryant, wait! Listen to me. Please.'

'George has five children, Rally. You have none, which I suppose is a small blessing for the world.'

The jabbering began. Rally could hear it issuing in a steady stream of fright; his lips forming words of beseechment that were falling on hardened, deafened ears.

The men shoved him towards the cliff. He thought they were going to push him over it and that was when Walter Rally did let go, wetting his trousers as he'd witnessed many a frightened debtor do. They weren't taking him to the edge of the cliff, he realised, but along its face, forcing him to stagger and stumble down the steps that had been cut into the rock face.

His breath was shallow, coming too fast. He could see it smoking out before him. It was freezing up here but he couldn't feel a thing at all. 'Where are you taking me?' he screamed.

'Down to a place all too familiar for most of these boys, Rally. It's a recent place of mass death so you'll be in the company of the ghosts of men you've leeched off for years.'

Rally surprised himself with a fresh vein of courage that

bubbled up and found its voice. 'When this is over, Bryant, I'll come looking for you and that family of yours. And when I do I'll start with your son and make you watch it all.'

'My son is gone, no longer in Cornwall. His debt is paid to you too. You're being taken to somewhere where no one will hear you scream. And when this is over, no one will even know where your body is.'

'Body?' Rally squeaked, his voice barely above a whisper. 'Bryant.'

Charles ignored the fresh shrieks, speaking calmly over them. 'See you around, lads. Each of you has a grudge against this man – now's your chance to act on it. I'm going to leave the money in the pre-arranged place. And you know I'm a man of my word.'

Charles Bryant strode away from the ugly scene. Although his heart was heavier for his part in this event, he felt better knowing that the evil man had now been obliterated, fifteen of the Bryant family's pounds rotting in his pocket.

He banished hate from his mind, let it fill with grief instead at the loss of his son. He knew he would never see Jack again, and he regretted with every fibre his inability to tell the lad that he loved him and was proud of him, despite all of the shortcomings and undesirable behaviour. Charles Bryant knew he had no one to blame for the boy's ways but himself; he hadn't been much of a father. Jack was right. Guilt had driven the father to unwittingly ignore his son and had now forced him to kill for him.

Walter Rally's body was never found. Levant had claimed one final soul to walk with its ghosts.

8

Through no fault of their own, Ned and Arabella found themselves cast onto the goodwill of others and finally cut adrift into the ocean of homelessness. Gently, Ned gave his sister a rose-coloured version of their situation during their final evening at The Strand, and Bella appeared to comprehend that both their parents had 'gone to heaven'. Ned told her only that their father had died of a heart attack and their mother in her sleep of a broken heart. He knew his sister loved the romantic idea that their parents were deeply in love, so she would find some comfort in this story, he hoped, despite her tears. Whether she had yet grasped the reality that they now only had each other was anyone's guess.

Initially, the Presbyterian church did everything it could for the orphaned Scottish children, but as the days wore on and the generosity of various families waned, the Sinclairs found themselves with only one option – to be put into the 'temporary care' of an orphanage.

Ned had loudly protested against being placed into the well-known SPG Orphanage for Boys while Bella went to its sister orphanage for girls. In fact, he refused to be separated from his sister, arguing passionately that they had already been through enough emotional turmoil in the last few weeks. His supporters – the general manager of the hotel, the deeply concerned Dr Fritz and various members of the European club – were not necessarily losing interest, but Ned understood that life for them must eventually go on. Finding a solution that gave these orphans a roof over their head, food in their belly and a chance to take stock of their situation was the priority.

But Ned stuck to his insistence that Bella remain with him, for he couldn't imagine what it might do to her to lose all her family in one swift stroke. As it was, she was already showing clear signs of unravelling. It was an impossible situation and in the end, it was Fraser – in his desperation to leave Rangoon but with a clear conscience – who suggested the non-denominational orphanage that had been set up ten years earlier by a group of do-gooder wives of various rice plantation owners. The orphanage had been hastily assembled in the burst of energy that had come with the women from Britain while they were still trying to feel useful and stamp their own mark on Rangoon. Now they had grown rich on their husbands' profits and lost interest, and they had left the running of the orphanage to a man named Dr Brent.

So, barely three weeks after their father's accident and their mother's subsequent suicide, the Sinclair children found themselves in the small, untidy settlement, surrounded by peepul trees, that was the All Burma Children's Home. Here, nearly forty boys and girls found a bed, a roof and two meals daily, along with an education of sorts. Funding trickled in from expatriates – guilty fathers who had long ago abandoned Burmese mothers to return to Britain and marry an English bride – and the endeavours of the children themselves, who made baskets to sell in Rangoon city.

There was no car to transport them this time. Their journey was made by horse and cart, which meant they arrived at the orphanage hot, dusty and parched. Bella did not let go of Ned's hand the whole way. If not for his sister, Ned might have taken his chances and headed off alone to find work on the plantations.

There were three main single-storey buildings and sundry

small ones dotted around an area of a couple of acres. The trees were thick in the distance and Ned wondered whether it was the beginning of the jungle he'd heard about. The bungalows had crumbling verandahs and cracked stuccoed walls. Shuttered windows hung off their hinges and their peeling paint only added to the general dreariness. There had been some poor additions to the original architecture and the once simple elegance of the main grand bungalow was complicated by unnecessary pillars and an incongruous porch.

A dozen or so youngsters streamed out to greet them with bright smiles, all jabbering in Burmese. They appeared to be around the ages of five to seven, Ned guessed, although there was one much older boy who hung back but still lifted his hand shyly in greeting. He smiled tentatively and Ned realised that, behind him, Bella was already waving to the boy. He was older than she was, from what Ned could tell, but younger than himself. Although he had black hair, the boy's skin was the colour of milky coffee, marking him as not only different to his dark-skinned charges, but also markedly different to the Sinclairs.

On the main verandah, a woman dressed in starched white garments done up to her neck shielded her eyes from the sun and waited for them to alight.

'Mr Fraser? I'm Matron Brent.'

'Ah, hello. Come on, then, Ned. Let's get you and Bella introduced, shall we?' Fraser said genially, although Ned could tell their escort was nervous, and keen to be gone. 'Don't worry about your things,' he urged, as Ned helped Bella down, and then he switched into the local language, issuing orders to the driver. Ned forgot about the older boy, but the excited little ones accompanied them into the main building, laughing and singing as they went. Their trunks were back at the hotel for safekeeping until final arrangements could be made, and Ned had never felt more dislocated from his life. Suddenly nothing but the clothes they stood in and Bella's hand felt familiar.

He held that hand tightly now and looked around. Even in his nightmares, he couldn't have imagined scenery more desolate. Almost anywhere in Britain, the pervading colour was green and the light was soft. Here he was scorched by an unforgiving sun in a sky bright enough to make a person wince but in air humid enough to make that same person droop to the brown earth. Only the foliage, dark and brooding green, suggested this place was alive. Everything else seemed in decay.

The village's name he couldn't pronounce and had taken little notice of anyway. He had no idea where they were, but already he thought about leaving here just as soon as he could. But for now this motley clutch of formerly whitewashed bungalows offered Bella a sense of safety, if not comfort.

Fraser threw a self-conscious glance at Ned as he led them towards Matron Brent.

'I promise you will not be here long, Ned,' he said over his shoulder.

Ned held his tongue and focused on Mrs Brent.

'Hello, Edward,' she said. 'And, Arabella, if I'm not mistaken. You may call me Matron.'

Ned let out a small nervous laugh when Bella decided it was appropriate to curtsey to this po-faced woman. He wanted to yell out that they were not meant to be here.

Instead he said, 'Am I the eldest here?' holding out his hand politely.

She didn't shake it but gave him a hard, brief smile that didn't touch her eyes. 'You are. But let me introduce you to Robbie.' She looked around Ned's shoulders and he took the opportunity to drag back the fringe of hair that had fallen across his eyes. He desperately wished he'd taken his mother up on her offer to trim it while they were still aboard the ship. Now he'd never again feel the soft touch of her fingers through his hair, the cool of her skin when her hand brushed against his forehead, or see the warmth of her smile. He forced the image of her face from his mind.

'Come here, Robbie,' Margaret Brent said and the older boy they'd noticed on their arrival edged his way before them.

He was slim, and clearly of mixed blood. 'Robbie is fifteen and he's been with us the longest. I'm sure he'll welcome some English friends.'

Ned offered a hand and Robbie shook it, his genial dark eyes beaming with pleasure to match his wide, white smile. 'Pleased to meet you,' Ned said.

Bella followed suit.

'You're like a princess from one of the books I love, Arabella,' Robbie breathed.

Ned warmed instantly to Robbie, who couldn't have said anything more appealing to his sister.

'No one calls me that,' she said, disarmingly. 'I'm Bella to everyone except Ned, who calls me Bell.'

Again Robbie's face lit up. 'Even more lovely.'

'Well, now,' Margaret Brent interrupted. 'Children, off you go. Robbie, get them back to their basket weaving, will you? Edward, Arabella, Mr Fraser? Perhaps you'd follow me and we can introduce you to Dr Brent, who is very keen to welcome you. But let's get you some water first. You must be thirsty? Nyunt!'

A slim girl appeared. She was not tall but her movements were graceful beneath her threadbare clothes.

'This is Nyunt. She has spent many years here and has stayed on to help us, particularly in the kitchens.' They all returned the shy smile of the young woman approaching them. 'She understands a little English but cannot respond so it's best not to ask many questions. Perhaps you'd like to go with Nyunt to the kitchen for some refreshing water.' She turned and spoke hurriedly in Burmese.

'Mr Fraser, you may come with me. Dr Brent will be taking tea shortly.'

Ned gladly disappeared into the cooler part of the bungalow with Nyunt, who smiled and gestured for them to follow.

Not long after, he found himself ahead of the girls and lingered outside a slightly open door where he overheard part of a conversation between Fraser and a voice he assumed belong to Dr Brent.

'Passports, any family documentation?' a man asked.

'None, I'm sorry.'

'Come, come, Mr Fraser. This hapless woman brought her children across the oceans. She would not have been permitted to leave Britain without papers.'

'I'm aware of that. But in our hurry we found nothing. They must be in her belongings somewhere and I will have them sent on.'

'I can contact the hotel management myself, I'm sure,' Brent replied dismissively. 'Now, about the payment . . .'

Ned heard Fraser sigh. 'I am giving you this money, Dr Brent, to ensure that the Sinclairs are well taken care of until I can track down someone in Britain who will take full responsibility for them. Do we understand one another? They are not to be classed as children without means.'

'Of course,' Brent replied. 'But I'm not sure I comprehend their status.'

Fraser sighed. 'I understand they have friends in southern England. I will hunt these good folk down and see if they can't be persuaded to give the Sinclairs a home – at least Bella. Ned might make his own way in time, back in England. He is, after all, turning eighteen shortly.'

'But who will pay their passage? Please don't expect me to —'

'I don't. I shall raise the money but this donation should take care of them for at least three months?'

'It will.'

'I shall be in contact in due course.'

'Until then,' the doctor said, with no genuine care in his voice.

Ned heard the girls arriving with Matron Brent. She spotted him.

'You may meet Dr Brent now,' she said.

Ned frowned inwardly as he knocked on the door. Three months, Fraser had said. He had hoped only weeks. And what if Fraser's sense of responsibility waned the moment he was rid of them?

'Come,' said the throaty voice.

Ned grabbed his sister's hand again and entered the room.

'Ah, the Sinclairs,' said Brent from behind a desk cluttered with paperwork, books, and a typewriter piled with files. A huge picture window looked out on the compound beyond but Ned's eyes were drawn to Brent, who was massively overweight. A clear jug of water sat on one corner of the desk, which he bumped as he rose. Its multicoloured, glass-beaded crochet cover glinted as jewels might. Bella was drawn to the glass beads that she'd seen many times over in Britain but not so beautifully illuminated by sunlight. It was the one pretty item in an otherwise drab room. He could smell the sour tang of Brent's perspiration, the dark damp patches showing through his pale-blue shirt.

'Welcome to our humble, happy place,' Brent said. His dark blue eyes, buried deep within the folds of his fleshy face, looked like the dull pebbles on the shingle beaches back home.

'We will not press upon your generosity for long, Dr Brent,' Ned replied, glad that he sounded so determined. 'I intend for us to be independent swiftly.'

'Indeed,' Brent replied.

'Yes. I shall write home immediately and seek help from my parents' friends. Where is Mr Fraser?'

'He had to leave. A ship to catch, I hear. Didn't he say farewell?' Brent made a tut-tutting sound. 'My apologies. It will be at least four to five weeks before we hear from him again,' he added, his gaze settling on Bella. 'What a pretty young thing you are, Arabella.'

'Thank you,' she replied and broke Ned's heart when she curtsied again so politely.

'So you are a doctor?' Ned asked.

Brent's hard eyes flicked back to him. 'With a calling to do some missionary work out here in Burma where my skills can be put to their best use,' he said. 'Of course, you're rather old to be in our care, Edward.'

'I realise that. Another reason why we won't impose on you for long, sir.'

'Oh, Arabella is welcome. I'm simply concerned that we have no one your age to engage you, although Robbie has longed for someone closer to his age. Nevertheless, I agree that this cannot be a long-term arrangement.'

Well, at least they were in agreement on something, Ned thought.

'Why don't you go and take a look around, Edward? Find your dorm, meet the other children. Arabella is welcome to stay here with me for a while.' He gave a soft, avuncular chortle. 'She seems rather mesmerised by my water jug.'

'She's had a lot to contend with recently, Dr Brent. I'd rather keep her close by, if you don't mind.'

'Hurry along, then,' Brent said coldly, all pretence at benevolence disappearing.

Ned nodded and reached for his sister's hand, pulling her out of the room and its claustrophobic atmosphere.

9

Ned found himself wandering with Bella by the henhouse. The caged birds reminded him of their own situation.

'What are we doing here, Ned?' she asked, her hair hanging in damp clumps around her sweet, cherubic face.

He hugged her, as much for his own consolation as hers. 'I just need a few days, all right?'

'To do what?' she asked, deep-blue eyes reminiscent of her father regarding him wide and seriously. There was so much trust in them.

'To work things out.'

'You won't die, will you?' Bella asked, anxiously searching his face.

He forced a tight smile, banged his chest. 'Hardly!'

'I miss Mama,' she said and he saw the tears well yet again.

'I know, I know, Bell, darling,' he said, echoing his mother's manner, feeling utterly helpless. 'I can't bring her back. I miss her too. I wish you weren't going through this.' Guilt raged through him again, imagining what his mother might think if she could see her daughter looking so bedraggled. Even from infancy Bella had hated her clothes to be creased or dirty.

'Let's go home, Ned,' Bella said, sniffing.

It made remarkable sense to him. No matter what hardships awaited them beneath the grey skies of Scotland, at least it would look and smell and taste familiar. He was qualified now. He could find work, perhaps enough to pay a live-in housekeeper for Bella. Electricians would be in big demand, so an income was guaranteed if he could just get them back. It sounded like a plan at least.

'We'll go home soon, Bell. But you'll have to be patient now because I have to work out how we're going to do that. That's going to take me a few days just to think through. Do you understand?'

She nodded solemnly. 'A few days? And then we can start on our way back home?' She asked with so much longing that her big brother could not deny her that hope.

'Yes,' he promised, almost inclined to cross his fingers behind his back.

Since then another week or so had passed and they had befriended Robbie James.

He'd sought them out at meal time on their first night, an occasion apparently not presided over by the Brents.

'Who are you looking for?' Robbie had sauntered over to Ned while Nyunt and two other older women had served the children. Nyunt was piling tiny pyramids of rice into bowls and ladling a watery broth over each.

'For Dr Brent,' Ned replied.

'He's not here tonight and his wife is taking her meal alone in her rooms.'

'Do they ever eat with the children?'

'No. Never. They sometimes appear to encourage us to give thanks or to sing for our supper, as you English say. Dr Brent likes to watch us sing.'

Ned heard something odd in Robbie's tone but couldn't quite place it. Perhaps he just hadn't latched onto Burmese humour or simply Robbie's quirky manner. 'Thanks for making my sister feel so welcome,' he said. They both glanced over to where Bella was stirring her food, her expression making it clear she didn't much care for what she was looking at.

Robbie said, 'Whether she likes it or not, she must eat.'

'Yes, since our mother died she seems to be losing weight by the second.' Ned gave Robbie a grateful smile. 'If not for you . . .'

Robbie smiled back. 'Miss Bella is easy to love. She is like an angel.'

'She's gone through a lot,' Ned said and then instantly felt embarrassed for he was among others who had little to boast about.

Robbie didn't appear to take any offence. 'You should eat too.'

'What is it?' Ned wondered, staring into the pot.

'I could give you the proper name but you will not be able to get your tongue around it.'

Nyunt laughed.

'It is good,' she said in halting English with her lovely smile and now Ned could hardly say no, even though it didn't look at all appetising. And for Bella's sake he should set a good example.

He reached for a bowl, fashioned from a half coconut shell, and allowed Nyunt to scoop some sticky rice into it, then ladle over the watery, near colourless broth. After Robbie had followed suit they joined Bella.

'All right?' Ned asked her gently.

She sighed. 'I'm not hungry.'

'You think you're not but your belly needs feeding, Miss Bella,' Robbie said gravely.

She giggled. 'I like the way you speak,' she said.

'Why? Am I not speaking good English?'

'Perfect,' Ned admitted and shared a grin with Bella. He too liked Robbie's singsong voice.

'I'm going to teach some of the children how to play cat's

cradle,' Bella said, pointing at the long piece of wool she had looped and tied off.

Robbie frowned. 'What is that? Cat's what?'

'Cradle,' Bella and Ned said together.

He looked at them quizzically. Bella gave a mock sigh, put down her spoon and in seconds had the wool's framework set up around her fingers. The wide-eyed children, who had been silently watching the trio talking, crowded around Bella within moments.

Ned grinned, glad to see Bell so animated. With a theatrical flourish, he too set down his bowl, then plunged into the wool and pulled it up and over onto his own hands.

The children gasped as one and then all laughed and clapped. Robbie stared.

'How did you do that?'

'It's a game,' Ned explained. 'I think every child in Britain learns it before they turn five!' He laughed.

Bella had the wool back on her fingers in a flash. Even Robbie looked enchanted and Ned wondered what sort of future Robbie had here. He'd probably end up like Nyunt, staying at the orphanage and working just for food and lodging and no doubt for a sense of belonging, something Ned could relate to. A wave of sadness washed over him as he watched Bella's beaming face. He knew he didn't want Burma to be home, and certainly not an orphanage.

He stood up suddenly. 'I might take a stroll around the compound,' he said. Bella didn't seem to mind. In fact, he could tell she was enjoying being the centre of attention and would not miss him for the time being.

Robbie found him later, going about the duties Matron Brent had allotted him. His daily tasks now included sweeping out and cleaning the floor of the older boys' dormitory. Ned knew the children wouldn't be in bed for another hour so he had got on with his chore. It helped to keep him occupied but gave him space to think. He'd already swept and was now onto mopping.

'Hello, Ned,' Robbie said, bringing in his own bucket of water and mop.

Ned gave him a smile. 'Where's Bell?'

'Learning some Burmese dance steps.' He wagged his head. 'She is very attractive in a longyi.'

'Well, she does love to play dress-ups,' Ned said. 'Thank you again for being so good to her.'

'Don't mention it,' Robbie said, falling in tandem with Ned's mopping, picking up the rhythm and moving alongside him. 'It is easy. If she were older, I would run away with her,' he said with a swashbuckling sword flourish of his mop. 'Have you read *Zorro*?'

Ned shook his head.

'Oh, it's very fine. Dr Brent let me read his copy.'

'That was good of him. He doesn't strike me as a particularly generous man.'

'He isn't!' Robbie said emphatically, and although Ned's head snapped up, Robbie had already turned his back and moved away.

'Tell me about where you come from? Your home in England.'

'My real home is Scotland,' Ned began, delighted to have the opportunity to talk about it aloud. 'Scotland is the very northern part of the British Isles,' he said, leaning his mop against the wall and forming a triangle with his hands. 'I lived in a little town not far from the main city, Edinburgh. It's a very old city with cobbled streets and beautiful Georgian buildings in the New Town. In the Old Town there's a castle that dominates the landscape.' He knew he was losing Robbie, but he didn't care. He wanted to be lost himself in his fond memories. 'Scotland is cold, wet, overcast for most of the year.'

Robbie frowned.

'It doesn't smell of orchids and spice, not like here. I lived in a seaside town, and that smelled of salt and fish and apple pies, of smoking chimneys spewing out their black coal dust, of fresh-mown grass and roses in the summer. It rained a lot but we were never damp. My skin is always clammy here,' he said, genuine irritation in his voice.

'Do you not like it here, Ned?'

He wanted to protect his new friend's feelings but he preferred to be honest. 'I don't. I would like to return to Scotland. I can find some proper work there. I'm sorry, I don't mean to be rude or ungrateful. I know this is your home,' he said, his nostrils suddenly assaulted by the smell of disinfectant that overlaid a general aroma of damp clothes.

Robbie fixed him with a gaze. 'This is not my home, Ned. This is where I live, that's all. I was your sister's age when I came here but you must get her away before she turns mad . . . before she even reaches ten.'

Ned stopped and stared him. 'What's that supposed to mean?'

'Bella strikes me as someone who is weak.'

'Weak?'

'No, that's not quite the right word. I mean something that could break.'

'Fragile?'

'Yes, that's exactly what I mean. My English, forgive me, but sometimes I just can't find the right word.'

'Robbie, you speak my language more clearly than a lot of the people where I come from. Who taught you?'

'Initially my mother. She was born in West Bengal but something went wrong for her in Calcutta. She never told me what happened. She ended up here in Rangoon.'

'Well, your English is very good.'

'Thank you. My mother insisted I persevere because my father was English. I need to improve my reading. Dr Brent has insisted

I speak only English and so it has improved a great deal over the years.'

'I'll help you with your reading, and so will Bell.' He wanted to ask more about how Robbie came to be the son of an Englishman and a woman from Calcutta but he thought it might be rude.

Robbie smiled his pleasure. 'That means a lot to me. While the orphanage says it teaches the children reading skills, it actually makes them spend more time on basket weaving to earn money, and on general chores to keep the place running. I am lucky I have access to Dr Brent's bookshelves – well, when he's in a good mood, that is. I think Bell would enjoy teaching me.'

That reminded Ned of Robbie's earlier warning. He sighed. 'Bell's so young. I can hardly blame her for appearing fragile.'

Robbie gave him a knowing look. 'This is only the beginning. The worst is yet to come, Ned. I won't lie to you.'

'What are you talking about?'

Robbie began mopping furiously. 'Look, I like Bella and you. I know we can be good friends even though I hardly know you. Do you understand?'

'No. Make it clearer. I'm past games right now.'

'This is not a game!' the boy said, leaning his mop up against the wall. He walked away.

'Rob—'

'Shh! Just a moment,' Robbie said, peeking out of one of the dormitory windows. 'You never know who is listening.'

'You've really lost me now.'

'Do you like Dr Brent?'

'Not especially. No, not at all, if I'm being frank. There's something sinister about him.'

'Sinister?'

'You know.' He mimicked a shudder of revulsion. 'He makes you feel uncomfortable.'

'Exactly! He makes one's skin twitch. Your instincts are telling you enough. So listen to them and get out.'

'Out?'

'Away from here as soon as you can.' Robbie was whispering now.

Ned frowned. 'The orphanage? We've only just arrived.'

'Yes, the orphanage, but also Burma,' Robbie replied, exasperated. 'There's a lot of anger in the city. There's talk of uprising. You people who stay at The Strand and go to your clubs, you have no idea of what's happening outside in the real Rangoon.'

'Really?' Ned began, his tone cutting. 'I am hardly one of "you people". My father was an infantryman in the war and then decided to go adventuring. My mother had to teach for a living. Now our parents are dead, I don't have a penny to my name, and we have no support at all!'

'All right, calm down. I'm sorry. But you're new here. You don't realise that it doesn't matter how ordinary your life was back home. Being British still means you're treated differently here in the colonies. I'd switch places any time.'

'We're both in this orphanage, aren't we?'

'Yes, but you are fair and blue-eyed, and you know who both your parents were, and you remember what they look like and you have papers to say your whole family is British.'

'That's not much help to me right now, is it?'

Robbie regarded him with eyes the colour of the dark chocolate his father favoured, although Ned could barely remember the taste. 'What?' he asked, exasperated.

'You're going to have to lose all that bitterness if you're going to survive. No one's going to help you and you can't help yourself if you swim in self-pity.'

'Spoken like a champion survivor,' Ned growled, throwing his mop aside.

'Yes, I'm a survivor. I told you, my mother was from Calcutta. For some reason she came here to work on a rice plantation. She was very pretty with a beautiful voice that I can still remember. I don't know who my father is. People say he was a soldier. Others told me it was probably the planter himself who liked to toy with the beautiful Indian workers. Either way, I think we know that whoever my father was, he was English.'

'What does that make you?'

Robbie smiled sadly. 'I'm what you call Anglo-Indian, Ned. Half-caste.'

'Well, given your name, you sound as Scottish as I am.'

'This is true. And I'm proud to bear the name of Robert James, but it's probably just a convenient name I was given.'

'What about your mother's family?'

'You don't know about the caste system in India yet, do you?'

Ned shook his head.

'Well, how can I explain it simply? There are so many separations in Indian society that no level crosses over the other. Some castes refuse to speak to each other, others consider it bad to even be in the same area as a caste they consider so low as to be ignored.'

Ned stared back disbelievingly.

'You think I lie?'

'I think you exaggerate.'

'And I think you have plenty to learn,' Robbie told him. 'Being of a caste is one thing. Being half-caste, neither one nor the other, is to live in a desert. My mother's people are merely servants in British households but they consider *me* lower than an untouchable – as one might look upon filth.'

'Oh, come on, Robbie —'

'Why do you think I'm here? My father abandoned us. My mother's people wanted nothing to do with us. My mother died of dysentery when I was around Bella's age. I know how much your sister is hurting.'

'So what happened to you?'

'Oh, I lived on the streets but I survived. That's all that matters. I helped visitors to find their way around the city, or I carried their things for them. I tried to earn my money, rather than just ask for it. I promised myself that I would never pickpocket. I don't like thieves. Anyway, one day I witnessed a theft. The victim was a ruby trader. He was negotiating with me to help him carry some stuff when a pickpocket struck. I couldn't have that – he was stealing my client's papers and with them his money and my payment. As the thief ran away I tripped him up and jumped on him.'

'What happened?'

'Well, the trader was very grateful and wanted to help me. I would have preferred money!' Robbie gave a rueful laugh. 'But he talked to some people and before I knew it, I found myself here. And then I grew up quickly.' Robbie continued his work, suddenly awkward and angry.

'I've only just managed to get Bell through a day without crying. I don't want to disrupt her again for the moment. What the locals do doesn't actually affect us, right?'

'You really think your British friends will keep you safe? They've already forgotten about you.'

'Mr Fraser said —'

'I know, but your Fraser is like my ruby trader. He swore he'd come back and help me – but that was five years ago. Your Mr Fraser will soon be on the other side of the world, Ned, and he's not thinking about the Sinclairs. You have to help yourself.'

'Like you have, you mean?'

That seemed to hurt Robbie. He turned and glared. 'I'm planning to leave, Ned. You can come with me if you like – you and Bella. Or you can rot here and watch Bella become Brent's plaything.'

Plaything? Ned wasn't sure he'd heard Robbie correctly.

'Don't waste your breath asking. I have experience. He's not choosy, Ned. He just likes his victims young . . . and preferably white. Bella will be his prize.'

Ned was filled with confusion and disbelief. 'Dr Brent used you to . . .'

'Yes.'

The hairs on Ned's neck were standing up. 'I don't know what to say . . . I . . . Robbie, I'm so sorry.'

'Nothing to say. But don't let Bella be his new victim. She's perfect for him, young enough to give him years of pleasure.'

Ned was still reeling from the story Robbie had just told him but he couldn't control his fury at this comment. 'Shut up!'

'He'll become her friend, act like a father to her, even —'

Robbie never finished. Ned's fist connected cleanly with his jaw and in the next instant the lad was slumped on the ground. Ned stared at his unconscious companion, incapable of rational thought while the rage pounded through him. But gradually his breathing slowed, and the powerful emotion slowly subsided.

And as it did, it changed, coalescing into something hard and implacable as stone. It settled in his heart, heavy and dark, before finally his rage spoke to him.

Leave, it told Ned. *Take Bella and get the hell away from here!*

IO

Ned sat self-consciously beside the bed. Bella was holding Robbie's hand while Matron Brent looked on disapprovingly in her starched white outfit.

'Haven't you got some work to be doing?' she asked.

'I finished the dormitory,' he offered.

One of the local workers burst in, apparently in high dudgeon needing her. Ned watched, relieved, as Matron Brent flounced out, glaring at him as she left. He knew he could not stay long.

One of Robbie's lids opened slightly. It was obvious from his arch look of intrigue that he'd been pretending he was still sleepy from being knocked out. 'Has she gone?'

Bella giggled. Ned felt a fresh gust of relief, not just that Robbie was well enough to joke but that Bella was cheerful. Robbie's easy likeability had penetrated her sorrow and Ned marvelled at how quickly a child could be won over through laughter, as well as the simple friendship of other children.

'How's your head? We can't find any damage,' Bella said.

'My head?'

'Where you bumped it,' Ned prompted, urging Robbie to rub his chin, right where Ned remembered clocking it. But before he could answer, Dr Brent breezed in, managing to create a draught within the stillness, such was his size and bulk.

'Ah, Robbie, I'm glad to see you're back with us.' He grinned expansively, the flesh of his cheeks folding in on itself in a fascinating manner. Ned noticed his gaze lingering on Bell's thighs where her frock had ridden up as she perched on the bed.

Ned reached for his sister and pulled her back. He made it appear natural enough. 'We should go, Robbie. We'll come back and see you as soon as —'

'Oh, don't leave on my account, Edward,' Brent protested, his wide face sheened with sweat. 'I need to speak with you, anyway.' He swung back to Robbie, leaving Ned trapped between the doctor and the exit. Ned glared at Bella. His look forbade her to do anything but stand quietly by his side.

'So what happened to you, young man?' Brent asked, all jolly roundness, damp still darkening his shirt and voluminous linen trousers.

'I slipped,' Robbie answered immediately.

Ned picked up the story smoothly. 'We were cleaning the dormitory.'

'Oh, yes. You decided to show me how to do a Scottish dance,' Robbie said, grinning.

Ned continued. 'You slipped spectacularly on the wet floor, and rather amazingly missed the pail, but I think you banged your head on the wall.'

Robbie groaned, rubbing the back of his skull. 'But I'm ready to get up and go back to my duties now, Dr Brent.'

Brent nodded. 'Good. Well, Matron Brent can see you shortly and make a decision,' he offered bluntly before turning abruptly to Bella. 'And you, my dear, Arabella. It's nice to see you smiling again.' Ned scowled. 'In fact, I think you're about ready to start taking some lessons.'

'Lessons?'

'We have to continue some sort of education for you. Can't have you growing up a savage, now can we?' He chortled. 'I'll take you under my wing and give you a few lessons myself.'

Robbie threw Ned an urgent glance.

'In fact —'

'I can teach her,' Ned shot in. 'Both my parents were teachers. I can read, write, do sums very competently. You don't have to worry about Bell.'

Brent straightened. 'Oh, but I do.' His voice was light but his tone had an edge. 'She is my responsibility, you forget.'

'Yours?'

'You're a minor, Edward. Not yet twenty-one. Surely you don't think Mr Fraser put you in charge of your sister. I'm afraid that's impossible.'

'Fraser?' Ned just stopped himself from yelling. 'Whatever made you think that Mr Fraser was in charge of myself or my sister, Dr Brent? He is nothing to us but a passing stranger. He wasn't even on first-name terms with my mother.'

Brent gave a soft chuckle. 'But Mr Fraser paid for your upkeep here. He has therefore taken on the position of guardian.'

'Guardian? He couldn't wait to be rid of us! He made it very clear he had no money for our welfare.'

'Precisely. This is an orphanage, Edward, for children without any parent. You and your sister have been formally given into my care by a responsible adult, who took the time and trouble to see that you were in a safe place. And as director of this orphanage, the decisions for your future rest with me. We are not equipped to keep young men of your age. Our cut-off is usually around fifteen. Young Robbie here is almost at the right age to go . . . but not quite.'

'But Mr Fraser told us to wait until we heard from him,' Ned murmured, alarm sounding through him.

'I'm sure he did. But until we do, you can't stay here, young man. I've had a word to the headmaster at a boys' school within the city limits of Rangoon. He's going to see what he can do to help find you some work, perhaps as an apprentice electrician?'

'I've finished my apprenticeship, Dr Brent.'

'Now, I'll brook no further argument on this, Edward. What I say goes. The school in Rangoon is not a permanent accommodation – Mr Jameson is doing this as a favour to me – but we can't have someone of your age hanging around here. You should be grateful to me for pulling some strings. Jameson is offering gratis food and board for the next three months, until we can sort out your future. Arabella will be very well cared for around children of her own age and I can assure you that I will personally oversee her schooling and welfare. How much more can I offer?'

Another furious glare from Robbie told Ned to end this conversation. So Ned gave Brent what he knew he wanted, in order to avoid suspicion. He slumped his shoulders and banished all defiance from his eyes.

'You're probably right. I need some time to come to terms with our situation and hopefully we'll hear from Mr Fraser soon after his ship arrives in England. I apologise for my poor manners.'

Brent's whole posture changed. All trace of the predator vanished, leaving behind only a warm smile and an avuncular air. 'Well, you impress me. Now you're thinking like the cool-headed young man I'd taken you for. This decision is wise and is best for Arabella. I'll make arrangements for you to be driven to Rangoon tomorrow. Why don't you take the day off and spend some time with your sister? We'll see you at supper.'

Ned surprised himself by finding a smile to reinforce the sincerity he was desperately trying to contrive. 'Thank you,' were the only words he could trust himself to say.

'Hurry along, then, you two. I'll just have a quiet word with Robbie here.'

Ned glanced at his friend, noticing how guarded he became as Brent's eyes fell upon him. Ned hoped what he saw in Brent's hungry gaze didn't mean what he feared it might.

Robbie found Ned before dawn sitting beneath one of the peepul trees; not even the slightest breath of wind was stirring its blanket of overlapping heart-shaped leaves. It was already claustrophobically hot.

The boys greeted each other silently, Robbie joining Ned on the ground. 'Good position, this. You can't be seen easily.'

'I'm glad you approve,' Ned said quietly.

Robbie handed Ned one of the blushing red mangoes he was carrying. It had been split at the top and Ned watched how Robbie peeled back the skin and began sucking on the golden flesh. 'You know, in the cooler months, when there is a breeze, these leaves sound like gentle rain.'

'What are you, a poet?' Ned scoffed, but not unkindly for he recognised too much of himself in Robbie. He chewed on the fruit and immediately had to start licking at his wrist as the ripe mango released its juice.

'I just like to escape through my imagination,' Robbie replied.

'Most English people would never have tasted this fruit,' Ned remarked.

'Tell me what fruit you eat in Scotland.'

Ned tipped his head to one side. 'Oh, apples, pears, gooseberries, rhubarb, blackberries, strawberries in summer, of course, blueberries as well, cherries in spring and plums in autumn.'

'What? No bananas or jackfruit, guavas, melons, pineapples or papayas?'

Ned laughed. 'I don't even know what jackfruit or papaya is.'

'We do come from different worlds, don't we?'

That was so true. 'Have you ever tasted a juicy, fat summer strawberry?'

Robbie shook his head.

'It's like heaven. I went strawberry picking with my father once. We were meant to bring home two big bowls. We certainly picked two big bowlfuls but we returned with only two strawberries for Mum.' He sighed. 'I loved to do things with Dad. My little man, he used to call me. He taught me how to ride a bike, how to fish, how to climb a tree properly, how to mend a puncture on my wheel, even how to tie my shoelaces.'

'It sounds like you were very close to your father.'

'Not really. I just have impressions and memories of moments together. I haven't really seen my father for near on five years. I was younger than you when he left for the war . . .' Ned's voice trailed off. He cleared his throat. 'We were going to start up a gem mining business even though I was qualified as an electrician. That was at my mother's insistence. She felt having a trade was important.'

'And she was right,' Robbie said.

'Yes. My father was a dreamer, Robbie, and look where his dreaming got us. I'm not going to be like him. I'm going to be as practical as I can be. When I get married, I'm going to give my wife all of me – my love, my money, my time. I want a family, and I'm not going to achieve that wasting away here.'

'You're young and handsome. You will have no trouble finding a wife.'

'Thanks. Anyway, more importantly, how are you feeling?'

'Fine,' came the flat reply.

'I'm sorry, about hitting —'

'Don't worry about it. Where's Bella?'

'Dozing in the girls' dorm. She's exhausted. She'll be up shortly. She's keen to learn how to weave a basket. Far more keen than learning to spell.'

'No one will teach her much of that here anyway, despite what Brent promised. Did she understand the conversation?'

'Parts of it. I think she only listens to what she wants to these days, poor thing. Who can blame her?'

Robbie nodded, said nothing for a moment or two. He tossed away the well-sucked stone of the mango. 'Ned, you can't leave her here with him.'

'So I gather. Tell me everything. Stop talking around it.'

There was a long silence, long enough that Ned wondered whether Robbie had taken offence, but then he finally opened up and by the end of it Ned deeply wished he had not insisted on knowing.

'Most weeks he'd find me. Since I've grown up I'm less attractive to him, I suppose, but still he likes to remind me that he has all the power,' Robbie concluded.

Ned couldn't swallow. He wiped his sticky hands against his trousers that had seen better days. 'He still does it?'

Robbie nodded. 'These days, though, his interest is only aroused very occasionally . . . like it was an hour or so ago.'

'What?' Ned rolled away and stood up, loathing and anger mingling with his disgust. 'It makes me feel sick!'

'Don't blame me, Ned. I was a little boy when he began.'

'You have to tell someone!'

'Like who? Wake up, Ned. We have no power here.'

'What can I do?' Ned growled beneath his breath. 'I feel so helpless without any money.'

'No, you don't. You just need courage.'

'What are you talking about?'

'I'm talking about escape.'

Ned glared at him. 'So you've said.'

Robbie stood up. 'I can see I'm wasting my breath.'

Ned stopped him with a hand on his shoulder. 'Look, Robbie.

I know I sound ungrateful but I think you're forgetting we only arrived off the ship a matter of weeks ago.'

'Yes, and in that time both your parents have been killed. You have a baby sister, no money, and you're in a strange country so far away —'

'Are you *mocking* me?' Ned asked, incredulous.

'I wouldn't dare. You've already knocked me unconscious once today. No, Ned, listen to me. No one cares! That's hard to hear but I've learned it the hard way, too. The only person who will help you . . . is you. And now me.'

'Why?'

'Because I'm angry like you. I'm angry at the world that made me the son of an Englishman who didn't lay claim to me and at my Bengalese mother who died on me. I'm angry at being alone in a world that doesn't care, that mocks me for my skin colour. But my real fury is at the man who has had power over me. And today he used that power for the last time.'

Ned stopped pacing. 'What are you going to do?'

'I'm going to escape. I'm leaving today.'

Ned's face dropped. 'Why now?'

'I've been planning it for months. But I'm not going to wait another day.'

'So, back to the streets for you?'

'No. He'll hunt me down. I know too much about him.'

'Where are you going?'

'India.'

'Calcutta?'

Robbie gave a snort of disdain. 'No. I'm going south, to a place called Bangalore.'

'What's in Bangalore?'

'Not what. Who. In that fair city is an English doctor. Dr Walker. I met him here in Rangoon and he and his wife took . . . how do you say? They took a shine to me. Mrs Walker is half Indian, originally from Bombay. They told me their address.' He tapped his head. 'I keep it here. They told me there would always be an open door for me at their house.'

Ned's expression had disintegrated into one of complete bemusement. 'Robbie, it's hundreds of miles away. How do you plan to make that journey with no money and on foot?'

'I'm desperate enough to walk it but with Bella that could be difficult. I think I'll have to find a way to take a ship.'

'Wait! Don't drag Bell into this . . . or me.'

Robbie stared at him. 'All right. You go off to the school in Rangoon, Ned. And if you're content to leave Bella in the hands of that – that devil,' Robbie spat, 'then that's your choice. He doesn't care about how much he damages a child. He doesn't care that it makes you hate the world and yourself. He'll have her pregnant and sent away somewhere by the time she's my age. You'll lose track of her. You'll never —'

'Shut your filthy mouth!'

'I speak only the truth. You must get Bella away.'

'To *India*?'

'To anywhere. But why not India? Ships leave more often for India than England. Dr Walker will help you to get home.'

'How am I supposed to get into Rangoon with a nine-year-old? Carry her on my back?'

Robbie's eyes blazed with eagerness. 'Whatever you have to do, you will do. I'm going. He's touched me for the last time. You can come with me or you can stay and take your chances.'

'Leave me alone, Robbie. I need to think.'

'Well, don't think too long. And don't miss a meal either. I'm sure Brent doesn't trust us. He knew we were lying today.'

Supper passed uneventfully. Ned did turn up for the meal of rice served on a banana leaf with soured beans and a few softly spiced chunks of meat that he didn't recognise. He lowered himself to the floor next to Bella. It no longer shocked Ned to eat on the floor, or to use his fingers rather than cutlery. Privately he enjoyed indulging in what seemed to be the height of bad manners from a British perspective. He'd been warned on the ship by a well-meaning Englishwoman that the local savages ate with their fingers. 'And you never know where those fingers have been,' she had tittered. But now that Ned had watched the locals eating, he noticed how neat their hand actions were. It was quite a skill to roll a pinch of rice, some of the curry, a bit of pickle into a small, delicious mouthful. And what's more, the palm of their hand was never touched by the food. Watching Robbie and the children, Ned had been determined to master it.

But right now he wasn't hungry. Instead he reached for his cup of water and as he raised it to his lips he caught Brent, who'd joined them this evening, watching him with keen interest. The eyes, though small and deep set, missed little. The water stuck in Ned's throat as he imagined what his friend had lived through all these years. And he thought of those fat sausage fingers reaching for Bella and felt sickened.

'Aren't you hungry, Ned?' Bella asked softly, rice clinging to her fingers.

'You go ahead,' Ned choked out, glad that his sister was hungry enough to eat. Her cherubic features had given way to a gauntness this past fortnight. She was a shadow of the child who had squirmed next to him in the car that fateful morning of their arrival in Rangoon.

She leant forward to help herself to thin pickings, for Bella did not enjoy the food of the east. Over the top of her bent head Ned caught Robbie's glance and nodded – just once. Robbie understood that Ned had just agreed to attempt escape.

Ned reminded himself to remain composed. He forced himself to pile a few meagre scoops of rice onto his own banana leaf. The meat dish was dry – the Burmese did not favour much gravy – but while Bella struggled to find any interest in side dishes, adding only some sliced fruit to her rice, he rather liked the spicy accompaniments, especially the salty soured beans. Nevertheless, it was a struggle to force any food down his gullet this evening. He kept talking, entertaining the youngsters around him with a story. Robbie kindly translated with lots of animated gestures that had the little ones giggling; he even managed to make Bella smile a few times, but all the while he felt Brent's gaze burning on his turned cheek.

II

Robbie rolled over in his camp cot. The only light in the boys' dormitory was a single tiny tea candle burning some spices to keep the biting insects at bay.

It didn't deter the constant scuttle of lizards in and out of cracks in the wall and small openings in the windows, Ned noticed. A crowd of moths banged uselessly on the window above the low candlelight, determined to get in.

Robbie guessed it was close to ten-thirty; all the children were in bed and the few adults who remained on site would have retired to their huts or sleeping quarters. Experience told him that all but one would be snoring by midnight. Dr Brent was a 'night owl' as he'd heard it described. Just then a lonely owl's low, haunted cry sounded in the distance, as though echoing his thought. He knew Ned would be wide awake, awaiting his signal that they could now hatch the next part of their plan.

Robbie took a moment to savour the enormity of what he had set in train. No longer was the escape just about him; now there was Ned, and Bella. Bella had stolen his heart. It was ridiculous – he knew it – but he had convinced himself that she was indeed a gift of the gods. Because of her he would change his life; because of the peril of her situation, he would take responsibility for his own and make the change he'd been promising himself for years.

He had always thought English girls were plump, but Bella

was petite and her movements graceful – more like the Indian girls he admired. Robbie loved the pale translucence of her skin and the light sprinkling of freckles on her arms and face, as though the gods had sent a gentle drizzle of gold to rain down over her. From the moment he'd seen her he'd wanted to touch her fair hair, and he'd known instantly that she would attract the worst sort of attention from Brent.

'Don't ever be a victim,' he recalled his mother murmuring on her deathbed. It hadn't made sense to him then but her words had begun to resonate in recent times, especially since the Sinclairs' arrival.

Brent's attraction to Robbie had diminished after the rains had come last year; the monsoon had coincided with the arrival of Robbie's body hair. Now Brent tended to use his slobbering mouth and fat fingers simply to remind Robbie that he still had power over him. He had on many occasions told Robbie that should anyone ever find out about their 'special friendship' Robbie would be killed. And no one would ever find his corpse, Brent assured him, except the vultures that would pick over his bones.

But Robbie was no longer frightened of the vultures. The real one was here, running the orphanage. His life was a living death. Now, his only goal was to extricate Bella from Brent's grasp. If he died achieving it, then he would give his life gladly.

'Ned,' he whispered.

'I thought you were asleep. I know it's not time yet, but —'

'Ned. We can't do it tonight,' Robbie blurted.

'*What*?'

'Shh.'

'This was your idea, you —'

'Listen to me,' he hissed. Robbie reached over and banged the side of Ned's bed. 'Brent knows.'

'Really? How?'

'He was watching us tonight, far too closely. Of course he doesn't know our plans, but he's cunning, Ned. You have to trust me. He won't sleep tonight. He'll be waiting for us to do something. That's why he turned up at supper tonight – he was letting us know he was watching us.'

'Have you forgotten I'm being sent away tomorrow?'

'No,' he pushed Ned back down. 'Don't sit up. Trust me. He is out there waiting for us to try something. I know it. He shouldn't even see our shadows moving.'

'I hope you have another plan.'

Robbie turned it over in his mind. 'I do, but it means you have to trust me with Bella.'

'Go on.'

'You must leave and go into Rangoon as Brent wants.'

'No. I cannot leave Bell.' Ned turned angrily onto his back, his hands behind his head.

'Ned, just hear me out. Go tomorrow. You must work out your own escape at the other end. Leave the same day. It will be your best chance when you are new and everyone is trying to be kind and welcoming. They're bound to give you some time alone. Do it as soon as you can.'

'And go where?'

'Did you ever see the markets at the end of The Strand?'

'Yes, vaguely.'

'Go there. Find a way. The school is in Rangoon city, so get your bearings and make for the hotel area, then head for the bazaar. I'll find you. I promise.'

Ned was silent for a few moments and Robbie held his breath.

'All right,' Ned finally said. 'I don't know how but I'll be there.'

'Go to the wet section, where the food is sold. Walk through that until you see the flowers. Bella will find it less scary there.'

'Which brings us to how you imagine you'll get my sister away from here and safely into the city.'

'Ned, I told you, you have to trust me.'

'How do I know you —'

'You don't!' Robbie said in an urgent growl. 'But I will bring her to you, I promise. She trusts me. You've got to trust me as well.'

'What will we tell her?'

'Leave it to me. Make sure you just look helpless tomorrow, when you leave. Make Bella all the promises you want – all the usual stuff. And she'll cry, Ned, you know she will, so be prepared for it. But go. He'll make you anyway, so it's fine to look upset and torn . . . even angry, but go. At least that's one of us in the city.'

Robbie watched Ned smack at his own face. 'Bloody mosquitoes,' he snapped. 'Why can't we have nets? Have you seen Bell's legs with all those bite marks?'

'She'll get used to it,' Robbie whispered with a silent sigh. He turned on his back, rarely troubled by the insects that whined around his head most nights.

'What about malaria? Our mother had quinine tablets the size of horse pills she said we'd have to take.'

'Malaria is the least of your problems right now.'

'Robbie, when will you get out?'

'By tomorrow evening, Ned, we'll all be together.'

'I don't know what to think,' he replied.

'Don't think anything. Just go to sleep. Tomorrow's going to be a big day.'

12

Ned woke early. In truth he hadn't slept well, simply dozed fitfully, worrying about what the day would bring. He stared at the dingy, mildewed ceiling of the boys' dorm. His sheets were damp and he could feel the itch of fresh mosquito bites around his ankles.

He longed for the comfort and gentleness of home – suddenly he craved an icy chill on his face, a scarf around his neck. Scotland. Would he ever see it again? It felt a long, long way away.

'Robbie?' he called.

'Yes?' He didn't sound sleepy either.

'I hope you made the right decision.'

'I did. Now, you stick to the plan. You have to be convincing. Give nothing away, especially not to Bella.'

Ned sat up. A gecko scurried away from his toes and disappeared. 'You just worry about your part,' he warned sourly and moved to the ablutions block.

Later, over a breakfast of rice that had been fried with some sort of pea he didn't recognise, Ned sipped the bitter but fragrant green tea he was getting used to, but it didn't stop him missing the taste of a good brew of black tea with sugar and milk. He looked at his sister, who hadn't eaten much.

'Did you sleep all right, Bell?'

'Not really. Matron is acting like Mummy now.'

'What do you mean?' he asked, blowing on his tea.

'She made me sleep in her house last night. But I like it better being with the children.'

Ned felt a thrill of fear pulse through him. 'You slept in the Brent bungalow?'

She nodded. 'It was just as uncomfortable as the dorm. When are we leaving here, Ned? I don't like it. I think we should go home.'

Ned's mind was racing. Brent wasn't anywhere to be seen. 'Bell, did you see Dr Brent last night?' He could barely breathe, waiting for her answer.

'No. I slept in the same room as Matron.'

Ned ran a hand through his untidy hair, anxious. He had to tell her what was happening.

'Listen, Bell.'

She stared up at him, trusting.

'I'm going into Rangoon today.'

'Can I come?'

'No, darling. I'm going to take a look at a school.'

'But you've already finished school.'

'That's true, but everything's changed now. You know that. They're going to see about helping me to get some work, just until we know what's actually going to happen.' He hated himself for being part of this lie. 'The school is where they might accommodate me temporarily.'

'But that means I'll be here and you'll be in the city.'

'Not for long, I promise.'

Her eyes filled with tears. 'But, Ned —'

He didn't want a scene here. He grabbed her hand and led her away from where the children were finishing their morning meal as gently as he could. 'Now, Bell, you have to pay attention and you have to trust me. Do you?'

She nodded but he could see she was deeply unhappy. He hoped she wouldn't cry. Tears were only ever a second away with

Bella, not that he could blame her. She wouldn't survive much longer here.

'Do you trust Robbie?'

'I trust you both,' she said, all but stamping her foot.

'I need to know that you'll do everything Robbie tells you to.'

'Why?'

'Because we've a surprise for you,' he said, desperately reaching for the lie that would ease this plan through.

Bella brightened. 'A good surprise?'

'Yes. But you mustn't tell anyone, all right?'

Her eyes shone. 'Deal!' she said and it made him think of his father's expression whenever he struck a bargain.

He grinned sadly at the memory. 'Good girl. So, I'm going to leave this morning and I know it's going to make you sad but this is the surprise . . . you and Robbie are going to slip away from here and we're going to meet up in Rangoon.'

'Why?'

He couldn't think of a single way to say it without it sounding dangerous. 'We're all going to have an ice-cream,' he answered.

His answer had instant impact. 'Really?'

'You can't tell anyone, though, especially not Dr Brent or Matron. Do you understand?'

She nodded seriously.

'I mean it. Just do as Robbie says and I'll see you later. All right?'

She shook her head, unsure, her hair frizzy and dull. 'But won't we get into trouble?'

'No, because we won't be caught. I hate us being separated, even for a moment. But it's best I go into the city first and make arrangements.' Ned shocked himself at how easy he was making it sound.

'But why is it all so secret?'

'Bell, if we tell anyone, everyone will want to come and I can't see Dr Brent allowing all the children into Rangoon, can you? So, this is just a treat for you and Robbie.'

'Can we see the grave?'

This was the question Ned had feared most. He, too, wished to spend some time at his parents' grave, which the English community in Rangoon had kindly organised, but he suspected it would be one of the first spots Brent would look. No, they must avoid their parents' final resting place.

'I'm sure we can.'

'Oh, then, I can't wait. But how will we get back?'

'It's all planned. Don't you worry about it. Right! I'd better go and let them know I'm ready.'

'Ned —'

'Go find Robbie before your lessons begin. He'll tell you what to do. I'll see you before I leave.' He hugged her tightly. 'Go on. You don't want to be late,' he said lamely and gave her a gentle push.

Reluctantly, Bella sped off and as Ned saw her joining the other children, her golden hair and pale skin so conspicuous in the group, he knew that neither of them belonged here. He would get her out of Rangoon and on a ship to some place where Brent couldn't touch her, even if it killed him.

———

'Ah, Edward, thank you for being prompt,' Brent said smoothly.

Standing in Brent's office was a tall, swarthy man whose black hair, combed back off his forehead, glistened with hair oil. He was neatly dressed in a lightweight suit.

'This is Horace Foster.' The English name was a giveaway. Foster was Anglo-Indian presumably.

Ned nodded at the stranger.

'Mr Foster is the deputy head at the school and he has kindly offered to escort you back into Rangoon.'

Ned played along as politely as he could. 'That's very kind of you, sir. I'd like to see about finalising my electrician's licence if that's possible.'

Foster tipped his head from side to side in what was, Ned realised, an Anglo-Indian trait, as Robbie displayed the tendency. 'We will certainly do our best to help.'

'Thank you, sir,' Ned replied, glancing at Brent. 'Of course, I'd need to be able to see my sister regularly. I'm all she has left of family and . . .'

'We understand, Edward,' Brent said, his voice as oily as his companion's hair.

'Besides,' Ned continued. 'Mr Fraser will be contacting us very soon with details of how we will be getting back home to Britain.'

'Of course,' Foster replied, but the look that passed surreptitiously between them told Ned that neither held out any hope of that. Frankly, he didn't either, but he had to keep reinforcing to all who felt they had power over his diminishing family that Rangoon was not where their future lay.

'Well?' Brent said brightly. 'Let's get you on your way, Edward. You've had some breakfast, I presume?'

'I have.'

'Good. Have you said goodbye to your sister yet?'

'No. I don't plan to either. I preferred to tell her I would see her soon.'

'Of course, of course,' he replied.

'I would like to say a farewell to Robbie, though. He's been friendly to us and I didn't get a chance over break—'

'Hurry up, then, lad. We'll see you outside in five minutes.'

He nodded and left the relative cool of the office, made marginally more pleasant courtesy of one of the orphans operating a fan of reeds using his big toe. Ned was glad to escape for once into the oppressive heat outside. He noticed the horse and cart and assumed the driver was waiting for him. Emerging from around the cart was Robbie.

'Is it time?' Robbie asked, dark eyes wide and alert, but sauntering casually in his shorts that were too big for him and his pale blue shirt that was clearly a size too small.

Ned nodded. 'They'll be right behind me,' he said quietly. 'Is this going to work?'

'It will if you stick to the plan. Just do exactly as I've said.'

'But how will we find a ship or —'

'Here they come. Act properly now. No anxiety. Sullen is best. I won't let you down, Ned. Now smile. I promise I will bring Bella to you.'

'Ah, Robbie. Saying your farewells?' Brent called.

Ned stuck out his hand. 'See you, then. Look after Bell for me, until I visit.'

Ned was sure there was a false note in his voice but Robbie seemed to have just the right tone. 'I hope you get a chance to visit the grave.'

'I plan to, as soon as I can. Bye, Robbie.' They shook hands before he turned. 'Goodbye, Dr Brent. Please let me know as soon as we have word from Mr Fraser.'

'Absolutely, my boy. You can be sure of it. Now, here's a small sum of money. Mr Fraser left this with me and I'm returning it to you.'

Ned stared at the envelope dully.

'So, off you go then,' Brent said, waving his hands as though herding Ned into the cart. 'Thanks, Horace.'

Foster nodded solemnly beneath his topi and gave instructions to his driver. The cart lurched and then they were in motion. Ned waved, feeling sick about leaving his sister, but also excited that stage one of their plan was finally in action. There was no going back now.

He cleared his throat. 'How long will it take, Mr Foster?'

'By road, about forty minutes.' Foster's English was flattened out by his Indian accent.

'Are we going straight to the school?'

'Where else did you think we might go?' Ned assumed there was no further point engaging the dour man in conversation.

The journey lengthened, as did the silence, and before long Foster was dozing, his head waggling with the motion of the cart. The driver had not said a word and clearly didn't intend to. Ned took out the envelope from Brent, slitting the paper open with his forefinger.

Inside were three pounds, two of them in ten-shilling notes and the rest in coin, no doubt a fortune in this part of the world, but Ned saw it for what it was. Brent's guilt money. He could now tell Fraser, or anyone else who came looking, that he'd done everything humanly possible for the Sinclair boy.

Finally the cart hauled to a stop. Already the various stalls in the bazaars had begun their food preparations for the evening. The sounds of car horns and braying cattle assaulted him and he could hear the rumble of the tram in the distance.

Foster jerked awake. 'Ah, we're here, are we?'

'The school?' Ned frowned. 'I don't see any —'

'No, Sinclair. This is a shop where I need to pick up some supplies.' He suddenly prattled in urgent Burmese and the driver nodded and leapt off the cart. 'Can you wait here, please?'

'Yes,' Ned replied, confused. 'Can I help?'

'No, just wait here and don't leave the cart unattended. We won't be long. All right?'

'Fine.'

Foster disappeared into the large, ramshackle building that

seemed to offer everything for sale from pots and pans to fresh food for sale.

Ned clambered down and stared angrily at the dark entry of the store. He could just make out Foster's back, heading towards a counter at the far end. Ned looked around wildly. The driver was nowhere to be seen. His heart began to hammer and his mouth turned suddenly dry. This was surely his chance! He would not get a better shot at it. During the hot journey he had tried to envisage his escape, but even in his daydream he hadn't imagined being left alone long enough to disappear into the throng of the city.

He gave himself no further time to think. Thinking was dangerous, his father had often said. Sometimes you just have to act on instinct. It was an argument that certainly suited his father's adventuring ways. Ned had nothing to take. Only his three pounds and the clothes he stood in.

The gods had certainly smiled on him and answered his prayer. Within seconds the horse stood alone, tethered to the cart, and Ned was running at full pelt as far away from imprisonment as he could, hurtling towards freedom.

A few minutes later Foster emerged and squinted into the sharp sunlight. He blinked, his pink lips thinning in his dark face as he looked around. The driver arrived carrying two huge sacks of rice and dumped them into the cart.

'So he took up the offer, Master?' he asked in Burmese, with a gap-toothed smile.

'Seems so,' Foster answered. 'Dr Brent will be happy.'

It felt to Ned as though he could run forever. He had deliberately taken the most zigzag path, twisting and turning deeper into the busy streets of Rangoon, finding himself in places where no white faces looked back at him.

He finally skidded to a halt, leaning back against a wall, breathing hard and suddenly realising he was now in a particularly quiet area. He'd run through so many alleys he couldn't begin to imagine where he was, but he could hear the reassuring traffic from the main roads.

The sight of a topi triggered a fresh panic and he spun into a door that opened, pushing past a swirl of saffron fabric and careening into a small group of young boys, dressed in red and orange robes. Their heads were shaved, their dark, almond-shaped eyes surprised at the sight of him, but he was touched by their wide smiles. They were chatting and laughing, like a flock of chirruping sparrows.

Ned paused, baffled, then realised he had stumbled into a monastery. Around him men – young, old – went about their rituals in a comfortable silence. Timber structures created separate areas along a winding labyrinth of stone-floored corridors, which led Ned further into the place of prayer and contemplation. As he walked, in silent wonderment, he noticed a monk taking a traditional bath, tipping water from a small vessel over his head. If the man noticed the foreigner passing by, he didn't pause. Nearby, Ned saw a circle of men sharing out a pot of rice and what looked to be a thin gravy of curry.

The smell made his belly rumble. He was hungry but it was irrelevant, given his circumstances, and he ignored it. Unlike the monks, he would not have to beg for food, which is what he imagined the stream of men heading past him were going to do right now. Full of smiles, seemingly not at all fazed by his sudden presence, the men flowed like a colourful river out of the monastery. In a moment of clarity, and feeling safer than he had done in days, Ned stopped one of them.

'Excuse me, sir?'

The man nodded, clearly unable to understand him.

Ned dug into his pocket and pulled out one of the two shilling bits. He pressed it into the man's palm. 'For you, for everyone here,' he said, waving his hand expansively. He knew it was plenty of money, could feed all of them probably for at least a day. 'In return, pray for my family,' he pleaded, and held his hands together in the pose of prayer. The dark-eyed, studious-looking man said something in Burmese. His words were unintelligible to Ned, but sounded comforting all the same.

Instantly, Ned felt more at ease. The plan was going to work. Somehow they would escape Brent's clutches and get away from Rangoon altogether. He looked up at the marshmallow clouds scudding across a perfectly blue sky, then left the monastery, picking up his pace again and running with even more confidence.

13

Ned scrambled his way into a covered market and found himself assaulted by the shrieks and calls of animals. He wasn't especially squeamish, but he didn't enjoy seeing animals slaughtered or butchered. He squelched through blood that ran in great rivulets beneath his feet.

He began to run again, moving blindly, hardly registering the people whose shoulders he knocked or feet he stumbled over. The smell of blood was overpowering and the squeals of frightened creatures and busy people made him dizzy.

He passed through a calmer area where incense was sold, Great spirals of the baked mixture, infused with perfume, uncoiled to form a beehive-shaped dome that hung from ceilings and burned for hours when lit.

The smell made him sneeze and a shopkeeper laughed at him as he ran by. He passed a stack of grey stone slabs and frowned, pausing briefly to suck in great gasps of air. A young girl tending the stall mimed grinding something on the slabs and then rubbing her face. Ned understood. He had seen many of the orphans using *thanaka*, a golden paste ground from the bark of trees, on their cheeks, mainly the girls. Apart from the pleasant fragrance and cosmetic beauty, it also had cooling properties and helped prevent sunburn.

Ned ran on. It was only the arresting smell of spice that halted him and then he doubled over, hands on his knees, sucking in air again. He was wet through; his shirt was clinging to his body, his pale trousers sticky and uncomfortable. He'd lost his topi somewhere and sweat was running into his eyes.

'Sir?' asked a gentle voice. 'All right?'

He looked up into the softly frowning face of a young woman. She was not Burmese – probably Chinese, with her smooth pale complexion that had a slightly golden hue. Her hair was glossy black, matching her feline eyes, and tied in a long ponytail. She was exquisite and petite, like an oriental porcelain doll.

'I'm fine,' he said, straightening. 'Thirsty,' he admitted, instinctively mimicking drinking.

She held up her hand. 'Please,' was all she said, disappearing into the shop that Ned now realised was a tea place of sorts. Tea shops dotted all of Rangoon and were popular meeting places. The young woman re-emerged clasping a delicate china cup.

'Try. Hot but cooling,' she urged and nodded, her gentle smile as much a tonic as her drink. She was beautiful.

It was green tea. Many people swore by it. He did not like it especially, but right now he was happy to oblige her.

'Thank you.'

He blew on the pale liquid and sipped as the grassy fragrance hit him first and then the slightly bitter, earthy taste nudged his tastebuds.

'This is good for you,' she said in halting English.

How could he resist her? He drank it all, then reached into his pocket.

'No, no, sir. My gift. All right, now?' she asked again.

'Much better, thank you.' He pointed to himself. 'Ned.'

'Li Li,' she replied. 'Hello,' she finished, getting her tongue around the English salutation.

It sounded as exotic and alien to him as she looked.

'Hello, Li Li,' he said haltingly.

She giggled deliciously. But then a shadow fell on him and an older man appeared, speaking to her in rapid Chinese. She made a deferential bow. The man cast an unfriendly glance at Ned. Ned didn't need to understand their language to know the instructions given. He handed back the cup.

'Thank you, Li Li. I feel well now.'

She smiled more sedately and gave a similar bow. 'Good day, sir,' she said carefully, and began backing away.

'Er, The Strand?' he asked, hoping for a last moment with the beautiful Chinese girl, but Li Li was urged back into the shop.

He moved on, stopping at various eating-houses until he found someone who spoke English and could direct him to the famous main road.

Finally Ned found himself on The Strand itself, facing the hotel. His heart leapt with the pleasure of familiarity, although that feeling was quickly followed by an equally heartfelt sense of sorrow. This would never be a happy place for him.

He arrived into its cool reception, with a sense of déjà vu. He didn't want to relive that ghastly moment when his life and that of his family had changed irrevocably.

In truth, he hated this hotel. He hated Rangoon.

'Yes, sir?' asked the man standing behind the desk pretending not to notice Ned's dishevelment.

Ned cleared his throat. 'I'm Edward Sinclair. I stayed here not long ago. May I speak with the general manager please?'

'He is not here, Mr Sinclair. He is in India at present.'

Ned's hopes plummeted.

'Perhaps I could help? I remember your family. I am Frank Jones, deputy manager.'

The man's English was impeccable and he certainly gave the impression of being British, yet like Robbie, he looked clearly foreign with his tawny skin and thick, dark hair.

'Thank you, Mr Jones. I'm wondering first if you would change some money for me?'

'Certainly.'

'I have two ten-shilling notes, thank you,' he said, handing over the notes bearing the portrait of King George V alongside Britannia and her great shield.

'This is a large sum of local currency, sir. May I put it into an envelope for you?'

Ned nodded.

'Can I also caution you, sir, if you plan to walk around with this in your pocket?'

'I will be careful. Mr Jones, can I rely on you not to mention that you have seen me here today?'

'We are very discreet at The Strand Hotel, sir.'

'Good. I hope I can count on that. Can you give me any indication of what a passage to Calcutta might cost?' He and Robbie had already agreed they would aim for Bangalore, which meant a voyage to Madras.

Jones handed him the money, giving away nothing on his expression, but Ned was sure his question surprised him. 'Er, you mean by ship, sir?'

'Yes.'

'I wouldn't know exactly. Of course, you could negotiate a passage. I would be happy to —'

'No, that won't be necessary but thank you. My family trunks. I'm wondering where our possessions have been kept?'

'In our storage rooms. Mr Fraser asked us to retain them until further notice.'

'May I see them, please?'

'Of course.' He rang a bell and a pristinely dressed man arrived swiftly. 'Is there anything else I can assist you with?'

'You've been very helpful, thank you. I will send word about our trunks in due course.'

'I understand. They are safe with us until you've made all your arrangements.'

———————

Fifteen minutes later, after reliving his despair as he looked over the contents of the two humble trunks, Ned had taken only some clothes for himself and Bella, and one of his own shirts for Robbie. The main reason he'd even taken this chance in coming to the hotel was to secure their passports. His father had told Lorna she'd need this new documentation to travel. He'd been issued with his at the outbreak of war, when the Allies felt it was important men had papers declaring their state of origin. And so Lorna had paid the sixpence for the new-fangled travel document that described her features, showed her signature and detailed her dependants as Edward and Arabella Sinclair.

He was glad the hotel had found Lorna's small leather satchel of documents that included this important travel paperwork, and placed that in one of the trunks. He could only wonder at where his father's documents were, but he was lingering too long over this. He took his mother's prayer book, her tiny watch, and stuffed one of her hand-embroidered handkerchiefs, still smelling of the 4711 Cologne his father had brought back from Europe, into his pocket and then rifled around Bella's favourite books. He couldn't carry them all. Their mother had loved sharing *Alice's Adventures in Wonderland* but Ned knew Bell secretly preferred *Peter Pan* and *The Wind in the Willows*. And then there was their father's final gift to her, a copy of Rudyard Kipling's *The Jungle Book*, which he claimed would whet her appetite for her new life abroad. Ned tucked that single book under his arm.

It felt terrible to close the trunks. They had signified the beginning of a happy new era as a family in peacetime, but now they stood for only death and sorrow. In closing them for what he knew was the last time, he was turning away from everything that was familiar. From here on, it would be steps into the unknown.

14

Robbie felt as though he was balanced on the edge of a precipice, preparing to jump. He crossed the compound in search of Bella, wanting to explain everything yet knowing he could tell her nothing. His normally expressive face was curiously blank.

'Robbie,' called a familiar voice. 'A moment, please.'

Robbie's heart began to hammer in his chest but he urged himself to act naturally.

'Yes, Dr Brent?' he answered, jogging up to the man he despised.

'Where is Arabella Sinclair? Apparently she's not in her lesson.'

'I don't know, Dr Brent. I've been running some errands for Matron.'

'I'm not interested in your errands, boy,' Brent snapped. Then he changed tack. 'That was a touching scene this morning with her brother.'

Robbie blinked, said nothing.

Brent cocked his large head to one side. 'You all seem very friendly.'

He nodded. 'Yes, Dr Brent. I suppose they are the first English children I've been able to know.'

'And what will you do now that Edward has gone?'

'I'll get over it. We really didn't have much in common.'

'Other than Arabella,' Brent said slyly.

'What do you mean?'

'It is obvious Edward loves her a great deal.'

Robbie forced himself not to fidget, not to swallow or show any sign of just how nervous he felt.

'Well, she is his sister,' he said carefully.

'But so, I fear, do you, and she is *not* your sister, so that is an altogether far more dangerous admiration. A love like that could prompt you do anything, try anything.'

Now Robbie did swallow, but held eye contact with Brent. To look away now would damn him. He desperately reached for the nonchalance he didn't feel. 'I like Bella, Dr Brent, but —'

Brent advanced on him. 'Bella, eh? That's a nicely familiar name for someone you hardly know.'

Robbie tore his gaze away from the sneering doctor and saw the laundry cart arriving.

'I should go, Dr Brent. Matron wants me to accompany the dhobi's chokra today. I have a message to deliver.'

Brent looked over at the dhobi's son climbing down from the vehicle, the back of the cart half filled with bundles of laundry. 'You tell the dhobi that I will kick his bony arse if he sends back laundry that is inferior. I will ensure he gets no work from the memsahib if he lets me down again.'

'I will, Dr Brent. Matron has asked me to watch everything they do and report back,' he lied.

'Good.' He cupped Robbie's chin in a parody of intimacy. 'Remember what I said. I want you to leave Arabella alone. I don't want you filling her head with thoughts of life beyond the orphanage. I'm actually quite surprised you didn't try to leave with her brother.'

'But this is my home, Dr Brent,' Robbie said in an injured voice. 'There is nowhere else for me.'

He glanced again at the dhobi's cart. Time was so short. He

had to get away from Brent or the whole plan could go awry. He cast a silent prayer that Bella was precisely where she should be and hidden from anyone who might be looking for her.

'Fetch me some water before you go, would you?'

'Of course. Let me replenish your jug.'

Robbie fled, first to the chokra boy by his bullock cart to give him some instructions to wait. How his heart was hammering. The plan was in motion. All he had to do now was hold his nerve and somehow keep Bella convinced this was all just a game.

He ran around the back of Brent's house, to the tiny outhouse. He'd already seen Matron leave for the day to oversee the purchase of the month's fresh dry supplies. She would be gone for at least another hour. Logically there should be no one anywhere near the house, other than Brent himself, and he had no reason to come here at this hour until his midday tiffin. Robbie was counting on it.

'Bella?' he whispered.

She emerged from behind the outhouse. 'Here I am.'

'Hello, Bella. Well done,' he said, relief flooding him. 'Do you remember our plan?'

'Of course I do,' she said, playfully. 'You're going to bundle me up in a sheet and we're going to escape.'

'That's right,' he said, nerves fluttering like a flock of birds in his belly. 'But, Bella, you have to stay silent – not a groan, not a giggle, not a sneeze. Any sound at all might give you away. And if you're found, Dr Brent will become enraged. You haven't seen him angry.'

'What will he do?' she asked, wide-eyed.

'Nothing to you. But me? He'll whip me, maybe send me away for good. He hates disobedience.'

'Oh, Robbie, let's not do this, then.'

'No, listen to me. It's going to be fun. We can meet Ned, have the ice-cream and you'll be back before anyone knows we're gone.'

'Hurry, hurry, then. Tie me in,' she whispered.

Robbie nodded and fetched the bundle of sheets he'd already stashed. 'Not a sound, Bella. And you only get out when I tell you it's safe.'

'I know.'

'Only when you hear my voice, Bella. Promise?'

'I promise.'

Bella was tiny, almost elfin, and her limbs folded into themselves with ease until she was wrapped deep within the sheets. Robbie tied her in. She looked like a beautiful butterfly just before it emerges from its cocoon.

'Stay loose and floppy,' he warned. 'No elbows or knees must poke anywhere. You need to imagine yourself as a bundle of sheets.' He heard her giggle. 'Hush now, Bella. It begins. Not another word until we get there.'

She made no further sound and Robbie hefted the bundle onto his back, glad his wiry body had done enough hard work to build strong muscles. He checked their reflection in a window as a last-ditch effort to reassure himself this mad plan could work. He held his breath and walked, reminding himself it was about confidence. From a distance no one would think anything was odd about this scene.

As light as Bella was, Robbie could feel her dead weight on his back. He forced himself to walk slowly so she didn't bang against him. He was almost at the cart when the voice he dreaded most called to him.

'Pardon, Dr Brent?' he called back, putting down the bundle.

'Come here, boy!'

Robbie had to approach the enemy. Brent stood perhaps thirty feet in front of him but it felt like the longest walk he'd ever made. The heat was already scorching the earth and he should have thought about a hat for Bella – if she survived the heat inside that bundle. He felt rising panic, his mouth turning dry. Robbie was convinced that guilt was written all over his face. Brent knew, he was sure of it, and now he was going to make Robbie pay.

'What are you doing?' Brent demanded.

Somehow Robbie held his nerve. 'I told you, Dr Brent, Matron asked me to make sure the chokra took all the laundry because he's been unreliable for the last couple of months. I was just helping to speed things up.'

'I see. You look anxious, Robbie. And my, my, you are perspiring hard this morning. Anything wrong?'

Robbie took a slow breath. 'Actually, I don't feel especially well, Dr Brent. I slept badly. I think last night's dhal upset me.'

'No one else is complaining.'

'It will pass. I will take more water.'

'Speaking of which, I thought I asked you to fetch me water.'

'I just thought I'd get the cart loaded up first.'

'You seem awfully eager to get away on the bullock cart for some reason.'

Robbie's insides froze. He hoped his fear was not reflected on his face. He couldn't feel it any longer – everything was numbed. 'I . . . I didn't want to let Matron down,' he stammered. Then reached one last time for a lie. It was his final parry. He had nothing more if Brent called this bluff. 'She said that if I ran all my errands before the dhobi sent back the washing this afternoon, I could visit the temple and make an offering for my mother.'

'Did she indeed? And why this treat, Robbie?'

'Because I've been so helpful to her recently, and she praised me for assisting with the Sinclair children.'

'Is that so?'

Robbie nodded.

'Well, I shall have to have a word with Matron. We can't single you out too often, especially as you have enjoyed my favour for so long.'

Robbie's pulse pounded in his ears and his head ached from

the pressure in his body. If this continued, he was sure he would quite simply explode in front of Brent.

'Arabella Sinclair has still not turned up to her lessons. I've got the servants looking for her. Did you see her?'

'Yes,' Robbie shocked himself by saying. 'I told her to hurry back to her classroom. She was hiding in a cupboard in the dorm. She was crying, Dr Brent, and I did my best to comfort her but I'm in a hurry, as you can see.'

'Yes, yes, and . . . ?' He clicked his fingers before Robbie's face.

Robbie's head snapped back. 'I think you'll find she's already with the others.'

'Good. Well done. Now fetch my jug of water, *jaldi, jaldi*!'

Robbie glanced at the bundle of laundry, sitting in full fierce heat, and realised there was nothing he could do for Bella at this moment.

He ran to the kitchen. The ayah was busy at her work, crushing garlic, ginger and onion on the grinding stone held nimbly between her crossed legs. She was humming to herself, her back to him.

He asked her if the water had been drawn from the well.

'There is some boiled water left, not much,' she replied. 'The rest is cooling.'

Robbie nodded and moved to the big pail where the boiled, cooled water was kept. His despair, his years of yearning to be free, his desperation to escape poverty and his desire to protect Bella against the monster that was Brent all joined to form a dark ball of festering hatred. It settled in his belly like a cancer that would consume him if he didn't heal himself by taking revenge. And there was only one way to heal his thirst for revenge.

Water.

Robbie had already lifted the lid on the pail of boiled water but now he replaced it quietly, hardly daring to breathe. Could he really do this? He needed to think it through but time was his enemy. Make a decision, Robbie.

Quickly Robbie filled the jug with unboiled water from the other container and, without a giving himself a moment to reconsider, he ran back to Brent's office.

'Here we are, Dr Brent.'

'Look at you sweating, Robbie. I do believe I've never seen you look so unhealthy.'

'I'll be fine.'

'No, we can't have that,' Brent said. 'Here, take a drink,' he said, pouring out a glass of the newly arrived water.

Robbie wiped his face with his shirtsleeve. 'I'm not thirsty, Dr Brent.'

'Well, you certainly look it.'

'I can have some on the journey. I really must —'

'Drink, Robbie. I insist,' Brent replied.

He had no choice. To defy Brent now would be to seal his and Bella's future. He could not permit that to happen. He reached for the glass, hoping his hand didn't tremble.

'Chin-chin,' Brent said, with a glint of pleasure. 'Finish it up and be on your way. Can't have you passing out from dehydration.' He laughed. Robbie steeled himself and drained the glass.

'Goodbye, Robbie,' Brent said. It sounded final.

Robbie left the hut, the sun not yet high enough to bake the earth but more than hot enough to send a pale-skinned little girl, unused to the heat, to an early death. He ran to the bundle still untouched by the cart. He couldn't say a word to Bella because the chokra boy was suddenly alongside and flinging his own linen onto the cart.

He hefted Bella, trying to make it look careless and easy, but stopped just short of flinging her.

'Bella?' he murmured, desperate for any sort of response. He glanced at the boy impatiently waiting for him to clamber up onto the bench.

The bundle remained ominously silent.

15

They finally arrived at the laundry with the bullock cart manoeuvring its ponderous way through the streets without incident. Robbie felt dizzyingly short of breath in his fear for Bella.

He leapt off the cart and as the dhobi himself came out of the gloom of the shop, yelling at his son and accusing him of lingering too long at the orphanage, Robbie was first to haul off the bundle that contained Bella. He made a show of adjusting the load, and in the meantime father and son had hefted their bundles onto their backs and were lurching into the laundry, still arguing.

It was Robbie's chance. He stumbled around to the side of the building, struggling with the knots that seemed to have tightened from the weight they held. He felt his panic take hold and fly.

'Bella!' he screamed. 'Answer me.'

He heard a soft groan and his poor, hammering heart stuttered momentarily with relief. She was alive! In a fever he bit through the fabric and ripped open the top sheet and there she was – his golden angel – bathed in sweat, her soft hair clinging like limp snakes to her face.

'Bella,' he whispered into her ear.

She moaned softly again. 'Ned?'

'It's Robbie. Come on. Can you stand?'

Her eyelids fluttered open and then closed again. She was dazed and Robbie feared heatstroke, which could kill.

'Bella, put your arms around my neck. Please, Bella, please. Help me.'

With an effort, he lifted her and staggered into the shop's entrance, darting around people ironing, and between sheets and shirts hanging from every inch of the shop, hollering for the dhobi.

The older man came hurrying out from the back, demanding to know what was going on.

In Hindi Robbie explained that he was bringing in the laundry when this young memsahib had collapsed. Two of the dhobi's women rushed to Robbie's aid, deferring somewhat to his paler skin and obvious Western blood, perhaps surprised by his fluency in their language.

Everyone began fanning Bella and fresh water was brought.

'Boiled?' Robbie demanded, covering Bella's mouth.

The wife batted his hand away. 'Of course!'

Life-giving water was dribbled between Bella's swollen lips and gradually she came back to them, her eyelids finally opening. She looked momentarily frightened by the dark faces looming over her, but then she saw Robbie and her confusion eased. Her eyes were bloodshot but she managed a smile. 'Is this where we get our ice-cream?' she murmured.

The dhobi seemed to grasp the last two words and grinned, revealing few teeth left in his head.

Robbie maintained his story that she was simply a passerby. He began discussing with the dhobi and his wife the possibility that Bella must have somehow become separated from her family and disorientated by the heat. Going by the concerned waggle of their heads, no one around him seemed to think the story implausible.

'What shall we do?' the dhobi asked.

Bella had closed her eyes again and was clearly of no help.

This was the opening Robbie needed. 'I shall take her into Rangoon.'

But the man frowned. 'Pah!' he said. 'How will you find the family she belongs to in Rangoon?'

'Easy enough. This girl is English, so the big hotel – The Strand – will be able to track down her people. Help me get her to The Strand. I can sort it from there.'

The dhobi looked doubtful but his wife prodded him.

'Hurry up, you fool,' she said. 'Get that bullock cart moving and get this girl to the hotel.' She wagged a finger in his face. 'If she dies here, you'll make lots of trouble for us.'

That threat galvanised the dhobi into action. He blasted orders at the chokra boy, who nodded continuously at both his father and Robbie. Finally, the boy beckoned.

'I'll take you now,' he said to Robbie.

They helped Bella to her feet. She was unsteady and claimed to be dizzy but Robbie could see that his prayers had been answered – Bella would recover. But there was always the lurking threat that Matron Brent might decide to pass by the laundry.

'Come on, Bella,' he whispered. 'We have to meet Ned. Take more water.'

'I can't. I can feel it all sloshing inside me. I'll burst. Perhaps I should go to a bathroom.'

Robbie nearly laughed, hysteria just a moment away with his nerves strangled and Bella's belief that a place like this would even have running water.

'We're going back to The Strand. Can you hold on until then?' he asked, imagining what she'd have to squat over if he asked if she could relieve herself here. It would be worse than the orphanage.

She nodded.

'It will be cool in the hotel,' he said, guiding her out to the bullock cart and helping her into it. 'Now we must shield you with this cloth. The sun on you again,' he said, looking up into the fierce light, 'is very dangerous.'

The bullock pulled out laboriously into the bustling traffic and the dhobi's farewell was swallowed up into the cacophony of the city.

———————

Ned wandered aimlessly around the bazaar. He was a familiar enough figure now and some of the stall owners chanced a smile at him. He'd filled his grumbling belly with a bowl of irresistible, silky-pale broth. He'd seen the soup simmering for an hour or more in a huge pot, so he knew it was safe to eat, and its exotic aroma made his mouth water.

Unlike his mother and Bella, Ned didn't mind the heat of chilli and the foreign tastes of ginger and garlic. The ship's galley had begun serving some Indian-style food once they'd left the Suez Canal behind, to get people acquainted with the spices and herbs they were likely to encounter further east.

Ned had been entranced by the rich colours of the curries, the rices striped with saffron and crispy onions, fried sultanas and little kidney-shaped nuts called cashews. On the evening called the Maharajah's Banquet, when everyone dressed in their finest, he had noticed with delight that the huge platters of rice were draped in tiny glittering foils of silver. One of the old waiters had assured him it was real.

Silver leaf, he'd called it. 'If this were a real banquet, for a real maharajah, this would have been one hundred per cent gold leaf.'

'Really?' Ned had exclaimed.

'No word of a lie. Gold means everything to these people. You'll see for yourself. Even the poorest people wear their money – a peasant woman will wear twenty-four-carat gold bangles. They even eat gold . . . but only royalty, mind,' he'd said, tapping his nose.

Ned bought a few bananas with the annas he found at the

bottom of his pocket, mindful only to show the smallest change. In the hotel he'd taken the precaution of taping the bigger notes to his chest. He had no intention of using them for anything other than their passage out of this place.

Once his hunger had been sated, he began prowling, never straying far from the flower stalls. He'd lost count of the times he'd circled this area of the bazaar, his gaze roving constantly for any sign of trouble but mostly for Robbie and Bella.

And so it was a moment of enormous wonder, his emotion welling up from somewhere deep inside and rushing out of his throat in a triumphant whoop, when he saw two familiar, slightly ragged figures stumbling into the hall of flowers.

———————

Their reunion was brief. Ned forced them both to take a bowl of soup as neither had eaten since breakfast and it calmed them both down. Bella seemed to have forgotten about the promised ice-cream, or had lost interest. Her complexion was pale, her skin dry and hot, no longer clammy. Robbie looked little better and seemed to be hiding something.

As Robbie drank the last of his soup, Ned asked the big question. 'What about Brent?'

'Don't worry about Brent.'

'Don't worry? You're joking, aren't you? He'd know by now.'

'Know?' Robbie jeered. Then he sounded suddenly sad. 'He already knew, Ned. He let us both go too easily. The one thing I don't think he'd counted on was us taking Bella as well. Now, that will make him mad.'

'What do you mean he knew?'

'It doesn't matter. We're here now. He won't think about the docks immediately, and by the time he does, hopefully it will be too late. If we can find a ship to take us, we should go tonight.'

'How?' Ned frowned.

'Finding a ship isn't hard. It's paying for it.'

'I have money.'

Now Robbie did look surprised.

'Brent gave me some. Guilt money, probably.'

'No, he wanted you gone, Ned. Don't you see? He was even giving you the means to be gone.' He gave a sound of despair. 'He knew. He let you escape. And I think he let me escape too, but in the end sealing our fate – you to the unknown and me, well . . .' His words trailed off.

'I don't care,' Ned said. 'We're here now and we're rid of him. Pull on this fresh shirt. It will be big but it's clean. I've already changed. Bella, you need to put on this dress. You have to look more respectable.'

'Over there.' Robbie pointed to a stall where an old woman sat, presiding over her flowers.

He guided them over and switched into Burmese, explaining that the little English girl needed to change and asking if, for modesty's sake, she could change within the confines of the stall?

The woman replied and Robbie interpreted for Ned. 'She said buy something first. She's seen you walking around most of the day and doesn't want any trouble. Give me a few annas.'

Robbie took the coins and gave them to the woman. She pointed over her shoulder but forbade the boys to go with Bella.

'Bell, change into this frock. It's your favourite, isn't it?'

She went without protest.

'She looks exhausted,' Ned said. 'You don't look so well yourself.'

'Slight bellyache. I'll be all right.'

Bella emerged looking much better, and though her appearance wouldn't have fooled a company of English women, Ned felt sure it would be convincing enough to the ship's crew to get her aboard. He dipped his old shirt into some flower water and cleaned up her face. Robbie clambered into his fresh shirt.

'Bell, look what I've brought,' Ned said, holding out the book and smiling at her soft squeal of delight.

Robbie peered at it.

'*The Jungle Book*,' she explained, and showed him. 'What about the others?'

'Oh, we can go back for those later,' Ned said, diverting her. 'I just brought this one for now. Ready?'

His companions nodded. 'Lead the way,' he said to Robbie, trying not to notice that Bella was no longer concerned with her treat or the fact that they were headed to a ship. He inwardly begged that she would not fall ill now.

As they turned, the old woman called out.

'You didn't take any flowers,' Robbie explained. 'Here,' he said, picking a tiny single bloom of yellow flowers and handing them to Bella. 'These are the national flower of Burma, called paduak. It is from the rosewood tree.'

The woman gabbled at him and he thanked her.

'It signifies love and romance, but also strength.'

Bella blushed as she took the beautiful spray from Robbie. She looked over and found a brief smile for the old woman, who laughed and pointed.

Bella tugged at Robbie's arm. 'What did she say?' she asked.

'She says she hopes you will always be happy,' Robbie replied, but Ned suspected the woman had said something far less innocent.

'Come on. To the ships,' he said, glad that Bella was looking so much brighter, although he couldn't work out what Robbie was thinking or why he was so pale; he looked even more worried than Ned felt. 'Are you sure you weren't followed?' Ned pressed.

'Sure,' Robbie said, too abruptly, then walked away, expecting the Sinclairs to follow without any further question.

16

Ned had no choice but to defer to Robbie in the matter of which ships to approach. He needed Robbie's language but mostly he was relying on their friend's well-honed street instinct. Ned held Bell back with him beneath the shade of a tree and let Robbie roam for as long as it took up and down the busy docks, his keen eye absorbing all the detail. There was constant activity and it was more than an hour before Robbie's willowy figure finally reappeared.

'Anything?' Ned asked, nervous.

'I think so. A passenger ship called *Aronda*. It should be relatively comfortable. She makes regular trips to Madras, next one late this afternoon.'

'We can get on?'

Robbie nodded, then looked down. 'Ned, it's going to cost the equivalent of about a pound for each of us. I know Brent gave you money but you're going to need it. You two go. Besides, I have no papers. I've already spoken —'

'We're all going, Robbie.'

'Listen to me —'

'No! I'm the eldest. I have the money. We use it all if we have to in order to get away from Rangoon for good. Money talks and we'll get around papers. No one's going to care about a kid. What happens after, we'll see. We'll work it out. But right now we're all getting onto that ship. We move as one.'

Robbie's chin trembled a little. 'All right, if you're sure.'

'We're not leaving you behind.'

The Anglo-Indian boy smiled but Ned saw only sadness there. 'Then come. She leaves at six. The three pounds is a bribe and should get me on. I'm sorry. I had to promise the man a pound each. I said there'd be two of us but I don't think one more will make any difference so long as we pay. I can probably travel as crew if he won't let me bunk down in your cabin. It's small but it will be private. They don't normally sell it to passengers. It's usually kept for staff.'

Robbie had wangled them an inside berth on the ship. It was small, airless and cramped with twin single iron beds and just a tiny washbasin, but after the orphanage it was a palace and Bella immediately curled beneath the sheets and fell asleep, fully clothed.

Ned was relieved that she was resting and locked her in the room, having scrawled her a note not to open the door for anyone. He had a key and was going on deck. She was to remain there until he returned, although she seemed to be sleeping so deeply he couldn't imagine much would wake her. He headed up onto the deck to find Robbie.

All Ned could focus on was being able to watch the ship pull away from shore. Only then would he begin to relax and accept that they had escaped Brent.

There had been nearly two days of exhilaration at being back on a ship and out at sea. No rules, no regulations, no threat or fear. And while the pain of their parents' passing was ever present, the joy of leaving Rangoon behind and all of its sorrows was irresistible.

Ned didn't even ask what Robbie had said to secure himself passage on board without papers, but whatever he'd presented had worked and he was even sharing their cabin, more than happy to sleep on the floor and roundly arguing when Ned said they could take turns with the bed.

They were eating with the second-class passengers and people hardly noticed the three unaccompanied youngsters, although Ned was beginning to believe that he no longer appeared quite so young. His plan to allow his beard to grow seemed to be working. He liked the beard and being addressed as Mr Sinclair. He was head of this family now and he would get Bell and Robbie to Bangalore or bust. That became their catch phrase those first two days at sea.

Then the serious cramps began and the first bout of diarrhoea struck Robbie.

Bella found Ned, as usual, up on deck staring out across the Andaman Sea that would soon become the Indian Ocean. He wasn't interested in deck quoits or any of the fun on board. He preferred to find a quiet spot and daydream about the future and how he was going to make a fortune in India and then take Bella and Robbie home to Scotland.

'Hello, pretty girl.' He wished he had brought her more clothes, although as precious as Bella could be, lack of clothes or toys had curiously not had much impact. He was saddened that his sister was being forced to grow up all too quickly. She was still tired and he wondered about the lasting effects of her heatstroke. But for now, given that the ship was serving ice-cream, he felt glad to have finally kept his promise to her. He noticed that her face was filled with anxiety as she came closer.

'Quick, Ned. You have to come. It's Robbie. He's sick.'

Ned ran a hand through his hair and could feel the salt thick in it. It was getting long enough to knot from the constant wind on deck. 'What sort of sick?'

She grabbed his hand to pull him along. 'I don't know but it's bad. He's groaning a lot. He's been running to the bathroom but he says he won't be able to make it soon. Now he's begun to vomit.'

Ned walked faster. 'How long has he been like this?'

'Since you left this morning.'

He checked his mother's watch that he kept in his pocket. 'I've been here for over three hours,' he said, realising he too had lost track of time.

Ned began to jog to the bowels of the craft where their tiny cabin sat amidships and was assaulted by the smell of sickness and waste when he burst through the door.

He gagged. 'Wait outside!' he ordered Bella, a familiar sense of dread returning to his heart. Another cautious look inside confirmed the worst; Robbie wasn't just feeling sick, he was in trouble.

'Bell, you must go and find one of the crew. I don't care who, but find someone and bring them here as quickly as you can. No, darling, don't cry. You have to be strong for Robbie now. He needs help and he needs it quickly. We need a doctor, tell them. Go, Bell. Run!' And run she did.

Ned let the door close and was at Robbie's side, pulling a handkerchief to his face to keep out the smell. 'Robbie,' he began.

Robbie turned his suddenly grey face to Ned. His lips were cracked. 'Ned, you have to listen,' he said in a choked voice. 'It's too late for me.'

'What are you talking about?'

Robbie groaned wearily. 'I know what this is. Don't tell Bella. Don't let her see me get worse. It will be over soon, I promise.'

'Robbie, you don't know what you're saying.'

'It's cholera, Ned!' he shouted, finding some sort of super-human strength in his voice as he pushed Ned's hands back.

It worked. Ned instantly leapt back from Robbie as if burned.

'Cholera?' The very word felt dangerous to utter. 'I don't understand.'

'Just be still. You can't catch it if you're careful. But keep Bella away. You too must leave. Tell them to throw me overboard – they'll insist anyway. I don't care. Let them burn everything. Ned, stay strong.'

Ned could feel his world shifting. Helpless tears – the ones he hadn't even shed for his parents – were now welling and blurring his vision. 'How did this happen?'

'He wanted water. He was threatening Bella so I did it.'

'What? Robbie, you're not making sense. Let me get you some water. Is that what you want?'

Robbie closed his eyes as pain hit him. It passed. He opened his eyes again, but they were bloodshot, rheumy, and his skin was dry and feverish. 'Ned, I gave Brent unboiled water.' He retched and began to vomit into a bowl. Ned looked away helplessly. The smell, the sound, they both made him nauseous. He pushed himself away to sit against the wall, his hands holding his head as he tried to make sense of this. He had left both Bella and Robbie sleeping soundly. How could Robbie be this sick in just hours?

Robbie fell back exhausted. 'You'd better get out of here.'

'Finish it!' Ned said. 'I have to know.'

Robbie sounded so weak, yet he obediently continued his tale. 'Brent made me fetch his water, but not before he threatened me and Bella. I couldn't stand it, Ned. I had to finally do something about him. He's a monster.' Robbie laughed but it sounded more like a cackle. 'Except he was cleverer than I could ever be.'

'I don't understand,' Ned urged.

'I had no choice,' Robbie whispered. 'It was the only way I could protect our secret . . . protect your sister.'

'What are you talking about?'

'It's cholera, Ned. I've watched cholera take people. There's nothing anyone can do.' His head turned slowly to face Ned and he already looked shrunken like a corpse. 'I'll be dead within hours. Just get yourselves to Bangalore.' He recited Dr Walker's address. 'Write it down somewhere, Ned. Promise me.'

The door burst open with Bella and two crew members who instantly shrank back at the smell. 'What the hell . . . ?'

Ned stood. 'He says it's cholera.'

'Cholera! Get out of there. Are you sure?'

Robbie began to cry. 'Ned, did you write it down? Promise me.'

'I won't forget it, Robbie. I've committed it to memory, just as you did.'

The crewman was yanking Ned away, yelling to his burly companion as he pointed at Bella. 'Get that child out of here. And alert the ship's doctor. We've got to let the captain know.'

'What about Robbie?' Bella shrieked as she was dragged away.

Ned looked helplessly at the crewman.

'I'm sorry, lad. We can't take any chances here. Look at the mess he's in.'

Robbie had begun to vomit and soil himself again.

'He'll be dead before the hour is up. I've seen it before,' the sailor said grimly. 'Now, that was your sister?'

Ned was so stunned he could do no more than nod.

'Right, and your name's Ned?'

'Edward Sinclair. My sister is Arabella. This is Robert James.'

'All right, lad. We need to get you and your sister straight to the doctor. Don't touch anything as we go. Come on. It's dangerous here.' He looked back. 'Hey, Robbie, lad, the doctor's coming. You hold on now.'

Robbie managed to turn his head. His once tawny complexion had turned pale grey and his lips had swollen. 'Bye, Ned.'

'Robbie . . .' Treacherous tears ran down Ned's cheeks.

'I'm sorry we couldn't go to Scotland together,' he whispered. 'No tears, Ned. I've never been happier than the last two days with you both.'

'I'm sorry,' Ned said now, pulling his arm from the crewman who was gently urging him out of the cabin. 'I'm so sorry, Robbie.'

'Bella's safe now.' Robbie fell back, all energy drained, and then twisted onto his side as a convulsion of pain erupted and liquid gushed from his body.

This time the crewman was successful in getting Ned out of the cabin. 'Key?'

'What?' Ned was suddenly disoriented. It was hanging uselessly in his hand.

The man stared at the key, obviously contemplating taking it, but thought better of it. 'Lock the door, lad, and say a quiet prayer of farewell for your friend. Like I said, he won't make the next hour.'

Robbie was pronounced dead by Grenfell, the ship's doctor, while most passengers on board were enjoying a midday meal. The Sinclairs had been taken to a new cabin, where a nurse oversaw Bella's bathing and the Scottish sailor ensured Ned also washed himself from head to toe with liquid disinfectant and bright-red Lifebuoy carbolic soap that made his skin feel raw, burned. Their few garments were thrown overboard immediately, along with their few remaining possessions.

Every last remnant of the life they had known before Rangoon had now been snatched from them. And now poor, loyal Robbie was gone, the kindly Dr Grenfell explained as Ned sat in the medical room, his hair still wet from his ablutions.

'Cholera takes its victims painfully but mercifully fast,' the doctor said, his dark-blue eyes filled with sympathy. 'I gather Robbie was Anglo-Indian?'

'He never knew his father but believed he was English. His mother was Bengali,' Ned said.

Grenfell offered a soft smile that gave his eyes a genial quality. Ned couldn't tell his age, guessed he was older than his father but not by much. Perhaps just past forty. 'My parents lived there,' Grenfell said. 'Both missionaries.'

Ned could tell the doctor was just trying to keep him talking, to get him past the shock. He had only kindness in his gentle voice and Ned sensed he could trust him. 'Where's Bell?'

'Sleeping. I gave her something because she was exhausted and the crying wasn't helping.'

'Thank you.'

'How are you feeling?'

'Numb.'

'I understand. No gripes, no upset belly, no thirst?'

He shook his head. 'How can it happen that fast?'

'It does. Hours, for most of its sufferers. I'm sure you and Bell will remain untouched by it, unless . . .'

'We haven't taken anything other than boiled water.'

Grenfell gave his shoulder a brief squeeze of sympathy. 'Tell me why we have three stowaways on board.'

Ned slumped forward, elbows on his knees and his head on his hands. He began slowly and told the doctor an abridged version of their story. He used the excuse that they didn't want to remain in an orphanage and preferred to take their chances in India to find a way back to Britain, keeping the whole ugly business of Brent from the tale. It just seemed easier to keep it simple. He didn't, however, spare the doctor his pain at the loss of his parents.

When he was finished, Ned sat back, his throat dry from talking. But there were no tears.

Grenfell held the silence for a short while. Their sad tale certainly took some digesting, Ned realised. Even to his own ears it sounded like it had been contrived for a novel: dramatic deaths, exotic setting, a daring stowaway on a passenger ship. He shook his head. 'This is all the truth,' he added. 'We couldn't even collect our few belongings. We have nothing but each other.'

'I'm sorry for all your losses, Ned. It doesn't seem right that you three have suffered so much and are still so young.'

'What will happen to Robbie?'

Grenfell began undoing the stethoscope from around his neck. 'Well, the captain is furious to have discovered a stowaway and obviously everyone is concerned about the potential spread of cholera. We don't know enough about this disease.' He gestured to the glass flask, urging Ned to finish the clean water. 'There've been two, no three, major outbreaks in Britain from Asiatic cholera. Doctors tried everything in the early days, from brandy to blood letting. But people took to sealing their doors and praying.'

Grenfell stood, busying himself with clearing away the implements he'd used to give Ned a medical check. 'Right at this moment there's a cholera pandemic raging through Bengal. It's been two years already and no control in sight. We know hygiene is important to stem contagion.'

Ned frowned as he thought this over. 'So Bell and I should remain well if we take all the right precautions?'

'Precisely. I believe you will both be all right. If Robbie only showed symptoms this morning, then he's been infected since before you boarded. Forgive me for sounding insensitive, but I do have to consider the people on board.'

'I understand,' Ned reassured him.

'If either of you were infected, we'd be seeing symptoms already, although some people infected may not show any symptoms.'

'That's confusing.'

'It's a disease, Ned. It can be as contrary as it likes,' the doctor said with a sad smile. 'We'll move you to the spare cabin next door so I can keep a close watch, but if you eat well, drink plenty, get lots of fresh air over this voyage, you will keep good health.'

'What about the captain?'

'Well,' the doctor winked. 'He can hardly make two polite and very pleasant young English civilians walk the plank. Don't worry, we'll work something out.'

'And Robbie?' Ned repeated softly.

'I'm afraid, son, that he will go overboard. It's their only option to bury him at sea.'

'May I attend?'

'If you're quick.'

'Bella will probably want to be there too. She wasn't allowed to see either of our parents after their deaths. She's already confused and unsure. To take Robbie from her now is tragic but I think she needs to see it happen – to understand that he is gone.'

'Well, it's entirely up to you. By the way, happy birthday for tomorrow,' Grenfell said, pointing to the passport.

Ned looked bemused. 'What day is it?'

'November 26.'

'I've lost all track of time!'

'Not much of a birthday for you, Ned.'

'Perhaps my nineteenth year will be happier than this one.'

'That's the spirit. Any plans for ashore?'

'There's a friend of Robbie's I'd like to make contact with. He's a doctor. He lives in Bangalore.'

'Ah, and what a lovely city to be heading for. Is there anyone at home in Britain you'd like us to contact?'

'No one, no. We have no relations.' It all seemed so hopeless all of a sudden.

'All right. Now listen to me,' Grenfell began. 'We arrive in Madras tomorrow. You've obviously got nowhere to go . . .'

Ned shook his head dejectedly.

'And you've got your sister to think about. Come home with me. I'll be staying on shore for the next eight weeks. I know my wife will be delighted to have some visitors – especially the pair of you – and it will give you some time to consider your situation.

Besides,' Grenfell said, smiling kindly, 'you should never spend a birthday alone.'

Ned could barely believe the man's generosity. He stared at the doctor, not sure what to say.

Grenfell put a hand on Ned's shoulder. 'We have no children, Ned. I think my wife would really enjoy the chance to spoil Bella . . . even for just a short while. So it's no hardship for us. We'd enjoy the company and my conscience wouldn't allow me to let you go without an offer of help.'

'That's incredibly kind of you.'

'Don't worry. You can earn your keep. We'll find plenty to keep a young man like you occupied – and now you're eighteen, there are endless government positions available in Madras.'

'Perhaps I can earn our passage home, but first I need to keep a promise to Robbie and find his Dr Walker in Bangalore.'

'That's agreed, then, and after you've settled in I shall help you find him.'

Ned stood and straightened the rough, ill-fitting clothes they'd quickly found for him. He held out a hand. 'Thank you for your kindness. I will never forget it.'

The doctor nodded. 'Welcome to India, Ned.'

17

April 1920

Jack Bryant stood on the deck of the *Naldera* and smoked an Ogdens Robin cigarette leisurely. They were expensive but the smokes had been an indulgence he'd allowed himself, just as the second-class passage had been a treat to himself on the Peninsula and Orient Lines' latest gleaming lady of the seas. They'd left Tilbury Docks behind several weeks ago but Jack's pleasure at being out on the ocean had not dissipated. If anything it had intensified, as the passengers became more comfortable with life on board ship and with each other.

Everyone was friendly, the women especially displaying a recklessness – a gregarious holiday mood – that a year or so ago Jack would have taken full advantage of. But Jack had no intention of creating trouble onboard a ship that offered no escape. Which was why he found himself up on deck during this balmy evening, smoking alone while everyone else was downstairs dancing the night away.

The cigarette tasted good. For years he'd resisted chewing a plug, as most of the Cornish miners did, the plug being the only method they had of enjoying tobacco down the shafts. And a pipe struck him as being the domain of older men, like his father. He'd rolled his own, of course, but these pre-made cigarettes were the new fad and he liked the colourful boxes and advertising that appeared on every shop, street corner and hoarding. To pull out a box of cigarettes and pluck one from the neat row was much more appealing than digging around in a tin to loosen the tobacco and then cramming it into a paper.

He inhaled deeply, tasting salt on his lips, and considered his decision to travel to Australia. Its mining industry was booming and he'd heard the southern part of the great continent had attracted a lot of his fellow cousin Jacks thanks to rich copper deposits. He'd been working as a labourer at Tilbury Docks, staying at a cheap boarding house, but as soon as he'd glimpsed details of the *Naldera*'s arrival, he couldn't get her out of his mind. And sailing aboard her seemed to be his destiny because he'd received a letter from his father telling him that the mining companies in Australia and India were actively recruiting in Cornwall. Jack made up his mind that day and booked a passage on *Naldera*'s inaugural sailing that would take her across the world to the sparkling Sydney harbour. The voyage was six weeks at least. Was Australia a better option than India? He wasn't completely sure, so he chose not to secure a job before he left. Ignoring his father's advice, Jack decided that if work was so plentiful, he could look for it on arrival, but in the meantime he could explore a little, get to know this great sunburned country, Australia, that he'd heard so much about. And if it didn't suit him, he'd use whatever money he had left to sail back to India – Madras probably – and make his way to the mining regions there.

That had been the plan when he'd boarded with a small piece of luggage and found his way to the double-bedded cabin he was sharing with an older man called Henry Berry. Berry was a slight fellow with a tic, whose shoulder twitched every minute or so. He described himself as simply a member of the Indian Civil Service – no family, no prospects of a wife, he claimed. Henry explained that he'd just finished his biannual holiday to England, and was now gladly making his way back to the steamy, manic, flourishing port of Bombay. To Jack it sounded as though Henry liked his work; did not suffer as much as others in the heat; and most of all enjoyed the way of life the colonies offered him. Even on his modest salary he could afford servants and a lifestyle that someone of his ilk back home could only dream of.

It was Henry who had first queried Jack's vision of Australia, and put the doubt in his mind.

'Are you mad, man? Australia? It's a desert. You can travel for days, I hear, and not see another person other than the natives. They've got biting insects the size of dinner plates in the air, and strange creatures in the sea – some with fatal bites. Crocodiles in their rivers, snakes on their plains and a sun that can kill you. And the majority of the few Europeans out there are mainly English convicts, let's not forget! We're talking thieves and murderers as your fellow workers, Jack. Fellows who'd happily slit your throat for a loaf of bread,' Henry had impressed, his voice rising with the dramatic scene he was vividly painting. 'No, the living is too hard there, too difficult to make a quid yet. That place has a long way to go before it can even begin to achieve the civilised life of British India.'

Jack was telling himself not to get carried away with one man's vision. 'So you think I should get off in India instead?'

'You'd be mad not to, old chap,' Henry replied, as he lay on his back in his bed, staring up at the ceiling. Jack echoed his pose in the bed opposite, heads behind his hands, enjoying the roll of the boat, the groan of the engine.

Henry turned over to prop himself on an elbow. 'You know, there's a place down south called Kolar Gold Fields that supports seven mines, each with its own thriving expat community. I went there once to gather some details for the government and I couldn't believe what a wonderful life they're all leading out there in the Indian bush. The clubs are superb, parties every night, picnics and dances. And the women, Jack! Gorgeous girls. Have you heard of the Anglo-Indians?'

Jack turned to face Henry now, his interest pricked despite his promise to himself to stay off women for a while.

'The Anglo-Indians are a curious community that's sprung up from intermarriages between the English and local people. I'm sad to say the sons of these marriages are all too dashing, with their dark good looks that put us pasty Brits to shame . . . but the women.' Henry had sighed. 'These girls are so exotic to look at and they possess all the charm and etiquette of English ladies . . .'

Jack grinned. 'So how come you haven't married one of these delicious beauties, Henry?'

'Ah, well, look at me, Jack. And while my status is alluring to some, these girls aren't keen to leave their families and live in Bombay. Now, London,' he said, with a flourish. 'That would be different! The Anglo-Indians act more British than we do. They talk about England as though it's home, yet most of these young women only know of it through magazines and what their fathers have told them.'

'You haven't answered my question, Henry.'

Henry flopped back onto the bed, dejected. 'I'm not very good with women, Jack. My tic seems to get worse around them. I can tell they'd flock around you. I suppose you've had hundreds!' he said enviously.

Jack laughed aloud and moved the conversation on. 'And work is plentiful in this mining camp?'

'The mines are screaming for good people. In fact, I was asked to prepare a report that John Taylor & Sons is using for its recruitment push in Britain later this year.'

'I think it's begun in Cornwall if my father's most recent letter is anything to go by.'

'You can bet on it, old chap. Seven mines – even a railway – and no more coal . . . it's electrified. This is why the area is flourishing and the population of Europeans is exploding.'

'Sounds as though *you'd* like to live there, Henry.'

Henry sighed. 'I would. It's a wonderful place. It's like being in a small English hamlet at times with the way people live there, almost completely isolated from the real world. Bombay can be so . . . well, quite mad sometimes. But I'd be lying if I didn't say I loved Bombay also. If I'm lucky, I may get a posting to Bangalore or perhaps in the Nilgiris down south. But in Kolar, you'd never be lonely. Everyone seems to know each other and it's an easy, good life, Jack.'

'You sound like you're on the payroll.'

'No, I just envy your position to be so carefree and able to choose when and where and what and how.'

'And the women,' Jack added with a grin.

'And the women,' Henry echoed.

'I don't think you're trying hard enough where girls are concerned.'

'You're right, of course. My problem is I want a very pretty wife but no very pretty single girl is going to look at me.'

'Nonsense,' Jack scoffed, trying not to focus on Henry's restless shoulder.

'No, it's true. Plain, bespectacled, chubby, shrewish – that's what I tend to be left to choose from. And so, denied beauty and grace, I've chosen to remain a bachelor.'

'Henry, you surprise me. A kiss from a plump girl is just as meaningful. And a plain girl can still have grace. Now, to be loved . . .' He sighed. 'Ah, that's the key.'

Henry shot Jack a look of scorn. 'The thing is, Bryant, you've probably never had to wrap your arms around a fat girl or ignore buck teeth or a spotty complexion. Please, don't deny it.'

Jack couldn't deny the accusation, but he had really meant what he'd said; he would give anything to be truly loved.

Jack stubbed out his cigarette. The fact was, it wasn't only Henry who sang India's praises. Most of his fellow travellers couldn't wait to get out, or in most cases back out, to India.

Conversely, even those he'd talked to on the ship who were bound for Australia assured him life was tough for a miner. Yes, fortunes had been made with copper and gold especially, but the great rush had already waned, and the fortunes been spent or certainly reinvested in the emerging pastoral and agricultural industries. Jack knew nothing about growing crops or herding sheep. One man was talking lustily about the fiery opals of a place called Coober Pedy. But, all in all, the lustre of Australia was fading – no club life, no partying, no exotic beauties with dainty manners, no servants, and huge distances to cover with only the dry days of Hades, dust and drinking to be enjoyed in what was still a very young colony . . . or group of colonies as some had corrected.

'Always alone, Mr Bryant,' said a husky voice, interrupting his thoughts.

He swung around from the ship's rail and recognised the woman; he had seen her a few times in the dining hall. 'Good evening, Miss . . . Er, you have me at a loss, I'm afraid.'

'Eugenie Ross,' she said, lazily. 'Care to light me?' Her gaze shifted to the unlit cigarette in her black, opera-length cigarette holder. It was far too big for her. He smiled and reached into his pocket for his matches, wishing he owned one of the newfangled lighters he'd seen around London. One day, he promised himself. One day soon.

He struck a match, cupped it in his fingers and was not surprised when his companion placed her small hand around his and pulled him closer.

She smiled as lazily as she spoke and then released him. 'Thank you, Mr Bryant. May I call you John?'

'It's my name,' he said, amused but on his guard. Eugenie struck him as dangerous, though mainly to herself. 'Although my friends call me Jack.'

'Jack? Mmm, that suits you. A rogue-ish name.'

He didn't respond, simply smiled back at her.

'Don't you think it's churlish of you to deprive all the single women of your company, Jack?'

In the low light on deck he couldn't tell whether her eyes were green or grey but they sparkled nonetheless. Her glossy lipstick glistened blood red and her small, perfectly straight white teeth flashed in a brief, contrived smile. There was nothing natural about Eugenie's pose, her highly coloured face or her manner. He realised she was still waiting for an answer.

'I'm not good company at the moment.'

'Oh? Why's that?'

Jack leaned back against the rail. 'I've got a lot on my mind.'

'Then a few turns around the dance floor will help to distract you.'

'I'm sure it would . . . if I wanted distraction.'

She smiled, as though sensing a contest. Daringly she ran a finger down his shirtfront and then placed her hand flat against his belly. He wanted to laugh; she was very young and had probably seen some actress perform that same manoeuvre in a film.

'Where are you headed, Jack? I do hope it's to Sydney. That way we can enjoy the entire voyage together.'

That was the moment Jack made up his mind. He would never forget it. Fate or destiny, or whatever it was, in the shape of Miss Eugenie Ross, had stepped in and pushed him from one path onto another.

'No, actually,' he replied, gently removing her hand. 'I'm getting off in Bombay.'

Eugenie looked surprised and Jack realised that she had likely already checked his destination with the ship's purser. Then she recovered herself, pouting. 'Is that so?'

'I only decided recently.'

'Well,' she said brightly. 'We still have over a fortnight to dance the nights away.'

'I'm flattered, Miss Ross, truly I am,' he said, 'but I'm not sure my fiancée would approve.'

She flinched as if stung. 'Good grief, Jack. You might have mentioned her earlier!' She slumped by the rail and sighed as she looked out to sea. 'I suppose you stand out here smoking alone, night after night, thinking about her.'

Now he did smile. 'Something like that.'

She blew smoke towards him defiantly.

'How old are you?' he asked.

'I'm nearly eighteen, if you must know, and perfectly capable of being with a man.'

Ah, he had definitely hit the target there. Young Eugenie needed protection from her own imagination.

'You know, Miss Ross, where I come from I'd reckon being with a man is something quite different to your girlish idea of it.'

She gave a sound of deep exasperation and flung her cigarette down, crushing it underfoot. 'I don't know why I bothered with you.'

'I don't know either. I'm quite sure I didn't invite the attention.'

'I shall tell the other women on board to ignore you, Mr Bryant.'

He grinned. 'That would be good of you, Miss Ross. Thank you.'

Her gaze narrowed to match the pursed line of her lips. 'There is no pining fiancée back at home, is there?'

'There's nothing back home for me, certainly no woman.'

That admission seemed to appease her. They stood in silence, staring out across the moonlit ocean, music distantly drifting up from below decks. It was a curiously comfortable moment.

'Look, Jack,' she said excitedly, 'a shooting star and it's moving towards you – so it's yours.'

'I see it,' he said, tilting his face up at the night sky and watching with wonder, enjoying her fanciful thought. 'I hope it means something.'

'It's a sign. I think India will bring you luck . . . possibly love.'

He looked at her and then bent to kiss her hand gently. 'I'll hold that thought, thank you.' She smiled back at him and it was genuine at last. 'You know, you're really very pretty . . . even prettier without all that rouge and lipstick.'

Eugenie appeared suddenly nervous. 'Oh, thank you,' she said, fiddling with the soft curls of her bobbed haircut. 'I'd better go back or the other girls will think I've been a little too successful with you.'

'Well, we shouldn't disappoint them, should we? Would you care to dance, Miss Ross?' he asked, holding out his arm, glad now that he'd invested in the tuxedo.

At first she looked incredulous, but then she smiled and linked her pale arm through his. 'I appreciate this,' she said softly.

'Your father isn't travelling with you, is he?'

She giggled. 'No. He's in Bombay waiting for me. So is my mother – we're going on to Sydney together. Right now I'm travelling with a friend and an aunt as our chaperone.'

Jack sighed privately with relief. 'One dance, Miss Ross.'

She patted his arm. 'One dance every night until Bombay.' She stared up at him hopefully. 'Just friends, I promise. Agreed?'

Jack smiled. 'Agreed.'

18

And so the long, lovely days at sea passed in a slow dream of genuine pleasure for Jack. Stepping ashore in Malta, while the ship was re-provisioned, made for a fun excursion with Eugenie and her party. Immediately the *Naldera* arrived in Grand Harbour, a flotilla of tiny craft surrounded them, offering everything from fresh fruit to laundry services done that day. And while the ladies made straight for the Strada Reale in Valetta and its famed lace shops, Jack couldn't resist a viewing of 'pickled monks' – men who had been embalmed from the Carmelite Order. Excited passengers arrived back on board carrying coral and silver among their purchases. Jack had bought only a postcard featuring a pen and coloured ink sketch of the harbour and the shopping street, which he duly sent to his parents with a brief message to say that he was well and enjoying the voyage. And while he never indulged in any romantic activity beyond a polite kiss to Eugenie's hand, he did keep his promise to dance a single song each evening as her partner, and they became close friends.

Perhaps the most bizarre event for him was a ritual that took place at the conclusion of 'Neptune's Ball' mid voyage. Jack and several other male passengers from second-class were sat down on the open deck and shaved by Neptune, comically played by the ship's purser. Neptune's court was in full attendance, of course, and the largest sailors, with the most luxurious beards and perhaps even the most obvious tattoos, were playing Queen Neptune and her daughters.

In good cheer, Jack submitted to being daubed with suds by what he was sure was a tar brush, then being shaved by a saw, before being plunged into a huge pail of salt water, much to the delight of the shrieking audience that included Eugenie, almost delirious with laughter.

'We used to do this for sailors on their first crossing of the equator,' the Queen explained in baritone, 'but now,' she said, with a wink and a perfectly timed pause, 'we'll take any excuse to dress up in frocks,' to a fresh eruption of applause.

Port Said was the stop everyone had been looking forward to. It was the first 'oriental' port and marked a milestone for the voyage; from here a whole new atmosphere pervaded the ship.

Passengers now exchanged their warmer clothing for summer garments. Again, Jack was grateful for the advice of his London tailor, who had insisted that a lightweight, light-coloured suit was a must for the colonies.

At the captain's orders no women were permitted to go ashore without escort, and so Jack was once again called upon by Eugenie's all-female party to act as their chaperone into a city purported to be alive with cutthroats, pick-pockets, beggars and magicians of all nationalities.

Jack was sure London's crowded streets had prepared him for most cities but Port Said was like nothing he could have imagined; everywhere was akin to festival day in Penzance, yet far more frenzied and infinitely more colourful. Their party was followed around by a small crowd of boys insisting they could show them to the best shops, cheapest goods, most prized purchases, as well as a horde of beggars and roaming purveyors of everything from embroidery to porcelain.

It seemed everyone who was new to India was pressed to visit the famous shop, Simon Artz, which seemed to stock absolutely everything but was renowned as the provider of topis – the hat every English man or woman was expected to buy for the tropics.

'Never be caught out in that Indian sun with a bare head,' Eugenie's aunt Agatha had stressed as she tapped the sturdy topi Eugenie selected for Jack. 'You only feel silly for a few days, then you won't be caught dead without it.'

The store was crowded with passengers he recognised but also many that he didn't. 'First-class passengers,' Aunt Agatha warned. 'They buy the Bombay Bowlers too. If you don't wear a topi, you're not considered tribe. And to be English and not tribe – when there's so few of us in India to rule millions – is to be just short of a traitor.'

Jack grinned and paid for the hat – but only after Aunt Agatha queried the price with words like 'preposterous' and 'robbery'. Afterwards he offered the women a drink beneath the shady stone arches of the port's main shopping area. The drink was cool and the company pleasant but the yelling horde still followed them and badgered them relentlessly to buy shawls or vases or sticky sweets.

They were frankly glad to return to the gleaming *Naldera*, where Jack noticed a metamorphism had taken place. The ship's officers had changed uniforms into all whites; the Europeans looked frankly ridiculous wearing their topis, but apparently it was the done thing; and the women were suddenly floating around in muslin and sheer fabrics. Hot soup was swapped for cold, and Jack noticed more adventurous food on the menu, dishes that were spiced, or contained intriguing pulses such as lentils, or sauces that might have appeared quite odd at the outset of the voyage.

Finally, when the ship signalled her intention to pull away from shore with one long blast of her horn, Jack noticed the excitement on board intensified because of the impending navigation of the marvel of the industrial revolution – the Suez Canal.

Personally, Jack wouldn't have minded sailing into the south

Atlantic via places like the windswept rock of St Helena – Napoleon's final resting place – or the more treacherous waters of the Cape of Good Hope and rounding the Horn of Africa. But the engineering revelation that was the Suez Canal, which had more than halved the travelling time to India, certainly intrigued him.

'The longing for Home never goes, Jack,' Aunt Agatha said, as they stood on deck and watched the port disappear. He tried to ignore his self-consciousness at the topi that he was sure must look like a fireman's helmet. 'But I can assure you that India is seductive and addictive.'

'Yes, I'm gathering that.'

'Your cabin companion,' she said, switching subjects without warning. 'I rather like him for his modesty, I must admit, but, Jack, the man is probably under thirty and he's already a district officer. Have you any idea of his power?'

Jack turned his gaze away from the shore and regarded Aunt Agatha. 'His power?'

She laughed. 'He's in charge of thousands of people. He's like a little dictator, presiding over villages and dispensing rules and regulations – not to mention justice.'

This did surprise him. 'I know Henry enjoys his work but he never really discusses his role. I had no idea.'

'He lives like a king, to tell the truth. He'd have a government-provided bungalow, servants, probably a car and driver.'

'But he assured me his income was modest.'

'It likely is. But that's the point! Everything is provided for him. Back home, he'd be a clerk in a dreary government department with a dreary life to boot. Men like Henry and my husband, William, who've tasted India, never want to leave her. She gives their lives genuine meaning.'

'That sounds rather dramatic.'

'Jack, I'm a realist. William might have been a bookkeeper at

best; I probably would have had to work too in a shop or something. And our daughter, Jennifer, would have left school to work
for a milliner or florist. She'd have met a nice young man – no
doubt another clerk from another government department – and
the whole cycle would begin again.' She touched his arm anxiously.
'And there's nothing wrong in that, don't get me wrong. But William dared to dream.' Aunt Agatha chortled and Jack smiled. He
really liked her. 'He brought me to India and I can't imagine being
anywhere else. Our lives are wonderful out here, and Jennifer's now
engaged to be married to a fine young officer in the Army.'

Jack finally began to understand what Henry had been talking
about. 'It all sounds like a bit of a fantasy.'

Aunt Agatha grinned. 'That's precisely how it is. But you
know, Jack, there is also a genuine sense of duty for most of the
people who live and work out here. I mean, my husband truly
believes in the British Empire and feels it's a mark of his patriotism
to devote his life to British rule in India. Most of the folk travelling
in first-class wouldn't see it any other way. Their children are often
born in India, sent home to school for years on end without ever
seeing their parents, and then those sons are plucked from their fine
public schools and sent back out to India. And they can't wait to get
back. The daughters too. Have you heard the jokes about the fishing fleet?'

'I'm not sure I grasped their meaning.'

'Well, there are so many eligible bachelors in India. English
spinsters are urged to travel out in droves for fun and to find a husband with prospects, hence the fishing fleet . . . you know, fishing
for husbands. Young Eugenie could be accused of that. She was
born in India after all and for most of the children born there,
India's in their blood.'

He sensed her gaze held a message. Jack up held his hands.
'I'm not looking for a wife, Aunt Agatha.'

'So she tells me. But don't worry, I won't pry . . . much as I'd like to, Jack.'

Grateful for her tact, he bent and kissed her cheek. 'Thank you.'

She looked around. 'Speak of the devil,' she said and winked.

Eugenie bounded up, wearing a flimsy summer frock, her new topi balanced precariously on her head, her face devoid of all make-up, he was pleased to note.

'Why did you buy this?' he asked, gently rapping the topi with his knuckles. 'Surely you have one from your first voyage?'

'I did, although that one was way too big for me because I was just three when I took my first voyage. I grew into it over the years. But as you'll see when you sail home, the minute you leave Port Said behind and enter the Mediterranean, it's custom for all on board to fling their topis into the sea.'

Jack laughed. 'Really?'

'Oh, yes. All very symbolic of leaving Mother India behind.'

'You people,' Jack said, shaking his head. 'Weep to leave London, yet you call India your Mother.'

'The gentry see India as an extension of home. Their land. It's British!' she said in a posh voice.

They all laughed.

'Well, my dears, I think I'll go have a lie-down before dinner,' Aunt Agatha said, turning to leave. 'Will you join us, Jack?'

'Thank you. May I suggest Henry joins us as well?'

'Of course,' Aunt Agatha said, departing. 'See you later. Eugenie, don't get burned.'

Eugenie turned to Jack. 'Must that twitching fellow be with us for dinner? I find him quite distracting.'

'He twitches because he finds you so beautiful.'

'Oh?' she said, sounding instantly ashamed. 'But he never so much as looks at me.'

'It's because he adores you.'

'While you, meanwhile, look me directly in the eye!'

'Because you and I are friends.'

'We could be more . . .'

He gave her a look of exasperation. 'Believe me, I'd reduce you to tears within months – no, weeks.'

'But why?'

'Eugenie, perhaps it would be better if I didn't —'

'Don't say it! I'm sorry. I won't tease you any further. I'll chat to Mr Berry and I'll continue to dance with you each evening and I'll let you go in Bombay. I promise. Don't desert us and don't stop being my friend.'

'All right, thank you, but only because I would be sad to leave Aunt Agatha.'

'I think I hate you, Jack Bryant.'

'Everyone finally comes to that conclusion,' he admitted, and while he made the comment to make her laugh, he wondered whether he hadn't ever said a truer thing.

It took them an entire day to travel the canal and Jack spent most of it on deck, beneath his topi, squinting out into the sharp sunlight, watching the children who scampered along the canal's shore yelling to the passengers; some threw coppers to them. At the town of Ismailia, more or less halfway, a flotilla of bumboats chased after the ship, selling everything from boots to monkeys.

The town of Suez was something of an anticlimax for Jack. He didn't know why he'd expected something special but it turned out to be a dull place with few diversions for passengers and almost no reason to leave the ship, other than a donkey ride.

A couple of days sailing on the Red Sea and Jack felt he was truly entering foreign climes. The landscape in the distance had become dry and dusty brown. It was unbearably hot during the day and even the sea breeze was too warm to tolerate. Jack wondered aloud whether the heat could send people mad. It seemed impossible, but the temperatures soared after Aden – day after day of relentless heat, forcing some of the passengers to sleep on deck. Even with a pair of ceiling fans in the second-class twin cabins, they sweltered, with Henry assuring Jack that it was more than a hundred degrees in their cabin.

'From here on, old chap,' Henry explained a week later, 'we live on deck by night.'

The crew rigged up a special divider using sailcloth to give the ladies some privacy. Men had taken to wearing shorts, which Jack found amusing while desperately wishing he had a pair.

Everything felt foreign, strange. The sea life changed around them, even the night skies looked different, and as they drew closer to the Indian mainland, new spicy fragrances wafted on the wind and assured Jack that his old life was now behind him.

———

The day of docking at Bombay finally arrived. There was a sense of high excitement aboard the ship but Jack was in no rush to disembark. *Naldera* had been kind to him these past four weeks and he'd come to see her as a friend. In fact, after only just a day away from her, in Malta or Port Said, it had felt like coming home each time he'd trudged back up the gangplank.

Jack had already said his farewells to Aunt Agatha and her two charges. He hadn't wanted a teary scene and he had a feeling Eugenie was not going to let him get away too easily. He really didn't feel a romantic connection with her. Although he had never admitted it, he had never felt the romantic connection with anyone like he knew his parents felt for each other. That's what he believed was real love. It was what he wanted to feel. It was what he thought Henry and Eugenie might achieve, if they bothered to grasp the opportunity, and why he had whispered to Eugenie, 'Don't let Henry Berry get away. He worships you and worship can't be bought.'

Now, Jack looked ahead to the natural harbour of Bombay and its three enclosed docks, all built by the British, or so Henry was now informing him. From the vantage point of the top deck, Bombay pier was a riot of colour and noise, with harsh-sounding languages being yelled on the dock and the bellow of oxen dragging carts of luggage trunks and cargo. Dark-skinned people ran around in seemingly endless frantic activity while the lighter-skinned crew gave orders and the loading and unloading of the *Naldera* began.

Theirs was not the only vessel in port, of course. Jack could see several others lined up, each requiring attention from a host of workers at the dockside. They scurried like an army of ants about their business, loading or unloading.

Jack could smell food cooking but nothing he could recognise. On board he'd learned about strange-sounding, bright-coloured flavourings from turmeric to tamarind. He'd agreed to taste the latter, wrinkling his nose slightly at the black, tarry plant paste that looked like a squashed date. Jack had taken the tiny mass and chewed it, arrested by the tangy explosion in his mouth. He was surprised to learn that it was a component of the Worcestershire sauce that the British used to spice up a dish, like Welsh rarebit or their Bloody Marys. The Lea & Perrins bottle was rarely missing from the *Naldera*'s buffet tables.

There was an earthy smell of humanity too, overpowering even the pungent smell of fish and fresh produce that pervaded every dock from here to London. He looked out at the city of Bombay, sprawling behind the port. He could see gas lamps lining the esplanade, elegant Victorian buildings, and large white bungalows in the distance.

Henry was droning on. 'Just over a decade ago we got our first electrified trams,' he said. 'Buses will be next, I'm told. Automobiles are surely just a blink away. The city is exploding; it's the centre of trade for the continent, and of course we have the railways expanding constantly, with routes from all over converging on Bombay.'

Discordant music drifted up from somewhere – the strange-sounding instruments added to the cacophony of squeaking axles, braying bullocks and yelling sailors. Lithe, dark men ran up ropes and over containers like agile insects, while Jack's gaze was drawn to the constant flow of passengers out of his ship, floating down the gangplanks and adding a sudden shock of paleness to the rich, jewel-like colours the Indians seemed to favour.

'Takes your breath away, doesn't it?'

Jack shook his head in wonder. 'You're right. It's exciting but daunting. I've never experienced anything like it.'

'Everyone feels like that the first time. I certainly did. But one gets used to it soon enough and curiously it all begins to feel familiar, even homely, before long.' He smiled kindly. 'I know I've asked this before but what are your plans, old chap?'

Jack shrugged. 'I'm no closer to knowing. I've let all who need to know that I'm not going on to Australia – much as I'd love to remain on board.'

Henry slapped his arm, clearly delighted. 'Good man! You won't regret it. But what now?'

'You got me into this, Henry. I suppose I'll take your advice and head to the goldfields of Ko . . .' He wasn't sure how to pronounce it.

'Kolar,' Henry replied. 'In that case you'll need to go to Bangalore first.'

'All right. I have no idea where that is.'

'South. And you can now – thanks to dear old Britain's industrial wizardry – get there by steam train.'

'Perfect,' Jack said, immediately liking the sound of that.

'What's more, we can travel together if it suits?'

Jack felt a surge of relief. 'Really?'

Henry grinned, his right shoulder moving rapidly with excitement. He held up a piece of paper. 'I've just got orders to go to Bangalore.'

'You got your posting?'

'No, not the one I want. This is just a short visit . . . yet another report to prepare on some of the hill stations in the south. But it means I can see you as far as Bangalore, perhaps look into an interview with the mines for you.'

'Henry, that's . . . well, I don't know what to say.'

'Don't mention it.' He gestured to shore. 'Welcome to India, old chap.'

Later, sitting in the relative cool of a bar on Marine Drive, sipping a gin and tonic that he had acquired a taste for aboard ship, Jack reflected on the long day of sightseeing.

Beyond the cultural sights, Henry had been proud to show Jack all the British buildings from the first cotton mill to the Grant Medical College and, of course, his favourite building – the central railway station known as Victoria Terminus.

'It vaguely reminds me of St Pancras with its Victorian architecture and red brick,' Jack had admitted and Henry had grinned.

'That's because it was modelled after it. We can't ever fully escape London, can we? Glorious, isn't it, with its amazing blending of the great gothic structures we know and Indian architecture? The engineer built it working from a watercolour made up by the draughtsman!'

The city had impressed Jack enormously and now, as he looked out over the huge crescent-shaped beach that marked the shoreline of the Arabian Sea, he understood why flocks of English came to Bombay.

It was an easy city to like if you enjoyed a hectic social life, the noise of people and the thrill of business. Jack didn't. London had been a means to an end and certainly not somewhere he wanted to live. Bombay, as vibrant and colourful as it was, would not suit him either. He hoped that the small-town life of Kolar Gold Fields would offer something closer to the simple lifestyle of his beloved Pendeen, but feeling the droplets of sweat gathering at his forehead, he wondered whether he could ever get used to India.

'In Bombay we have the luxury of the sea. We're in the hot season now. May can be unbearable and then monsoon begins in June, when it will rain frequently – and I mean rain, Jack, but it's brief and not unwelcome. Anyway, where you're headed, you'll enjoy a temperate climate. Bangalore has a high altitude and cooling breezes.'

'I'm looking forward to it.'

'You'll love Bangalore. I'll inquire about some train tickets in the morning. We may be able to take an evening train.'

They raised their glasses and cried, 'Cheers!' in unison.

19

Ned travelled to Bangalore alone. For the first time since leaving England he didn't have Bella at his side. His sister and Millie Grenfell had taken to each other instantly, and Millie was soon like a favourite aunt. Ned was relieved that Bella finally had a maternal figure back in her life. He'd had many sleepless nights worrying about how he was going to raise a young girl on his own.

While the death of their mother especially was an ever-present cloud, the Grenfells had brought a sense of tranquillity to the Sinclair children's lives. Dr Grenfell lived in a large old bungalow within the boundaries of what was known as White Town in Madras. It provided the first secure accommodation Bella had known since setting sail for Rangoon five months earlier. Ned was old enough to understand that in her reckoning that period was a lifetime. He also appreciated that the large bedroom with its big shuttered windows and beautiful bed of clean white linen, the regular meals, the large garden to play in and the servants to do the chores was more than simply seductive.

Ned had no reason to fear that Bella would mind if he went away to Bangalore. In fact, he was fairly sure his sister would hardly feel his departure. The Grenfells led a full, active and thoroughly pleasant life, but they needed someone to lavish with love. Bella easily accepted the mantle of being that beloved child and, during the weeks following their arrival, Ned watched his sister become comfortably entrenched in her new existence. There would be no withdrawing her from Millie's loving clutches – and no need either, he had told a worried Dr Grenfell when he began making serious noises about moving on.

'She is safe and happy here,' he assured the good doctor when Grenfell finally asked if Ned was feeling obliged to leave Bella in their care. 'I wouldn't dream of disrupting her life again – so long as you are both happy to look after her. I really think I should be asking you and Mrs Grenfell whether you mind, rather than the other way around.'

'Happy?' Grenfell asked with gentle irony. 'We're overjoyed that she's in our life. That goes for you too, Ned. We have come to love you both. Are you sure you have to leave?'

'I must find Dr Walker. I promised Robbie I would.'

'Of course. I understand and I'm glad that you have this respect for him. But will you return to Madras?'

'I plan to. But would you forgive me if I say I'd rather not be held to that? Does that sound ungrateful?'

Grenfell had smiled. 'A little but only if it was taken out of context, son. I know you're a restless soul. I suspect that with all that has happened to you you need to work something out of your system and I hope you find some answers on your travels. And you're a man now. I left home at seventeen. I shake my head when I think of it now and how it upset my parents, especially my poor mother. Somehow that sounds so young. Of course it's not and you must find your own way. Millie and I both understand. But I think it's important to say this and for you to know that there is always a home here for you.'

'I'm really at a loss to know how to thank you for all your kindness. Our clothes, our welfare – you've been so generous. Of course I will send money for Bella once —'

'Oh, tosh! Bella will want for nothing. Now, listen to me,

Edward. We want you to take this.' He picked up an envelope from his desk and handed it to Ned.

Ned froze momentarily when he realised the envelope was filled with rupees. 'I can't —'

'You can, you will. This is not something I'm prepared to debate, young man. My wife and I have talked this over and if we must let you go, then we want to know you have sufficient money to cover your travelling expenses and incidentals.'

Ned shook his head. 'I can't take this. You've already done so much, and keeping Bella safe means everything to me. I'll make my own way.'

'It's a loan, then. I'll not hear any more about it. When you can, you can repay it. But we have more important things to discuss than money, Ned.' He handed Ned a folded piece of paper. 'I think you'll need this.'

'Is this Dr Walker's address?'

'Yes, the address you had is correct. He lives in central Bangalore.'

Ned's eyes shone. 'All I seem to say is thank you to you.'

Grenfell held up a hand. 'There's more. I might as well come clean.' He smiled to prevent the inevitable torrent of protest. 'I have contacted Dr Walker.'

'What?'

'I hope you don't feel offended. I wrote to him. And he has replied to me. I have not told him about Robbie. That's for you to do. But I mentioned you were trying to reach him. I kept it all deliberately vague.'

'So he's waiting for me, you mean?'

'Indeed. He is expecting a visit and has offered to help find you some work, get yourself established . . . if that's what you choose to do. Many people are making their fortunes here, young man.'

Ned smiled. 'Well, I'm in no hurry to leave India. My parents are buried in this part of the world, my sister is happy. I might as well see what I can make of myself here where the work is plentiful . . . because it's not back home.'

'I'm sure you're right. Well, young man, shall we go tell the ladies of your decision? And then I think we should immediately book your first-class carriage to Bangalore.'

After what had felt like an endless series of train carriage changes and long waits at stations in the middle of nowhere, Ned finally found himself standing on the platform at Bangalore. The scenery he'd moved through had been one constant vision of dusty, dry tan earth. Flashes of colour erupted as the trains had passed through level crossings where people, carriages, heavily laden bullock carts and waving children waited for the train to chug by. At one point Ned had undone a window to half hang out of it as he looked around to get his bearings. He noticed, with shock, a pile of scruffy male passengers were travelling open air, on the top of the train.

It was early evening and the Bangalore City Station was teeming with people, many of whom were soldiers. Ned had learned that Bangalore was essentially a military base but it was the military that had turned the city into the elegant, party city it now was. The British military, their wives, families and the huge civil service that had grown up around it during the heyday of the British Raj enjoyed an enviable lifestyle in this city, cooled by late-afternoon breezes due to its high elevation. Bangalore was the first city in India to be electrified and that meant a sophistication in its daily life that was unrivalled throughout the rest of the continent.

While Rangoon had been a surprise in more ways than one, Ned had not had the opportunity to appreciate it as he'd been able to with Madras. And his time with the Grenfells had prepared him for crowds, beggars, traffic, noise, filth, colour and wonderment at almost every turn.

Now, as he pushed his way through the hordes clamouring for his attention at the station, he did his best to ignore the beggars without sight, without limbs, some so hideously maimed it hurt to look at them. Experience had taught him that to dig into his pocket, even for just a few coins, and give it to one of the needy, meant he would be set upon with fresh urgency by others determined to win his favour. However, a quiet young girl – far too young to be a mother – leant against a pillar with a near newborn cradled in one arm. Her free hand was extended, palm cupped, but her eyes were cast down; it was actually an exuberant puppy dancing around her toes that caught his attention and his sympathy was pricked into action. He reached into his inside pocket, where he'd taken the precaution to leave some loose change, and carefully dropped the equivalent of a rupee into her hand. He knew it was a small fortune to her.

Using one of the few phrases he'd picked up from Dr Grenfell, who'd found it very hard to pass beggars, he whispered 'feed yourself' in Tamil, hoping she would understand.

Presumably she had, for she put her hand containing the money to her heart and muttered something, still not raising her eyes. When her hand opened again, the money had disappeared. Ned smiled inwardly. She might be young and desperate, but she was smart enough to know how to hide her money from the other equally hungry or desperate people.

He walked on, steeling himself against the throng of beggars who just stopped short of jostling him. As he neared the exit of the station, he risked a look back and noticed that the young mother had gone. Emerging into the main street, Ned caught the delectable smell of fresh peanuts being roasted and it reminded him that he was famished; he was tempted to buy a small cone, fashioned from a piece of newspaper, but his belly was just becoming accustomed to the spicier foods, and he was not prepared to risk the consequences of the street seller's goods on his still-fragile gut. He'd already lost a stone since leaving Scotland and his frame now looked hollow. He shook his head at the young man cutting up guavas at the roadside using a vicious-looking knife that he expertly dipped in salt and chilli powder. With a mouth still watering from the offer of food, he hailed one of the throng of rickshaws, and clutching to his knees the small leather bag the Grenfells had given him, he gave the wiry old runner the address in nearby Sheshadri Road.

With a lurch and a yell at the traffic, the man took off and Ned, trying not to feel self-conscious at being dragged around by a man who looked old enough to be his grandfather, sat back beneath the canopy and let his first impressions of the garden city of Bangalore wash over him.

20

Dr Walker was every bit as welcoming and charming as Robbie had painted him and his shock of steely grey hair and deep voice gave him a distinguished manner that suited Ned's vision of him. Ned had been ushered across the threshold of the large, white-washed house on the quiet, tree-lined boulevard and taken into the spacious sitting room that could have been dark if it wasn't dominated by three tall arched windows, where he was now introduced to Walker's wife.

Obligatory ceiling fans revolved slowly above them and the room had a pleasant, comforting smell that hinted at flowers and tobacco, spice and perfume, wax polish and oiled timber. He felt instantly at ease with the rhythmic tick of a rather grand old mantel clock, the flowery fabric on the sofas and the worn rug beneath his shoes.

'This is Flora,' the doctor beamed as a round, darkish-skinned woman rose to greet him with a wide smile. Even though Ned was not especially tall, he towered above her hair that was pinned up in a bun and shot through with threads of silver. She had to be in her late fifties, Ned guessed, but her gentle plumpness and unlined face made her seem ageless.

'Pleased to meet you, Edward,' she said in perfect English flavoured by an Indian accent. 'I imagine you must be very tired after your long journey.' She nodded to the hovering servant, who held out a tiny glass on a tray. 'Sherry?'

Taken by the warmth in Flora's smile and the genuine concern in her voice, Ned took her hand and bent to kiss her cheek. 'Thank you so much for making me welcome.'

'Please, sit,' she said, gesturing towards the wide, heavy-based sofa and pile of cushions that he sank into.

'Get this down you,' Walker urged. 'You look as though you could use some.'

Ned grinned and joined in the cheers, raising his sherry to his hosts, mentally pinching himself to check he was actually still in India and not in some quaint drawing room in England.

'He likes to be called Ned, dear,' Walker explained.

'Ned it is,' Flora agreed. 'But you look half starved, child. Are you hungry?'

'Famished,' he admitted.

With that admission he watched Flora switch effortlessly into one of the local languages. In amongst instructions to her servant, she glanced his way. 'I'm organising supper to be brought forward. No one goes hungry in this house, Ned,' she said, with a soft glare at her husband. 'Now, no more of that sherry, Harold, until this boy has some food inside him. Please excuse me,' and she was gone with a second flurry of Tamil to the tall manservant who opened the door for her.

Walker laughed at Ned's look of surprise. 'We've been married for nearly thirty years and she never tires of organising me – or indeed anyone else, so don't say I haven't cautioned you,' he said, sipping at the final dregs of his sherry.

'I'll consider myself warned, Dr Walker.'

Ned looked around him and took in the heavy wood panelling and matching dark furniture. Beautiful well-used rugs hugged the rich brown timber floors. The trio of windows framed a pretty garden he hadn't noticed as he'd approached the house down its short pathway from the street. Now he saw the large English trees alongside exotic plants he couldn't name.

Dotted around the room, on the mantelpiece, in fact on every flat surface, including the walls, were framed photos. From a distance he could see that there were lots of family group shots, pictures of the Walker family as they grew up. They looked happy and playful in every one – he envied them.

Walker was pouring himself another tiny measure of sherry at the great oak sideboard. 'So, you've been in India for how long?' he asked, turning to offer Ned one.

Ned shook his head to decline. He wouldn't dare after Mrs Walker's warning. 'I was in Rangoon first, that's how I met Robbie, and Dr Grenfell and his wife took in my sister and myself after we arrived in India about six weeks ago. I suppose Dr Grenfell has told you of our situation?'

'He has. We were very sad to read of your losses. Finding the right words is . . .'

'There are none, Dr Walker. It was a shock and we're coming to terms with it. It's been easier to bear since arriving in India.'

'I can imagine.'

Ned had been dreading this moment but it had finally arrived and he knew he could not avoid it. 'I'm feeling rather guilty actually. Leaving my sister behind was not easy and yet I know she is happy and secure there. At the same time, I do feel relief at no longer having to worry about Bella's safety.'

'Perfectly natural, son,' Walker replied.

He'd needed that assurance. 'Dr Walker, there is a reason that I've travelled to Bangalore to see you.' He took a deep breath. 'I promised Robbie I would.'

'Before you go on, Ned, I suspect that you don't bring glad tidings of that fine young boy. Grenfell said little but I was able to read between the lines and the mere fact that you are here and Robbie is not confirms my grave suspicions.'

Ned hated himself for feeling a new gust of relief. 'He died on the ship to India. It was cholera. I'm still at a loss —'

He didn't finish what he was saying because Flora arrived and announced supper was on the table. 'Don't let it get cold, Harold,' she warned, wagging a finger at him.

Walker gave Ned a conspiratorial wink. 'Come on, old chap. Let's get you fed and watered.' He put a friendly arm around Ned. 'I'm very sorry to hear of Robbie's death. We hardly knew him, to tell the truth, but what we did know was that he was a sweet child, desperately keen to belong to someone, and it's true I did say that he could come to Bangalore and stay with us any time. I'm glad he didn't forget that and I'm grateful to you for wanting to share this difficult news with us in person. It was good of you to come all this way.'

And so it was done. With Walker's gentle words closing that chapter of his life, Ned found himself being guided into a sparse but elegantly decorated dining room of lace tablecloths and dark wood where Flora awaited him, her beaming smile echoed by the two female servants ready to wait on them.

Ned became lost in a pleasant early evening of conversation and simple, delicious fare that masqueraded as local food but in fact tasted more like a slightly peppery chicken stew.

'We weren't sure how accustomed your tummy was to Indian food,' Flora explained, 'so I had the servant make up the chicken we give all our new visitors just out from England. I hope you're not offended.'

'Mrs Walker, it's scrumptious. I could eat this all day.'

'Have you started getting your palate more used to the superb Indian fare?' Walker asked.

Ned grinned. 'Yes, I love Indian food. So where is your family from, Mrs Walker?'

'Daddy was English but my mother was a local girl from

Bombay. We settled here and of course I met Harold and had a family here. We have six children, all grown up now.'

'Our youngest is Iris. She's around your age actually and easily the most spoilt of our bunch,' Harold admitted.

'And your favourite,' Flora chimed in, as she helped the ayah to rearrange dishes.

'Don't say that, dear. She's just the last and my little princess. What can I say? She's adorable.'

'I hope I'll meet her,' Ned replied.

'She's gone to Ooty, son,' Flora explained. 'She's teaching in an orphanage up there and will probably be gone for the rest of this year.'

'Pity,' Ned said.

'Oh, I'm sure you'll meet her some time, although she's thinking she'd like to travel to England. Harold has a few relatives scattered around but I'm hopeful you'll meet all in our family.'

'You're not planning to rush away from Bangalore, are you?' Walker asked.

'I'm not sure what I'm doing yet.'

'Grenfell said you're a qualified electrician.'

'I am. I hope I can use my qualifications to find some work in Madras and . . .'

'Madras? No, I say stay here, son. Bangalore is the place where it's all happening. This is where they have need of fine young qualified men like you. But listen here, why don't you consider KGF?'

Ned frowned. 'I don't know of it.'

'Kolar Gold Fields. Booming, my boy, booming! Gold running out of the shafts. That's my next posting.'

'Really?'

'Yes, in fact I'm supposed to be taking up my position there by end of June. I can ask around, if you're interested.'

Ned looked unsure. 'I have to think about Bella – what's best for her.'

'Bring her down.'

Ned's frown deepened. 'She's just so happy in Madras. The three of them make a great family, I'm almost sad to admit.'

Flora Walker leaned over and touched his cheek in a way only a mother could. Ned felt a twinge of sorrow that his own was lost. 'Oh, my dear, how sad you are. I understand you'd want to be near your baby sister. Well, whatever you decide, you are both most welcome and we'll do what we can to help you.'

Walker was lighting up a pipe and the sweet smell of tobacco began to fill the room. 'I think you should definitely take a look at KGF before you make any decisions, Ned. Any coffee coming, dear?'

She gave him one of her affectionate glares. 'Yes, my love.'

'Are all your children in the goldfields?'

'Near enough,' Walker said. 'The boys are involved with the mines in some form or another. 'Christine is working in the north. She's a nurse. There's Iris, of course, and then our middle girl, Florence, is married to an army fellow, so she moves around a lot but we hear he is coming back south around September. Then we have Geraldine, who will probably marry someone locally in time. We're hoping they'll be able to settle down in Bangalore.'

'I'm very pleased for you,' Ned replied, and even he could detect the envy in his voice.

'Ned,' Flora began, with far too much tenderness. He had to clear his throat and concentrate hard on not letting his emotion get the better of him. 'We were captivated by Robbie during the short time we knew him. Your news is so sad I can hardly bear to think of that lovely boy. And it's obvious you became fast friends. There was something special about that child. He seemed to have a sixth sense. No, Harold, it's not just because he was Anglo-Indian. I really believe he was touched by the heavens. And Robbie chose Ned and his sister Bella to be special in his life.' Flora regarded Ned seriously now. 'You are welcome in this house, young man, and in our lives. And until you can start a new one of your own, I suggest you make yourself feel part of this family. I can tell you're a person of high morals and so, Ned, I like you and I know the rest of the family will too.'

The lump at the back of Ned's throat had doubled in size and he cleared his throat again. 'I'm not sure what to say.'

Flora banged her small hand lightly on the table. 'There is nothing more to say. Until you can find yourself somewhere you'd like to live independently or perhaps until we leave, you must stay here with us.'

'I'm really so grateful,' Ned stammered, overwhelmed by the kindness of these people.

'That's settled, then,' Flora said.

Ned grinned at them both. 'Thank you. My main plan was to come here and fulfil Robbie's wish that I meet you. He was so determined.'

'Oh, that poor boy,' Flora said. 'I suppose we must be grateful that neither you or your sister were infected by the cholera.'

'Enough gloom,' Harold said, allowing a stream of smoke to escape the side of his mouth. 'So, my boy, let's get you down to the club and initiated into the Bangalore scene.'

'Club?'

'Look lively, lad. No, leave all that. Flora will organise to clear up here. Come on, we'll make tracks.'

Ned walked around and kissed Flora. 'Thank you for everything.'

'Your room will be ready by the time you return,' she said, hugging him back. 'Welcome to Bangalore.'

The rickshaw driver dropped them outside a grand colonial stone, single-storey building surrounded by manicured lawns. Its wide verandah was lit and Ned could see people – men mainly – drinking and talking quietly while Indian men in starched whites and rich red turbans hovered to take care of their every need.

Harold paid the driver and guided Ned through the gates. 'This is a favourite of the Anglo-Indian community, which is very large in this city. I should know, I've added six of my own to it.'

'Did you meet Mrs Walker here?'

'I did. I came out with the East India Company and she was such a delicious little thing. And so shy. You wouldn't think that now, would you?'

Ned shook his head and shared a smile with the doctor.

'Oh, but she's a good woman and I love her as much now as I did then. Our children have all enjoyed this club's facilities. I still prefer the Bangalore United Services Club but it's a bit stuffy for my lot and children aren't particularly welcome. With a large brood, it was easier for us to use this place. Besides, The Institute has always been very welcoming to the Anglo-Indian community and Flora feels comfortable here.'

To Ned it looked like a fairyland. 'Am I dressed all right?'

Walker laughed. 'You look fine, son. You're well enough dressed for the BUS club!'

They climbed up the steps onto the cool verandah. Its tranquil atmosphere was stirred only by the ceiling fans and the odd burst of laughter from its guests.

'Here, let's take a pew. Inside, people can amuse themselves in the billiards room, or there's a magnificent library and a quiet reading room, but you have to be brought by a member.' Music struck up distantly. 'Come the weekend there are balls and dances and lots of gaiety. People your age can have a lot of fun here. Iris hated to miss the opportunity to dress up in her party frocks.'

'And there'll be none where she's gone?'

'She's in the mountains, son. There's absolutely nothing there. In fact, it's why she's gone. Those orphaned children have so little. Iris took up several chests of toys and clothes. I'm glad she felt the calling but then Iris has always been the gifted one. She's good at everything and seems to be able to achieve whatever she sets her heart on.'

'And your other children?'

'All fine upstanding citizens, I'm proud to say.' He sighed. 'Their mother misses them dreadfully. She'd have us all living together in one huge compound if she could.' He stood and tapped Ned on the shoulder. 'I'll sign us in. You order some drinks. Make mine a single shot of Scotch. Tell them the Chivas.'

'I know it well, sir,' Ned said, reminded suddenly of home.

Walker disappeared but not before stopping several times to talk to people along the verandah. When the attendant arrived and murmured a soft 'good evening, sir' while bobbing his head politely, Ned felt like pinching himself. Suddenly his nationality gave him status and this much older man was bowing to him! Ned remembered his manners, wished the waiter a good evening back and ordered the whisky and a shandy for himself. After the man had soundlessly left, Ned sat back and looked out across the lawns, feeling vaguely happy for the first time in a long time. He promised himself he would write to Bella this evening.

As he relaxed in the relative quiet of their corner table, he allowed himself to soak up the gentle hum of activity around him. Ahead he watched as a small army of people worked quietly in the distance, setting up for what looked like a party. He recognised the popular song 'For Me and My Gal' as it struck up on a gramophone somewhere but it was muted and didn't disturb anyone. The waiters worked fluidly around the guests, clearing glasses and refreshing drink orders. Next to him two men were laughing quietly. He glanced over. One seemed to be nearing his thirties. The other looked around Ned's age. Ned caught snippets of their conversation, which moved from talk of a voyage from London to making a new life in India. This was reassuring. Ned was clearly not the only young newcomer to this exotic land. He hoped he would soon make some friends of his own age and feel as relaxed as his neighbour appeared to be, sipping at a beer and laughing with his colleague.

He stopped eavesdropping and sighed. Somewhere over the course of his journey he'd accepted that he would make a go of this new life in India, so now he had to seriously consider finding work. It was a comfort to know that Dr Walker was investigating positions in the goldfields. If Ned's father had taught him anything in their brief moments alone, it was that being financially independent was the single most important step a young man could make. Ned had responsibilities now. He had to earn enough to send money to Madras for Bella's education and he had to be able to pay for his own board and upkeep.

Walker arrived just as their drinks were being delivered.

'Perfect timing,' Ned quipped, noticing that the pair next to them chose that moment to push back their chairs.

'Enjoy your evening,' the younger one said, nodding at Walker and throwing a broad, bright grin Ned's way.

'Thank you. I plan to savour every last drop of this single malt,' Walker replied.

They had both moved on before Ned could respond and he could have kicked himself for not being quicker off the mark. It was a lost opportunity, he decided, as the two men retreated. The friendly one was tall with a confident lope of a walk, his black hair carelessly swiped back from his tanned forehead. He looked like a man at ease with himself and his surrounds even though he was a relative stranger to Bangalore.

Walker settled into his chair. 'You're all signed in, young Sinclair. So here's to you,' he said, picking up his tumbler. The light sparkled through the amber liquid. 'Cheers, old chap.'

Ned lifted his chilled glass, its contents fizzing deliciously. 'To you, sir . . . and thank you again.'

Walker sighed his pleasure and Ned was determined to next time order a proper beer. Looking over at the empty beer tankards on the neighbouring table, he felt suddenly childish sipping a shandy.

'Did you know those two gentlemen, Dr Walker?'

'The elder of the two struck me as vaguely familiar – I've probably seen him here before.'

'I could swear I detected a west-country accent.'

'You probably did. You're going to meet people from all over Britain out here.'

The conversation turned to jobs and the potential at Kolar Gold Fields. After a couple of drinks, Walker suggested he give Ned a tour of the Bowring Institute. They ambled down the cool corridors as Walker pointed out the quiet reading rooms through dark arched doorways, continued along smaller pathways until they could hear the sound of men's laughter.

'And now we've reached the billiards room. Care to take a look?'

'Why not?' Ned said, stepping into a smoky atmosphere of low lighting, a host of bearers standing around the large room setting up fresh trays of balls or serving drinks. A bank of windows lined the back wall, and the other walls were lined with tiered bench seating for an audience. Men in rolled-up shirtsleeves drank, laughed and laid bets on the green baize of the huge tables. Among them he saw the two men he'd noticed earlier. Only the younger one was playing.

Ned wandered over to watch as the young man took a long look at the seemingly impossible shot he was going to attempt to win a small pile of coins.

'Florins,' Ned murmured to Walker, who had joined him.

'Well, it's certainly not Indian currency. A whole pound on one shot. The young man is mad!'

'Or very confident.'

They watched him line up for his shot and Ned noticed how still the man became, how his smile gave way to a more focused expression. Gently, the man pulled his right arm back, his left not even wobbling, then took a breath and held it. With a fluid movement he struck the white ball and with a hard clack it cannoned into the black, which flew to the far end of the table and careened back, then dropped with a satisfying clunk in the pocket. Men watching erupted into applause and the two opponents shook hands.

'I won't be betting so freely next time,' Ned heard him say as he watched the winner pocket his coins.

The young man grinned fiercely and then took Ned by surprise by shooting him a friendly glance and raising a hand.

'Good to see you again,' he called over. 'Fancy a flutter?'

'I don't know how,' Ned said.

'Come and have a go, all the same,' he said, wandering across. 'Good evening again, sir,' he said, shaking Walker's hand. 'I'm John Bryant. People call me Jack.'

'New off the boat, eh?'

'Is it that easy to tell?'

'You're not tanned enough. I'm Dr Harold Walker and Edward Sinclair is a guest staying with our family,' he added, nodding towards Ned.

'Arrived a few weeks ago into Bombay and I've been in Bangalore just days,' Bryant said, offering a hand to Ned. 'Good to meet you, Sinclair.'

'It seems we're both new to these parts. I've been in Madras for some weeks but only got into Bangalore today. Call me Ned, by the way.'

Jack introduced his companion. 'This is Henry Berry.'

The men shook hands. 'Pleased to meet you, Dr Walker. Do you work at the Lady Curzon Hospital?'

As the doctor and Henry fell into conversation, Jack caught Ned's eye and nodded towards the snooker table. 'Shall we rack up?'

'So long as you don't mind me being useless.'

Ned watched Jack signal to the servant to chalk up some cues. 'Are you Cornish?'

'And proud of it. I detect a slight accent too.'

'I hope you hear only Scottish,' Ned said indignantly and just a bit hopefully.

'Is that what it is?'

'Well, if you'd guessed Welsh, I'd have had to hit you with this cue.'

Jack laughed. 'I'd like to see you try.'

Ned grinned. 'I'm quick,' he warned.

'Let's see how you strike first before you shoot your mouth off,' Jack said, clearly enjoying the banter.

And so began the first tentative steps of a new friendship. Jack was so easygoing and confident; Ned felt his spirits lifting as Jack guided him not only in the game of snooker but also in the notion that India was the future for both of them.

Jack winked as he slammed the final black ball home. 'You'd owe me about twenty pounds by now,' he said, putting the cue behind his back and stretching his shoulders. 'I should have insisted.'

Ned laughed. 'I'm wise to you, Jack. I think you're a shark. I suppose you play cards too?'

'All the bad habits. And probably why I find myself here in the colonies,' he added, sagely, as he returned the cue. 'We're finished, thank you,' he said and withdrew silently.

'Well, thanks for your company. I've enjoyed this evening. Listen, are you really thinking about heading to the goldfields?'

'I'm a miner, Ned. It's time I found work. You should take Walker up on his offer to find some work there.'

'I'm thinking about it.'

'Don't think, act. KGF is booming and Henry assures me a man can live a grand life out there. It's good wages – he even thinks something can be wangled to make me a covenanted man and that means I'll be given accommodation.'

'Lucky you.'

'I need some after my run.'

Ned looked at Jack quizzically.

'I'll tell you more one day. Right now Henry's yawning and I think as he's my host I should let him get his sleep. He's off in a day or two to Ooticamund, or Ooty as they call it. It's a long trip and poor old Henry needs his rest.'

'Perhaps we can meet again?'

'Definitely. We're at the Bangalore Club. It's not far from here. Why don't you meet me there on Friday and I'll show you around Bangalore? I've got my bearings now and it's a most attractive city. If not for the heat, you could almost swear it was part of London. Amazing parks and wide streets.'

'I've seen nothing but the inside of a rickshaw.'

Jack grinned. 'I'll take you for a ride in a jatka.'

'What?'

'Horse-drawn cart. Much faster. Even less comfy!'

They both smiled and shook hands. 'I'll see you Friday, then,' Ned said.

Dr Walker and Henry Berry arrived. 'Come on, young Ned,' Walker said. 'Mrs Walker will be cranky with me if I don't get you home in time for her to wish you goodnight. She hasn't got anyone to fuss over with our Iris gone. I don't count, you see.'

Henry laughed. 'It was a pleasure to meet you both. Good-night, Ned. I'm glad you two hit it off. Jack will have some company while I'm gone.'

'I've arranged to see Ned again on Friday.'

'Excellent. That suits me because I'll be out all day with Mrs Walker. Thank you, that works out well. By the way, we're trying to keep him here, Bryant, so show him the best side of Bangalore.'

Jack tapped his nose conspiratorially and the four of them laughed, Ned especially, because for him suddenly the world was righting itself.

Life is good, he told himself later that night, after all Flora Walker's fussing was done and he found himself lying beneath a billowing mosquito net in a large, four-poster bed. Its four legs were placed in tubs of water to keep the insects away and the bedroom shutters had been thrown open to let in a cooling night breeze. And on its breath it carried the delightful scent of a flower that Flora had explained was called Queen of the Night.

Its fragrance brought to mind the night of his mother's suicide, but Ned decided firmly that nothing was going to ruin his hopeful mood.

21

'Has Harold told you about the phone call he took this morning, Ned?' Flora asked.

'Thank you, Sabu,' Ned said, as the butler refreshed his china cup with steaming hot tea. They were sitting on the back porch overlooking the garden, where Flora liked to take breakfast. 'No, he hasn't said anything.'

'Oh, that man!' she said, her eyes widening with exasperation. 'Sabu, has the master gone out?'

'Just briefly, madam.'

She looked back at Ned apologetically. 'I suppose you've noticed that he likes to take a morning stroll.' They both heard the main door bang behind them. 'Ah, here he is, back already.'

Walker arrived, muttering about how Bangalore's traffic was on the rise. 'A man can hardly cross the road for fear of being run down by a jatka and I thought the rickshaws were bad enough. I counted no less than ten motor vehicles on the road this morning too,' he grumbled. 'Any tea going, Sabu?'

'Yes, sir,' Sabu said and rushed off, no doubt to make another fresh pot.

'Morning, Ned,' Harold said.

'Hello, sir, and before you ask, I slept like a baby. I don't think I've slept in years as well as I have the last three nights.'

'It's the cool Bangalore air, son. Another reason to stay. And

I insist you stop calling me sir. My staff do that.'

Ned smiled his thanks.

'Harold, tell him about that telephone call,' Flora scolded gently.

'I was going to, Mother.'

'Well, hurry up, men,' she said.

Ned was getting used to Flora's singsong way of speaking and how she added 'pah' or 'men', on the end of her sentences that were meant to berate.

Harold addressed Ned with a sigh. 'I'm not sure whether to say it's fortunate that we have one of these newfangled telephone things or whether to complain that I am suddenly so contactable. Either way, we took a call this morning and it was about you.'

Ned put his cup down. 'Was it Dr Grenfell? Bell's all right, isn't she?'

'Absolutely fine, as far as I know, son. No, this wasn't Grenfell. It was a doctor though. His name is Brent.'

'Dr Brent?' Ned felt suddenly sickened. 'From Rangoon?'

'That's the one,' Walker said, looking pleased. 'He sounded so glad to have hunted you down. He told me he'd been trying to follow your tracks for a few months now.'

'Ned, dear. You look pale suddenly,' Flora said, frowning.

Ned's new sense of wellbeing instantly evaporated. He had broken into a sweat and his throat had seemed to close.

'Ned?' Flora repeated, putting her own cup down. 'Are you all right, son?'

He gathered his wits. 'Yes, er, yes, I'm sorry,' he stammered. 'I think just the mention of Brent brought a lot of bad memories flooding back.'

'Oh, of course it did,' Flora said, glaring at her husband. 'We're so sorry. How insensitive of us.'

'It's not your fault, Mrs Walker.'

'It is. And, Ned, just call me Flora. We don't need to be formal.'

He thought he murmured a thankyou but his mind was in chaos. 'What else did Dr Brent say?' he asked, his tone as casual as he could make it.

'Well, just that he's going to be in Bangalore and is looking forward to seeing you. He has something for you, apparently. Perhaps he's brought your belongings from the hotel in Rangoon?'

Ned recalled the story he'd given the Walkers that followed the same gilded truth he'd given the Grenfells. He couldn't change his story now. 'I suppose it could be,' he said miserably. 'Do I have to see him?'

Walker looked astonished. 'But don't you want to? Brent sounded so pleased that you are both well.'

A new thought struck Ned. 'Has he seen the Grenfells?'

'Yes. Expressed his delight at seeing Bella looking so bonny.'

An ice-cold clamp seemed to fit itself snugly around Ned's innards. 'What did he say?'

'Oh, just that he's in Bangalore.'

'He's *here*?'

'I've told him to come to the house. What's wrong, Ned?'

'Nothing,' he said quickly. 'I'm just . . . just a bit churned up.' He took a steadying breath. 'What time is he expected?'

'Oh, not until later. Probably early evening. I suggested any time around six should catch you. I know you were planning to go out with that Bryant fellow today, weren't you?'

Ned nodded dumbly.

'It's just that I can't promise we'll be back in time to meet him, unfortunately.'

Ned stared at the Walkers now.

'Remember, we're going to KGF today and it's a long journey, there and back,' Flora said, concerned.

He snapped himself out of his shock. 'Of course. No, you go

ahead. I'll see Dr Brent, although I can't really see him for long. Jack asked me for dinner at the Bangalore Club,' he lied.

'Well, well,' Walker said, clearly impressed. 'You'll enjoy it, Ned. By all means offer Brent a sherry and then see him on his way.'

'Of course. Well, if you'll both excuse me, I'd better get ready for today's sightseeing,' he said, feigning a brightness he certainly wasn't feeling. 'I'll be down to see you off.'

Upstairs in his spacious room Ned fought to steady his careening thoughts. Brent had hunted them down. But why? What could possibly have dragged him from Rangoon to India?

Ned felt very alone, once again. He had no ally this time. As slight and young as Robbie was, he'd been a partner in their escape and had masterminded the whole event. Now, though he was surrounded by the generosity of the Walkers, and Bella by the vast affections of the Grenfells, they were still alone.

Ned didn't feel he could tell either of the doctors the truth of their escape. He should have given them the ugly details from the outset but it was too late now.

'So be it,' Ned thought, but although the words sounded confident as he murmured them, they brought no peace. He rinsed his face, then dried it on a soft pale towel in an effort to calm himself and his suddenly hot cheeks. He had no one to share these fears with. No friend to confide in.

Just then he heard a familiar voice asking for him downstairs. He *did* have an ally. Perhaps Jack Bryant would have an idea of how to approach this.

He grabbed his jacket and hurried down the stairs, once again schooling his features to hide his internal anxiety.

'Jack! You're early.'

'It's going to be a hot one,' Jack said from the reception area where Sabu stood alongside him, holding their guest's topi. 'I thought we'd get going?'

'Fine with me,' Ned said, shaking Jack's hand. 'Come and meet the Walkers. I'll just say my goodbyes.'

After the introductions, Ned explained that they were heading out early.

'Take your helmet, Ned,' Flora warned. 'You have to get used to wearing it all day. How are you boys getting around?'

'I've negotiated with a jatka-waller to be our guide,' Jack confirmed.

'No more than a couple of rupees, I hope, Bryant?'

'No, sir. Five, in fact.'

'Five? Robbery.'

'He has a family, he told me,' Jack said, genially defending himself.

'We'll be home after dark, son,' Walker admitted.

'I've already told the ayah you won't need dinner. Nice of you to host Ned for a meal at the Bangalore Club, Mr Bryant,' Flora said.

Jack barely hesitated as he threw a glance Ned's way. 'I thought he'd like to see the place. Henry's already signed him in for me.'

'Excellent,' Walker said. 'Well, have fun. Don't forget Dr Brent for six, Ned.'

'I won't, sir,' he said, guiding Jack back into the dark reception hall, with Flora's bowls of flowers everywhere, and the waiting Sabu.

Once they were uncomfortably balanced in the back of the jatka that lurched forward precariously, Jack finally turned to Ned. 'Well, what was that all about?'

For some reason Ned couldn't explain, he sensed his secrets were safe with Jack. He found himself telling his new friend everything, and somehow by sharing his fears with Jack, they didn't seem so bad.

Jack listened intently, his face growing more serious and his expression darker as Ned's story wore on. It only became animated when Ned's voice stopped almost in synchrony with the jatka.

'Cubbon Park, Master,' the driver said over his shoulder.

Jack didn't move, just stared hard at Ned.

'Say something,' Ned said, instantly self-conscious, despite the general noise of the streets.

'Let's get out,' Jack replied, easing from the jatka. 'Can you wait here?' he asked the driver. The man wobbled his head in the Indian way that said yes. 'Let's get some air,' Jack said grimly.

Ned followed him through the park's gates and onto one of the pathways. Jack lit a cigarette and glanced over at Ned.

'He's got something in mind.'

'Yes, well, I didn't imagine he'd come here to ask me how I was. What do you think he means to do?'

Jack shook his head and took another long drag on his cigarette. 'I suspect he's going to threaten you.'

'Why? I'm out of his life.'

'Not really. You're out of his clutches, all right, but you can still do him damage from afar.'

'I don't want anything to do with him!'

'Ah, but he doesn't know that. He doesn't know you haven't begun telling people about his perverse ways. He has no idea whether authorities are already on their way to ask him some difficult questions.'

'And so he's coming to find out,' Ned finished.

'No, from what you tell me, I suspect he'll want to take some action.'

'Like what?'

'At the very least I imagine he'll threaten you.'

'With what?'

'Think, Sinclair! What's the one thing you fear most? He already knows your weakness.'

'Bell,' Ned said, angrily.

'Yes, Bella. She's his trump card. He knows where she's living and he's already paid a visit to the family in Madras. Is that right?'

Ned nodded.

'Well, presumably he's established that they know nothing of what occurred in Rangoon. Why didn't you tell the truth about him?'

'I had no proof. Robbie was dead. Brent's extremely well respected in Rangoon. It would have been my word against his and frankly, Jack, I was just happy to be rid of him. I thought we'd left him behind for good.'

'You'll meet him, of course.'

'I don't want to even see his face —'

'Ned, you have to meet enemies and stare them down. Find out what he wants. He could be coming to beg your silence. Buy it, even.'

'I don't want his money!'

'I know that. But find out what his intentions are first. Then you can make your decisions. Either way, you have to front him . . . and be resolute.'

'He makes me sick. When I think of Robbie —'

'Don't think of Robbie. Robbie's dead. Think of your sister and just focus on getting him out of your life for good. '

Ned sighed. 'You're right.'

'I usually am.'

'You're much too sure of yourself, Bryant.'

Jack laughed. 'Come on, you've got all day to churn this over in your mind. You might as well enjoy yourself rather than moping.'

Ned made his best attempt. 'So, where are we? It's lovely.'

'This is Cubbon Park, named after one of the commissioners. Built by the British, for the British – a little slice of home, even in the colonies. You'll see flowers, trees, shrubs, all reminiscent of the plants we know. It's quite incredible. If you look across there, you can see all the way through to Holy Trinity Church. These two landmarks encase the cantonment in a way. That's South Parade, and further on is Ulsore Lake, where many of the Brits here like to take picnics. Beyond that they've set up dairy farms, growing barley and wheat. Even some small vineyards.'

'Really?'

'Well,' Jack said, pulling a wry expression. 'I think we like our fresh milk, our bread, our beer, and even the officers like their wine too much to suffer any local produce. Do you fancy drinking goat's milk or oxen's?'

Ned wrinkled his nose. 'The park looks huge.'

'A hundred or so acres, I'm assured.' They said good morning to a pair of middle-aged women walking with a troupe of children. The entire party was dressed in pastels and the women carried umbrellas – a sure sign of status. 'Just like Kew Gardens.'

The two young men began to exchange stories of their lives, Ned learning that Jack was a miner and Jack hearing about Ned's upbringing in Scotland.

Ned stopped talking suddenly. 'Great music,' he commented.

'I was leading you to the bandstand. This way.' They turned onto a new path, shaded by huge old European-style trees. 'I think they're rehearsing. It's the Royal Air Force. They'll be playing on Saturday night. Look, here's the statue of Queen Victoria. Over there,' he pointed, 'is the memorial to King Edward VII.'

'Ah,' Ned said, smiling, as they emerged. 'The bandstand.'

Right enough the RAF big band was practising, belting out the latest foxtrot.

'Do you dance, Jack?'

'Never got much of a chance in Penzance, but yes, I can dance.'

'I can teach you. This is called white jazz or a foxtrot.'

'Why don't we come here on Saturday night?'

'I'm not dancing in public with you!'

Jack burst out laughing. 'Nor I with you! I was thinking we could meet some girls.'

Now Ned's eyes widened. 'I'd like that.'

'You see, plenty to look forward to. Come on. I'm going to take you to a place called Three Aces on South Parade where they serve great coffee. I've got a big day planned.'

Over what Ned had to agree was a superb European-style coffee, served in silver crockery by dark men, once again in their starched white traditional dress with blood-red turbans and sashes, he returned his thoughts to Brent.

'Jack, I was wondering if you could come by the Walkers' house this evening?'

'I figured you'd ask that.'

'It is cowardly?'

'It's wise. But you should meet him alone. I'll drop by a little later. You can use me as an excuse to get away. Six o'clock he's coming?'

'About then. What if you come by at six-twenty?'

Jack drained his cup. 'Done. Right, I'm going to show you the madness and colour and fun of Commercial Street now. Anything you want to buy is there.'

'Anything?'

Jack arched an eyebrow. 'Well, well, Sinclair. Not so naïve after all, eh?'

Ned found a grin, already feeling as though the Brent episode was no longer something to fret over but simply something to get past.

22

It felt strange to be in the house without the Walkers but at a quarter to six precisely, Sabu politely showed Ned onto the cool back verandah. He could see a gardener still toiling in the vegetable patch.

'A drink, sir?' Sabu asked. 'Perhaps a gimlet?'

Ned wasn't sure what a gimlet was, but he certainly wasn't going to say no to something that sounded like it wasn't a soft drink. Minutes later the butler returned bearing a tray, and on it a tall tumbler, ice clinking and a slice of lime balanced on its rim.

'Thank you,' he said. 'Sabu, I won't be offering drinks to my visitor.'

'Yes, sir.'

'Where should I see him, do you think?'

'Mrs Walker said he is to be shown into the drawing room.'

'That will be fine. He will not be staying long.'

Sabu wobbled his head in the way that was now extremely familiar to Ned and withdrew into the shadows of the house. Ned steeled himself by taking a gulp of his gimlet. He had noticed the thick rivulets of a syrupy liquid swirling in the drink when he stirred it with the glass cocktail stick. And now he tasted that it was Rose's Lime Juice – unmistakeable – and he suspected he was drinking it with a healthy slug of gin. There was no giveaway spritz of soda on his tongue and he took another big sip to steady his nerves. He wanted to be forthright and as aloof as possible with Brent.

Jack was right. He had to face him. But he was reassured that Jack would arrive soon too and then, hopefully, the ordeal would be over. Ned tugged at his collar to loosen it and sipped again. The gimlet was nearly finished. He inhaled the mild evening air, mercifully cooler today. The crickets were already chirruping – or were those cicadas? And as usual the heady fragrance of the evening blooms wafted gently across the garden. He thought he heard a distant voice and a fresh spike of fear stabbed through him, but he drained his glass and forced himself to settle. Ned felt the liquor hitting his empty belly.

Sabu returned. 'Mr Brent is here, sir,' he murmured.

'How is he?'

'Not at all like you and Mr Walker, sir.'

Ned swung around. 'What do you mean?'

'He pushed me out of the way when I answered the door and asked me not to breathe on him, Mr Sinclair, sir.'

'That's because he's a fat, arrogant, English swine, Sabu.' Ned saw the recognition flare in Sabu's expression. 'I despise him, which is why we shall be polite simply because he is a guest in Dr Walker's house but I shall rid us of him as soon as I can.'

'Yes, sir,' Sabu said in his deadpan manner, but Ned noticed his eyes glittering.

'Let's go.' Ned straightened his jacket and tie, glad to note that his voice sounded steady. He followed Sabu through to the entrance of the drawing room and nodded before silently taking a long, deep breath and opening the door.

On the opposite side of Sheshadri Road Jack watched. He'd seen the heavyset Brent arrive, by foot curiously. Obviously the man had been dropped close to the house but he was cautious enough to have taken his time to stroll to his destination, no doubt taking stock of his surrounds. A careful man, then. He was dressed in pale linen and the suit looked lived in. Jack could tell by the confident walk, the apparel, even the arrogant way Brent tapped a beggar out of his path with his cane, that this was a man who was at home in the colonies – had been here long enough to know the ways, to cope with the heat, and to feel comfortable in his superiority.

From what he'd gleaned it appeared that Brent had been happy for Ned to disappear, but because his sister had escaped as well, that meant Ned was free to say whatever he liked about the scheming doctor. Jack suspected the visit was to warn Ned against opening up.

He watched Brent rap on the door, then he was over the threshold in a blink, pushing at the butler's chest aggressively. Just as the door was closing, Sabu caught a glimpse of Jack. The butler hesitated only for a moment but in that split second Jack had felt naked. Why did he feel guilty? He shouldn't, but what would the servant be thinking?

Jack bit his lip. Should he arrive earlier than planned? That way he could remark that he'd seen the visitor arriving and hadn't wanted to encroach on the household at the same moment. It sounded contrived but he was sure he could make it work.

***

Brent turned from the mantelpiece where he was standing and smirked at Ned. 'Hello, Edward.'

'What are you doing here?'

Brent made a clicking sound of admonishment. 'That's not a very polite welcome, is it, young man?'

'That's because you're not welcome here.'

'Dr Walker invited me to make myself at home.'

'You're not staying.'

'Not even going to offer me an hospitable aperitif? Where are your manners?'

'How did you find me?'

Brent regarded him with contempt. 'It was easy.'

'I asked you how?' Ned's tone was so dry it sounded brittle enough to break.

The man fluttered his eyelids as he shook his jowls and shrugged. 'A child could have tracked you down, Sinclair. After talking to the hotel in Rangoon I figured you'd try and get on a ship somehow. I asked around. And then I learned there had been an outbreak of cholera on a ship – it was in the local newspaper, in fact, and it reported that the single victim was an Anglo-Indian youth aged fifteen. Every chance it was Robbie, but I wanted to be certain. I was patient. I waited for the captain to return and of course discovered that the victim was a stowaway, travelling with two others, a sister and brother.' He grinned malevolently. 'You can see just how easy it was to slot the jigsaw pieces into place, Sinclair. You hardly covered your tracks in your desperation to get away.'

'Go on,' Ned seethed, reining in his anger.

Brent opened up his hands in protest. 'What's to tell? It was a simple enough task to track down the ship's doctor – I'd already been told that he'd taken charge of the two English stowaways. I contacted him and spun a beautifully crafted story about being the worried director of the orphanage, concerned for Miss Sinclair, who was my charge, after all.'

'That's a lie!'

'No one cares. Perception is everything, Sinclair. You should learn that. And I am a responsible figure in Rangoon. I am trusted. You are an orphan of no means, a mere stowaway . . . an urchin. So is your sister. Dr Grenfell was most relieved to hear from me and was especially welcoming when I suggested he and Mrs Grenfell might like to consider formally adopting Bella.'

Ned paled. He hadn't heard about this turn of events. 'You had no right,' he murmured, stabbing a finger towards Brent. It sounded like a threat but he was calm and that was a relief to him.

His remark won only laughter from Brent. 'I say again, who cares? Grenfell was delighted to hear I was passing through Madras.'

'Get on with it, Brent. Whatever you came here to say, spit it out and leave this house.'

'Well, well,' Brent said, moving lightly on his toes towards an armchair. 'I presume I am permitted to take a seat at least?'

'Don't make yourself comfortable. I'm going out.'

'Oh? Bangalore's quite a buzzy place if you fall into the right circles. And it seems you've fallen into the bosom of a respected family.'

'Brent, what do you want? I didn't think I had anything more to say to you.'

Brent's demeanour changed. 'Did you not? Well, I certainly have things I wish to discuss with you.'

Ned glanced at the clock on the mantelpiece, ticking loudly. 'Someone is picking me up in fifteen minutes. I'll give you five.'

Brent smiled again, oily and sinister. 'How self-possessed you've become, Edward. You obviously feel more secure in these salubrious surrounds than when we last met. I suppose it is comforting to have the backing of a good family, when your own parents lie rotting in muddy graves in Rangoon —'

'Good evening, Dr Brent. I shall call for the butler to show you out.' Surprising himself that his voice sounded so controlled, even though he felt as though he were teetering on a precipice of rage, Ned turned and opened the door, making straight for his room. Come on, Jack, he begged inwardly. 'Sabu!' he called.

'Not so fast.' Brent trailed him down the dark, slightly musty hallway. It seemed Sabu had not heard Ned's call because for once the tall Indian did not materialise from the shadows. Ned had no choice but to continue into his room. To his dismay, Brent followed.

'Get out!' Ned snarled.

'You thought you could beat me, didn't you, Sinclair?'

'We did!' he hurled at Brent, backing towards his wardrobe, his ears straining for the knock on the front door.

'Robbie didn't.'

'No, well, cholera's a random killer. I hope it catches you one day.'

'Oh, there was nothing *random* about Robbie's death.'

Ned's mouth opened and nothing came out. He could sense his cheeks burning even though he felt suddenly cold. 'What?' he finally whispered.

'Oh, dear. Did Robbie not tell you?'

Ned was sure his shocked expression told Brent more than enough. Brent approached him and Ned flinched.

'Robbie tried to murder me. Did he mention that?'

Ned shook his head dumbly.

'Probably all the excitement of his escape, which I will say was most ingenious. Perhaps you realised it was all too easy? You fell perfectly for my plan. That was a wonderful moment hearing that you'd . . . disappeared.' He clicked his fingers before Ned's face. 'For good, I'd hoped. What I hadn't foreseen was Robbie's resilience. I take my hat off to him, but of course by the time Robbie had left the orphanage grounds, he was already dead.'

Ned shook his head with confusion.

Brent smiled, filled with the familiar menace Ned recalled from months earlier. 'I asked him to refill my water jug but given his nervousness I made him drink from it first.' Brent laughed but it sounded like admiration. 'He did! Without hesitation, I might add. That's why I let him go that morning. I figured if he'd drunk the water, then my suspicions that you two were up to no good were unfounded. He left with your sister knowing he would likely die, for the water he drew was not boiled, I now realise. He was trying to kill me, the little snake.'

Ned's breathing had become ragged. Now he understood. Robbie had deliberately drunk infected water – to protect Bell.

'Still, I didn't trust the water,' Brent was saying, but Ned had switched off. His thoughts had become chaotic as a fresh fury overtook him.

He heard the front door knocker bang and then distantly a voice. It focused him again.

'Ned?' Jack called from the hallway.

Sanctuary . . . safety. 'I'll be right out.' Ned returned his angry gaze to Brent. 'Get out of my room, get out of this house, Brent. If I have to see you again, I won't be held responsible for what I do.'

Brent guffawed.

'Why are you here?'

'Well, I am here on business, believe it or not. A happy coincidence for me, it seems, because it means I can remind you that I am very well connected, especially in Madras. It would be a great tragedy, now, wouldn't it, should something happen to your darling sister? Just remember that if you, or anyone connected to you, start casting aspersions about my good name, it will be so much the worse for Bella. One snap of my fingers, Sinclair. That's all it would take. Keep your mouth shut about me.'

Jack, who'd stolen down the hallway and had heard the final minutes of the conversation, returned silently to the front room when he realised Brent was leaving.

He dashed to the window and watched as the big man lumbered down the short garden path and turned towards the city, the back of his suit marked by sweat stains.

He thought about it only momentarily before knowing his plan was the only solution to Ned's dilemma. He marched by a surprised Sabu to Ned's room and opened it without knocking. Inside, he found Ned, still frozen to the spot, staring at the ground, his fists clenched.

'Ned?'

'You were right, Jack. He openly threatened Bell.'

'So I heard. The thing is, Ned, she is safe, or can be made so, but others aren't. He's buying your silence so he can continue his life untroubled by any claims you might have considered making.'

'I hadn't thought that much ahead. I just wanted to put Brent far behind me. He and I both want the same thing – to forget our paths crossed.'

Jack considered this, then nodded. 'Bella was the lucky one who got away. There will be others who aren't nearly so fortunate.'

Ned turned an angry stare on Jack. 'What do you want me to do? Risk Bell?'

'Oh, get a grip, Ned. The man is making empty threats. How do you reckon he snaps his fingers and people jump in Madras? How? It's thousands of miles from Rangoon.'

'Telephone?'

'Really? And you think every dodgy crim in India has a phone that Bully Brent can just call on a whim?'

Jack was right, of course. 'I suppose not.'

'You suppose not? It's time to grow up, Ned. You've got to deal with this swine now.'

'What do you mean?'

'I mean, you have to call his bluff.'

'Bell —'

'Is untouchable,' Jack interrupted, exasperated. 'Send a telegram to Grenfell today if you have to or put through a telephone call. She's safe if you act swiftly.'

'And what do you suggest?'

'Well, first, follow Brent. See where he's staying. Come on. I hate bullies like him. The fat, sweating slob is on foot. We can catch him easily enough.'

'Jack —'

'No time. Talk as we walk. Come on!'

Ned found himself bundled out of the house past Sabu.

The light was dim and evening was falling rapidly. Jack's sharp vision just caught sight of their prey hailing a horse and carriage.

'Got any bikes here?' Jack murmured, never taking his eyes off Brent.

'What?'

'Bicycles, quick!'

'Sabu!'

The butler appeared. 'Sir?'

'Have the Walkers got bicycles?' He mimicked riding.

'In the shed, Master.'

'Get them!' Jack ordered and waited while Ned and the butler disappeared.

Brent was now hauling himself up onto the seat.

Ned returned with two old bikes.

'You get the girl's one. Come on!' Jack urged, leaping onto one and pushing off.

Ned followed suit, giving chase alongside Jack. 'What have you got in mind?'

'We're going to threaten your Dr Brent right back,' Jack replied. 'Hurry, now. We can't lose him!'

———

Brent looked to be staying at the Bangalore Club. From a safe distance they followed him off the Richmond Circle and into the grounds, hopping off their bikes at the entrance and adopting a casual air as they walked the cycles through the entrance guarded by whitewashed pillars. The lights were just being lit by the staff and the whole club began to sparkle in the fading light. Brent was swallowed up beneath the arches and through the main, elegant entrance.

'Okay. Let's get rid of these.'

'What do you mean? I'll have to get them back to the Walkers.'

'Just hide them behind the trees. You can pick them up later if they're precious.'

Ned glared, but disappeared with the bikes.

A servant was approaching up the drive. Jack waited for him to arrive, using the time to casually pluck a cigarette from the silver case he'd won at cards recently. He banged the cigarette on its lid before taking it between his lips and reaching for his matches.

The bearer finally arrived. 'Good evening, sir. Did you have a good day?'

Jack took note of the man's name on a badge. 'Evening, Ramesh. I had an excellent afternoon, thank you,' he said, glancing towards Ned's back, hoping Ramesh hadn't noticed him. 'Um, was that Dr Brent I just saw arriving at the club?' he asked innocently.

Ramesh beamed. 'Yes, sir. Do you know him?'

'Of him. He's from Rangoon, I believe.'

Ned hung back, deep in the shadows, terrified but impressed by Jack's nonchalance.

Ramesh waggled his head. 'A very important man in Rangoon. He tipped young Kumar handsomely.'

'I'll bet he did.'

Ned's eyes widened in the darkness.

'He is here giving a talk, I understand. He wants to find new patrons and open more homes in the north and south of India. He's a good man, sir. I'm sure you'll meet him in the bar.'

'Which room is he in? I might drop him a note,' Jack said over his shoulder.

'Twenty-three, Mr Bryant. His talk is tomorrow morning.'

'I'll stop by.'

'Good evening, sir,' Ramesh said, and glanced at Ned in the shadows, bowing his head before hurrying the passing chokra boy about his duty.

'That man is a fount of knowledge.'

'Jack, what are you doing?' Ned asked nervously.

Jack pulled his friend aside, so they were hidden again from the view of the main entrance. 'Ned, as I told you, sometimes you just have to stand up to bullies.'

'It's all right for you. You look —'

'I didn't, that's just it. When someone needed me to stand up for them, I ran away.'

Ned frowned, confused.

'It's just another reason I'm here. I watched a man being tortured not so long ago. I wasn't really in a position to do anything heroic but, Ned, I didn't even try. Instead, as soon as I had my chance, I ran away . . . as fast as I could. I didn't want it to happen to me, you see. And the bully got his way.'

'But —'

'But not for long, it seems. My father dealt with him.'

'I don't follow.'

'It's a long story and I think he always thought I'd never know the truth – and probably hoped I wouldn't – because it was everything he stood against. But I heard that my father took care of the man so that no one else ever suffered his cruelty again.'

'What did he do?'

Jack shook his head and gave a mirthless burst of laughter. 'I don't want to think about it. If my mother knew . . .'

'Jack, listen —'

Ned found his jacket suddenly bunched in Jack's fists. 'No, you listen to me. You've got a chance to stop Brent by not running from him. This man uses his power and his influence to hurt people. He enjoyed telling you how he engineered Robbie's death. Unless you stand up to Brent, Robbie won't be the last. These are *children*, Ned. They have no one to fight for them. Now, you know what he's doing and you could at least warn the authorities about him. You can't let it go because you're too scared or you don't want anything more to do with it. It will be his word against yours, of course, but at least he'll know he's under scrutiny. And mud sticks, Ned. Word will get around. You can stop him!'

Jack was close enough for Ned to smell his hair cream. He glanced sideways to see who might be watching. No one was. 'Let me go, Jack.'

Jack dropped Ned's lapels as if burned. 'I'm sorry.'

'What do you suggest I do? I'm no match for him.'

'You've got Brent scared. Why do you think he's here? He's frightened of what you might do! Tell him he shouldn't plan to appear at the talk tomorrow or you will too – and that you'll be making a public claim as to his crimes.'

'But you're forgetting the most obvious point here. *I have no proof.*'

'You've got to make Brent believe you know enough to jeopardise his reputation.'

'How do I do this?'

'Just play him at his own game. You want justice for Robbie and revenge for what Brent wanted from Bella. Well, he's right here. You'll never get another opportunity like this.'

'For a miner you're rather philosophical.'

'Ah, there you go. Making the mistake that so many others do. I'm a miner, yes, but I was educated, Ned, possibly better than you. You don't know me, you don't —'

'Jack, stop. I'm sorry. I know you're right. He's not going to stop harming others. I know he thinks he's scared me enough to prevent me saying anything to anyone.'

'Just scare *him* and send him packing. You'll always regret it if you don't take control now. No regrets, Ned. That's what I promised myself when I left Cornwall. It's not a bad creed.'

'But you weren't being hunted by a swine like Brent.'

'Don't be so sure of that. I wish I had my chance to set things right. Instead, it seems my father cleaned up my mess. I'll never let that happen again. You've got a chance now to save some helpless children from a terrible fate.'

'What should I say?'

'Tell him you've spoken to your sister over the telephone. Tell him Bella has already been removed and that you're going directly to the British police in Bangalore. Tell him you'll do everything in your power to have him arrested and charged. That's a good start.'

'And then tell the authorities everything I know?'

'I'll be nearby in case he does decide to push you around. He won't, though. This sort of man has no weapon but his cunning. Whatever happens, at least you'll never look back with regret that you didn't try. This way you force Brent's hand. He is the one who has to deny the accusation.'

'Yes, but I'm the one who has to come up with convincing proof.'

'Not necessarily. Once your accusation is made public, no matter how much Brent denies it, the more he protests, the more guilty he'll appear. Sow the seed of his guilt in the minds of the right people, then you've achieved something, and perhaps someone more powerful than you will bring about Brent's fall. But it has to start somewhere. Think about how brave Robbie was to drink that water. That's how badly he wanted Brent to suffer for his sins, Ned. That's how loyal he was to you and Bella.'

Ned cast his eyes down, looking suddenly ashamed of his previous fear. 'Robbie had everything to lose but on the other hand he had nothing to lose.'

'And in risking everything, including his life, he gained self-respect. He gained courage from his defiance. He won.'

Ned nodded. 'All right, I'll do it. Room twenty-three?'

'Yes. I'll be near. You just have to call.' Jack pushed him. 'Now go! Don't lose your cool but make him understand that he's the one who should be looking over his shoulder. Tell him to get the hell out of Bangalore and to stay well clear of Madras. Remember, Brent brought the fight to you. Now you're going to finish it.'

23

Ned took a deep breath, relieved that his nerves had calmed. Suddenly it felt right to confront Brent – and defy him. He knocked. And waited. He knocked again.

The door was pulled back angrily. 'I asked not to be distur—' Brent looked shocked. 'What are you doing here, Sinclair? I've nothing more to say to you.'

'Yes, but I have something to say to you. Now, we can have our conversation in private, or we can have it out right here in the hall . . . or in the bar over a drink if you'd prefer,' he said, impressed by his own daring. Jack's nature was rubbing off, it seemed.

Brent's face flushed red. He opened the door wider.

Ned stepped across the threshold, resisting the desire to throw a glance back at Jack, who was watching from a distance.

'Very well. Speak if you must. But quickly. I have better things to do with my evening than to listen to a pathetic squib like you.'

Ned forced himself to keep his voice even and low. 'You found us because you could and because we left tracks, but there are no more tracks to Bell. I've seen to it with a single telephone call to Madras. As for you, you'll find it pretty hard to achieve anything from a stinking prison cell.'

'You think you can call my bluff, young man? You have nothing! Do you suppose the Walkers will believe your stupid story?

Where is your evidence? Your only proof is now bloated fodder for the fish, lying cold and dead on the ocean floor.' Brent smiled to see Ned's expression turn pinched. 'You haven't got another card up your sleeve, Sinclair. I can see that. You're pathetic. Your whole family's pathetic!'

Ned began to clench and unclench his fists. A clammy, invisible hand seemed to be squeezing his lungs. His breath came shallowly as Brent raged on, clearly delighting in his tirade.

'Your no-good father left you all, and then your weak-willed, good-for-nothing mother also abandoned her children, indulging herself in the ultimate cowardly act. Both dead. Both useless parents.'

Ned knew his lips were moving but wasn't sure whether any sound was coming out. He could hear nothing but the angry rush of blood through his ears and a howl of rage that was so loud within himself it disoriented him.

Suddenly Brent was looming, his meaty finger jabbing Ned's sternum, his ugly face leering far too close . . . so close that Ned could smell his sour breath of old garlic and neat whisky. It offended him. Everything about Brent was offensive. Ned could feel a new ringing in his ears. It felt as though he was losing control of himself, his eyes narrowing and his mouth twisting into a bitter snarl.

'You don't come from good, strong stock, Sinclair. No, you'll follow form, and just like your weak, poverty-stricken parents before you, you'll —'

Ned watched as surprise and confusion ghosted across Brent's face. Then the man staggered once, before crumpling to the tiled floor, flopping onto his back.

Ned dropped beside him and heard Brent murmur something unintelligible before he convulsed, his bulky body twitching as though an electrical current was being passed through him. That rapid spasm changed into a sort of flopping. Ned, half fascinated, mostly horrified, watched the man's fists ball – his final throe – before his body relaxed into the death pose, his face palled into a mask, eyes staring upwards to the ceiling fan that continued its soft whirr of activity, oblivious to the shocking scene below.

Ned crouched alongside Brent's corpse for what felt an eternity, but he could see from the man's wristwatch that barely two minutes had ticked by. He shook his head and raised his eyes to once again look upon Brent's lifeless face, stained by sweat and a dribble of saliva making its way to his shirt collar.

He didn't need to reach for a pulse; it was clear Brent was dead. Stunned, Ned finally pulled his gaze from Brent's slack face and looked with disbelief and shock at what he was holding – a large glass paperweight. The weapon he had slammed into Brent's head was as big as an apple and on it was etched a map of the world. He half expected to see blood smeared across its continents but the globe glinted clean in the soft light. Absently, instinctively, he rubbed it across his soft shirt as if to rid it of any taint of death.

Still dazed, but his thoughts gradually clearing, Ned reached over to Brent's head, unmarked, its skin unbroken, and felt around the scalp. Sure enough, on his left temple was a small depression in the skull where the paperweight had killed him instantly.

Ned put the paperweight down and stood slowly, wiping his clammy hands self-consciously down the front of his suit jacket. Looking around, he caught sight of himself in a mirror and his suddenly haunted reflection had near bloodless lips. He barely recognised himself for his face had also seemed to sag. It was the face, he realised, of a killer . . . a murderer.

He began to gag and turned first towards the closet but knew he wouldn't make it. Instead he took two steps to pull open the shutters, grateful that the window was open. He had the presence of mind to keep his retches silent but the acid in his throat burned with accusation.

Fortunately, Brent's room backed onto a small garden and his window was well concealed. No one could have seen Ned and outside looked deserted. He wiped his mouth and dragged a shaking hand across his clammy forehead.

He turned around, half hoping to see Brent twitch again, or give some sign of life that Ned could raise the alarm for. But Brent's body remained treacherously still and silent.

The chaotic blur of the previous minutes cleared slightly to allow the first rational thought through. Jack! He rushed to the door but then took a deep breath. He should not be broadcasting the events that had unfolded in this room to other guests or any of the servants. Not yet. Not until he'd spoken to Jack.

Smoothing his hair and adjusting his collar, Ned blinked angrily and opened the door.

———————

Jack had long ago lost interest in the newspaper. He had folded it, risen and strolled up and down the hallway, looking away as two servants passed by.

In the end he had walked around the garden area behind Brent's room, but he couldn't see anything. He made his way back inside, strolling aimlessly, cigarette in hand. He even wandered past his own room and was tempted to go in and wait but he passed it by, walking as slowly as he could, finishing his smoke and finally ending up back at his reading nook and his newspaper. Just as he was resigning himself to staring at the familiar pages again, the door opened and Ned looked out.

Jack stood and smiled as Ned approached. 'All right?' he said softly, expecting Ned to close the door and walk towards him.

But Ned didn't. He beckoned instead. He looked pale, urgent.

Jack frowned, hurried his step. 'What's going on?' he murmured as he got closer, noticing that Ned was looking around nervously now, as though checking that they weren't being seen.

'Come in.'

'Why?'

'Just come in!'

Jack noticed a tremor in Ned's voice and his friend definitely looked rattled. He didn't say anything but stepped inside as Ned closed the door behind him.

'What's happ—' Jack's words died in his throat. Sprawled on the floor was Brent. Jack leapt to the man's side. 'Ned! What the fuck happened?'

Ned inclined his head towards the glass paperweight beside the body. 'I hit him.'

'Hit . . . ?' Jack looked back at Brent, speechless. He shook his head from the barrage of questions that leapt to mind. 'But . . . how? Why?'

It was Ned's turn to shake his head. 'I . . . I didn't even know it had happened until he dropped. I lost control, Jack. He was cursing me and threatening me. I just . . . felt this rage. Actually, I didn't feel anything. I just reacted, I think.'

'He didn't slip or stumble or —'

'I hit him, Jack! I picked up this paperweight,' Ned said, marching over and picking up the orb again, 'and smashed it down on his head!'

Jack stood, both hands raised in a defensive fashion. 'All right, Ned, all right. Shhh now. Let me think.'

'Yes, think! This is your fault! You made me do this.'

'What?'

'You made me confront him. Look what happened.'

'I didn't say murder him!'

Ned pointed angrily. 'And look where talk got me. I'll get life in prison. In a stinking, rat-infested jail in India, rotting, and for what? For Brent? All because you forced me to defy him.'

Jack grabbed his friend by the lapels for the second time that evening. 'Be quiet, now. Let me think!' He let go and Ned flopped back like a rag doll.

'What have I done? What possessed me?'

'Indeed,' Jack murmured softly to himself. 'Be still, Ned, I mean it.'

Mercifully, Ned became silent, his shoulders hunched over, face in his hands. Jack took a deep breath and stared down at the body. It was unmarked. He checked Brent's skull. The skin was miraculously unbroken. Further scrutiny into the man's greasy hair revealed there was no sign of blood.

'All right,' Jack began slowly as he stood again. 'Here's what we're going to do. We're going to call the cantonment police,' he pulled out his handkerchief and reached for the paperweight. 'And then,' he carefully rubbed the glass clean of all fingermarks or smudges, 'I'm going to tell them I found him like this.'

'What?' Ned said, startled out of his shock.

'Did you touch anything else in the room?'

'No, what? No. Yes!'

Jack gave Ned a stern look. 'Remember everything you touched. Your fingerprints could lead to a lot of questions we don't want.'

'The door handle.'

'That's fine. What else?'

'The windowsill.'

Jack walked over and went through his routine of cleaning down the sill. Henry had already told him that all prisoners in India were fingerprinted and many used their fingerprints as signatures. At last Henry's seemingly useless information was coming in handy. It could save Ned a prison sentence or even a death sentence. He shuddered inwardly at the thought.

Ned watched Jack deliberately touch the sill himself and the handles of the shutters. He frowned, said nothing.

'Now, you're sure,' Jack persisted, looking around the room, avoiding glancing at Brent. 'You touched nothing else?'

Ned shook his head. 'What's going on, Jack?'

'I'm giving you an alibi.'

'You don't have to. I'll tell the truth.'

'And go to jail for manslaughter.' Jack decided not to mention what else could happen should Ned be found guilty of murder.

Even so, Ned took a step back as if Jack had just slapped him. 'People will understand. I'll tell them everything . . . the orphanage, Robbie, Brent's threats, and I'll —'

'Still be a killer. You will go to jail, Ned. They're very strict here, apparently. And yes, Walker and even your friends in Madras can speak on your behalf, but the fact is you've killed a man. And the law interprets that as murder and not self-defence. A court will hear that you came to his room and, no matter what transpired, you used a weapon and killed him,' Jack urged, his voice a growl now and so low that even Ned was straining to hear him. 'We have to act now. People may have seen our shadows moving around in here. We must raise the alarm immediately. But you must go – get out of here. Stay calm, walk briskly but don't run. If you run, you'll be noticed. Move through the gardens and use the trees for shadow and cover. Leave by the back entrance but don't forget the bikes. Speak to no one. Go home and continue the night as normally as you can. Don't go out again, and try to be seen by others, Ned, do you understand? You must create an alibi for yourself.'

Ned nodded, but only because Jack's stern gaze was insisting he did.

Jack continued. 'We ended up not having dinner because we'd had a big lunch. I'll do the talking. I'll wait here with him another hour, just in case you're seen.'

'Jack, I don't think this is —'

Jack shook his head with irritation. 'No time now, Ned. Move!'

'Why are you doing this?'

'God only knows! Because you're so helpless, I suppose. I hate all the bad things that have happened to you, and there was so much to look forward to. Brent was a pig, by all accounts, and a criminal. I'll be doing the orphans of Rangoon a service if I cover for you. They can't pin anything on me. But you have to do exactly as I say and perhaps you'll be able to put this behind you.' He pointed at the corpse. 'You've stopped him. If people only knew, they'd quietly thank you.'

'I should answer for the crime, Jack. I'm thinking more clearly now.'

'You'd give up your life for this piece of slime? You'll give up your future? Bell? Your life's only just beginning. Brent had no remorse for the hardships and pain he caused. You've done the world a favour, Ned. And now the world owes you a chance to leave this behind. I'm giving you that chance.'

Ned stared again at Brent. 'All right.' He turned. 'I'll never forget this.'

'Our secret,' Jack said softly.

'Secrets bind, my mother always said.'

'Then we're bound in friendship.'

Ned offered a hand. 'I owe you.'

Jack shook. 'One day you'll help me when I need you to.' He pointed to the window. 'Go the back way. Take care not to be seen.'

Jack assumed that army officers and certainly someone who knew the Superintendent of Police would be in and around the club, and he was right. Within minutes various senior people had crowded into guest room twenty-three, including the military police, but now there was only a senior officer from the Indian Police and his offsider, the club's manager, a man from the morgue assisting the doctor in charge of Brent's corpse, plus Jack. Everyone but the doctor and his assistant had their backs to the dead man.

'What time did you find him?' the police officer asked.

'Nearly an hour ago now,' Jack answered. 'I was hoping to introduce myself. I'd heard he was staying here.'

'Why would that be, Mr Bryant?' He was a rotund man with bright white teeth, a pitted face and dark circles beneath his sharp chocolate brown eyes.

Jack frowned momentarily. 'Well, I can't quite remember where I'd heard about him – probably on the ship coming out – but I knew of Dr Brent's work in Rangoon and of course then I met Sinclair, whom I've mentioned earlier, who also knew him and I thought I should say hello.'

The officer showed no expression at this response. 'And you walked in and found him like this?'

'Lying like this, but not dead. I told you, he seemed to know it was grave; asked me to convey his affections to his wife and —'

'That he's sorry, yes,' the man finished.

'That's right.'

'For tripping over.' The policeman couldn't quite hide the slight hint of sarcasm in his polite tone.

'It's what he said. I told you he kept reaching to his head and telling me he banged it when he fell. It was the second time he'd tripped over the rug today,' he said, nodding towards the faded Indian carpet. 'I told him to be still and that I would call for help but he wouldn't let me go. He was frightened. And then he seemed to convulse and die as I crouched beside him. I couldn't be sure and so called for help immediately.'

The short policeman seemed to bob lightly on his feet. 'Forgive me, Mr Bryant, but logically he would have hit his head at the front.'

Jack shrugged. 'I wasn't here, Officer Guha. I'm sorry but I can only tell you what I know, and what I saw.'

'Well, if you ask me,' the army doctor said, getting to his feet with a sigh and a groan of protest from his knees, 'the unlucky bugger has most likely hit this,' he said, pointing to the glass paperweight. 'That seems to suit the depression on the skull.'

'He didn't mention it. Well, I imagine he didn't know what he'd hit.'

The doctor nodded. 'A post-mortem will likely show his whole skull has cracked like an egg. It just hasn't broken open completely. Blood will have probably flowed into the head cavity and constricted the brain,' he said, making a squeezing gesture with his fist. 'What an unlucky fellow.' The doctor sighed. 'Well, Officer Guha, my bit's done here. We'll hand over directly to your people now that we know none of the military are involved in this death.'

Jack's heart raced with hope that this was his cue to leave. 'Are we done here? May I leave now? I could use a stiff drink.'

Guha nodded. 'One more question, sir, if you don't mind. This Mr Sinclair you've mentioned.'

'Yes?'

'Where can I see him?'

'See Ned? What has he to do with this?'

'Simply that he knew the man. He may shed some light.' Guha beamed Jack a bright, patient smile.

'By all means. He's staying at the Walkers' house on Sheshadri Road.'

'That's Dr Harold Walker,' the doctor said, pulling on his jacket. 'Good man. You'll find him at number four.'

Guha didn't wait for the doctor to close the door. 'Thank you, Mr Bryant. I'm most sorry you have experienced such an unpleasant evening in our beautiful city,' he said in perfect English. 'Perhaps you would permit us to come back to you with any further questions?'

'Yes, of course, although I was planning to leave Bangalore shortly.'

'Oh I see,' Guha said. He bounced lightly again on his toes. 'Where are you off to, sir . . . if I might inquire?'

'Kolar Gold Fields. I have a job arranged there.'

'Ah, KGF,' he corrected with a small shake of his forefinger.

The doctor slapped him on the back in farewell. 'Well, you'll have plenty of fun there, son.'

Jack contrived a smile.

'I'll be on my way, Guha,' the doctor finished. 'Have the corpse brought around to the morgue and, if you need me to, I'll be happy to perform a post-mortem, but I suspect we know he died of a head trauma due to a fall.'

Jack risked it. He had to know. 'Did anyone see anything out of the ordinary to suggest it wasn't just a tragic accident?' He tried not to show that he was holding his breath.

'Indeed, sir. No one we've spoken to saw anything, although two servants remember seeing Dr Brent arrive back at the club this evening. Where he had been earlier today is really what we have to find out. It's early days yet.'

Jack felt his insides turn to ice.

———

Walker looked shocked. 'Dead?'

'I'm afraid so, Dr Walker,' Guha replied, seeming to relish the attention.

'But how can that be? He was apparently hale and hearty in my home just earlier this afternoon. How did he look to you, Ned?' he said, swinging around to find Ned frozen by the sideboard, almost hoping not to be noticed.

Ned swallowed and straightened. 'As you describe. He's overweight and he was perspiring a great deal but he didn't say he was unwell. Gave no indication of being ill certainly.' He knew he should not embellish any further, so he stopped talking abruptly.

'How long was he here, Mr Sinclair?' Guha asked.

Ned deliberately frowned, trying to appear casually concerned. 'Not long at all. Perhaps a quarter of an hour at most.'

'And what did you talk about, sir, if I might be so bold?'

'Nothing important. Dr Brent had been hoping to see me since discovering I was living here.'

'Why is that, sir?'

Ned felt his cheeks burn and desperately hoped his flushing wasn't showing up in the low lamplight of the room. 'Well, he was wondering what to do with our family's belongings that we left behind in Rangoon.'

'I see. You left them behind?'

Walker interrupted and gave the man a stern glance of rebuke. 'The boy lost both parents in tragic circumstances and Brent was good enough to provide food and lodging at his orphanage before Ned and his sister came south into India.'

'You left the orphanage in difficult circumstances it sounds like?' Guha persisted.

'My sister and I did not want to live as orphans, Officer Guha, and we certainly didn't want to be separated. By the letter of the law, I suppose we came to India as stowaways, but we didn't want to miss the ship. I should tell you that we did indeed pay for that passage, and the crew knew we were on board from our first day.' It sounded awfully thin but Ned pressed on, trying to contrive a story as easily as he had seen Jack do earlier.

'And you didn't see Dr Brent again today after he came here this afternoon?'

Ned shook his head, too frightened to answer immediately, but had the presence of mind to admonish himself that this looked guilty. He sipped from his glass of sherry when Guha suggested he take a brief moment to gather his wits. He was saved by the loud and boisterous arrival of Flora Walker.

'Harold, is it true?' she asked, horrified. 'And, Ned, there's a Jack Bryant waiting in the hall for you. Ah, here he is. Come in, Mr Bryant.'

Ned straightened. 'Hello, Jack,' he said as Jack entered the sitting room that felt suddenly crowded.

'Hello again,' he said, directing himself briefly at Guha, before walking towards his host. 'Dr Walker, forgive my interruption but I thought Ned might need some support on hearing this news. It must be such a shock for him.'

'Thanks for coming, Jack,' Walker acknowledged. 'Yes, this is a very regrettable business. Officer Guha, this is my wife, Mrs Walker, and you've obviously met Bryant.'

'Please forgive me interrupting your evening, Mrs Walker, and for being the bearer of such sombre tidings.'

'I heard it was an accident,' Flora said. 'Our butler, Sabu, is the eyes and ears of this household.'

'Ah, may I speak with him?' Guha asked.

Ned wanted to yell a frantic no and saw Jack blanch, but of course the Walkers gladly agreed.

'Call him in, my love,' Walker said. 'Sherry, Jack?'

Jack shook his head and moved closer to Ned.

Guha bowed. 'No, Dr Walker. Don't disturb yourselves any further. You've all been most generous. Perhaps I could just speak with Sabu?'

A warning glance from Jack told Ned to hold his nerve.

'I'll take you,' Ned offered. 'This way.'

In the parlour they found Sabu muttering to the ayah, who was cleaning the pots and pans from the Walkers' late supper.

'Sabu,' Ned began hesitantly, 'this is Inspector Guha. He wants to ask you a few questions about this afternoon. You've probably heard that Dr Brent died accidentally tonight.'

Guha smiled politely at Ned, although Ned could tell that he was not pleased to see Sabu so fully briefed. Nevertheless it startled him and Jack when Guha launched into rapid Tamil. The ayah stood alongside, her eyes wide.

Ned stole a worried glance at Jack from behind but Jack had eyes only for Sabu, whom he locked onto with a stern stare. Sabu never took his eyes from Guha, but Ned was sure that the butler was only too aware of Jack's searing glance.

Sabu answered several questions, hands gesticulating and head moving constantly.

It was when Jack and Ned heard their names spoken that they realised Guha was asking leading questions. Ned felt his knees go weak.

'Excuse me, Guha. I heard my name spoken. Please translate what you just asked this man,' Jack said. 'I think it's only fair.'

'Of course. Forgive me, sir. It is just so much easier to get quickly down to business if I speak in our own language.' Ned noted the hint of reprimand there. Perhaps Guha was one of the modern Indians who had begun to show resentment to the British presence in India. 'I simply inquired whether Sabu heard any of the exchange between Mr Sinclair and Dr Brent.' He turned to Sabu. 'Reply in English, Sabu,' he added and Ned definitely heard the word English said as though it were a dirty word.

Sabu stole a brief glance at Ned. 'I was in the parlour,' he replied in his singsong way. 'I heard nothing that I shouldn't.'

'What does that mean?' Guha asked.

'Dr Walker does not like me, how you say, eavesdripping.'

'Eavesdropping. You are not in any trouble, Sabu. Tell me what you heard.'

Sabu looked surprised. 'I heard nothing, sir. I showed the visitor to the front room as I was asked, fetched Mr Sinclair and then I went about my duties. I was in the parlour and then in the garden sorting out the gardener and the chokra.'

'How long were you in the garden?'

'I cannot say, sir.'

'Well, when you returned who was in the house?'

'Other than the servants, only Mr Sinclair, sir.'

'I see,' Guha said, eyeing Jack.

'Why has my name come up?' Jack asked and Ned wished he wouldn't press this fact.

'I did ask Sabu if he'd seen you here at the time of Dr Brent's visit.'

Jack turned to look again at Sabu with contrived astonishment on his face. Ned had to admit it – he was good!

'Sabu said he let you in this morning after breakfast but has not seen you again until just now.'

Jack turned slowly to Guha. 'Then I am at a loss. Officer Guha, I have acted in good faith on this very sad matter but somehow I feel you are looking for something more sinister.'

'Forgive me, sir. That is not my intention. My job is to seek the truth and now I have it. I will go away and make my report. I have satisfied myself that Dr Brent's death was accidental.'

Ned wasn't sure he'd heard right. 'So it's over?'

Jack gave him a sharp glance.

Guha smiled at Ned. 'I'm sorry to have taken up your time but we must – as you Brits say – cross all our Ts and dot our Is. No, I will not require you any more in this matter. Thank you, Mr Sinclair, Mr Bryant. Your part in this is done.'

'Good,' Jack said, not even looking relieved, Ned noticed. 'Because Mr Sinclair and I are leaving Bangalore soon.'

'I didn't realise you were both leaving for KGF. And what will you do there?' the policeman asked. Ned wasn't ready to make such a decision and yet he didn't want to spend another moment in Bangalore. He shrugged to consider an answer and to relax his shoulders, lose his nervousness. 'I'm told the work there is plentiful. I gather

KGF was the first part of the whole Asia region to have electricity. As a qualified electrician, you can't blame me for making a beeline.'

'I see. When do you leave?'

'Tomorrow,' Jack answered for Ned. 'I've managed to get us a lift with some John Taylor staff who are coming for another tour at the mines.' He smiled charmingly at Guha. 'They're driving up and I've squeezed us both in.'

'I suspect you won't have much to pack, Mr Sinclair,' Guha replied, with an equally benign smile, 'considering all your belongings are still in Rangoon.'

Ned said nothing. Jack gave Guha a hurry-on sort of shrug. 'Well, if that's all, Office Guha . . . I, er, I would like to return to the club and continue with my preparations.'

'Of course.' Guha turned to Ned. 'Please pass on my thanks to Dr and Mrs Walker. I won't disturb them again.'

'I'll see you out,' Ned offered, as he gestured the police officer towards the parlour's door.

Jack watched as Ned followed Guha and they disappeared into the main house, leaving him staring at the butler. The ayah took one look at them both and she too went back to her business.

'Why did you do that?' Jack's question didn't need elaboration.

Sabu took several moments before he replied. 'The Walkers treat me as one of their own family. But there are others – most of the British, in fact – who treat us all like low-caste beggars. I am of a higher caste, sir. We are called Kshatriya.'

'Shah-tree-ya?'

'Very good, sir. I am from the warriors.'

'The caste system is very complicated.'

'It is how we live. And while I do serve, I still need respect. It is how it is.'

Jack understood immediately. 'Brent treated you without respect. He ignored you as a person.'

'As if I were mere filth to be pushed aside.'

Jack nodded. 'Is this your revenge?'

'No, sir. He was bad to me and I could hear he was being bad to Mr Sinclair, who treats all of us politely and kindly. I am not a man of revenge, sir, but I have pride. I am not sad the fat man is dead and I do not care how or why he died. I cannot hurt him through my silence.'

Jack stared at Sabu a moment longer, considering his logic. He thought for a second about giving the man money for providing him his alibi. But something in the man's dark, sombre eyes told him that would be an insult. Instead, he held out his hand. 'Thank you, Sabu. I am grateful that you did not mention my presence later today. I came only to protect Mr Sinclair.'

Sabu gave a single nod; it was just short of a bow. 'Then I am glad you both are safe.'

Jack intensified his grip on the servant's hand.

'Can we keep this secret between us, for Master Sinclair's sake?'

And Sabu almost made him smile when he blinked slowly and replied, 'What secret, sir?'

PART TWO

PART TWO

24

October 1926

Jack and Ned had both come off the night shift and were sitting on the cool verandah of the KGF Club, looking out across the manicured lawns at the small army of gardeners who buzzed like bees around beds of flowers, trimming shrubbery and watering the grass, not one of them wearing a hat.

It was the start of a new day for most, but for the two men it was the end of their working day.

'You have to pinch yourself sometimes to believe this isn't actually Britain, don't you?' Ned put his beer down and sat back in the cane chair.

Jack wiped his sleeve across his mouth and then sighed as the chilled beer hit the spot. 'Not the Britain I recall. I come from Penzance, man! Steep granite cliffs and wild seas and freezing cold . . . not this garden party picnic scene you seem to like.'

'Oh, go dip your head, Jack. I'm sure I heard you ask Gwen Davison whether she'd like to go for a picnic only the other day.'

'Ah, but that wasn't to eat cucumber sandwiches and look at the scenery.'

'You're a bad boy, Jack.'

'Never claimed to be good.'

Ned sipped his beer again and after a short silence, sighed reflectively. 'We got lucky in Bangalore.'

Jack didn't need any elaboration to know what Ned was

referring to. He stayed quiet for a moment, remembering their narrow escape. 'That was six years ago, Ned. You've got to let it go.'

'You think I should find it easy to simply forget I committed murder?'

'You're determined to ruin my peaceful morning.' Jack put down his glass, exasperated. 'Listen, Ned, the verdict was death by misadventure. Get on with your life. I don't want to talk about this any more.'

'Because you feel guilty? I'm the one to blame.'

'Of course I feel guilty! But you need to make peace with your own conscience, as I have. Look at us! I'm suddenly a senior engineer, for heaven's sake. I'd have waited years for this opportunity in Cornwall. And you're near enough managing the electricity department already. Ned, this is old, old ground. We've trodden it once too often. I'm tired of it.'

'You're right, I'm sorry. We won't speak of it again.'

Jack grabbed his glass and raised it. 'I'll drink to that!'

Ned picked up his glass too. 'To our secret,' he said quietly.

Jack leaned back, relieved, then knotted his hands behind his head. 'This is the life, Ned, especially now that monsoon is past. But what you really want, I suspect, is a wife and a brood of children.'

'Nothing wrong in that.'

'Nothing, if your name is Sinclair. But mine's Bryant and I prefer to think of myself as a Pirate of Penzance. Free as the wind.'

Ned scoffed and threw a peanut at him. The Indians roasted them and flavoured them with chilli and coriander. They were delicious. He swallowed a mouthful. 'You've got a nerve. Daphne Ellis is heartbroken.'

'Daphne Ellis will be heartbroken for a few hours and then she'll move on to her next target.'

'Don't be cruel, Jack. She's a nice girl.'

'Then you take her out.'

Ned grinned. 'No, I'm waiting for Iris.'

'Ah, the elusive Iris Walker. How many times has she apparently been packed and ready to leave England?'

'This time I think she's definitely on her way.'

'Well, at the risk of sounding like a parrot, I'd advise against dating a girl of parents you know well. Destined for doom.'

'Harold and Flora know we've been writing to each other for years. I always get the impression Flora's encouraging it. They worry about Iris. She's sort of a free spirit.'

'And you think Mrs Walker sees stability in her dating the dependable Edward Sinclair?'

'Well, she could do worse . . . she could date you.'

Jack laughed. 'What if she has a glass eye?'

'Keep laughing, Jack, because here's a photo of her at seventeen.' He opened his wallet and pulled out a small family photo. 'That's Iris,' he said eagerly, pointing to a slim, dark-haired girl in the middle with her arms coquettishly wrapped around her father.

'Hmmm,' Jack murmured, not prepared to give too much away. But he was surprised. Even in the grainy photo she looked deliciously pretty with her wide, dimpled smile. And she seemed to be staring straight at him. 'Not bad.'

'Not bad? She's gorgeous and you know it.'

'It's a shocking photo. For all you know, one day soon she'll limp off the train, dragging her club foot, and —'

Now both of them dissolved into laughter and Ned flung an entire fistful of nuts at Jack. 'Well, you'll meet her soon enough. The Walkers left for Bombay this morning. They want to see her off the ship and I shall meet them with the rest of the family when their train draws in from Bangalore.'

'Well, good luck to you. I hope she finds you irresistible.'

Ned grinned. 'Just keep yourself well away is all I ask.'

'She's all yours. What about Bella?'

'She's so grown up. I had another letter yesterday. Her social life sounds extraordinary – Grenfell did a special six-week stint in Calcutta so she's been the complete social butterfly for the last month and a half!'

'Is that what you wanted for her?'

'I couldn't have given her one quarter of that life. And Bell suits being a socialite. When I was in Madras last year she had more poise and confidence than some of the women twice her age. Bell's very different to me. All I've ever wanted is a family life. I just hope the man she falls in love with is wealthy and will give her all she desires.'

'When are you going to bring her down?'

'Now she's finished school, and she's almost sixteen, I'm hoping in the next couple of months.'

'Good. Now, what's happening about housing for you, by the way?'

Ned sighed. 'I don't have the comfort of being a covenanted man, like you.'

'Yes, but you're on the company payroll. It's not as though they've got qualified electricians banging down the door, and old man Lawson can't even read the dials.'

Ned gave Jack a look of soft rebuke. 'Lawson's all right, you know, and he's a good boss. I've learned so much from him. I've got no desire to push him from his perch, although he's definitely due and I'm certainly capable.'

'You're being modest. You're all but running the place.'

'I'm only twenty-four, Jack. They won't give me the status or the house that goes with it.'

'I think they will. I'll see what I can find out.'

'Oh no, don't.'

Jack held up a hand to stop Ned's protests. 'I've only been in my own place for a couple of months so I know how sick of the lodgings you must be. I have nothing against the Italians, but if Vince Batista sang one more rendition of "O Sole Mio", I was going to drop him down Harry's Shaft.'

Ned gave him a look. They both knew how dangerous the work was in one of the deepest mines in the world. 'Don't even joke about it.'

'Well, I know how different life is in your own bungalow. And I'm offering you somewhere to stay. Was that your strange way of saying, thank you, Jack, for being so thoughtful and yes, I'd like to stay at Marikuppam?'

Ned smiled at him. 'I'm grateful for the offer, Jack, but I think I'll let you stew out there alone, scowling from your new verandah at all who dare pass by. I'll get my own place soon. Are you coming to the Champion Reef picnic, by the way? You can meet Iris.'

'I'll come to the dance afterwards just to satisfy myself that my love-struck friend isn't planning to marry someone with an arse like an elephant.'

Ned nearly spat out the beer he'd been nursing.

Jack waggled a finger. 'Always look at the mothers.'

'Stop!' Ned said, laughing helplessly. 'You're wicked.'

Jack stood. 'I'm off for a sleep. I've got a longer shift this evening.'

Ned watched his tall friend heading away from the club, realising he was left to sign for the drinks. He didn't mind. Jack was generous in all things towards him. He motioned to the servant and while he waited he watched Jack striding down the pathway that separated the pristine whitewashed club buildings from the road. He wondered whether Jack would ever find a woman to suit him; somehow he doubted it.

They'd enjoyed a fun-filled handful of years in Kolar and everyone thought Jack Bryant was a philandering opportunist. Only Ned knew him for the deep thinker that he was, and while

Jack was happy to let the KGF community believe he was every inch the handsome rogue without a heart, the truth was that he was lonely. Ned sensed this – always had – and deeply believed that when Jack finally fell for a woman, it would be one of those intense, fiery loves that consumed everything in its wake.

He shook his head free of Jack and instead let his mind fill with thoughts of Iris. It was her first letter, arriving out of the blue, that had ignited his helpless infatuation. No girl had ever written to him before, and if he were honest, no girl had ever really noticed him, let alone taken an interest in his life. Since then he'd dated frequently, could even now consider himself a popular addition at any dance or around anyone's dinner table. But no other woman held the same fascination for him as Iris, despite the fact that they had never met.

Iris's letters were always full of questions, and she didn't seem to mind in the least that her parents treated him as a son. The letters included sketches of a squirrel she'd seen in Hyde Park, a swatch of fabric from a dress she'd recently had made, a ticket stub from the Theatre Royal in Brighton. And so it went. Snatches of her exciting life in London arrived frequently for him. Ned had taken to refusing to open her letters until he was alone and had the time to savour them. He often caught himself smiling as he read and he would always read them several times after the first eager skim-through.

She had always been affectionate, but the relationship had deepened over the years. Ned had never admitted how he felt, yet he sensed she was looking forward to their meeting every bit as much as he was. Every time he thought about her arrival, his throat seemed to tighten. Would she be disappointed? Would he be too short, too reserved, too adoring, too boring? His fears grew but then her latest letter suggested that their relationship had blossomed to a new level.

It had arrived accompanied by a photo, a close-up of Iris. She said she'd had one taken of herself for her parents but on a whim had enclosed a copy for him. *So you know who to look for when you pick me up.* Her words had oozed expectation and confidence that he'd be waiting. On the back of the photo she had scrawled in an elegant hand: *For Ned. I x*

His heart began pounding twice as hard the moment he saw the photo and its cryptic note. Perhaps he was reading too much into it; perhaps Iris was this affectionate with everyone. He had wanted to show Jack, but for some reason held back, needing to keep Iris to himself.

Jack didn't mind the long walk home. It always helped to clear his thoughts and, if he blurred his eyes and ignored the red earth and the dark skins of the people moving around, there were moments when the mining structures – winding wheels, engine houses, the buildings surrounding a main shaft – echoed a life back in Cornwall. He missed it. He missed the cold, and while KGF was astonishingly verdant due to the constant irrigation, beyond people's gardens the landscape was very arid. He missed the green seas off the Cornish coast on a bright spring day and the green of the fields surrounding those rugged granite cliffs. And while he would never complain about club life, there were moments when he genuinely missed the anonymity of a Cornish pub and the smell of fresh pasties baking.

Jack never allowed himself to indulge in too much reminiscing or he dipped into a bleak frame of mind. But it was comforting now and then, and he carried a sense of hope that one day he would return to Penzance.

For now, though, KGF was home, and there was much to love about the place. Henry had been right all those years ago. This was a thriving community made up of plenty of British and Europeans. And while the bulk of the actual mining was done by a legion of Indian workers, it was the Anglo-Indians who 'owned' KGF and gave it the flourishing lifestyle everyone enjoyed. Their families were large and the mix of blood gave their offspring a handsome, exotic look with very thick, almost black hair framing everything from a pale complexion through to tawny and even dark skin. They were a fun-loving, party-going society who worked hard and played hard; who followed the etiquette of the British but happily sat down to spicy curries and strange-sounding Indian fare that would send their British counterparts running.

There was a clear segregation in KGF when it came to housing. The club itself was an obvious demonstration of this – no Anglo-Indian was permitted to approach by the main road that led members into the grounds. Only the British were granted membership, so only the British could use that roadway. If an Anglo-Indian needed to visit, he entered via a special side road. As for the Indians, their only reason for being on the manicured grounds was to tend them or to serve food and drinks to club members. And so the low, majestic-looking building loudly proclaimed its colonial heritage with its impressive circular drive and stairwell that led onto the sprawling verandah framed by arched colonnades, providing a cool retreat for guests. The arches were continued in the bank of picturesque windows, with their hundreds of tiny panes of glass that sat proudly beneath the steeply angled, clay-tiled roof. English trees stood alongside palms and other tropical plants, all set against lush green lawn and styled beds of glorious flowers.

As he walked, Jack admired how beautifully kept KGF was. Breezy, bungalow-style houses sat back from the road, each within their own well-tended and creatively planted gardens. Grass was watered and mown regularly, so a carpet of green extended as far as the eye could see. The British, who were mainly the senior mines management, had the pick of the houses with tall hedges and bigger grounds. The more important Anglo-Indians were next in the pecking order for the larger bungalows with high-grade fencing and exquisitely tended gardens. What impressed Jack most was that every family was provided free housing by John Taylor & Sons – in fact, not just their houses, but their electricity and all manner of special allowances.

Little wonder the region was such a popular spot. Even the Indian workers, who made up the bulk of the community, were given excellent housing in the Miners Lines, simple, robust dwellings called tatti houses that were made from bamboo strips and highly desired by the Indian families who made their living from mining gold.

As he approached the Oorgaum Bridge, the trolleys thundered overhead, taking their quartz to the mill on the other side. Jack waved to someone who was just stepping into the library on his right. It remained one of the most popular spots in all of KGF – a place where many a whispered item of gossip was exchanged. A lot of that gossip was about Jack, as it happened. But he wasn't thinking of the very attractive girl he was planning to see later that afternoon. The one person whose face kept swimming into his mind was Iris Walker. When he'd looked at her picture, the fancy had struck him like a bolt of the electrical current Ned controlled so well to all the mines. Iris was staring out of that old photo and straight into his heart. The notion had rocked him. Jack had long ago learned to be careful with Ned's emotions, for they were fragile, and this thing he had for Iris Walker was very real.

Jack couldn't help wondering how Iris would live up to Ned's vision. He hoped she was every inch the princess Ned believed her to be, but Jack saw something in her glance that told him differently.

Ned wanted little more than a secure family life. Jack couldn't help but feel sorry for his friend. As much as Jack would have liked to see his mother again, perhaps impress his father that he was making something of himself, he didn't want to feel as though he needed anyone – not in the way that Ned constantly needed people around him.

He smiled ruefully at the very thought of trying to impress his father. He imagined trying to explain to William Bryant how he had covered up the death of a man – a bad man, but it was murder nonetheless. All his stern advice to Ned, advice he had truly believed as he'd delivered it a few years ago, fell away to leave him feeling suddenly filled with the self-hatred he'd become accustomed to back home. He tried to imagine how he'd explain it to his father.

'A man was murdered . . . and I never said anything. In fact, I went out of my way to cover it up.'

Jack shook his head, clouds of regret settling about him. He suddenly wished he could see his father again. He hadn't thought about Walter Rally in years, yet now the cruelty of Wally came back to haunt Jack. He had run away and let his father pick up the pieces.

As he strode up Funnell's Hill, feeling suddenly gloomy, he wished he could apologise to his father for being a coward as much as a liar. And then he made a promise to himself. He would go home one day and find those right words and the courage to stand up and tell his father of his ugly deed in Bangalore. His father might never forgive him, but perhaps that would release him from the burden of trying to live up to his high expectations.

Jack wasn't hungry or thirsty. In fact, he was exhausted. Nevertheless he steered towards the tiny 'petty shop', little more than a kiosk, by the side of the road. Jack had never felt lonelier than he did in that moment, and he was grateful for the sight of another person on the road for it made him stop and snap out of his dark mood.

'Hello, Chinathambi,' he called.

'Mr Bryant, sir!' the shopkeeper exclaimed, his hands coming together as though in prayer, a smile beaming. 'I did not expect you today.'

'No, well, I just thought I'd call in and see if you had some fresh eggs,' he lied.

The tall, reed-thin Indian with a deep sing-song voice waggled his head. 'Yes, yes, very fresh, sir. Laid only this morning.' He hissed at a young chokra boy. 'Marimuthu, go get the eggs. *Jaldi, jaldi,*' he urged. 'How are you, Mr Bryant, sir?'

'I'm tired.'

'Finished your shift and ready for the shut-eye, as they say,' Chinathambi said, grinning.

'Indeed.'

As the son arrived back holding half a dozen eggs, so did a tall girl – his sister, going by her features. Jack had seen her before, instantly recognising the fluid way she walked. It was more of a glide really; like the dancers he'd seen in London. She was barefoot, but golden jewellery around her ankles jangled prettily like bells and her bright-yellow sari was a blaze of colour in the otherwise dark shoebox of a store.

'Is this your daughter?'

'Yes, sir, this is my daughter.' Jack loved the Indian accent speaking English. Daughter came out as 'darter'. He was equally sure that any English person speaking Tamil would sound just as amusing to an Indian. He tried to avoid it for that reason. 'She is called Kanakammal,' Chinathambi said proudly.

She recognised her name and averted her gaze. Chinathambi growled something to the girl and she reluctantly turned to Jack and nodded behind the veil of her sari that she'd drawn across her face. Jack was struck by the shocking lightness of her eyes. They were an arresting dove-grey, and set in the deep chocolate tone of her skin, they were mesmerising.

'You have beautiful eyes, Kanakam,' he blurted, taken aback by her piercing gaze. As he worked his tongue around her difficult name, he knew he hadn't succeeded in saying it properly.

The shopkeeper laughed. 'Their grandmother on their mother's side was from Persia. She is my favourite, this one. And she loves her daddy, brings me my meal each day at this time, as you see, sir?' He gave his daughter a hug.

Jack noticed that the girl carried a small dekshi wrapped in a linen cloth, its corners tied to form a makeshift handle.

'Smells good.'

'Dhal and rice, sir,' Chinathambi explained, his hand twisting upright in the air – another trait that Jack liked. He'd seen it used to mean many things. 'Six annas, Mr Bryant, sir.'

As he waited for Jack's payment, Chinathambi issued orders to his children. Jack took his time handing over the coins.

'Is there anything else, Mr Bryant, sir?'

He reached desperately for a reason to keep him here. 'Er, yes, actually. Now I come to think of it, I do need some Indian ink.'

'I have only black.'

'I didn't know it came in different colours,' Jack replied.

'Oh yes. Blue, and there is talk of red and green, but black is all I ever have.'

'That's fine,' Jack said, imagining a letter in green. He glanced at the daughter, patiently waiting behind the counter. She was as still as a statue, her curious eyes downcast. 'Do your children speak English?'

'Only she does,' Chinathambi admitted, apology in his voice. 'But she needs some practice. No time for school and language for the others. Ah, here it is.' He returned. 'Five annas, sir.'

'Well, just in case she doesn't understand me, will you tell your daughter that she looks as bright as the sunshine today?'

Chinathambi grinned. He turned to the girl and prattled in Tamil. Her eyes flashed to him momentarily before she looked down again, pulling her veil closer.

Jack emerged into the morning sun and felt the first promise of what was to come. By mid-morning it would be unbearable. And it was October . . . the worst was behind them. He plonked his helmet on, hating to wear it but knowing he couldn't defy the sun. He detested the heat, could never get used to it, even as he watched others acclimatising. Jack was sure the high temperatures of summer profoundly affected his moods.

His thoughts turned to the picnic for the ladies. Would he go? No. But he would definitely go to the dance as he'd promised. He felt he had to, if only for Ned.

He looked at the ink he was carrying and decided that it was an omen; today he would write to his parents. He couldn't remember the last letter he'd sent home; and it was possibly a year or even longer since he'd heard from them either. The last letter said they were both well and business was flourishing. His mother had finally cut her hair shorter and the house was being repainted.

Today he would begin to build a bridge with more regular correspondence, he promised himself, and that bridge would lead him back to Cornwall one day.

25

Ned waited impatiently on the crowded platform at Bowringpet Station, wondering whether he would even be noticed among the throng waiting to board and travel on to Madras. He could barely hear himself think for the noise of people talking, and porters shouting as they prepared goods to be loaded, dragging trolleys in between passengers. As usual the colours of the women's saris were an assault on his eyes but Ned never tired of their beauty.

Today was a special day as the town took part in the Karaga Festival that was so important to this region. The Indian women were dressed to the hilt; even the poorest looked superb in their fabulous silks. Ned glanced over at the Walker women and once again was struck by the difference between British and Indian. The Indian women looked elegant and feminine in their floaty gowns. The Anglo-Indian Walkers looked starched and stiff in their creams, whites and khakis that emulated British tropical wear. Why did they copy the English? He would give an arm for such exotic good looks.

The Walker family had decided to meet at this platform, where most travellers changed trains. Rupert Walker had borrowed a car and planned to drive his parents back into KGF. Everyone else would have to find their own way home by whatever means they could. Ned had no idea how he would return yet but he had the following day off work, so he was not worried. What Ned *was* worried about was a small stain on the bottom of his fashionable new cuffed trousers. They were all the rage right now in Britain, Jack had assured him. Ned cursed under his breath. He wanted Iris to notice only his positive attributes, not his imperfections.

He looked at the flowers again, a posy of azaleas, camellias and baby roses.

'Hmm,' the florist had said at the beautiful arrangement. 'Deep meaning in these flowers.'

'Really? All good, I hope?'

'If you're in love, definitely.'

'I had no idea,' he'd said, feeling the colour rise in his cheeks. 'I've never even met her,' he added, hoping to deflect her scrutiny. Now that he had learned their significance, he was pleased with his choice and the embedded message they carried in their petals and perfume. But would they touch Iris's heart? Would she even like him on sight? They were, after all, simply pen friends.

Rupert strolled over. 'Nice flowers, Ned.'

He sighed inwardly. 'Thanks. They're wilting.'

'So am I.' Rupert pulled out his watch from his waistcoat pocket as the telltale whistle of a train shrieked in the near distance. 'Ah, any moment now. Bang on time, thank goodness. I can't stay, actually. I have an appointment later.'

Rupert was older than Iris but was her favourite brother, Ned had learned. It pleased him that he got on well with Rupert, a senior clerk who had recently moved into the assay department at John Taylor & Sons in India. Ned had often wondered how Iris and Rupert hit it off so well, considering her outgoing personality and his far more reserved manner. Rupert did possess a dry wit that Ned appreciated. What's more, Ned liked him simply because he was short. He barely stood over five foot seven in his shoes. 'It's been so long since you've seen Iris. Will you even recognise her?' he asked, just to kill a few more nervous seconds.

Rupert had to shout over the scream of the approaching train.

'Iris doesn't change. She'll always be the baby, the princess . . . the spoilt one. I imagine she's going to look even more lovely with her London frocks and big smoke ways. So no, I'm sure I won't recognise her until I hear her voice and that lovely laugh and then I'll realise how much I've missed my little sister.'

People were hauling themselves to their feet, babies were being rearranged in arms, and children were being gathered up by their mothers, as fathers tried to marshal all the luggage, from chickens in cages to bundles of ragged-looking clothes. Ned had never had to travel in anything but first class on Indian trains. He couldn't imagine the noise and the smells and the cramped conditions in the other carriages. Even now he could see men perched on the train's roof. Ned smiled to himself, feeling a tremulous bond with the stowaways. He would never forget his escape from Rangoon.

'I haven't had a letter from her in ages,' Rupert continued.

Ned felt a rush of pleasure. He heard from Iris regularly.

'And then, of course, we have to see if she likes my fiancée. Iris can be terribly jealous, you know. But she's nearly twenty-four now, so she probably has far more interesting things on her mind than who I've chosen as a bride. Anyway, here we go,' he said, nodding down the track.

Ned's head whipped around as smoke billowed and the engine whined as it slowed to a stop. People surged and his heart leapt. He was finally to meet her. He smoothed back his hair and straightened his jacket as he craned his neck to see over everyone's heads. He picked out Harold Walker, who had already spotted his family and was waving.

And then there she was!

Iris Walker squeezed past her father, pushed out of the window and began waving enthusiastically to her siblings. Ned jealously watched as her gaze roamed and locked onto her eldest brother. He so wanted her to pick him out but it did give him time to let his own gaze linger on the vision in pale-blue and white. Her beautiful, dimpled smile turned into a beam. And while her bobbed hairstyle was a shock, it had a lustre that made him want to touch it, plus its short length only accentuated her slim neck that led his eyes help-lessly, treacherously to the flawless, tawny skin above her breasts.

The train lurched to its final halt and doors began to swing open. People started to spill from its carriages and Ned lost Iris in the few frantic moments that followed. He had become separated from the rest of the Walkers and found himself pushed aside by a huge family heading for third class with a mountain of baggage that included a goat and four ducks. Ned dropped back and stood on tiptoe. He glimpsed a flash of powder-blue and his pulse surged. If only he were taller. Jack would stand head and shoulders above this crowd, damn him.

'Hey, Ned, over here,' someone called. He thought it was Rupert and he began to push his way forward again, tripping over a disgruntled rooster and an old woman who was clutching it, scowl-ing at him from her swathe of pale-pink sari.

When he finally regained his position, Iris was buried beneath a mound of hugs and family arms. Harold Walker held out a hand in the meantime.

'Hello, Ned. My, my, what a crowd. Thanks for coming.'

'Wouldn't have missed it for quids,' Ned replied and hugged Flora Walker. 'Good journey?'

She touched his cheek. 'You look thin. Come to dinner tonight.'

He nodded and grinned. And, as if on cue, the siblings parted and there, standing in the middle, was his vision, wearing a dar-ingly cut dress that even showed her knees. He tore his glance from Iris's irresistible legs and tried to ignore her enticing décolletage to gaze on the face he had so longed to see. It did not disappoint. Iris was stunning and she was smiling brightly at him. She shook back her loose long sleeves, also cuffed in white satin, and drew a few wisps of her hair from her face. It was an action that made his heart pound. Everything about her was so much more elegant and beautiful than he'd imagined.

'And you must be Ned! At last!' she cried.

Without any further warning he felt himself gripped in a wild embrace and pulled into a cloud of heady perfume. 'I can't believe it!' she continued and then kissed both his cheeks.

'Hello, Iris,' he said shyly. 'You look so lovely.' The words were falling out before he could censor them.

'Thank you,' she replied, delighted, with an abashed curtsey. 'Are those flowers for me?'

He had completely forgotten he was holding them. 'Oh, yes, they are. Oh, I'm sorry. They look rather forlorn.'

'Well, *I* think they're exquisite,' she said, reaching for them. Her gloved hands touched his and he felt momentarily dizzy.

'Well, come on, everyone. Let's not wait about here,' Walker urged.

They emerged into the main street that was also vibrant with people. The festival was in full swing and a host of bare-chested young men were roaming down the street, brandishing their swords in honour of the heroes of the past.

Iris gave a theatrical sigh. 'I've missed India.'

Her father smiled delightedly. 'I'm glad to hear it, dear,' he said, and hugged her close. 'Now, Rupert, what's the plan?'

'I'm taking a jatka back to work – I'm running late as it is – and Jim will take you, Mum and Iris back to the house. He's borrowed a car. The others are making their own way. I'll see you all tonight.'

Rupert kissed his mother and Iris farewell as the others pressed in to give hugs goodbye. Finally, they'd all dispersed to make their way back to KGF, and from a distance he hadn't consciously created, Ned watched as Harold Walker clambered into the big black car. James lifted a hand to wave farewell to Ned, then also got into the car.

Ned sighed. She was gone almost as soon as she'd arrived, and her attention for him had been fleeting. He couldn't help feeling a fraction forlorn.

He turned away, wondering now about how to get himself back to KGF.

He spun around at the tap on his shoulder. 'Iris,' he said, surprised.

'We insist that you come home with us.'

'Are you sure? Perhaps you'd like some quiet time with —'

'Oh, Ned! I've spent the last five days with Mummy and Daddy. Now I'm looking for company my own age. Unless, of course, you have someone else to answer to?'

'Er . . . no. I'm very much single.'

'Good!' she said, linking her arm around his as she led him towards the car. 'I hear there's a dance on in a few days. Perhaps you'll take me to it?'

Ned felt a surge of warmth rush through his body. It was as though every dream he'd ever had was suddenly coming true in this moment as he stopped still and stared into her beloved face and deep hazel eyes. 'I wouldn't allow anyone else to.'

Iris laughed. 'That's a little dramatic, Ned, but I'm all yours.'

He knew he was grinning like a loon now.

'Come on. The oldies get cranky as they tire. But then you know my parents better than I do right now, I'm sure.'

'Your parents never seem to get tired!' Ned climbed into the car after Iris, trying once again not to stare at the perfect turn of her ankle or the tiny blue vein at the back of her knee.

It was a journey Ned would not forget. Those hours squashed next to Iris Walker in the back seat, her left thigh pressing against his right, were some of the best in his life. And while from this position it was difficult to see her face, he used the time to enjoy the sound of her voice washing over him and to study her ever moving hands while she talked excitedly about London and her travels through Europe with the very wealthy Fitzgibbon family who had offered her a full-time position as governess to their daughters.

Ned worked hard not to stay silent, even though he would have been more than happy simply to listen to Iris. She was so energised and full of laughter.

'I've never understood what Karaga actually is,' Iris remarked as they watched a pack of bare-chested men whoop and jump alongside the car before running ahead.

'I only know a little about it,' Ned obliged, deciding this was a topic he could at least be vaguely interesting about. 'It's one of India's oldest festivals, but only celebrated in this Karnataka region. The Karaga itself is a vessel, which contains a secret. Something to do with health, I think. The carrier's arrival is heralded by the young braves.' He pointed out of the car window. 'And do you see the blades they carry?'

'Dad would never let us watch that part of the ritual.'

'They do their firewalking at night.'

Iris's mouth dropped open.

'I've watched it.' Ned was thrilled to be impressing her. 'Have you seen it, Harold and Flora?'

'We have, yes,' Walker replied. 'It's all a bit crazy for us.'

Ned grinned. 'Apparently the warriors can slaughter the vessel bearer, should he drop it. Perhaps in centuries gone they might have done that. These men will walk across burning embers showing no signs of pain or injury, then hit themselves with their blades, often nicking their skin, drawing blood.'

'But they're all in a trance, aren't they?'

'Yes. It's why they don't feel the pain.'

The conversation moved on to plans for a special birthday for

Florence, one of the sisters, and Rupert's engagement party.

Ned was happy to remain silent until they began to see the green hills and mining structures of KGF.

They drew towards the circular patch of bright garden that was one of the landmarks of the region.

'This is Five Lights, Iris,' Walker explained. 'The five great lamps that hang from this lamp post spotlight the individual roads that intersect at this point and lead off to different parts of KGF.'

'It's a rather romantic spot really, isn't it?' She looked at Ned as she said this, perhaps noticing for the first time how quiet he'd become. 'It's so pretty. I imagine it's lovely at night. How far now?'

'Oh, we're as good as there,' James piped up. 'Ten minutes at most.'

'Good. I'm famished and I'm exhausted. I hope the house is cool.'

'It is,' her mother replied, in a tone suggesting she was being tolerant of Iris's bleat.

Ned noticed Iris glance his way; he was sure he'd fallen too quiet again. 'Actually, Iris, it's one of the prettiest homes in Oorgaum. I . . . er, I don't work too far away from it because the electric department is directly opposite – as the crow flies, anyway. It's still a cycle ride up to your place, though.'

Iris smiled sideways at him. 'I'm glad you plan to visit, Ned.' She blinked and something in that gesture spoke volumes.

He felt his heart skip again and turned self-consciously to stare out of the window. He knew he wasn't mistaken; Iris was definitely flirting with him. They'd been sitting so close for so long that he couldn't feel where his thigh ended or hers began and he dared not look. Iris was definitely interested in him!

'That's the school up there,' Walker said, pointing.

'Have you spoken to them, Dad?'

'Yes, and of course they want to talk to you about a position. They always need good teachers.'

'Why don't we drive through quickly?' James suggested. 'That way you can get a good overview of KGF. Ned, you're not running late for anything, are you?'

'No,' he answered quickly.

'That's the club and golf course on the right – and behind there is St Michael's Church, my girl, where we go. Perhaps you'll get married there,' her mother said, and tittered as Iris groaned.

James took up the reins of the guided tour. 'On the left is the electric department, where Ned works,' he said, pointing to a large white building. 'It supplies all the electricity for the mines. Right, Ned?'

'Yes, all very modern here, Iris,' he said with a soft smile.

'We're essentially now in Champion Reef. That road leads to Robertsonpet – it's a nice little town with the civil hospital.'

'I'll never remember all this,' Iris said.

'You will,' Ned murmured. 'It's really very small once you get to know the different areas.'

And so it went, James guiding Iris past all the places Ned had come to know so well. He tried to remember what it was like when he first came through but that felt like a lifetime ago. Bella had opted to remain in Madras, despite being desperate not to hurt his feelings. Ned had understood; he too had changed and his life wouldn't have suited a teenager and all her needs. The Grenfells had given her a wonderful life and education; Robbie and his plan had blessed them with so much more than just escape.

'You know my friend, Jack, the one I've told you about? That mine is where he works. It's called William's Shaft, part of Top Reef. I know you're going to like Jack,' Ned said.

'Even though he's a bit of a rogue,' Walker said.

'Rogue?' Iris repeated as if unsure what they meant.

Ned laughed. 'I think your father's being polite and really means to say that Jack's a bit of a rake.'

'Really? Well, I can't wait to meet him.'

'Oh, you will. I've persuaded him to come to the dance next Tuesday night.'

'Well, that'll be a first,' her mother murmured.

As they swung the car into the small circular driveway, Iris squealed with pleasure. 'Oh, it's lovely. I love that big tree.'

'It gives us beautiful shade, dear. Your father likes to take his afternoon tea beneath it.'

They poured out of the car, stretching and pulling their clothes straight from where they clung to their bodies in the sticky heat. The talk had moved into the mundane about the house, its servants – all of whom were waiting on the steps to greet Miss Iris. Ned felt he was now imposing.

'Jim, will you need some help with the trunks when they arrive? I thought I might make a move, if not.'

'Don't rush off,' Dr Walker said. 'You're most welcome . . .'

It was tempting but Ned didn't want to outstay his welcome. 'No, sir. I'll get some errands done that I've put off for weeks. This is my first free day in an age and it's been lovely to share it with you, but I think you could all use some family time now.'

'You are family, Ned,' James said, checking that nothing had been left in the car.

Ned nodded gratefully. 'Everyone's tired. I'll be back, don't you worry.'

'All right, Ned. We'll see you later. Come for supper, if you'd like. Otherwise we'll see you at the picnic.'

Ned was already retreating. 'Please say goodbye to the ladies for me, Harold. I won't interrupt them.' Hopefully Iris would be disappointed by his departure.

Walker gave him a mock salute and disappeared into the shadows of what was clearly one of the best bungalows in the district. Ned wondered how Iris would cope with life in this tiny oasis in the wilderness of southern India after her hectic years in London. She would certainly be the belle of the ball for a while and her looks would make her a target for every eligible bachelor – of which there were plenty, most with far more to offer than Ned.

He would have to make his move swiftly and declare himself to Iris as soon as he found the nerve. Perhaps he would even have to drag Jack's help into this; no one knew more about winning a woman's heart than Jack Bryant.

───────────

Iris watched Ned from her window as he retreated down the pathway. He truly was everything she'd imagined he would be. So often she judged people and got them wrong, but Ned had completely lived up to the shy, cautious, intelligent man she'd assumed he was. It was clear he was already very close to her own family, obviously because he had none of his own, although he had written so fondly of his sister.

What she hadn't known was what Ned looked like and this was a surprise. She'd pictured him taller, darker for some reason, even though he'd once mentioned his family was fair-haired. In her mind's eye he wore glasses, and had a studious air. The man who met her earlier today was far more handsome than she'd anticipated. His smile, when it came, was bright and infectious. She loved the timbre in his voice – it had a velvety quality that made listening to him a pleasure.

Although Ned was careful, when he looked at her he was direct and held her gaze firmly. Even so, his blue eyes held a naïve, almost wistful quality that confirmed her overall impression that Ned was a dreamer.

She smiled and waved, even though he probably hadn't seen her. He looked back over his shoulder only briefly, and she liked the excited thrill his glance prompted in her. She turned and stared at his flowers that her mother had arranged to have put in her room already. They were gentle in colour and shape – just like Ned seemed to be. She couldn't imagine him raising his voice. That was reassuring after witnessing her employers' marriage behind closed doors and the way the wife often wore long sleeves on a mild day. Iris recalled being woken by soft cries during one night. She'd risen to check the babies in her care were not disturbed by their parents arguing, or their father's drunken behaviour and the sexual demands he made of his wife.

No, even on this first meeting Edward Sinclair lived up to her expectations; he was a safe, reliable and gentle person. What's more, he looked to be a man in love. She hugged herself. In love with her! She had always been used to attention; she was the youngest, the prettiest, the one most likely to go far, or so it had seemed. She'd left India on a wave of confidence but Britain had demoralised her. Over there, she was simply the exotic servant girl with a 'curious' accent.

She'd met so few men that her hopes of falling in love overseas had quickly faded. And then Ned had arrived in her life, his letter landing on the front doormat of the family home. The telltale postage stamps of India combined with the unfamiliar, neat and confident script excited her. And inside she found a charming note, carefully worded but imparting much information – how Ned had come to be linked with her family, the sad details of his own background, and even a suggestion to treat herself to an ice-cream sundae at Fortnum & Mason's fountain. The latter was a pilgrimage he had always promised himself and never achieved. Since meeting Ned she'd realised just how entranced he was by her, long before they'd even met.

She smiled coyly to herself. He was definitely husband material, so easy to like ... perhaps even easier to love, given her parents already approved so wholeheartedly. It would make them so happy.

She had wondered whether coming home, to KGF rather than her familiar family home in Bangalore, would be disappointing . . . but lovely Ned Sinclair! What a delicious turn of events.

Iris reminded herself not to appear too eager. She had watched the young socialites from a distance in London playing admirers off against each other and they always ended up getting their way.

'Having a man jealous over another's interest in you is precisely where you want him,' one bright young thing had remarked to another in Iris's hearing one evening. 'It keeps them more eager than you can imagine, more likely to say yes to anything and everything.' And the women had cackled lightly at the notion.

The comment had remained with her but Ned seemed solid; a good man with good intentions. She couldn't wait to get to know him better.

26

'Are you awake, Master Ned, sir?' the chokra boy said through the flyscreen door.

Ned had been asleep after finishing the night shift. He knew the electrical manager found the long evening stretches hardest. Ned had offered to take over the night shift as often as he could, and he didn't mind. It would mean more time to spend with Iris, for as trusting as the Walkers were, they were not going to let him take their precious favourite out at night alone very often.

Ned loved his work. Supplying the mines with their power was an important job and a huge task. He would never have been given such a senior opportunity back home and now there was a very good chance he would be offered the most responsible position in the whole department. There were moments when he needed to pinch himself, and Jack was right – they had to let go of the past because the future was looking so bright for them both.

'Oh, hello, Joseph. Is there a problem at the Walkers?'

'No, Master Ned. Madam thought you might like to help with the kul-kuls for the dance on Tuesday.'

Ned laughed, standing at the door in his pyjamas, and scratched himself. He wouldn't miss an opportunity to spend time with Iris. And being formally asked to join the kuk-kul production party was an honour, usually reserved for close family members. 'Tell Madam I'll be along shortly. And, Joseph, please thank her.'

The boy scampered off. Ned wasted no time getting ready. Already well accustomed to the famous 'Ganges' shower achieved with bucket and mug, he clambered into a fresh shirt within minutes and left the small rooms he lived in. He didn't think the Italians would mind if he borrowed one of their bicycles. After all, they'd borrowed his not so long ago and returned it with a bent front wheel and now it was at the repair shop at Nundydroog. Living so close had its advantages and disadvantages. Technically, he shouldn't even have this accommodation, which was essentially for officers and covenanted men, but somewhere along the line – probably Jack had wangled it – he'd been offered three small rooms in the row of tiny cottages and he had happily lived in them ever since. Jack had recently moved out into his bungalow up on the hill.

At the Walker household, production was already underway. Ned smelled fresh coffee and could hear laughter as he approached. As usual Sabu said nothing but his manner was always respectful, dignified.

'Morning, Sabu.'

Sabu nodded but made it appear as a courteous bow.

'Kitchen?'

'Dining room, sir. Making quite a mess.'

'Good morning, all,' Ned said, ducking through a curtain tied back at the doorway. He scanned for Iris but couldn't see her. Disappointment knifed through him. Seated were Flora Walker and two of her daughters. He felt suddenly ridiculous. 'Please don't tell me I'm the only male here.'

They all giggled. 'You are, my boy,' Flora admitted, 'but I was sorry you didn't join us for supper the other night.'

'It was a family time.'

Flora held up a finger. 'You are family, Ned. You must never think otherwise. Iris is sleeping in, lazy scamp, but she won't be long.'

Ned's spirits lifted instantly.

'Sit here,' Christine offered, shifting along a seat.

'Now, do you remember how to do this?' Flora inquired.

'Well, he did enough a couple of Christmases ago with us, Mum,' Geraldine replied. 'Coffee, Ned?'

He nodded, grinning at her.

'Have you eaten?' Flora asked.

'I'm not hungry, thank you.'

Flora made a shooshing sound. 'Ask Sabu to organise some of the curry puffs with the coffee, dear.'

His belly grumbled at the mere mention of Flora's renowned little savoury pastries.

'You said they were for the dance,' Christine complained but without any heat. They were all fond of Ned and begrudged him nothing.

'Yes, but a man needs a full stomach. Ah, here's sleepy-head. Morning, darling,' Flora said, rising to peck her youngest daughter on the forehead. 'Go sit next to Ned.'

He blushed. 'How are you feeling, Iris?' he asked after everyone's mumbles had died down.

'Strange . . . it feels very strange to be here but wonderful too.'

'Oh, good,' he said, standing to make way for her. He felt a thrill of excitement as she brushed past him and he quickly sat down.

'The dance will do it, my girl,' Flora assured. 'You'll see a few familiar faces, I suspect, from Bangalore, and it will feel as though you never left India.'

Iris smiled. 'I suppose so. Now, what are we doing here. Oh, I want a fork.'

'I thought you should roll, dear, as you haven't formed them in so many years.'

Iris mock-glared at her mother as she took in Ned's hand,

poised with fork at the ready. 'And you honestly believe Ned Sinclair can form a better kul-kul than I can? He's not even Anglo-Indian!'

The coffee arrived on a tray with the delicious aroma of freshly baked curry puffs lending a festive air.

Opposite Ned, the women continued rolling small balls of dough to about the size of the king marbles that Ned remembered playing with as a child. They worked evenly, the conversation meandering quietly from Elsa Drummond's bridal gown to whether Mrs Irvine's russam pepperwater was as good as their mother's, which Flora firmly denied.

Meanwhile Ned and Iris's job was to flatten the perfect little spheres over the backs of the tines of a fork. The dough was then rolled up again, curling in on itself with a ridged outside.

Flora stood after a while. 'Ned, the curry puffs are cool enough to eat now, but your coffee's getting cold. Let me take that load for deep frying – you can have a break.'

The daughters continued rolling and Iris began a new tray alone as Ned sat back to do as Flora had bid.

'What about you?' he said, gesturing towards the puffs.

'Oh, I couldn't. I'm still full from last night's feast. Mum's making a banquet each night and we've had so many visitors that it's endless fruitcake or vadais!'

He laughed. 'You couldn't have had a vadai in years!' he said, thinking of the scrumptious deep-fried lentil snack, flavoured with onions and coriander, unique to south India.

'Oh, I'm not complaining, but in London everyone's so conscious about their figures.'

Ned glanced at her tiny waist. 'I really don't think you have anything to worry about.'

'Well, in England they warn that every girl should look to her mother, and ours is hardly svelte.' At the gasp from around the table, she didn't back down. 'Am I lying? It's all right for all of you, you've left home, but Mum's got me in her sights and in her house. I'll be fed until I burst as she laments all her brood fleeing the nest.'

Her sisters laughed as one.

'How can you not miss her delicious home cooking?' Ned asked. He loved the savoury food of south India but had realised long ago that the British had adapted many of the recipes to suit their own palate. It was how Anglo-Indian food had come into its own.

'Well, you're right. I'd take Mum's dhal over a lump of roast beef any day, but these loose lines have their days numbered,' Iris said, pulling at her drop-waisted soft pink dress. She wagged a finger. 'And mark my words, you'll be thanking me for the warning when the new cinched waist and very curvy lines take off.'

The girls chortled in gentle scorn.

'No more flat busts!' Iris continued. They laughed louder. 'Every curve of your —'

'Iris!' Flora entered the room to find Iris cupping her breasts.

Iris gave a soft squeal. 'Have I embarrassed you, Ned?'

'Don't mind me,' he said, trying not to blush.

The girls exploded with amusement and Ned felt that was his cue to excuse himself. 'Really, ladies, it's been a lot of fun, but I think I'll go find Jack and chop down a tree or something.'

'How is the handsome Mr Bryant?' Geraldine asked. 'I hear he broke Daphne's heart.'

'One in a long line of broken hearts,' Christine chirped.

Ned could see Iris paying close attention to this conversation.

'Oh, hush, Geraldine,' her elder sister continued. 'I don't think you've ever got over Jack Bryant not falling for your flirtations.'

'Rubbish!' Geraldine said, her swarthy skin still managing to show a hot flush. 'And don't you dare say that in front of Ken.'

'Don't worry. Ken would still marry you. But it's not Ned's

fault Jack won't be pinned down. Anyone who dates Jack Bryant needs to keep their eyes wide open.'

'And their legs firmly closed, obviously,' Iris finished, and then slapped her hand to her mouth at her mother's horrified gasp.

'When did you get so bold, my girl?' Flora wagged her hand. 'Don't leave on my wicked daughter's account, Ned.'

'No. I must, though. But I'll want a share of those kul-kuls once they're fried and coated in sugar.'

'You'll get plenty at the dance, son, don't you worry,' Flora said, touching his cheek. 'I'll see you out.'

'Bye, Ned!' It was a chorus of farewells from the sisters but his gaze lingered on Iris.

She gave him a flirty smile.

He took his chance. 'Er, Iris, do you want to go to the . . . the club tonight or something?' As the room fell silent he felt a need to fill the void. 'We have so much to catch up on.'

Iris looked unfazed. She stared back at him, her dark eyes glittering. Then she shifted herself and shook her head slightly, reaching for another ball of dough. 'I'm not allowed into the club, Ned, or had you forgotten?' she said, airily.

He wanted the ground to open and swallow him. He had forgotten it. It was something that hadn't been an issue until now because his friends were mainly British, and the Walkers – including their father – seemed happy enough in their own facilities. He did meet Dr Walker from time to time at the KGF club, but the doctor was one of those people who could seamlessly encompass both sides of the community with ease.

Ned stammered an apology. 'I think it's all right actually for a member to take you along as a guest,' he added, trying to make amends.

'Thank you but I'll have to pass. I've agreed to meet Ivan Chalmers this evening.'

'Chalmers? From the Miners Hospital?'

'That's him. We went to school together in Bangalore. I think we're going to bingo. I plan to win the Jaldi Five.'

Ned stared at her as though trying to fix her features into his mind. In truth he couldn't believe what he was hearing. Bloody Ivan Chalmers getting in first! He composed himself quickly, realising that everyone was staring at him. 'Well, have a good time tonight – make sure you win,' he said, overly brightly. 'I'll see you at the dance.'

She smiled and it hurt his heart. He followed Flora out to the front door feeling a mixture of anger and self-pity. He'd obviously misread the signs.

'Thanks for coming today, Ned,' Flora said.

'I don't really know what good I was,' he said, forcing himself to sound cheery and self-effacing, 'but it was fun,' he lied. 'I can't imagine how well my particular kul-kuls will turn out, but —'

'Ned, dear,' she said, stopping him mid-sentence. 'My invitation to you was nothing about making kul-kuls. I asked you over to ensure my daughter doesn't miss the best catch in KGF.'

It took Ned a moment to digest what Flora had just said.

'You know?'

'It's obvious.'

'You approve?'

'Wholeheartedly.'

He wrapped his arms around her and kissed her loudly. 'Really? And Harold?'

'Couldn't think of a son-in-law he would like more.'

Ned was speechless. 'Does Iris know?'

'Oh, I suspect she does, but you haven't known her long enough. From when she was a little girl Iris has needed to be the centre of attention. She likes to entertain, be indulged, be enjoyed. I imagine she knows she's got you eating out of her hands.' She tapped her nose. 'But I also know that Edward Sinclair was all she was talking about on the journey south from Bombay and again last night . . . certainly not Ivan Chalmers.' Amusement sparkled in her dark eyes.

'You're not just saying that?'

She laughed. 'We couldn't shut her up.'

'But she's not acting as though I'm on her mind.'

Now Flora gave him a knowing look. 'Then I've taught her well, haven't I? No daughter of mine should be an easy rose to pluck. It's up to you now, Ned. I would be lying if I didn't warn that there are several young men interested in Iris and some who've held a candle for her for years.'

'Oh, God.' He was deflated.

'Don't worry. Iris has her head screwed on.' Ned nodded disconsolately. She patted his hand. 'Just keep reminding her of why you're her best choice. I'm counting on you . . . and I'll help wherever I can.'

This brightened him. 'I'll stay close . . . and patient.'

'Good boy. Now, you'd better go home and see if you can't catch a couple of hours of sleep. I'm sorry I interrupted it for silly kul-kuls but it was an opportunity I couldn't let you miss.'

'It was worth it.' He leapt down the steps with a new spring in his stride. 'See you on Tuesday night.'

'Oh, Ned? I meant to warn you. Don't talk too much about your friend Jack Bryant, will you?'

'Oh?'

'He's dangerous around women . . . and Iris has always been blindly attracted to people who don't fit the mould. That's why you have nothing to fear from Ivan Chalmers. He's as predictable as the monsoon.'

'Jack is the opposite,' Ned breathed.

'Exactly.'

So just what does that say about me? Ned wondered.

———

Jack was bone tired but the message to go to the chief's office at the end of his shift was not something to be ignored. He'd run over his past few days of work in his mind and there was nothing out of the ordinary, no errors, no one unhappy, as far as he could tell. He'd only had a few dates in the last couple of weeks, nothing serious and no offence given to anyone, he was sure.

Although he kept himself to himself, recently he had helped out at a fete to build the gymkhana stand. He'd changed the wheel on Dr Walker's motor vehicle when the old man found himself stranded near Nundydroog, and he'd not taken any notice of Geraldine Walker, who'd been batting her eyelashes at him. That wasn't so hard, he had to admit – none of the Walker girls was especially good looking. He would reserve judgement on Iris until he met her.

He felt bad that he hadn't even seen Ned over the last couple of days to find out how the meeting at the station went.

He hung up his overalls and checked his appearance in the mirror of the changing area. Hardly neat and tidy but not too dishevelled. He was unshaven, he realised, as he ran a hand over his rough chin, but it would have to do. He said goodbye to the new shift's team in the engine room and stifled a yawn.

Jack walked out of the engine room and across the mine yard, striding quickly towards the brick building, well away from the shaft. He walked up the stairs onto the shady verandah, still attempting to tidy his hair. He ran a glance over all the doors, until he found the Mine Superintendent's plaque.

'Come in,' came the reply at his knock and Jack entered. 'Ah, Bryant, good. I'm glad it's you. Sit, sit,' Drew said, dragging a big white handkerchief from his pocket and wiping it over his face.

The man was perspiring heavily and it didn't look as though the morning heat was entirely responsible. Drew was a huge man, as wide as he was tall, and Jack wondered how long it had been since the manager had seen his toes. Despite his size, Drew daintily sipped on black tea and lemon.

'How're things going, Jack?'

It was such an open-ended question; Jack wasn't exactly sure what the man wanted to hear.

'All fine, Mr Drew. Is there a problem?'

'Problem? No. What gave you that idea?'

'I'm not really sure why I'm here.'

'I'm just wondering how you are and how work is? I notice you've moved out of the cottages.'

'Yes, sir, I have. It's cooler up on the hill, more private. I really like the house and have already settled in. I . . . er, well, I've asked the mine management if I could rent it off Taylor & Sons. No one else seems to want it.'

'But you can live for free in the lodgings?'

Jack nodded, then gave a small shrug. 'It's not a lot. I have some family money and it's my only real expense. It was that or a car . . . and I'll be happy with a motorbike, to tell the truth. Some peace is worth paying for.'

'Well, I think we can help alleviate some of that cost for you.'

'What do you mean?'

'You're being promoted, Bryant. You've been doing a good, steady job for us and old Tom had decided he wants to make a trip back to England while his bones can still cope with the cold. He's decided to retire early and although you're young, we think you've got it in you to take on the role of senior engineer.'

Jack couldn't believe what he was hearing. He'd never imagined he could take over Tom's job. Drew was grinning, shaking Jack's hand.

Jack grinned back, bemused. 'Did you say senior engineer? Are you sure, sir?'

The Super slapped Jack on the back. 'It's a very responsible job,

Jack. I'm sure you know it. I'm putting you in charge of winding in particular, but you'll run the engineering department alongside Tom until he leaves at the end of the year and then you'll take over completely. We think it's time to blood a younger man, who can grow into the role and give us some longevity in the position. We think you're that man. Frankly, you're the best-trained man we have across KGF right now. We're counting on you, so don't let us down.'

'I won't, sir. Do I begin immediately?'

'From tomorrow's shift.'

'Thank you, Mr Drew. I think I'll probably have to double-check that I didn't dream this.'

Drew smiled.

'Well, I'll get on, then,' Jack said.

'Bloody hell, man. Aren't you going to ask about money?'

'Money?'

'There's a significant salary increase for starters, and that house you've rented – we'll be letting you live there at no cost. Now go home and get some sleep.'

'Yes, Mr Drew.'

'Oh, and Bryant?'

'Sir?'

'Get a shave! You have to set standards now.'

Jack grinned. He was headed straight out to Cresswell's to get some fresh blades.

At the store he met Ned, who was buying some boot polish, but Jack was not in luck – they were out of blades. They exchanged news; Ned was thrilled to hear of Jack's promotion and went on to detail the conspiracy between himself and Flora Walker to win the hand of Iris. Jack clapped him on the back and walked out with him into the hot sunshine.

'So you're definitely coming to the dance, right?'

Jack didn't say anything immediately.

'Don't even think of letting me down, Jack. I need your help.'

'To tell Iris how brilliant you are and what a good husband you'll make? Don't be pathetic, Sinclair.'

'I've never wanted anything more in my life than this. She represents my future happiness. Without her, I'll only ever think I've got second best.'

'Don't be so dramatic. She's a girl. There are dozens of them in KGF, let alone Bangalore. What makes Iris so special?'

'She's the one, Jack.'

'All right, all right,' Jack said, raising his hands in mock defence. 'I'll help. But don't say I didn't warn you when it all goes pear-shaped.'

Ned laughed. 'It won't. See you at the dance.'

They parted company and once again Jack made the trek up Funnell's Hill. He called into Chinathambi's store.

'Ah, morning, sir,' the older man welcomed. 'What is it I can get you?'

'Blades, please. For the Pall Mall.'

The older man's eyes widened with recognition. 'Wilkinson's Sword,' he muttered and went hunting for the small packet.

'How's your family?' Jack asked to pass the time.

'All well, sir, thank you.'

'How many children did you say you have?'

'Nine, last count,' and then he laughed at his own joke. 'Another baby on the way.'

'Nine? How do you keep them all fed?'

Chinathambi waggled his head. 'Kanakammal, my eldest, can work now, and if she gets a position in a household then perhaps her younger sister can join her. We shall see. God will provide.'

Jack looked surprised. 'So you're Christian?'

'Yes, Mr Bryant, sir. I was converted into Catholicism when I was about Kanakammal's age, through a missionary family where we're from.'

'Kanakammal?' Jack repeated slowly, enjoying the way the strangely rhythmic name rolled off his tongue.

'Yes, sir. There's something very special about that girl,' he admitted, rolling his r's heavily.

Jack remembered the elegant daughter with the strikingly pale eyes. There was something mysterious about her and, despite the language barrier, he'd seen amusement dance in those eyes when she'd lifted them to his. Perhaps he could help the family and give her a better start in life? It must have been his mood, lifted by this morning's good news from management.

'Chinathambi, bring your daughter over to the house on the hill at Marikuppam this afternoon. Pale-blue shutters. Can you do that?'

'Yes, sir. I know the house. But, why, may I ask?'

'Can she cook? Clean? If so, I shall employ her.'

'She is an excellent cook, sir. Taught well by her mother. She will clean happily for you. And her sister, Namathevi, will be a very good help to her if you would consider both, sir.'

'Your daughters don't speak English as well as you do.'

'Kanakammal is fluent, sir. She has an ear. Her sister is learning but not so good.' He noticed Jack's look of surprise. 'I was forced to learn English. Most of today's children aren't so ready to give up their own language.'

Jack didn't want to get into a political discussion. He paid for the blades. 'It seems I will have less time to myself soon, Chinathambi, and will need some servants. Bring your girls this afternoon and we'll sort it out.'

The shopkeeper all but danced around the counter and took Jack's hand. 'Thank you, sir, thank you.' He raised both arms to the heavens. 'My wife will be so pleased.'

Jack grinned. 'See you later.'

'Yes, you will, sir,' he said, clapping merrily to the astonishment of two other shoppers who'd just stepped in.

'Morning, ladies,' Jack said politely as he pushed past, realising too late that one of them was Daphne's mother.

She scowled at him but nothing was going to dampen Jack's mood this morning.

Much later that day, as Jack sat on his verandah watching the sun dip low, collar open, unshaven and newly awoken from his sleep, he watched three figures walking up the hill. They had to be coming to his house because there were no other houses close by. It's why he liked its position and high vantage.

It was far too big for him, of course, its echoing rooms adding to his loner status, but he didn't mind. He loved its silence. The front garden needed some work but a butler would have the grass mown short into a crisp, green carpet soon enough. The back garden was ringed by tall trees, including several fruit trees. If Chinathambi's daughter wanted, he could have a full vegetable patch planted out the back with all her herbs and spices, as well as other vegetables. He had also populated the henhouse with four hens and a strutting rooster.

Jack really only lived in the front two rooms – his own bedroom and a sitting room. He had a bathroom attached to his bedroom, so the entire back of the house he essentially had no use for. Perhaps with a woman's touch the house would feel a lot more like a home.

He was looking forward to having some help. He might even start entertaining soon, as his mother had taught. Smoke from his cigarette drifted into his eye, making him squint slightly. He couldn't remember the older girl's name. She was tall, carried herself with the fluid grace he remembered from that first meeting. Her younger sister skipped unselfconsciously alongside, chatting animatedly. Jack smiled at the happy family and was glad he could do this for them.

Chinathambi walked with an umbrella for shade, while his daughters strolled beneath the direct gaze of the sun, untroubled by the heat. Jack raised his hand in welcome. He had not so long ago employed a butler and he also had a butler, who appeared two or three times a week to run errands. But to have full-time household staff to cook and clean would be a genuine luxury.

It made him think of Mrs Shand from the house in Pendeen. Jack had taken it for granted then – clean linen on his bed each week, his shirts laundered and ironed, his socks darned, a hot meal always available, which he often turned down. He wished he could be back home right now to thank her properly, perhaps spend a moment with her to ask about her son or inquire after her health. It was only now, so far away, that he could appreciate how good life had been for him in Cornwall. He'd love to tell his father about his promotion, about the new house and staff and how he was taking responsibility for himself. This would please the old man and thrill his mother.

He had written to them today with his news but perhaps he should plan to sail home. He was permitted six to eight weeks leave. As soon as he was feeling comfortable in his new role, he'd speak to the boss about it.

Jack couldn't remember a time he had felt happier or more relaxed.

'Hello, Chinathambi.'

'Hello, sir,' the shopkeeper said, arriving with a smile and his arms full. 'My wife asked me to bring you this.' He held out a dekshi.

'I can smell it from here. It makes my mouth water.' Jack

inhaled the seductive aroma of the spicy lentil dhal, a staple of the region he could never tire of. 'Thank you.' His butler, Gangai, stepped forward to take the pot. 'Boil up some rice. I'll have that for my evening meal.'

Gangai nodded and disappeared. Jack turned his attention to the girls. The youngest stared up at him, wide-eyed and curious. She too had the wonderful light eyes but none of her sister's presence. He glanced at her elder sister, who looked down. This time it was respectful but not, he noticed, in any way servile. He liked that about her immediately.

'I have brought Kanakammal as you asked, sir. This is Namathevi. She is nine.'

Jack's gaze didn't waiver from the eldest. 'Kanakammal. That's it,' he said, hearing the familiar but tricky name again. 'Welcome.' He watched the father utter something under his breath to his eldest.

She finally looked up and nodded at Jack, saying a few words in Tamil that Jack could not hope to understand, then to his surprise she uttered them in English. 'Thank you for the job, Mr Bryant, sir. I will speak only English in your presence now.'

There was something defiant about her – well couched beneath her deference, but definitely there. He smiled. 'Come in, come in and see the house, the kitchen, while I speak with your father.'

The girls immediately moved, ushered up the steps to the verandah as Gangai reappeared.

'Gangai, will you show . . .'

'Kanakammal,' she prompted.

'Thank you. Will you show Kan-naka-mal,' he pronounced slowly, making Namathevi laugh, 'and her giggling sister around, especially their rooms at the back.'

'Yes, sir.'

They followed him into the house.

'Is she comfortable with this, Chinathambi?' Jack asked.

The man gave a single shake of his head from side to side and beamed. 'Very happy, sir. We are too. She wants to work. Wants to help the family.'

'She's so young.'

'She's strong and . . .' he searched for the word. 'Ah, and independent,' he said, triumphant to have recalled it.

'What about the little one?'

'She worships her big sister, sir. Besides, if Kanakammal has her sister to boss around, it will make her feel more at home.' The man laughed. 'She will be very reliable, I promise you, sir.'

'Well, so long as she'll cook my meals and help Gangai with duties, we'll all get along just fine,' Jack said. 'Now, how does twenty-five rupees a month sound? Of course, all meals, accommodation and two new saris for each girl, each year, will be provided at my expense.'

'It sounds very good, sir,' Chinathambi said.

And with that, they shook hands and Jack suddenly had a new job, three full-time servants and a new home to call his own.

27

The dance was well under way when Jack arrived. The hall was crowded with merry-makers, mostly Anglo-Indian but many English guests also. Dozens of embittered women's eyes glared at him from the moment he slipped inside the double doors. Jack flicked away the insects battering at the lamp above his head.

Junie Evans nudged the arm of Daphne Ellis. 'There he is!' she murmured. 'Oh, Daphne, how did you let him get away, child!'

Daphne didn't want to look at Jack Bryant; she had promised herself she was strong, even made an oath that there would be no more tears, no admission that her heart felt as though it were being torn in two. She sucked in her breath at the sight of him, cutting a dashing figure in his tuxedo.

Jack was looking every inch the god tonight – especially tall, especially broad and with that dark wavy hair, he could pass for the son of Zeus any day, she decided, but Daphne's weren't the only eyes arrested.

Inwardly she felt something give and prayed that she would not let herself down. She must face this test and pass it. She'd been the envy of her friends a couple of months ago, but now she was reduced to the small legion of broken hearts, each once believing that they'd be the one to tame Jack Bryant and win his love.

She watched him walk around the dance floor. It wasn't really a swagger, as others had often said. No, Jack just possessed a distinctive lope; if he were an animal, he'd be a tiger, not frightened of any other predator, walking slowly, head high, muscles rolling as he strode proud and aloof. Daphne had lost her inhibitions when Jack's lips had found hers and even now she blushed inwardly to imagine how far she might have let him go if time had been on their side.

Jack seemed to be looking for someone in particular.

'I don't understand why he's here,' she groaned, the memory of Jack's deep kiss haunting her.

'Ned Sinclair's probably asked him along to join the Walkers.' It was a new voice, edged with slight disdain.

'Hello, Joyce,' the girls said together. Joyce Kent was seven years older than they were, and hadn't found a man to marry her yet. Daphne knew Joyce had also been out with Jack once or twice and felt her colour rise at the thought that Joyce had probably done a lot more than just dance cheek to cheek with him.

Daphne sighed to herself. Did anyone get over Jack Bryant, she wondered?

'He's probably making a beeline for that Iris Walker, back from England and full of smiles and stories,' Joyce said, moving on.

Joyce was probably right. Well, perhaps it was Iris Walker's turn to have the Bryant treatment, Daphne thought sourly, taking uncharitable pleasure in imagining Jack breaking the Walker girl's heart too.

'It's only a matter of time,' Joyce said conspiratorially over her shoulder, and then nodded towards Iris.

———————

The Auxiliary Indian Force band was doing a pretty good job with 'I'm Forever Blowing Bubbles'. It was clearly a favourite with many of the youngsters who had come along with their families. A couple of them even had some soap suds and a wire wand and were blowing bubbles into the fray of dancers twirling around the room.

The hall was decorated with paper bunting, giving it a festive air. Jack smiled, imagining how anything as glamorous as this event would even take off in Pendeen on a Saturday night. And yet here in a tiny community in southern India the girls were dressed to the hilt and the gents looked dashing in their tuxedos and waxed hair. By tomorrow morning a few would be working thousands of feet under the earth, but for now it was all glamour and merriment.

Tables and chairs were pushed to the side of the room. Tomorrow they'd serve another purpose for the Jaldi Five Bingo Evening; in the meantime they were the domain of the elders – mostly the matriarchs and their minions – from various family groups, seated like sentinels, watching their young daughters and nieces drift around the dance floor. Their job was to ensure no gentleman's hand strayed to the modestly bared flesh on shoulders and backs. As for a couple using an excuse to 'step out for some air', the alert gatekeepers would ensure no one left the hall unattended by ageing uncles or fathers, who casually tagged along to frustrate plans. The older women swapped news but mostly they commented on the dresses on display, the eligible bachelors, and especially they gossiped about each other.

Jack didn't receive many invitations to these dances, but he always enjoyed them when he did go along, usually at Ned's behest and most often as a guest of the Walkers. Unfortunately, he wasn't sure quite how welcome he might be this evening. He knew Geraldine considered him well out of favour and he felt vaguely offended by this. He'd only taken her out twice. Once, Ned had cornered him into escorting her to one of the mine dances, and the second time was simply in a group outing to the movies. Geraldine had invited him casually enough and it would have sounded churlish to say no. Since then he'd refused all further interest. He liked and respected Harold Walker and had no intention of doing the wrong thing by any of his daughters.

He sighed and searched for the Walker table. It would no doubt be one of the biggest. There it was. He moved around the edge of the dancers. He was desperate to move to one end of the hall where a lot of the older men had gathered to smoke, avoid the gossip of their women and admire the pretty young things skipping through the French chalk used to make the floor slippery enough for some of the more complex dance steps. Instead, he dutifully looked for Flora Walker to pay his respects.

Iris and Ned had barely stopped dancing since they arrived.

'I really should dance with Ivan,' she groaned.

'Please don't encourage him,' Ned replied, turning her around and away from where Ivan Chalmers stared at them. 'Iris, I could dance with you all night.'

She giggled. 'You'll draw attention to us.'

'I don't care. I want every man in the room to know that at the Friday night dance next week, they'll have to queue in vain.'

She laughed openly now. 'Ned, you hardly know me.'

'I know you, Iris. I know you're the one —' But her attention was suddenly elsewhere.

'Who is that?' she murmured, her gaze fixed around his shoulder.

Ned turned and saw Jack's unmistakeable outline. 'Now, why can't my tuxedo look like that on me?' he groaned and then grinned.

'His is white, for starters. You lot are all behind the times wearing black. Who is he?'

'That's Jack.'

'Oh, let's go meet him,' she suggested.

Ned wasn't ready to let her go. Dancing innocently with Iris was the closest he was going to get to her until he could declare himself, he was sure, and Jack had already interrupted his first attempt. 'After this tune, eh?'

'Mmm?' she said, not really listening. 'They're right. You two are an odd couple.'

'We have a lot more in common than you could imagine,' he said, wishing the image of Brent lying dead on the floor didn't erupt in his mind.

'So you keep saying.'

He sighed theatrically. 'We're both great lovers,' he said, surprising himself with his daring.

She looked at him, eyes widening in mock horror. 'Even though you say so yourself, Edward Sinclair!'

The tune ended. Iris linked her arm through his. 'Come on. Introduce me. I'm intrigued.'

Ned dutifully led Iris towards Jack; his friend was talking to Harold, and Ned inwardly begged that he'd treat Iris with his usual offhand manner. In fact, he suddenly hoped that Jack was in one of his darker moods.

―――――

Walker's attention was suddenly diverted. 'Ah, here they come,' he said, and Jack turned, his breath catching in his throat as a ravishing dark-haired, dark-eyed beauty sauntered up, arm in arm with Ned. Harold Walker kissed the top of her head. 'You shake a fine ankle, my dear.'

'Thank you, Dad. We desperately need a drink before they strike up a Charleston. It's so warm this evening.'

Jack watched, mesmerised, as she fanned herself dramatically with her hands.

'Hello,' she said, her bright white smile startling him. For a moment he'd felt as though he'd disappeared and she wouldn't notice him staring. 'Isn't anyone going to introduce us?'

'Hello, Jack,' Ned said. 'Let me introduce you to Iris Walker. Iris, this is my very good friend, Jack Bryant.'

'At last,' she said, holding out her hand. 'I've heard so much about you, Mr Bryant. *Enchantée*.'

Jack took her hand and stared at her rudely, he was sure. His breath felt ragged all of a sudden. It was as though everyone else had suddenly disappeared into a blur. Time stood still and within the bubble of this moment there was only himself and Iris; her heart-shaped face, punctuated by dimples and a dazzling smile, her eyes sparkling with mischief and flirtation.

The bubble burst when Ned said, 'That's French, Jack. Iris learned that in London.'

Jack gathered his wits swiftly. He cleared his throat and returned her smile, even bending to kiss her hand. 'Likewise, Miss Walker. Frankly, Ned can't stop talking about you.'

Everyone around them laughed. Did anyone notice, though, Jack wondered, that her hand lingered in his and that he was in no hurry to let it go? He dare not look at Ned: 'Perhaps you'd dance with me later?'

'Why not now?' she said.

'Er, well, is that all right, Ned?'

'Don't ask Ned, ask me,' Iris corrected.

Jack flicked a glance at Ned, whose eyes had narrowed, and felt trapped. Either he allowed Iris to belittle him, or he risked Ned's ire.

He grinned. 'Would you care to dance, Iris?' he said, bowing theatrically to convince Ned and the Walker family that he was simply being chivalrous.

'Thank you, Jack. Lead the way. Sounds like a waltz striking up. My favourite.'

Within moments she was in his arms, floating around the dance floor within his careful embrace. She was petite and slim; he felt like a bear holding a fairy doll, and while he tried not to stare, he found himself entranced by her. Her skin was so silky and unblemished. Many of the Anglo-Indian girls had swarthy complexions but Iris was just softly golden – not pale but not olive, not freckled, no moles, no birthmarks. She was perfect; light on her feet, gentle of voice and, he realised with dismay, awaiting an answer.

'Pardon?'

'Jack, you're not even paying attention. I was warned about you but I didn't think you'd be distracted quite so fast.'

'Forgive me. I was just marvelling at how attractive you are.' He felt instantly cross with himself. He really hadn't meant to say that aloud.

She giggled. 'Well, in that case, stay as silent and distracted as you wish.'

He frowned.

'Are you tongue-tied, Jack?'

'I think I am. I'm not used to such directness.'

'From what I hear you're only used to adoration.'

He shrugged, regaining some of his poise. 'I wouldn't say that.'

'Plenty do.'

He moved to safer territory. 'How does it feel to be back?'

'Strange, wonderful, tedious, joyful.'

'All at once?'

'Absolutely! KGF is a mystery to me. Bangalore I know, but not this place, so I suppose I'm a bit nervous but also excited to be here. I love being home with my family, of course, but London was thrilling.'

'Was it really? I don't remember London that way at all.'

'You've been there?'

'I'm from there,' he said indignantly.

'I was under the impression you were from Cornwall.'

'I am. But I spent a long time in London before I sailed to India. I found it dirty, expensive, lonely, soulless.'

For the first time, Jack saw her composure slip.

'Did you?' she asked, looking suddenly forlorn.

'I was an outcast – a cousin Jack taking a Londoner's job. My west-country accent singled me out. I just didn't fit comfortably into any part of its society. I envy you fitting in so easily.'

She bit her lip, studying his face. 'I didn't,' she blurted quietly.

He looked at her, surprised, but said nothing, waiting for more.

She obliged, her eyes suddenly misty. 'I was never made to feel fully welcome. I went as a governess but was treated like a servant. I sent home jolly letters because I didn't want my parents to worry and I felt I was to blame, but, Jack, London was horrid to me. I couldn't wait to get back, to be honest.' Now she looked teary, her beautiful dark eyes glistening.

Jack was shocked. He hadn't meant to set off such a serious conversation. He glanced across the dance floor and noticed Ned politely dancing with Eleanor Jones. 'Iris, would you like to get some air?'

She nodded and he deliberately didn't hurry her away but walked towards the bar, veering to the counter where they were handing out lemonade, and slipping her out of the side door. He was sure someone would notice – someone always did – so he deliberately stood apart from her, making a show of lighting a cigarette, handing her his handkerchief from his breast pocket.

'Oh, no, don't,' she said, sniffing. 'You'll spoil your perfect look.'

He gave a snort of derision, took a puff on the cigarette and leaned against the wall. 'Are you all right?'

She nodded, dabbed her eyes quickly with his handkerchief. 'I'm sorry about that. No one knows.'

'Not even Ned? I thought you were so close.'

She sighed. 'We are but I wanted them all to believe I was having the perfect time. You know, everyone in that hall just dreams of going to England. I couldn't bear to shatter those visions.'

'Yes. I've never quite understood it because they're all born here and they say where you're born is always in your heart. Me? I would love to see Cornwall again simply because it's my home, but if I never clap eyes on London again, it won't matter a hoot. I'd probably miss the life out here more than London.' He was relieved to see that her tears had dried up.

'I'm sorry about that, Jack. It came out of nowhere. I am so happy to be home – that's the truth of it. They can keep England.' Her tone turned bitter. 'I was given a top private-school education in Bangalore. I graduated with flying colours. I speak English better than many Londoners, my clothes are all hand-tailored, I had savings, and yet I was looked down upon like some sort of poor immigrant.'

This was a surprise for him. 'I don't understand.'

'Neither did I. I applied for a job as a governess but the family I went to treated me with real disdain. My mother would never speak to our ayahs the way Mrs Fitzgibbon spoke to me. I heard her refer to me in front of her friends as "coloured" or "the Indian girl". She made jokes about the way I spoke. Some people actually talked to me in a sort of pidgin English because they didn't think I'd understand. And the final straw was when she asked me not to teach Louisa and Millie any rhymes because she didn't want them speaking with my accent. Oh, it still makes me furious!' she said, stamping her foot.

'What about the society parties Ned told me about and . . . Paris?'

'Fibs, I'm afraid. I did go to Paris but I had to sleep on the floor in the girls' room – like a dog – while they slept on beds in satin sheets. It was so humiliating. Oh, I don't know why I'm telling you all this, Jack. You don't deserve the privilege of my secrets when we hardly know one another.'

'Then why are you telling me?'

'Because you're Ned's best friend and he trusts you and I trust Ned completely.'

'Not with the truth, though, obviously.'

She looked instantly chastened. 'Don't be cruel. I will tell him. I just wanted to put that whole unpleasant time behind me.'

'I don't blame you. I'm glad you came home.'

Her gaze snapped up to his. 'Why?'

He shrugged to cover his sudden self-consciousness. 'Well, it makes Ned happy, for starters.'

'Oh,' she said, and he thought she looked slightly disappointed. 'That's nice of you to say.'

'Iris?' a voice said softly into their silence, making Jack feel even more awkward.

'Ned.'

'Everything all right?'

Jack could feel the thrum of their intimate conversation still buzzing in the air between them and he wondered whether Ned could too.

'I just came out for a smoke,' he said, thanking his lucky stars it was still smouldering in his hand.

'We were talking about London,' Iris said brightly. 'Jack spent time there before coming out to India.'

'I had to save for my passage out,' he lied.

Ned smiled. 'You've never really told me much about that time, Jack. I suppose you won your passage gambling on cards, eh?'

'Something like that,' Jack drawled, flinging down his cigarette stub to crunch it underfoot. 'Anyway, I might make a move.'

'So soon?' Iris said.

'Oh, I didn't expect him to even turn up, let alone stay for a dance,' Ned said, knowingly. 'Jack only came because I asked him to meet you,' he said, shyly taking her hand.

'Yes,' Jack said, 'to let you know how many hearts are

breaking that you have whisked in from London and stolen one of the most eligible bachelors in KGF.' He grinned to cover how awkward he felt but at least he'd kept his promise to Ned to help.

Her eyes sparkled, amused. 'I see,' Iris replied, her gaze fixed on Jack now. 'Don't you enjoy putting on your dress suit and coming to these dances?'

'They're fun,' he replied.

'Don't waste your breath, Iris. His looks are wasted on him.'

She laughed. 'How are you going to meet a nice girl, Jack, if you don't come to the social gatherings?'

Ned gave a snort.

Iris must have noticed the expression Jack gave him. 'What does that mean?'

'Nothing,' Jack said. 'Goodnight, Iris. Thank you for the dance. It was lovely to finally meet you. You and Ned make a very handsome couple.' He took her hand, kissed it. And then he was gone, pushing his way through the crowded hall to slip out of the front door.

Ned and Iris watched him leave. Neither could know how his heart was hammering.

———————

Kanakammal heard the door slam. She made a mental note to ask the bearer to get it fixed. Master Bryant had returned. She could hear him moving about in the main part of the house. She and Namathevi were accommodated at the very back of the dwelling in a small room and although she had nothing but two iron beds and a simple chest of drawers, it was a palace in comparison to what she'd left. She was used to sharing a very small space with a crowd of siblings, not to mention three grandparents plus her own parents.

Here, with Namathevi sleeping on the other side of the room, Kanakammal could actually hear herself think. Silence was a marvellous new treat in her life, although going by the noise the master was making, perhaps the quiet was going to be transient. Leaving home so suddenly had been a shock, and being given over to this stranger as his servant was an even bigger one, but she had already been told by Gangai that the master would require very little of her other than a single cooked meal each day and some light cleaning duties. She knew her parents were counting on the money and retaining this job was very important.

She got up from bed. She wasn't sleepy anyway; her head was too full of the tension of finding herself in this new setting and she was determined to give a good impression and make her parents proud. She dressed quickly into her sari and splashed some water on her face from a bowl on the sideboard, before quickly plaiting and tying up her long hair.

She could still hear the sounds of someone pottering around, but clearly achieving little. He was much closer to their room now, so she hurried out of her chamber, following those sounds to the kitchen.

'Good evening, sir,' she said, hesitating at the doorway, unsure if she were interrupting his privacy.

He swung around and she saw a mixture of confusion and perhaps anger on his face. She waited for him to say something but then steeled herself. 'Can I help?' While her English was very good, her nervousness made her stammer.

'I'm looking for a glass.'

She nodded silently, hesitantly pointing to a cupboard behind him, glad that she'd spent the last few hours acquainting herself with the kitchen and setting it up how she wanted it.

'Bring me one, can you? I'm going to hunt down a bottle of Scotch.'

She remained as still as a statue, eyes downcast as he loomed past her. He looked suddenly huge in the doorway and in that instant she caught the smell of the cream she'd noticed on his dressing bureau. She didn't mean to inhale the scent but it was irresistible – a manly smell, even though her father scorned such product – and she admonished her indulgence as she hurried to find a short glass. She needed Gangai's help to find the right glass but he was having a night off with his family. Bryant gave him two nights away from the house each week and in those times she would be responsible for any of the master's needs. Gangai had assured her she would not be called upon, impressing upon her that Bryant was a very private, quiet person. This was her first night in the house and already Bryant needed to be waited upon at an odd hour. She chose a glass, held it up to check it was clean before she put it on a small tray and rushed out to the front room.

He was not there when she arrived barefoot and as quietly as she could. She looked around the room carefully, not moving from the doorway. He was definitely nowhere in sight. She heard him clear his throat and realised he was on the verandah. She stole out of the front door, the creak of the wretched flyscreen giving away her arrival before the bells around her ankles heralded it.

He was seated in a chair, leaning back against the wall of the house, the moon drenching him in a stark, somewhat ghostly spotlight. Kanakammal froze. She could see his half-naked body. He had pulled off his jacket, which was now slung on the wall of the verandah; his braces were loose around his waist and his bow tie was hanging carelessly about his neck. His shirt was unbuttoned to his waist, and his fair skin – made all the more pale in the soft light of the night – was so sensuous, so perfect. She averted her gaze but it was too late by then; she'd absorbed all of the information on his strongly sculpted body that those few shocked moments could afford. She imagined the hard muscles of his belly were earned from his boxing. Gangai had told her that Master Bryant competed in the mines' boxing competitions and was hoping to capture the trophy this year.

She instinctively glanced at his knuckles but could see little in this low light, other than the fact that he had huge hands – large enough, she was sure, to encircle her waist . . .

'Well, bring it here,' he said. 'I'm not going to eat you.'

'Sorry, sir.'

'Kan . . . Kana . . .' He gave a sound of exasperation.

'Kanakammal, sir,' she murmured as she placed the glass down. She darted backwards, instinctively raising the veil, covering her hair, and was tempted to draw it across her face but she resisted. She was sure he could see little in the shadows where she stood.

'I struggle with your name each time. Is there a shorter version?'

She stared at him, uncertain of what he meant.

'You know, a family pet name or a nickname?'

'I do not understand, sir.'

His grin was sad and brief as he ran a hand through his hair, so that it now partly flopped forward across an eye. It gave him an even more rakish appearance. 'That makes both of us. Don't worry about it. You'll just have to get used to me mangling your name or perhaps we pick a new one for you.'

'Yes, sir,' she said, stepping back still further and watching him pour a slug of the Scotch and knock it back without pausing for breath. He made a sound like pain as it went down and then he sighed, proceeded to pour another. 'Will that be all, Master Bryant, sir?' She could see what was coming, had witnessed it often enough with the men of the township drowning sorrows or simply just drowning reality.

'No. I want you to talk to me,' he said, surprising her. 'Keep me company for a few minutes – at least until I get drunk.'

She was at a loss for what to say or do. The temptation was to flee but she couldn't let her parents down on her first night.

'Drunk?' she repeated, feeling stupid but unsure of herself and the correct procedure.

'I'm going to finish this bottle,' he said. The small mercy was that it was barely a quarter full anyway. She wondered how long it would take him. Not long, perhaps, at this rate.

He'd demanded she talk to him, so she made an attempt at conversation. 'Why is being drunk a good thing?'

'It helps to dull everything.'

She remained still, eyeing him cautiously as he tipped another shot of the fiery liquid down his throat.

He turned to her and she could tell the liquor was beginning to work on him; she'd seen that glazed look in men's eyes before and she didn't like what often came after it. Too many times she'd slapped away wandering hands of her father's acquaintances after they'd shared some of the local arrack. But he seemed quite comfortable in his chair, rocking back on two legs and regarding her through a narrowed gaze.

'I've decided what to call you,' he said, smiling at some private amusement.

He pointed with his glass in his hand. 'I'm going to call you Elizabeth, after my mother. What do you say to that?'

She halted the shrug that came as a natural response, instead straightening and taking a short breath. 'My name is Kanakammal. But you are my employer, so you can call me whatever you want.'

'Well said,' he slurred. 'And I choose to call you Elizabeth because I can say it and because it's a name my father and I love and I haven't heard it in a long time.'

He was rambling now. He would be asleep soon.

She kept up the pretence at conversation. 'Was the dance lovely, sir?'

'Iris was lovely,' he answered, leaning back and closing his eyes. 'Iris was beautiful and fragile.'

She watched the glass dangling in his hand. It would drop soon. She tiptoed forward so lightly that even the muted jangle of her bells and her bangles didn't disturb him. She eased the glass from his fingers. 'Who is Iris, sir?' she asked softly, more to make a soothing sound than out of any interest.

'Iris is the woman I love.'

She blinked. Gangai had warned her – with pursed lips and a knowing look – that the master had many women friends although no one special, but here he was talking about love.

'I am glad for you,' she murmured, trying not to look at his bare chest.

'Don't be,' he said and it came out as a soft, slurred growl. His eyes were closed now. She couldn't remember their colour.

'Why, sir?' She carefully lifted the bottle from his lap and set it down soundlessly beside the glass.

'Because . . .' she watched his tongue dart out and moisten his dry lips, '. . . she belongs to Ned Sinclair, but she will be mine and it will tear our friendship apart.'

28

A week had passed since the dance and Ned still hadn't seen Jack. He was desperate to ask him what he thought of Iris; she certainly had seemed to approve of him. He'd seen plenty of Iris in that time, though, deliberately making suggestions for entertainment with everything from card nights with the family to a movie night and even a game of bingo at Mysore Hall. She'd had no time to be courted by any other bachelors in KGF. Even now he had persuaded Iris to come on a bicycle ride with him as far as Five Lights; he was hoping she would agree to a milky coffee at the small café just to give him more time to gear up to his big question.

They were riding leisurely side by side and it was nearing dusk but still light enough to see well.

'I hear Jack has got himself a promotion,' Iris remarked.

'Yes, to senior engineer. Brilliant, eh?'

'No wonder he can afford to live in that big old house alone. He must enjoy the peace.'

Ned smiled. She'd given him the perfect opening. 'Is it a bit crowded at your house, Iris?'

She gave him a wry glance and then sighed. 'It's so good to be home but I'm not a little girl any more and I feel as though I'm asking permission every time I want to go out. When I suggest going into Bangalore, my mother frowns. I'm twenty-four! I've been in London. Bangalore is not a scary place for me.' He made a soothing sound but she ignored it. 'And have you seen the stream of visitors that come and go from our house on any given day?'

He knew all too well the Walkers' open-door policy but Iris still had much to learn about the KGF community's way of calling in on people unannounced. 'They've surely always been like that, haven't they?'

She groaned. 'I suppose so, but I didn't notice it so much when I was younger. But here, I feel housebound and there's no privacy. If I stay in my room, the aunties think I'm rude; if I come downstairs but remain quiet, they think there's something wrong with me. If I go out, they think I'm being too "fast". If I don't go out, they worry that I'm becoming withdrawn.' She tossed her hair with exasperation and it made Ned's heart flutter in his chest. He wanted to run his fingers through it. He so wanted to kiss her tonight, but she seemed distracted and irritated.

'What do you want, Iris? What would make you feel content?'

She shook her head as she stood up slightly on the pedals to see ahead. 'Oh, I don't know, Ned. I'd just like some time to myself.'

'Just to yourself?'

'Oh, you know what I mean.'

He did. He could solve her dilemma with just a few words if he were game enough to utter them. But they stuck in his throat, the fear of rejection too great.

'Jack's not the only one with a promotion,' he said, instead.

'Oh, Ned. Let's ask Jack and go to Bangalore for a day.'

He blinked, uncertain whether she'd heard him. She continued, without pausing for his reply. 'We could go and have a great day in the city. It's so much cooler there and there's plenty to do. We could go to Ulsore Lake and have a picnic and an ice-cream. Oh, come on. Say yes. My parents won't object to me going with you. And it would be good to see Jack again.' She looked away, suddenly embarrassed. 'I hardly spoke to him that night at the dance.'

Ned had a different recollection of the night, but he didn't want to appear churlish.

'Have you seen him?' she pressed.

Ned cleared his throat, intensely irritated that Jack was dominating the conversation he had hoped would be about himself and Iris. He stopped riding.

'Ned? What's wrong?'

'Iris, you haven't listened to a thing I've been saying.'

'Don't be ridiculous. Of course I have.'

'Then why are you asking questions I've already answered?' He deliberately didn't mention his friend's name, as if its sound alone might prompt him to feel anxious about Iris and her feelings.

She softened her expression and walked the bike back to where he stood. She linked an arm through his. 'I'm sorry, Ned. That was rude of me. I am listening but I think my mind is just a bit scatty at the moment. Have you got some good news to share?'

He grinned, relief exploding like lightning through him. She was instantly forgiven. 'I'm being groomed for the electrical manager's position.'

She looked awestruck and it thrilled him. 'But that's impossible,' she said, slapping his arm in mock disbelief. 'You're so young.'

'Yes, but I'm now officially training for it. In less than two months, if I pass all the right stages to full competency, I'll be the mines' electrical manager. The boss is retiring. What's more, I'll be given the bungalow next to the department.'

She squealed and hugged him. It was so spontaneous and unexpected that he nearly toppled backwards. He laughed, loving her exuberance and the feel of her against him. In that brief embrace he felt her breasts press against his chest and it made his head spin with possibility.

'Thanks, Iris. I thought you'd be pleased.'

'Pleased? I'm as proud as punch for you. Manager at twenty-four! Well, aren't you two going to be the toast of KGF?'

Ned's expression clouded. 'Oh, you mean Jack and myself.'

'Of course I do. Handsome, dashing Jack Bryant and quiet, enigmatic Edward Sinclair – what a duo you make.'

Something rankled inside Ned and his brain wasn't fast enough to prevent the words slipping out. 'So I'm not handsome?'

Her smile faltered. 'I didn't mean it like that.'

He looked down and then back up at her, his face sombre. 'It's how it sounded – and certainly how it looked last week.' There, it was out! He hadn't even realised he'd formulated such a thought.

Iris stared at him, her expression hard to read. Tension stretched like a taut rubberband between them. 'What do you mean?'

Ned scratched the back of his head, instantly embarrassed. But he was on this path now, even though it was all his own fault; he had forced Jack to come to the dance and he had all but thrown them together. Somewhere deep down he'd known it was unwise and yet he had so wanted his two favourite people to be friends. She was waiting, looking offended. 'Oh, I don't know. A few of the men were having a joke at my expense about you and Jack leaving the hall.'

Now she openly glared. A hand moved to her hip and her manner was instantly closed, defensive.

'Iris, whatever it looked like, I —'

'What did it look like?' she snapped.

He wished they could go back five minutes in time. Ned took a breath but her hard expression was not softening. Truth was best. 'You know Jack has a reputation.'

'Oh, I see. And you think I'm an easy catch, do you? That Jack Bryant can twirl me around the dance floor for a single tune and suddenly I'm swooning in his arms and wandering outside with him so he can do whatever he wants with me? Is that what you really think of me, Ned?'

'No, Iris. No.'

'Oh, this makes me mad! Typical small-town gossip. This is why Bangalore is better for me, Ned.'

Ned was in despair. The evening was ruined and there was nothing he could do or say to make it all right again.

'Iris, I'm sorry. Truly I am. You owe me nothing. I just wanted to tell you that —'

Suddenly the ground shook beneath them as the sound of an explosion rent the calm of the evening. It felt like an earthquake and as the bikes toppled, he and Iris instinctively reached for each other and clung together. It felt like an eternity but the shifting of the ground and the trembling of homes lasted only a few seconds and then all was deathly still; there wasn't even the sound of the evening birdsong.

That silence was almost instantly punctuated by shrieks and screams from the houses of the Indian mine workers. Women and children flowed from the scores of tiny dwellings that Ned had always thought looked like dolls' houses, fringing the main town. The voices of the women combined to form an otherworldly shrill keening. It was joined by the even louder braying of a siren.

'What's happening?' Iris's face filled with shock.

Ned's mouth was open in disbelief, his heart suddenly hammering. They'd rehearsed for this sort of event over the past six years but he'd never imagined it would happen. He knew this was no drill. They were listening to the sound that everyone in KGF dreaded.

'Ned! What's going on?'

The oath he expelled was lost in the noise and the sudden frantic activity all around him. 'It's an accident, Iris. There's probably been a rock burst beneath the surface.'

'Rock burst?' she repeated, her eyes frantically searching his.

'A sudden collapse in one of the mines during excavation,' he shouted over the screaming of the villagers as they ran up the hillside towards the shaft.

'Which mine?' she shrieked.

'I think it's William's,' he said.

Iris stared at him with such dread, her hands flying to cover her mouth, that Ned wasn't sure what to say next. 'Don't be frightened, Iris. I'll get you straight home.'

'Rupert!' she cried, her eyes wild with panic. She broke free of Ned and began to run down the road.

Ned ran after her, confused. 'Iris, wait!' He caught up easily enough. 'What do you mean about Rupert?'

'He's leading a time study in William's today. He's down there, Ned. He's in the mine!'

It was a shock, but ever since the death of Brent, Ned had accepted that panic was never an answer to any stressful situation. He was pleased he could take the lead and guide Iris out of the fright that had her frozen to the spot.

'Iris, we must go. They'll need every able man but I might also be needed at the electric department.'

'You can't leave me, Ned.'

'I'll get you to the shaft. I know your family will be waiting there. But I have a responsibility. It's part of our drill. So come on, take my hand. We need to get moving now.' He watched her look around. 'I've got your purse. Don't worry about the bikes. Come on, Iris. We must run.'

They hit their stride until they found themselves in the midst of the wailing Indian women of the community streaming up the hill, anticipating the worst, begging their god to deliver them from it.

Jack was on the early morning shift this week and taking full advantage of his time off, learning how to play golf, which he'd decided was the gentleman's sport of choice. His prowess in snooker and cards was envied by many but it gave him little other status, other than that of a cad. Until now that had never troubled him, but until now he'd never wanted to impress anyone.

He'd found he had a natural swing and powerful drive down the fairway. He still had a lot to learn but his caddy was giving him plenty of helpful advice and he was surprised at how much he enjoyed the game that he had formerly scoffed at.

He was feeling especially pleased with himself, having avoided all of the bunkers and landed with his chip onto the far rim of the green, when the earth moved beneath him, followed by a loud explosion. The trembling continued as he hauled his golf buddy from the bunker.

'Rock burst!' he yelled, familiar with the fearful sound.

One of the caddies was on his knees, terrified, while a second found himself on his backside in the sand. But Jack didn't dawdle in his surprise. He yelled some orders to the caddies before turning his attention to his playing partners. 'Let's go. All hands on deck!'

And they were running as fast as they could towards William's Shaft.

Jack arrived first into pandemonium. The rescue centre's team, which had only been set up the previous year, was yet to hit the scene and worried men were already forming into groups as no one wanted to wait. Defying the new rescue protocol, eager volunteers were being asked for but only people with deep-mine experience were being selected.

Jack didn't hesitate. 'Mr Collins,' he called to the shaft's duty supervisor. 'Let me go. I've been to many an accident in the Penzance mines.'

'None this deep, lad. It's happened at seven hundred feet, we think.'

'Don't worry. I've carried enough men up on my back in my time. Let me go.'

Collins nodded. 'Get geared up. We're lowering in the next few minutes.'

Jack ran over to where he counted fifteen men, who were pulling on whatever safety equipment they could assemble between them, which wasn't much now that there was a dedicated rescue squad.

'How many down there?' he asked.

'Possibly twenty-five to thirty, one white and one Anglo-Indian included.'

Jack knew the last comment shouldn't be relevant, but in this tight-knit community, it was overwhelmingly important. The first wave of the Indian families whose husbands and brothers, uncles and fathers, were potentially buried hundreds of feet down beneath killing rock arrived at the shaft. A cordon had already been set up to keep them back and the loud keening escalated as women began to beat their chests and wail for their men.

'Should we wait until the rescue team arrives?' Jack wondered aloud.

'Can you stand by and wait? Look at the fear in those faces. We have to do something.'

'You're right.'

'Let's go,' Collins yelled. 'Divide into teams of three. The rescue squad should be here any minute but hopefully we can feed them the information they need to make a successful retrieval.'

Jack formed a trio with a couple of men he knew – Arnold de Souza and Charlie Jones – and was soon being wound down in the cage that could carry up to twenty-six men in two layers. He'd been down several of the shafts in KGF, mainly out of curiosity to see how gold mining differed from tin mining, but also to feel as though he was still part of the underground community. Surface workers like Jack were often on the receiving end of scorn from those who did the 'real work'.

Right now, though, he wanted to be part of the crew that brought these men back safely. He knew in his heart it was an empty hope. The sound of the explosion suggested it had been a big one, so deaths were a foregone conclusion. He could feel the tension in the cage as the rescuers were all wrestling with the same notion.

'Do we know anyone down there?' he asked the man standing next to him.

He nodded. 'You're thick with the Walker family, aren't you?'

Jack frowned.

'One of the Walker boys is down there, I'm afraid.'

He felt a surge of fear. 'It must be a mistake.'

'No mistake. Rupert has been moved to the assay department recently. I gather John Drake is with him.'

'I know Drake. He's senior.'

'And a good man. He was on leave from Saturday. He should have been packing up his desk.'

Jack ground his jaw, memories of the Levant disaster crashing back into his mind. 'We're going to find them.'

'I hope so.'

The cage juddered to a halt and the men were engulfed in dust. Those who had breathing apparatus counted their blessings for it. Jack was imagining what this terror would do to the Walkers, and Iris in particular. Billy's face with its cheeky grin swam into his mind. He hadn't been able to save Billy but he had every intention of delivering the Walkers their son . . . alive. But there were many other sons down here, who all had families that worshipped them, needed them. He didn't want to care about them any less, but since hearing about Rupert, it felt like fate – as though he had been chosen.

Try again, the heavens were saying. This time, don't let him die.

He could barely see anything in the darkness, despite their petromax lights. The heat was intense. Jack was already soaked through with sweat. He'd forgotten the heat of a mine and the core temperature of the rock this deep was vast, plus he realised that electricity was not available. The explosion would have knocked out the lights of any who had them.

Arnold de Souza's tone was filled with indignation when it punctured the silence that had enveloped them. 'I lost my father to one of these rock bursts. But nothing's changed in ten years; the company's still as greedy and ruthless as ever. Safety conditions are —'

Collins interrupted. 'All right, de Souza. We've got a job to do and lives to save.' He turned to Jack.

'Bryant. You, de Souza and Jones take tunnel nine A. We know the assay was being done across nine.' He directed others to tunnels nine B and nine C. 'Listen to me carefully now. I want all survivors called in by runners, back to this point where I'll station someone. But only survivors. Is that clear? We've got families waiting and the rescue squad will be working alongside us too. We can't do anything for the dead right now so we've got to get the living out first. We've got two of our own down here, good men both. Let's find them alive, please.'

The men murmured their determination.

'Get going, you nine. The rest of you, follow me.'

De Souza led their small group with grit. At the mouth of the tunnel was a steel arch, reinforcing the entrance. Once again Jack marvelled at the construction of the South Indian mines, so much more sophisticated and advanced than any he remembered in Cornwall. Taylor & Sons spent a small fortune on modern technology and engineering to ensure these mines in KGF led the way for the rest of the world. And still accidents happen, Jack thought.

'How will they breathe?' he asked.

'Pockets of air. It won't all be like this,' Jones said. 'I was caught in one of these when I first started and we were fine – the lucky ones. We had a good supply of air but we lost about eighteen workers in that one.'

'No more talk of loss,' de Souza growled.

'I'm not resurfacing until one of our parties has good news for the Walkers,' Jack said. 'Come on.'

They walked into the dark furnace, following the ore trolley lines that looked like miniature railway tracks – another amazing engineering feat Cornish miners could only dream of.

To Jack, walking beneath the steel reinforced arch that welcomed him into tunnel nine was like entering the gates of hell.

Ned arrived at the shaft, which was now a hive of frenzied activity. The rescue centre squad was in place, pulling on their new safety equipment and bellowing orders.

He turned to Iris. 'They seem to know what they're doing.'

She bit her lip; her face was tear-stained, her clothes dusty and the strap of her shoe torn. Nearby women wailed, others stood by in shocked silence, while small clumps talked and pointed, muttering between themselves with pinched expressions, often stifling tears. Children clung to mothers and older sisters. The atmosphere was so tense that Ned believed people might start throwing themselves down the shaft in their grief and despair.

He was stirred from his thoughts by the arrival of the Walkers, and as Iris ran towards her family, he schooled his features and hoped for good news.

Ned watched Iris crumple against her father's chest. Rupert was definitely down there. Ned swore under his breath and then steeled himself to greet the Walker family, which was gathering in its entirety on the fringe of the shaft's opening.

He picked his way through the sea of colour. Saris shimmered as twilight settled, the sky looking like one of those layered jellies his mother made him to go with ice-cream on his birthday. The deep violet of evening had yet to claim the ultramarine blue, which fought to hold back night from the dusky pinks and fiery oranges closest to the sun. The night sky laid herself across KGF, gradually bathing the traumatic scene in muted shadows and soft silvering moonlight.

Ned sped up to see the Walkers. He was met with a solid wall of gloom.

'It is true?' he asked, kissing Flora Walker.

She wept. 'My Rupert's down there, Ned.'

Ned swallowed. 'They'll get him out, you'll see.' He turned to Iris, who was still sobbing at her father's chest. 'Iris, I need to help where I can.'

'What can you do?' Harold asked.

'Well, I can rig up some extra lighting. I'm sure every bit helps.'

It was as though he'd magically overheard the comment because the chief of the rescue team ran over. 'Sinclair! The guys can barely see anything for dust.'

'I'm heading over to the electricity department right away.'

'Good lad.'

'How many unaccounted for?' Harold asked the man.

'At this stage we believe it's twenty-eight. I'm so sorry, Mr Walker.'

Walker nodded, as if to say no apology was required.

'We've learned that a dozen or so men have already gone down. They didn't wait for the professionals.'

'What?' Ned said. 'Are they mad? You people have the best equipment in the country. The safety plan should have been followed to the letter.'

'They were keen to do what they could. Very brave. I have to admire them. In fact, your friend's one of them – very quick to raise a hand.'

'Jack's down there?' Iris blurted.

'He's not even an underground man. I have to take my hat off to him. I had him down as a career miner.'

'Will he be safe?' Iris asked, her voice shaking.

Ned glanced at her, jealousy nagging at him.

'No one ever is down there, Miss Walker. But they've got fifteen minutes on us. They could get lucky and find your brother. We're counting on them to pull off a miracle.'

'Jack will find Rupert, Mum, and he's strong enough to carry Rupert out if he has to.'

Ned frowned. Iris sounded as though she'd known Jack all her life.

'Well, thanks for the extra lighting. It can't come too soon,' the rescue leader said.

Ned ran back down the hill. By the time he returned, twice as many people had gathered. A battery of Anglo-Indian women had flown into action, setting up trestle tables and running mugs of tea and coffee – even snacks – to the men working hard on the rescue.

Ned acted swiftly with his electricity workers and before long a new skeleton with wires and plugs had been erected around the shaft entrance. When Ned threw the switch, the whole area was flooded with light. People clapped, but the applause died quickly as the rescue chief bellowed for quiet. The team needed silence to hear their colleagues and cries for help below.

Ned backed away, happy and relieved that his part had been acquitted smoothly.

'Excuse me, Master Sinclair,' said a voice.

He turned at his name, and looked into the exquisite face of a young Indian woman. 'Yes?'

She immediately covered her face with her veil. 'You are a good friend of Master Bryant, sir?'

'I am.'

'I am Master Bryant's new . . . I work in his house and we are worried because he has not come home. We heard the siren, sir, and . . .'

Ned nodded, mesmerised by her intense grey eyes. 'Sorry, what is your name again?'

'He calls me Elizabeth but my name is Kanakammal.'

'Well, Kanakammal, I'm sorry to tell you but Master Bryant is part of the rescue effort.'

'Have we heard from him, sir?'

'I'm afraid not. Not yet. We're hoping we will soon.'

The young woman seemed to understand. 'Thank you, Master Sinclair. I will let the household know.'

'Hopefully both our prayers will be answered,' he encouraged. Ned watched her retreat with long, graceful strides, her pale-grey sari silver in the moonlight. She looked like a glimmering angel as she floated lightly on her feet up the hill. She was beautiful.

'Who was that?' Iris asked from behind. He swung around.

'Er, a woman who works for Jack. Apparently he calls her Elizabeth.'

'Oh?' she said, squinting slightly to pick her out. 'She seems to have disappeared.'

'She was like an apparition anyway,' Ned remarked.

They were walking through darkness, save what little pool of light their lamps cast. The dust had begun to settle but even so it was impossible for Jack to see his hand held out in front of him.

'Do we know what's ahead of us?' Jack asked, suddenly realising they too could be walking straight into a natural trap.

'I know the channel well enough,' de Souza replied, 'but who knows if it's intact? I think it's better for one of us to scout ahead with care, just in case.'

'All right,' Jack said. 'I'll go.'

'No, you're stronger than me, Bryant. If we need to carry anyone out, we'll be relying on you. Are you feeling all right, Charlie?

Your breathing sounds strained,' de Souza said, pausing now. Jack had noticed it too.

Charlie Jones sighed. 'This dust, it's making my breath ragged.'

'Go back,' Jack said immediately. 'It's too dangerous. Is it asthma?'

'Not since I was a child,' he wheezed, then bent over and coughed. 'I'm sorry, lads.'

Jones wasn't an underground man but he could never have been taken for someone with weakened lungs. He led the KGF choir and was always shouting the loudest at football and hockey games.

'You can't come any further, Charlie,' de Souza warned. 'You'll have to go back.'

They all turned to stare into the blackness behind them. In that instant Jack and de Souza both realised it was probably more dangerous to let Charlie walk back alone.

Jack ground his jaw. 'I'll get him to the rendezvous point. I'll be back quickly.'

De Souza nodded. 'Be careful.'

'You too. Just wait here. No heroics, all right? If we stick together, we've got a better chance of getting out. Have you got matches, just in case?'

De Souza dug a pack of Tiger matches from a pocket and shook them.

Jack and Charlie headed back down the lonely path they had just come. It took Jack at least another fifteen minutes to deposit Jones at the meeting point. Jack set straight out again alone, passing beneath the steel of the tunnel again and noticing the huge steel fire doors this time. He was more sure now of his footing and could move faster through the murky tunnel. His lamp cast an eerie glow and dust particles danced in the air. Jack held his lamp higher; large sections of the tunnels were reinforced with pine liners, interspersed with steel for additional strength.

The glitter of a vein of gold running at about shoulder height caught his attention. He had seen this only once before and couldn't help but marvel at the glinting line that tempted men so deep into the earth. He touched the seam of gold in quiet respect. KGF's combined mines yielded roughly two massive blocks of gold per month. 'If you can pick it up, you can keep it!' said a sign in the smelting room, where impossibly heavy ingots were poured.

About halfway back to de Souza he heard a loud rumble and instinctively he crouched, covering his head with his arms, awaiting the landslide of rock. Nothing happened. He was crouched in a black silence.

'Arnold!'

The only reply was his own voice echoing into the void. He tried again. He knew he was close enough for de Souza to have returned his yell. A knot tightened in his belly as he straightened in the blackness and tentatively felt his way forward. After five minutes of agonisingly slow, careful steps, he felt sure he had reached the point where he had left de Souza.

'Arnold, are you there?' he yelled and once again he heard his own voice echoing down the passage, mocking his fear.

He was torn. His head told him he should turn back; alert the teams that he believed there'd been another rockfall. The rescue squad needed all the information it could muster. But his heart overrode his head. His instincts told him that de Souza might be in trouble and to turn away now was to desert someone in need. Then he heard a muted groan. He held his breath and waited, his ears straining for a sound – anything that would give him more information than he had right now. He began to think he was simply hearing his own heartbeat. But then he heard it again. A man's voice, calling his name.

'Arnold? Arnold, where are you?'

'Jack.' The voice was louder, but not by much.

'Tap on something. Guide me to you.'

'Keep back!' the voice warned. There's nothing in front of you.'

'All right,' Jack said, soothing de Souza's fear with his own forced calmness. 'Are you hurt?'

'I'm trapped,' de Souza said. 'I feel numb.'

'Is your light working? Can you shine your lamp in front and I'll do the same?'

'No. I must have dropped it.'

'Then bang on something.'

Jack heard a small stone on the wall. 'I think I have you. Now, just be still.' He held his own lamp high, but what he saw before him was devastating.

Jack bit hard on his lip as he took in the scene of a huge boulder crushing Arnold de Souza beneath it. Only de Souza's torso was visible, his hips and legs presumably mangled beneath hundreds of pounds of unyielding rock. His position meant that he couldn't raise his head easily, and he was faced away from Jack.

'I can see you, Arnold.' He didn't know what to say, so he uttered the obvious. 'How much pain are you in?'

'No pain. Can't feel a thing,' came the laboured reply. 'I have no feeling in my body right now, but I have eyes and my hands can tell me there's a fucking great rock on me,' he said and shocked Jack by laughing.

'Arnold, shh, just save —'

'No, you be quiet. I'm as good as dead. We both know it. But listen, Jack – I heard voices before, I'm sure of it. There are others alive down here.' De Souza began to retch. 'Just let me die. You can't move this fucking thing and neither can I. No one can in time.'

'Wait,' Jack said, trying desperately to push away the inevitable. 'I can see a path through to you.'

He gingerly picked his way over the debris. For now, all that mattered was to hold the hand of the dying man in front of him. Jack reached de Souza and not a moment too soon.

'Bryant,' de Souza stammered. 'Tell Amy I love her and the children. Tell her I'm sorry to leave her.'

'I'll tell her, Arnold,' he said, squeezing the man's hand. 'She'll be proud of you.'

De Souza smiled and it was filled with a radiance that broke Jack's heart. He died in the next breath, his hand suddenly limp in Jack's hand.

Jack stared at him for a moment, silently saying a prayer for his soul. He reached into his pocket and found a handkerchief, which he used to cover de Souza's face. It seemed right. Jack blinked away his tears of frustration and then straightened. With an angry determination, he picked up his lamp and headed deeper into the tunnel.

Jack was going to hunt down those voices, for Arnold's sake and in his memory.

29

At the surface Ned saw Charles Jones being helped from the shaft. Harold Walker was already standing by for the first casualties and they watched him give instructions for Jones to be laid on a stretcher.

All the Walkers held their breath when Harold sent a runner to them.

'I am to tell you, madam,' he said in his clipped Indian accent, 'that there is no news yet of Mister Rupert.'

Flora didn't flinch, although her lips pursed tighter still. She continued rearranging teacups and refilling her sugar bowl.

'Mister Jones was part of the early rescue crew. Mister Bryant sent him back.' He waggled his head.

'Is Mister Bryant all right?' Iris asked anxiously.

'I do not know, Miss Walker,' the runner admitted, then departed swiftly.

Ned turned to Iris. 'Jack will be fine,' he said brusquely. 'I think I'll go and talk to some of the other families. They need reassurance too.'

She pouted. 'They live with this every day; it's not as if they aren't aware of the dangers.'

'That's a little uncharitable, isn't it?'

'Well, you know what I mean, Ned. These people know mining life. They live with its consequences.'

'*These people*? Iris, the Brits and the Anglo-Indians, well they —'

'Why do you separate them? Do you forget my father is as British as you?'

He stared at her, shocked. 'No, not at all. We're all the same, Iris, including the Indian families.'

Her face softened. 'Yes, you're right. I think we're all so anxious, our emotions are spinning too fast, too hard. Forgive me.'

Ned put an arm around her. Despite the heat, he loved the feel of her warmth against him. Suddenly, nothing much else mattered but the love he felt for Iris and how he was going to make her the happiest woman in all of KGF. 'Iris, let's both go and talk to some of the families, try to reassure them as best we can.'

'Oh, Ned, I don't think —'

'You can do it.' He took her hand. 'They'll remember your kindness – and so will I.'

Iris allowed him to lead her around to various families. She put on a cheerful manner and shook hands with the Indian women, even spoke in rusty Tamil. Ned had become relatively proficient in the language himself, and was often surprised by how few British bothered to learn the local language.

Both he and Jack had made a point of practising from the moment they had arrived in KGF, entertaining everyone from butlers to chokra boys, forcing them to speak back to them only in Tamil. He liked that Iris slipped into Tamil, but a thought nagged at him that she was obviously more comfortable using it to give instructions, rather than to inquire after someone's wellbeing, as she was now.

As Ned moved into the thick of the Indian families he could smell spices and sandalwood oil. When their rough hands cupped his, their many glass or gold bracelets jangled in a light cacophony and he felt humbled by their gentle bows of gratitude and murmured voices, filled with worry but still so full of hope.

He suddenly wished he was down there with Jack. Jack at least was doing something. Ned glanced up the hill and saw Kanakammal, standing aloof and alone, ethereal in the moonlight.

Iris saw her too. 'There's that woman again,' she breathed. 'Did you say she has someone lost?'

'No. She's here for Jack.'

'She hardly knows him, surely?'

'Yes, but look at her face. She's as concerned for his safety as we are. I'm going to talk to her again.'

'Wait for me,' Iris said.

The tall woman watched them clamber up the hill. She looked ghostly in her pale sari, away from the floodlights. 'Hello again, Kanakammal,' Ned said.

She bowed to them both, her large pale eyes regarding them unblinking, her face giving nothing away.

'Kanakammal, this is Miss Iris Walker. The Walker family live at Oorgaum.'

'I am pleased to meet you, Miss Walker,' Kanakammal said.

'You're working for Mister Bryant, I hear?' Iris remarked, sounding lofty.

The girl lowered her gaze humbly. 'Yes, madam. My sister and I are living at his house.'

'Living in? Well! How very modern.'

Ned made an exasperated face.

'What?' she said, tartly. 'He's a bachelor, Ned.'

Kanakammal looked away, over their heads. 'Something is happening, sir,' she said, clearly glad to change the subject.

He swung around, noticed activity at the shaft mouth. 'Well, hopefully we'll have Mister Bryant back in his house before long.'

She gave him a look of gratitude. 'Goodbye, sir, madam,' she said, and then with her wraith-like ability, she melted away and joined the crowd of onlookers, who were all pressing forward, hoping for fresh news.

'That wasn't very subtle,' Ned said disapprovingly as he led Iris back to her family.

'Come on, Ned. Don't tell me her looks escaped you.'

'Well, yes, I think she's incredibly beautiful, and so poised.' He could tell he was annoying her now. 'But I just don't see your point.'

'My point is that she is clearly very young, and single. And Jack is a bachelor and something of a rake.'

'Not something of a rake, Iris. He is one! But he's single too, and whoever he chooses to spend his time with – British, Anglo-Indian or villager – is his business. I think you're reading far too much into this.'

'Ned! I was looking out for her wellbeing, that's all.'

He bit back on what he wanted to say about her noticeable preoccupation with Jack Bryant and instead reached for her hand. 'Iris, we have to focus on Rupert now and getting him back safely. That's all I care about. Him and Jack returned to us unharmed.'

She nodded and smiled, but he wasn't reassured. The whispers intensifying in his mind were becoming impossible to ignore.

Jack was burning up. His lungs felt scorched by each new breath of hot air he took in. He knew he was too aware of his breathing. His father had once told him about this phenomenon, which could strike men below the surface. 'Breathing happens without you concentrating on it. Your body knows how to do it,' his father had explained.

And so now Jack tried to stop thinking about it. 'Focus, Jack,' he growled to himself.

After what he thought was perhaps ten minutes of inching progress, he began to doubt himself again. He was blindly moving deeper into the earth, into a tunnel he knew nothing about, after people he couldn't even be sure were here.

He stopped, slid down the wall and held his head. It was aching from the heat, his throat was dry and his water canister had long been emptied. Should he turn back?

It was in that instant of doubt that he heard voices, clear as anything. Now he was torn. Should he go back to the rescue team or should he press on to where he was now absolutely certain that Rupert and his companions were trapped?

Jack made a snap decision to press forward. He could never live with himself if he had to look Iris in the face and admit he had turned away from her brother.

That vision alone drove him on.

––––––––––

Jack found Rupert dazed, slipping in and out of consciousness.

'Rupert, talk to me! Come on, I heard you cry.'

His head was lolling. A nasty gash had torn away part of his scalp and he was bleeding heavily. He looked like he'd just clambered out of the trenches. Jack wished he had some smelling salts. He reminded himself that the rescuers could only be a minute or two away now. Until then, his job was to keep talking to Rupert, who seemed to be rallying.

'God, it hurts,' he groaned. 'Is that really you, Bryant?'

'I'm afraid so.' He squeezed Rupert's hand for reassurance. 'I need you to just stay calm, stay conscious. I won't sit you up with this head wound.' He dared not say anything about Rupert's mangled right arm that looked worse the more he glanced at it. 'There's a rescue squad right behind me and they're going to get you out. Where's Drake?'

Rupert began to weep. 'He's gone.'

'Gone? Gone to find help?'

'No, gone! Down that big black hole over there. The whole wall collapsed and took him with it and I think it took my arm. I crawled over here but I couldn't go any further. I must have . . . must have blacked out.' Tears began to roll down his face.

'Listen to me. Your arm's here, right where it should be,' Jack reassured, allowing himself to believe he was only telling a white lie and Rupert's arm might yet be saved. He heard another deep rumble not far from where he'd just been.

'Oh, God. It's going to happen again, Jack. We're going to die down here.'

'Be still, Rupert. That's just the aftershocks; the earth is settling.'

Rupert snorted in scorn, despite his pain. 'Start saying your prayers, Bryant. That was exactly the sound we heard before it blew. It's going to do it again, I tell you!'

Jack heard the approach of the rescue squad and ignored Rupert, relief flooding through him. They were going to be safe now. He tried not to think about John Drake and Arnold de Souza, or the dozens of men whose names he didn't know who were likely trapped, injured, dying or already dead. They had loving families too, but the mine would not see to their needs as it would the families of de Souza and Drake – with compensation payments, special pensions, counselling and all manner of other benefits. The Indian families would be left with a dead body to cremate – if they were fortunate enough to retrieve it.

He looked over at Rupert, who'd gone quiet.

'Rupert. Come on, man. You'll be on the surface shortly. Your whole family's waiting. You want to be conscious to reassure them, don't you?'

Rupert mumbled something and Jack was satisfied he was still awake.

'Here!' he yelled, now that voices were evident in the distance.

'Bryant?'

'Over here! Be careful of the —'

He got no further. At first it was a deep rumble but that gave way almost immediately to a screeching sound. Instinctively, Jack pulled Rupert towards him, covering him with his body and protecting his own head with his arms. And then, a huge fissure yawned open and rocks the size of small huts fell away. Jack could no longer see a thing and so he clung to Rupert, awaiting a death blow from the earth.

The high-pitched sound was his own long scream, he realised, barely audible above the far more powerful voice of nature. His head hurt and his body was taking some punishment as rocks and debris fell across his back and shoulders. But he held onto Rupert, while images of his parents and Iris flashed through his mind. He saw Ned, his face full of accusation, and Brent with his head caved in. He saw Arnold de Souza reaching out to him, and then he thought he saw an angel welcoming him, beckoning him towards her, but then realised it was his new servant, Kanakammal. She was wearing a floaty grey sari with silver thread running through it, sparkling amid the apocalypse, and she told him to survive.

A sharp pain roared back at him when he shifted position but he welcomed it. The pain told him he was alive. He reached behind his head and felt the telltale wetness and now realised his face was sticky with blood too.

'Rupert . . . Rupert!'

Walker groaned beneath him. Jack was grateful in that instant that they'd both survived the landslide. His attention turned to the men of the rescue squad.

'Hey!' he yelled into the dark, his voice bouncing back quickly. Only now he understood they'd been cut off. He didn't dare move. In this blackness he could step straight into a hole, lost for good.

Fear reclaimed Jack. He was trapped in tunnel nine, wounded, bleeding, and with a man so badly injured he would die if he didn't get medical treatment quickly. Jack scrabbled around for his lamp but realised he couldn't risk relighting it anyway. A naked flame was too dangerous with all the gases that had been released. He couldn't imagine things could get any worse, but Rupert's groans dragged him from his despair.

'Walker . . . Rupert! How's the pain?'

'How do you think?' he growled.

Jack wasn't offended. At least Rupert was showing some gumption. He'd need it if they were going to escape. Jack would rather die on the move, fighting his way to the surface, than sit here.

'Right, there is no rescue party now. Can you stand?'

Rupert sighed, fully lucid now. 'I doubt it. My whole right side took a battering in the first blast.'

'Let's try, shall we?'

'Why not? It should be entertaining, if nothing else.'

Jack stood up, careful where he stepped. He felt dizzy at first but his head cleared quickly, despite the pain. He gave a sigh and then leaned down. 'Your turn.' He reached under Rupert's arms. 'Use your good leg to push up if you can.'

'Yes, thank you, Bryant. I reckon I can work that out.'

'Then get on with it, you old woman.'

Impossibly, Rupert began to laugh. And Jack joined him. It didn't last. Rupert was screaming within seconds as he tested his weight on his right foot. And then Jack was lowering him swiftly.

'Broken ankle?' he inquired politely.

'At least that,' Rupert replied, through short, shallow breaths.

'Right,' Jack said, wiping blood from his eyes. His head was bleeding and his own shoulder was on fire but that was the least of their problems right now. 'We need to move while you're lucid.'

'Well, if it's any consolation, the pain has certainly woken me up. I actually feel more alert.'

'That's good, Rupert. That's really good. Well, I'm ready to hear any suggestions.'

Rupert took a longer, deeper breath and Jack remained silent. He was hoping for a miracle, but miracles did happen, so why not now?

'If my memory isn't playing tricks on me, there *is* a way out of here,' Rupert began. 'Nine A connects with C further down, but unfortunately not on the same level. We'll have to hope the ladders are in place.'

'What then?'

'If the old ladders are intact, we might be able to get onto the higher levels and attract some attention, or find our way from a safer level to the cage.'

It was sound thinking. Jack was impressed. 'Listen, if worst comes to worst, I'll carry you up those ladders all five hundred feet if I have to.'

'You know, Jack, you'd move a lot faster without me.'

Jack snorted. 'I don't particularly like you, Walker, but I'd rather risk my own life hauling you up those damn ladders than face your mother without you.'

'So, to tunnel C it is. Shall I try to hop?'

'I think I'll have to carry you. I still can't see in front of my nose, so we're going to have to feel our way and pray for some luck.'

'Remember to follow the trolley tracks. They'll keep you straight and on target.'

'Right. And before we set off, I'd better put a tourniquet around your arm.'

Within moments Jack had his shirt torn into some useable shreds of fabric and eventually fastened them tightly in place, then hefted Rupert onto his back.

Jack lurched off into the darkness. Rupert's weight was not an issue, he was as lean as he was small, but in the darkness Jack knocked Rupert's arm and that set off fresh groans.

Soon he lost all track of time and distance, his sole focus on safely putting one foot in front of the other. His mind was mostly blank. He wasn't even sure if Rupert was still conscious; his intense pain would have been made worse by the tourniquet.

Jack thought of home, Pendeen, and the church graveyard where they had buried Billy; buried all the sons of Pendeen who had perished in the Levant disaster. It wasn't going to happen again. It wasn't!

'Bryant!' Rupert suddenly bellowed.

'What?'

'I think we should start looking for where the tunnels meet. I've been counting.'

'What?'

'Your steps. Miners are taught this, in case of this very emergency. I reckon we're close.'

'What do we do?'

'Start feeling around for the opening. Sorry I'm not much help.'

'Why don't I set you down, then I can move faster?'

It hurt them both but finally Rupert was back leaning against the tunnel's hot, dry wall and Jack was sucking in big breaths. 'I don't suppose you have a water flask?' he asked.

'I do! Or at least I should do. Here.' Rupert guided Jack's hand in the dark. 'Attached to my belt.'

'Please say there's some left.'

'There is. Have you got it?'

'Yes,' Jack said, tipping the contents down his throat. He could have drunk all of it but stopped after the first two gulps. 'Here, you have some.'

'Thanks,' Rupert said, taking the flask and sipping from it. 'There's none left, Jack.'

'We won't need it. The next drink we take is going to be in the open air.'

'You keep that promise,' Rupert warned.

'And then we're both going to get drunk.'

'I'll drink to that.'

At the surface the first casualties were being hoisted from the cage. Ned watched with despair as women began to beat their chests and tear their clothes. Already three men had been declared dead, another had died minutes after arrival at the surface and five others were critically injured.

Ned watched Harold Walker move carefully from patient to patient, performing triage. A team of doctors and nurses had been rushed in from both the Mines Hospital at Champion Reef and the Civil Hospital from Robertsonpet. Ned felt helpless. He offered to drive a car with the wounded in it but they really didn't want volunteers right now. There were actually too many people crowding around the site and that was hampering easy access.

'Ned, get people to stay back, will you?' Walker pleaded. 'The ambulance needs access.'

And so he'd found himself foreman of a tiny patch of ground, keeping onlookers at bay. He'd lost track of Iris but could still see Kanakammal staring at the shaft entrance, her gaze unwavering.

Ned had just got word via Harold Walker that one of the rescue teams had communicated with Jack before losing contact after a second tremor. They knew nothing more.

'Arnold de Souza was found dead,' Walker sighed. 'He was with Jack when they sent Charlie back up.'

'Dead?'

'Crushed. Jack had gone on. Don't ask me why. I have to keep hoping he heard my son, because there's been no news of Rupert from anyone else.'

They stared at each other in silence.

'Well,' Ned began, 'then we have to pray.'

'Indeed. Not a word to my wife, Ned. Besides, it's speculation. Either way, there's no good news yet. Just hold this position, will you? It's only going to get worse.'

'If Jack's with Rupert, he'll get him out, Harold.'

The old man smiled sadly and then retreated to his makeshift emergency centre.

30

Jack couldn't help the elation. 'I found it, Rupert! You were right!'

'You see, my mind is like a vice!' Jack had a newfound respect for Rupert Walker and that grudging admiration was deepening all the time. 'Can you get up into the next tunnel easily enough?'

'The ladder is there!' Jack even clapped, but he regretted it immediately, as shock waves ripped through his shoulder.

'Well done,' Rupert said, but Jack detected a false note. 'Listen, I'm not sure I'm going to make it. I want you to go on alone and —'

'Don't be stupid, man! We've got this far. We're on the home straight now.'

Rupert seemed weak and breathless suddenly. Perhaps the bleeding had begun again.

'I'm not leaving you down here.'

'You have a chance without me . . .'

'I am not leaving you,' Jack said slowly, firmly, crouching beside his companion. 'Now rally, man! Rally as your father would expect you to and help me get you onto my back. We've got a lot of ladders to climb.'

'Do you want to know how many?' Rupert mumbled.

'Shut up, Walker. Now, just get on my back and let's do this. I'm dying for a beer.'

They began to laugh; the shared nervous laughter of those with no other path to take. Once again they resumed their former position, this time with Jack's hands firmly gripped beneath Rupert's knees. He didn't trust Walker not to slip off his back if he lost consciousness.

Iris brought Ned a cup of coffee sweetened with condensed milk.

'I don't know how your mother keeps going,' he remarked, sighing from the syrupy, comforting taste.

'It helps her to stop panicking. But she's on the edge right now . . . over eight hours since the rock burst.'

'You must stay positive. We all must.'

'Every second man is so hideously injured. Either that or he's dead,' she said and crumpled, the tears streaming down her face. 'I couldn't bear it if I never saw Rupert again.'

Ned was desperate to reassure her; to watch her weep broke his heart. 'Listen, you have to swear you'll say nothing to Flora. But there's a chance Jack got through to Rupert and John Drake.' Her expression was a mixture of confusion and delight. He bit his lip and then decided to tell her everything he'd learned. 'But, Iris, this is all speculation,' he warned, as her smile broadened.

She hugged him tight. 'Jack will bring him out safely, Ned. I know it. Jack won't let me down.' She turned, invigorated with fresh hope, and returned to help her father tend to the walking wounded.

Ned stared after her, a hollow pit opening in his belly. Iris was smitten by Jack – he hadn't moved fast enough to secure her . . . and now it was too late.

Once again Jack blanked his mind. Rupert had found some last reserve of strength to hang on, and slowly, painfully, they had ascended the ladders, step by killer step.

Many a Cornish miner had dropped to his death from nothing more than fatigue, Jack recalled, knowing he now risked a similar fate. He was exhausted, aching, bleeding and frightened. But he couldn't tell Rupert that and he barely dared admit it to himself, so he focused instead on the beer he had promised himself and the sight of the Walker family and their joy.

Rupert had fallen silent again but Jack could hear his ragged breath.

Jack paused. 'I have no idea how far we've come.'

'Just over two hundred steps. We have at least that yet to go, perhaps even more.'

Jack groaned. 'I didn't need to know that.'

He set off once more. The first twenty to thirty steps were the hardest as he tried to find the rhythm again.

'Sing with me, Rupert.'

'Don't be daft.'

'Come on, no one can hear, not even me. My heart's beating too loud.'

'No strength.' Rupert laughed mirthlessly. 'Do you take requests?'

'For a price?'

'I'll pay you a rupee to sing my mother's favourite song.'

'Tell me, then,' Jack replied, dreading it was going to be one of those Al Jolson numbers he couldn't stand.

' "What'll I Do",' Rupert said.

Jack knew the song; liked it. 'What'll I do,' he began in a weary voice that was hardly singing but would do, and was surprised when Rupert, despite his fading energy, joined in.

And so, murmuring Irving Berlin, two wounded soldiers dragged themselves up another two hundred and forty-five rungs from the dark, bleak battleground and into the murky, silent dawn of survival.

The atmosphere surrounding the Walker clan had become thick and bleak, like a fog. Ned felt the family's heartbreak so keenly that his teeth ached from clenching. Silence had long ago descended among them. There was simply nothing more to say. Where at one point the family had huddled with arms around one another, praying and reassuring each other that Rupert would be saved, now they stood close but separated, as if bruised.

Iris looked inconsolable. She had retreated from him, moving closer to her brother Jim, and her mother, whose silence was perhaps the most heartrending of all. Flora continued to fuss with cups and bowls of sugar, teaspoons and tins of milk, but anyone could see she was oblivious to her own actions. Her mouth was uncharacteristically turned down. Her neat hair, normally twisted into a tight bun, now looked ragged, with silvered hair loosened and falling down. She seemed to have aged a decade during the night.

Even though he was so close to the Walker family, Ned felt like an interloper – an observer who kept watch over them, but wasn't fully part of them. Once again the isolation that had plagued Ned for most of his life echoed strongly in his thoughts. He stood just a few feet away from those he loved, knowing they did not love him in the same way they loved each other. He belonged to no one.

Many people had intermittently strolled over to offer quiet commiserations. They no longer sounded like words of support but more like condolences. No one was holding out much more hope. He watched Walker adopt the stiff upper lip that the British prided themselves upon as he worked through his despair, tending to those who needed his skills. But his wife and his children found it easier to show their emotions; Jim wept openly for his brother.

All the Indian workers had now been accounted for, and their families had dispersed to tend to their wounded, to pray over their dying or to offer a vigil for their dead. Only Arnold de Souza's body hadn't been recovered. It would need some heavy equipment to retrieve his corpse from beneath the enormous boulder.

As for Bryant, the last sighting had him alive, but there had been no word of Rupert or Drake. No one was comfortable about pronouncing the lost trio dead, preferring the softer-sounding term of missing, but to Ned and the Walker family it meant the same.

Ned felt sick, just as forlorn as any of the other mourners and more isolated because he was so alone. Pricked by this sad realisation, Ned remembered one other person who was here for Jack. He glanced across to where the servant girl stood as still as a marble statue. The mythical stories he'd enjoyed as a child came to mind, where goddesses watched from on high and now and then deigned to interfere in mortal life. That's how Kanakammal struck him; she was here but not really involved in the scene. There was little expression on her face and even close up he found her pale eyes unreadable. But there was something lurking behind that calm façade; her passions burned deep, Ned guessed, but she had learned how to contain them.

Dawn was breaking. Only the Walker family kept a united front, hoping against hope. He cast a final glance towards Kanakammal, wondering when she would give up her lonely vigil and accept that her new employer was gone and that her hopes of a steady income were dashed for the time being. Ned assumed her family would be relying on it; no wonder she was willing Jack Bryant to survive.

Suddenly she turned her head sharply to the left, away from him and the main shaft, and in the direction of one of the three adits – the small access shafts – that linked with it. He assumed she was resigning herself to defeat. For some reason, he couldn't bear to watch her give up on Jack and he deliberately turned away.

Kanakammal saw them first, her gaze dragged to a separate access shaft that linked to the mine. From her high vantage on the hill, where she had stood alone through the long hours, she saw the unmistakable silhouette of Jack Bryant in the ghostly grey light of the dawn. He was on his hands and knees, while another man lay flat on his back next to him. She watched the man she was convinced was Bryant flop to the ground now. He was spent. The other did not move.

Both were covered in blood from head to toe and she paused a moment to stare at Bryant. She had reached out to him in her prayers through the night. And she had pictured herself travelling to him in spirit, finding him, urging him not to give up, to follow her back to safety.

And here he was. She had found him. And he had found her.

Kanakammal shouted, raising the alarm, pointing and gesticulating. She knew the Walkers had given up hope. They should have had more faith.

She was certain that the man lying next to her master was none other than the missing Walker son. Drake was much older but the man with Bryant was young.

People began to run.

The nice young Edward Sinclair was among the first to react to her cries. Amid the hysteria he took a moment to share a meaningful glance at her as he charged towards the adit, where she pointed. And Kanakammal nodded at him once – in joint relief – before she turned away and walked down the hillside.

31

Flora Walker described it as ghosts returning from the dead. Although Ned had reached the injured pair first, the Walker family had descended as one, screaming their joy until they registered the scope of Rupert's injuries.

Jack remembered little of that time. As soon as he had reached the surface, he had blacked out. He recalled only the sensation of a soft breeze caressing his bare skin and the banishment of the dark. As they'd got closer to the surface he did remember urging Rupert to stay conscious, stay strong and to look up; he wanted Rupert to see the light streaming down the tiny access shaft. It had felt like the eye of God smiling down upon them. It was in fact the dawn; they'd made it before an everlasting night had claimed them.

Now he was sitting up in a hospital bed, his arm in a sling, his body tight with bandages and every inch of him throbbing in pain.

Harold Walker, who had personally attended to his injuries, was now sitting on the edge of the bed. 'How are you feeling?'

'Sore,' Jack croaked, his voice like fresh sandpaper scratching on old paint.

The doctor nodded. 'Let me give you the litany of your injuries,' he said, smiling kindly now. 'They're impressive.'

Jack gave a lopsided grin. 'I reckon I can guess. Ribs?'

'Several broken. A sprained shoulder, or so you screamed when we tried to turn you over. Your back is a mass of contusions.'

'The rock slide in the aftermath.'

'Rupert has no such bruising. Did you shield him?'

'I can't remember,' Jack said.

Walker's eyes narrowed; Jack was being modest. 'You're seriously dehydrated. We've got you on a drip. Just be patient. I have no idea how you bore the pain carrying my son. It is a miracle either of you made it out.'

'Rupert?'

'Not as robust as yourself but he's a fighter, Jack. He'll come back from this.'

'His arm?' he croaked, hardly daring to hear to the answer.

'We amputated it a few hours ago.' Walker looked away, hiding the tremble at his lips. He cleared his throat. 'It's all very clean now. He'll learn to live with one good one.'

Even though Jack had anticipated it, the news was still a kick in the guts. 'Is he conscious?'

'Not yet. Rupert will need some time to adjust.'

'What about his leg?'

'His ankle was smashed up. We saved it but he'll limp, I suspect. When you've lost an arm, what's a limp?' His attempt at a philosophical approach fell short and sounded hollow.

'He lost a lot of blood.'

'Yes, he did. Your tourniquet saved his life, Jack.'

'Anyone would have done the same.'

Walker paused. 'I'm not sure that's true. Rupert was more or less a stranger to you, and our family hasn't been overly gracious towards you either. We've always considered you a dangerous influence over Ned, whom we care plenty for . . . and no doubt recent relations have become more frosty with Geraldine's interest in you.'

'Dr Walker, Geraldine —'

'Jack, you don't have to explain. I know it has been unsolicited and that's her burden, not yours. We owe you a great debt for your courage and your strength, your tenacity and your willpower.'

'Dr Walker, we kept each other going. We were blind down there but Rupert knew how to find the opening even in the pitch black.'

Walker nodded. 'He's a stickler for detail. But the point is that you chose to stay, to risk your own life for our son. I have to wonder why you did.'

Jack swallowed. His throat hurt. His mind was racing. 'I did it for Ned,' he lied. 'You're all the family Ned has and I know how much he loves you all. I couldn't have faced him if I didn't try – he's the closest friend I've ever had.'

Walker looked thoughtful. 'Well, I'm grateful for it, Jack, and I want you to know that you're welcome at our house, around our table, at any time.'

'Thank you, Dr Walker, and for patching me up as you have.'

'Don't mention it.' He held out a hand and Jack had to shake awkwardly with the wrong one. 'Ned's waiting outside. In fact, expect a long stream of visitors, all of them Walkers!' He smiled again and the warmth in it touched his eyes. Jack could see Iris in that smile.

Ned walked in, his face all but shining from a shave, his hair still damp but neatly combed. He held out a bottle of Scotch triumphantly. 'I'm not allowed to leave this here,' he said, beaming, 'but we're going to drink it when you're out.'

Jack whistled. 'That must have cost you a week's wages.'

'And the rest!'

They locked hands.

'I thought we'd lost you, Jack.'

'You can't get rid of me that easily.'

They laughed.

'Blimey, but I'm thirsty,' Jack complained.

'Your lungs must be charred.'

Jack wet his cracked lips. 'No one's told me how many made it out.'

'Seven dead. Two still clinging to life. Among the dead are Arnold de Souza and John Drake.'

Jack nodded. 'I held Arnold's hand as he died.'

Ned looked shocked. 'I had no idea.'

'If he hadn't guided me to Walker, I would have headed back.'

'Have you heard about Rupert?'

'Yes. He showed real courage.' He thought he could avoid the subject but she roared into his mind, defying his resistance. 'How's Iris taking it?'

'Badly. They're close. She's worried about what this will do to his state of mind. Rupert's ambitious and his career will stall.'

'It doesn't have to.'

'Try telling that to him.'

'I will. I'll tell Iris too.'

'You make it sound so easy, Jack. You always seem to get what you want, so you think everyone else can too.'

Jack let it go. He feigned a smile. 'Do you know what I really want? A motorbike.'

'What?' Ned looked at him as though he had suddenly started speaking in tongues.

Jack gave a crooked grin. 'I promised myself that if I got out of that damn hole I was going to treat myself to a motorbike. I'm going to buy a Francis-Barnett 292cc.'

'You're mad. You can't even use your arm.'

'I won't be like this forever.'

'Are you sure you didn't get rockfall on your head, Jack?'

His friend's laughter was reassuring. 'You'll love it when I drive you to Bangalore on it.'

'Can I get you anything? Bring you anything from home?'

'Food,' Jack replied, without hesitation. 'I need some decent food. It's like gruel here – all watery lentils. I want spices, I want some meat. Tell Gangai to buy some mutton and have the girl curry it up.'

'You mean Kanakammal?'

'How do you know her – and how on earth do you remember how to say that name?'

'She waited all night at the mine. She was the one who saw you emerge. She raised the alarm.'

Jack looked astonished. 'Are you sure?'

'She was there all night, I tell you. She didn't move. She looked like a guardian angel in that silvery-grey sari of hers.'

Jack gave a soft snort of confusion as a memory nagged on the rim of his mind. 'Well, she can cook my curry.'

'I'll go there now. Oh, by the way, I've been promoted.' He laughed as Jack's face lit. 'Anything you can do, I can do better.'

'That's great news, Ned. You deserve it. So, manager of the electricity department, eh? Looks as though we'll both have to be acting responsibly.'

'Not just that. I can get married now.'

Ned's comment brought with it a tension neither man wanted to acknowledge.

Jack cleared his throat. 'Really? Have you asked her yet?'

'No, but I'm about to.'

Jack's emotions were suddenly so mixed up he was at a loss; he knew he should congratulate Ned but he felt a stab of jealousy. 'Well, exciting times,' was all he trusted himself to say. He let his head flop on the pillow as though he were exhausted.

'I'll see you later, Jack. Heal,' Ned warned, wagging a finger. 'Don't rush it.'

Jack didn't know how to feel. Iris was Ned's girl. There was no two ways about it. But he couldn't get her face out of his mind and he hadn't been imagining it; Iris had flirted with him and given him all the signals – inadvertently or deliberately – that she wasn't fully committed to Ned Sinclair.

What a messy situation. Perhaps he should just avoid her, ignore her, and the feeling would pass. Once she and Ned were engaged, perhaps he would find it easier to set thoughts of her aside?

Jack's lids felt heavy and he drifted into another world some-where between consciousness and sleep.

———

Iris tiptoed into the room where Jack lay. Muslin curtains muted the sharp sunlight so the area around his bed was bathed in a soft golden glow. She had avoided Ned, guiltily watching from the long hospital verandah as he left the premises and sauntered across the beautifully tended gardens towards the main road. Once she was sure Ned had left and none of her family was nearby, she had found Jack's quiet room at the very end of a corridor.

Stepping silently across the floorboards, she held her breath, arrested by the sight of Jack's body, naked to the hips, the sheet carelessly draped across his lower belly.

Iris drank in the sight of him lying motionless and beautiful, like one of the marble statues she had marvelled at in the museum in London. Part of his torso was bandaged tightly. Her father had mentioned broken ribs. But the sight of his sculpted body, browned from the sun, dark nipples punctuating the rise of his muscles across his broad, hairless chest, the bones of his pelvis starkly contoured, making his belly dip, the space between sheet and skin at that point creating a shadow – it all made her heart race. She pulled her gaze away.

Now she began to notice the hideous criss-cross of bruises and scabs.

She looked at Jack's poor arm, held in a sling and propped up by a pillow. She had to resist the urge to smooth back the lock of hair that had flopped across his eye but she noticed the dark lashes beneath, the slightly frowning eyebrows as though Jack was deep in thought, even as he slept. He made little sound; just the faintest breath escaping his lips, the shallow rise and fall of his chest.

She couldn't help her hungry eyes from traversing his body again, even though she knew this was wrong. She felt herself blush as she imagined bending down and touching her lips to his, slightly open and so inviting. Iris coughed softly, almost hoping it would wake him and give her an excuse to kiss him brazenly, covering her real motive with a rush of thanks for saving her brother's life.

Iris looked over her shoulder. All was quiet outside and within. She took a breath and risked it, pulling off her glove. Gently, she laid her fingertips on his chest. Slowly, tenderly, she flattened her hand to Jack's warm skin. The bandages chafed against her palm, reminding her that she was on forbidden territory. Iris kept skin to skin for a few seconds longer, feeling his strong heartbeat in rhythm with her own, then lifted her hand away and imprisoned it again within the safety of her glove.

Mindful of the traitorous heat gathering at her neck, flushing her cheeks again and shortening her breath, she silently lowered herself into the chair beside the bed, where the man who loved her had sat just a few minutes earlier.

Iris waited.

———

Jack awoke in serious pain, with a raging thirst and a desperate need to urinate.

He swung his head around searching for a nurse and found instead Iris Walker sitting demurely by his bed, like a fresh spring flower in a buttery-yellow dress, trimmed with white. She looked achingly pretty and the mere sight of her calmed his distress.

'Hello, Jack,' she murmured coyly, as though she'd been caught peeping.

He couldn't speak. He looked towards the beaker of water.

'Oh, let me.' She leaned over him and carefully lifted his head from the pillow to help him sip.

The sweet scent of violets enveloped him and his eyes dipped instantly and helplessly to the spectacular glimpse of her satin brassiere cupping the curves of her breasts.

The effect on him was alarming and immediate. Jack jerked his knees up to cover his embarrassment.

'Oh, I'm so sorry. Did I hurt you?'

'Just a spasm.' He reached for the beaker from her hands. 'Thank you,' he groaned.

She smiled sweetly. 'Just ask if you need more.'

He wouldn't dare. A short, awkward pause stretched before them.

'How long have you been here?'

'Half an hour maybe. I didn't want to disturb you. But you were restless.'

'I was dreaming.'

'Yes. Even so, it was nice to watch you sleep. I mean, it was nice you were resting after all you've been through.' She sounded nervous. Her eyes kept flashing to his naked chest. 'Jack, I don't know how to thank you for what you did for Rupert, for our family.'

'Oh, that's easy, Iris. Save a dance for me.'

She laughed. 'Such puny payment.'

'It would make me feel rich,' he replied, an inner voice telling him this was dangerous ground.

'Then I'm all yours at the next opportunity for a dance, Jack Bryant. You've earned it.'

She stood, smiling. Jack's pulse raced at the thought of holding her in his arms again. She lifted a pot from the floor and pointed to a small tiffin, tied up in a teatowel, secured by its four corners. 'Mum's mulligatawny. All-healing,' she warned with a wink.

'Excellent. Thank you.'

'I'll visit again,' she promised and then surprised him by leaning down and placing a soft kiss on his cheek.

He caught her hand. 'I want that dance to be in Bangalore, Iris. At the bandstand in Cubbon Park.'

'Bangalore?'

'Promise me,' he said, not letting go of her gloved hand, even though she looked around self-consciously. 'I want to dance with you without your family breathing down my neck.'

She grew more serious. 'I-I can't do that,' she stammered.

'Oh, come on. Surely you owe me that much?'

Iris nodded. 'I don't like owing anyone. One dance.'

'One dance, in Bangalore, no family around.'

'All right,' she finally said. 'I promise and then the debt is paid.'

A fortnight later, with his shoulder more mobile and feeling much stronger, Jack returned to his home on the hill above Marikuppam. The servants had draped the verandah with fresh, fragrant blooms they'd painstakingly sewn into garlands of welcome. Jack was enveloped in the heady fragrance of the dense, waxy flowers, which would later be placed at small altars to give thanks for his return.

Gangai had the whole household – the butler, the chokra boy, the new gardener, the new girls and himself – lined up on the stairs to welcome Jack home. They all clapped as he climbed out of Harold Walker's car, followed by Ned.

Jack shook hands with each of the staff. Kanakammal looked down as she loosely gripped his hand and then let it go quickly. Her sheer pink sari, worn with a deep crimson choli, did little to hide her superb figure. Jack consciously averted his gaze from the creamy brown skin of her midriff.

'Thank you for your delicious food, Elizabeth,' he said. 'Each day it was something to look forward to. I'm sure it's why I am returned to such good health so quickly.'

She nodded but would not raise her eyes to him. 'You are welcome, sir.'

Soon enough, Jack and Ned found themselves alone on the verandah.

'Back to work tomorrow, Jack?'

'I can't wait. '

'What about the sling?'

'I'll manage, even if I just direct my men. Besides, the shoulder's feeling much better now. I'm even planning to go up to Bangalore at the weekend.'

'Why?' Ned sipped on the rich, sweet and creamy coffee that Gangai had served.

Jack reached for one of Elizabeth's small hot potato and onion savouries. 'My motorbike,' he struggled to say, trying to cool the spicy mouthful on his tongue.

'My God, you're serious! I thought that was delirium talking. That or morphine.'

Jack laughed. 'No, I intend to ride everywhere from now on. One day soon I'll buy a car. But I'll begin with my bike.' He wiped his hands on a starched napkin, impressed that his staff had thought of everything. 'What's happening with Bella? She's due any minute, isn't she?'

'I'm picking her up tomorrow. I can't wait to see her again. It's hard to believe she's finally going to be here and meeting the people I care about.'

'I get the impression you're hoping to persuade her to stay.'

'I am, Jack. That's exactly my plan. So I'm calling on everyone's help. The Grenfells have been so generous, but she's my sister, my only family. I want her to love Iris and for Iris to love her and hopefully she'll want to stay with us.'

'And Bella has no idea, of course, of your evil plan.'

'It will be her choice, come what may. She'll be a fresh breath of air after everyone's anxiety over Rupert.'

'He'll be fine.'

'You were very good to him in hospital, visiting him daily, I hear, and keeping his spirits up.'

'I was glad to see him recovering.' Jack recalled how he'd been careful to avoid being caught in Rupert's company when Ned and Iris dropped by, and was aware that Harold Walker on his rounds had always found a way to drop into the conversation if Iris was calling in on her brother. Jack realised he was being manipulated by the Walkers to avoid Iris, but that was all right. It suited him.

'How's it going with Iris?' Jack asked, looking away.

'Oh, well, Rupert's recovery has overshadowed everything, but I see her every day.'

Jack kept his voice even. 'Have you popped the question?'

'No,' Ned snorted, as if disgusted with himself. 'But we're close and I don't think it will come as a surprise to her.'

'What do you mean?' Jack said carefully, reaching for his coffee to hide the fact that he was grinding his jaw.

'Oh, you know. I'm not a fast mover like you, Jack, but we've certainly become more intimate.'

'I'm pleased for you,' he replied, feeling his gut twist. 'So, tell me about this promotion.'

'Everything's falling into place. Next week I'm going around to each of the mines. I'll be speaking to the managers about their power supply, what improvements we can make, how we can streamline the service. I know some of the smarter villagers – particularly shopkeepers – are trying to pinch electricity when we're transporting it from Shivanasamudra Falls, but they're going to kill themselves if it continues. One fellow is already dead.'

'How ingenious of them.'

'Everyone knows electricity is the future, Jack. It will make many men rich. Anyway, next week I won't be around much.'

Jack nodded, storing this information away. 'What about Bella? You're not going to just leave her, are you?'

Ned looked offended. 'She'll be fine. I'll leave her with the Walkers.'

'Well, why don't I take her out for a day?'

'Really?'

'Yes. Why not? I don't mind taking her into Bangalore. I can rearrange my shifts. I'll take her to the soda fountain, perhaps the movies at the BRV. I might even organise a guided tour for her.'

'Excellent, Jack, thanks. She'd love that.'

'It's a deal, then. When do you leave?'

'Monday morning.'

'All right. Tell her to be ready early on Monday and I'll pick her up. Clear it with the Walkers, though, will you?'

'Why don't you tell her yourself? Presumably we'll all meet up before then?'

'You're right. Why don't you bring her over tomorrow evening? I've got a cook now and can entertain fine company.'

Walker had lent Ned his car so he could collect Bella from Bangalore in comfort. Nothing was going to prevent Iris coming along too, and as they drove down the bumpy, potholed 'highway', Ned held her hand in a haze of bliss.

'Are you happy, Iris?' he said, breaking the comfortable silence between them after Iris had told him a long story about visiting the Redhill Street Mills in England's north and seeing all the beautiful textiles her employer's family sold. He continued to wonder why Iris had ever come back, given the starry-eyed way she spoke about her time in England.

'You know I am.'

'I mean with me. Are you happy with me?'

'Of course. What's brought this on?'

Now seemed as good a time as any. He took a deep breath. 'Well, I want you to be my wife,' he blurted.

'Ned! This is hardly the place to propose!'

'Why not? We're alone, we're holding hands, I feel happy. I've never been happier, to tell the truth . . . and I'm in love, Iris. In love with you.' Ned braked harshly, stopping the car with a skid that kicked up a pile of dust on the road and startled a bullock that had been ponderously pulling its load towards them. He leapt out of the car, held his hand up in apology to the bullock drover, and ran around to the passenger side. He yanked open the door and dropped to one knee.

Iris began to laugh. 'Ned, don't be a —'

It was as though he had wings and he was soaring high above the clouds, such was the lightness in his heart. 'I love you, Iris,' he began, grinning helplessly. 'There'll never be anyone else for me. I could never feel about anyone the way I feel about you right here, right now, so there's never been a more perfect place for me to say this.' Ned took her hand and kissed it before he looked into her dark eyes. 'Marry me, Iris. Say you will and make me the happiest man alive.'

They stared at each other for a few long moments before she touched his cheek and he covered her hand with his.

'Please, Iris.'

Her expression clouded. 'I need some time, Ned.'

'How long? An hour? An afternoon?'

She laughed. 'Ned . . .'

'Tell me.'

'By the next dance.'

He did a quick calculation. 'Nine days?'

'Yes.'

He felt crestfallen at first, but at least she hadn't refused him – and he had sprung it on her without warning. She was going to think about it, which meant she was probably going to talk it over with her parents and he knew they were already on his side. He felt confident as he returned to the car that Iris would accept him.

In fact, he was positively chirpy by the time they parked at the Bowring Institute. He and Jack had both taken out memberships there and at the Bangalore Club, so they always had somewhere to stay when they came up to town. It didn't matter to him that Iris had turned more pensive and their conversation was all but non-existent by the time he had eased her father's car into the manicured grounds of the club. Ned refused to believe that Iris wouldn't soon share his elation; he convinced himself that she was just being sensible and waiting for her family's official approval.

As he helped her from the car, Ned couldn't resist pushing his cause a little further. 'Iris, I've talked with your father about this.' At her sharp glance, he hesitated, then pressed on. 'It felt like the right thing to do . . . I mean, to get his permission.'

'Ah. And what did Dad say?'

Ned gave a wry shrug. 'Well, he said it was your decision, not his, but he and your mother would be very happy for us to be engaged.'

Iris nodded. 'They're very fond of you, Ned. But let's not talk about it any more now. It's all a bit much to take in . . .' Her smile helped allay his sudden anxiety, but he couldn't help feeling the smile took too long to arrive. He banished that notion and allowed himself to be diverted from all further discussion about marriage and the future.

'So, what about the station?' she asked brightly. 'What time is Bella's train in?'

'Not for another two hours.'

'Two hours! Why are we here so early?'

Ned reminded himself that this was a happy day. 'I'm taking you to Commercial Street,' he said, planting an affectionate kiss on her cheek. 'I want to buy you something. A gift. Whatever you want.'

His heart soared again at the way she laughed. 'You're mad,' she accused.

'Madly in love. Yes, officer, definitely guilty.' He grinned at her as they linked arms. 'Come on. Let's go shopping.'

Ned always enjoyed strolling through the warren of tiny vendors who formed a bazaar that sprawled out behind Commercial Street. One day soon he'd have to make an appointment to see his tailor who had a permanent shop in this area. There was a whole street of tailors – but his, the one Jack had found and recommended – was second to none and could cut a man a suit just by looking at him. Nevertheless, Mr Rau insisted on detailed measurements and could have the first fitting within seven hours. He was a magician, Ned was sure of it! He pointed out Rau's shop to Iris.

'A suit for you today, Master Sinclair?' the tailor inquired, emerging from the shadows of his shop to the open shopfront where his four workers sat on tiny stools, sewing on small treadle machines.

'Not today, thanks. I'm looking to buy Miss Walker here a gift.'

'Ah, sir,' he said, waggling his head and a fat finger in tandem. 'Do try Mr Ramesh's silk emporium around the corner. I hear he has some exquisite woven stoles in. Real pashmina, sir, from Kashmir. Very beautiful and genuine chyangara wool, sir. You can trust him, sir. He's my second cousin.' He smiled benignly.

'We'll take a look.'

'Ask to see the two-colour shawls. They take your breath away.'

They nodded, strolling on, Ned deliberately guiding Iris down the street of jewellers and assuming that what needed to be achieved would be easy because women and precious gems were like magnets, utterly irresistible to each other's pull.

He chatted amiably, pretending to be distracted and hoping something would happen soon. He was almost embarrassed that Iris was so predictable when he felt his arm dragged sharply in tandem with a small cry from her. The magnetic pull had occurred.

'Oh, Ned, look at that gorgeous ring!'

'Hmmm,' he said, deliberately vague.

'Look,' she said, pointing. 'I love sapphires.'

'Really? I would have picked you for a diamond girl.'

'Oh, I love diamonds too, of course. Which girl doesn't? But that setting is so beautiful. It would be an amazing stone if it was twice the size.' She sighed.

'Come on, Iris,' he urged, taking note of the store. 'I'd like to see those pashmina stoles.'

Reluctantly she allowed herself to be pulled from the window and even more reluctantly allowed him to buy her a superb dusky-pink pashmina stole that could be worn on its pink side or its smoky dove-grey side. But she was all but trembling with delight to own the delicate stole when he presented it to her. She wrapped her arms around him and kissed him briefly, joyfully, on the lips. He was sure he could have flapped his hands and flown from the shop he was feeling so light-headed.

'Ned, this is too much.'

'Rubbish. I like spoiling you. Besides, you're beautiful, Iris, and I want you to have beautiful things. I have no one else to lavish my earnings on.'

'There's Bella,' she reminded him.

'Bella has plenty and she's my sister. You are the twin half of my soul, Iris.'

At this ridiculous statement she kissed him again, laughing. 'I do love you, Ned. Thank you.'

He had heard men describe the feeling of being in love as though your heart were so full it could burst. Ned now understood the claim – his heart was swollen with so much happiness he was certain it was getting ready to explode. 'Right. I'd better get us to the station before I start kissing you passionately right here in the street.'

She gave a mock gasp. 'My parents would kill us. Come on. Let's not be late for Bella.'

32

A tall, golden-haired young woman alighted from the train and recognised Ned immediately. She waved furiously, her smile wide and open. If not for that smile, which reminded him achingly of his father, he would not have known Bella. The child was gone and in her place stood a lovely young woman.

He rushed towards her and swung her up into the air. She was slim and feather light and her laugh was exactly like their mother's. It brought tears to his eyes.

'Bell!' he exclaimed, his voice choked with emotion. He hugged her close. 'I can't believe it's you.'

Tears streamed down her face. 'It's me, Ned, but look at you! I always thought you were Mum all over again but you've definitely become Dad. Well, at least what I remember of him.'

'And you look like both of them rolled into one. You're a picture!'

'Thank you,' she said, pirouetting for him on the platform so he could admire her all grown up.

He grabbed her hand. 'Come on. I want you to meet someone very special.'

Iris had hung back, not wanting to intrude on the reunion of brother and sister.

'Iris,' Ned said breathlessly, looking fit to burst with pride. 'This is my sister, Arabella Sinclair.'

Iris didn't wait for Bella; Ned had warned her that she might be shy so she gathered Bella into a big affectionate hug. 'Welcome, beautiful Bella. Ned's told me so much about you. I'm Iris Walker, a friend of Ned's.'

'Bell,' Ned said, a mock tone of horror in his voice. 'Iris is not just a friend. She's the woman I hope will shortly agree to marry me.'

Bella's eyes widened with delight as she let out a squeal and hugged them both again. 'Oh, wonderful,' she gushed. 'I'm so happy for you. Ned's written so much about you, Iris. I feel as though I do know you. When's the wedding?'

Iris and Ned both laughed awkwardly.

'Well, he only asked me today,' Iris said, rescuing them from a difficult silence.

'What are you waiting for? He's such a catch,' Bella said, squeezing Ned's cheek. 'I have to pinch you to be sure I'm here.'

'Yes, he *is* a good catch,' Iris admitted quietly, more to herself than to Bella and Ned, who were talking excitedly. 'I don't know why I'm hesitating.' She gave a soft sigh.

Ned organised for Bella's two large trunks to be loaded onto a horse and cart and driven back separately to KGF. In the meantime he took a second carriage with the women back to the institute.

'Let's have a drink here before we head off down the dusty track to Kolar.' He glanced at Iris and gave her a reassuring smile. 'I'd be hard-pressed to find two more beautiful guests in all of India.'

Later, sipping fresh lemonades, Iris watched brother and sister as their conversation predictably turned to their past.

'I've often thought about visiting the orphanage again, seeing if there's anything I can do.'

Ned frowned at her in query.

'And, you know, close off some doors in my mind,' she said.

'It's probably best you don't go back,' Iris said gently. 'That wasn't a very happy time for a young girl.'

Ned thanked her with his eyes. 'Iris is right, Bell. We shouldn't be recalling it.'

'I disagree. It's the reason we're both here in India. I've come to terms with losing Mum and Dad – in fact, I'm often embarrassed that I forgot to miss them. The Grenfells have been so influential to me, a part of every day for the past six years. And they've given me a wonderful life – one I couldn't have had back in England or Rangoon, even if Mum hadn't died.'

Ned looked hurt, Iris noted. 'You make me feel so guilty.'

'Oh, don't, Ned, please,' Bella soothed.

'How's Arthur?'

'Would you forgive me if I said he's been more of a father to me than our own ever was?'

Ned felt a stab of pain on behalf of their father. 'Of course I would.'

Bella reached over and kissed Ned tenderly on the cheek. 'I know you loved him. Oh, listen to us. We should be celebrating being together.' She gave Iris a watery smile. 'Forgive me, Iris. I promise from here on it's all joy and laughter.'

Iris smiled reassuringly in return. 'So you're enjoying yourself, Bella? I mean, Madras suits you?'

'Oh, it's wonderful. While I didn't love school work, I did love school. I've made some great friends and there's talk that I can visit some of their families in Britain.' Iris could tell immediately that Bella's experience would be a far cry from her own, and even though Arabella Sinclair was an orphan, she was still born on the right side of the world to be instantly accepted. 'And I'll probably become a governess or teach French or something – I'm fluent now.'

'In French?'

'I've been learning it from one of the French wives. They lost their daughter rather tragically and she took a shine to me.'

'You've certainly landed on your feet,' Iris said, trying not to sound envious.

'I know! All my life needs now is a nice Englishman in it and it will be perfect.'

All three of them laughed, but while it was said entirely light-heartedly for some reason Iris chose to hear only cynicism in the remark.

———

Ned and Bella talked non-stop all the way back to KGF. If Ned noticed that Iris had become quiet, it didn't seem to trouble him.

'You see these trees that line our journey, Bell? They're mulberries.'

'Of course. We had one at home. Mum used to complain about our stained fingers inside the house.'

'Good memory.'

'I have so few, really, but the ones I do have are very vivid.'

'The miles and miles and miles of mulberries are because this region is famous for its silkworms.'

'Really?'

'Southern Indian brides are married in silk. Not everyone can afford it, but most families try to make sure their daughters have a pure silk sari for their wedding day.'

'Amazing.'

'The poor old worm has to die to keep the silk cocoon intact. They pierce them with needles or drop them in boiling water.'

Iris and Bella made sounds of disgust in unison.

'So, when do I get to meet the great Jack Bryant, Ned?'

'Well, he's asked us over for dinner. I hope you're up to it?'

'Oh, yes! Are you coming too, Iris?'

Iris looked around, slightly flushed. 'No. I haven't been invited, have I, Ned?'

Ned stared at the road ahead. 'Well, it's not like that. I think Jack just thought he'd like to do the right thing and make Bella welcome. I'm away next week.'

Iris felt a twinge of jealousy that Bella would enjoy Jack's undivided attention, but she checked her treacherous thoughts before they spiralled out of control. Ned had only hours earlier asked her to marry him.

'And before I forget, Bella, Jack's offered to take you out next Monday. It's a hike back to Bangalore, I'm afraid, but he'll make sure you have a wonderful time.'

'Lovely,' Bella exclaimed, clearly used to lots of attention. 'I do hope he's handsome,' she added, laughing, but neither her brother or Iris joined in.

Jack was looking forward to playing the host. Gangai and Kanakammal had set a fine table with the new European damask linen Jack had sent for from Bangalore. Setting up house was not cheap but Jack had spared no expense, finding himself unexpectedly in funds.

The house had been freshly painted inside and out and the gardens had been given a facelift. A tired, weatherbeaten property had been transformed into a grand gentleman's bungalow. You couldn't miss the house, set back from the dusty roadside with a circular drive. Jack felt like something of a country squire looking down on KGF from his wide verandah.

He was surprised to have received a letter from the family's Cornish lawyers while he was in hospital, informing him that a special fund had been allocated by his father to help him establish himself in the colonies. It was very curious after six years of polite but innocuous letters between himself and home. The first and unexpectedly generous allocation was wired to Jack's English bank in Bangalore and he suspected it had to do with the fact that his father had been ailing. Nothing serious, his mother had said, but Jack wondered whether the old man was softening; perhaps he was even missing having his family around him.

Anyway, he had already decided how to spend it. Lying in his hospital bed with too much thinking time, he'd decided he wanted to try his hand at business, just like the old man. He'd figured that the old shop at the top of Funnell's Hill could mint money if an investor took it on. He had no intention of giving up his new promotion but he could employ a good manager and have the best of both worlds; remaining in mining but being in business too. The shop had been vacant for more than a year and was falling into disrepair. It was begging for someone to open up a general goods store. It would be a grander scale of the petty shop of Chinathambi's. People would flock there if he ensured there was a constant supply of English goods, from jams to paper patterns for clothes. He'd have to find a manager to run it and a couple of staff, but there were so many large Anglo-Indian families and not everyone wanted to work for the mines. He'd wasted no time in quietly making an offer on the property, and by the time he left hospital he owned the deeds.

And that wasn't all. He intended to buy a house. He knew exactly where, too – just off St Mark's Road in the heart of Bangalore city. Within this area was an enclave of elegant, understated English-style bungalows. He was convinced that as the city developed, these leafy, quiet streets would become extremely desirable for British and Eurasians – especially so close to the private college for ladies and its companion Bishop Cotton Boys School.

As he had slowly dressed, hampered by his shoulder, he'd had

Gangai prepare a gin and tonic to privately toast himself for his acumen and his father for his sudden generosity. The promotion, the new business, the properties, his motorbike . . . life was looking very good. All he needed to make it complete was a wife; but here his daydreams faltered, for there was only one woman for him now.

He banged down the glass, his wonderful vision for the future shattered as he imagined Iris kissing Ned, sharing his bed as his wife. He knew he had no right to covet Iris as he did, but his feelings for her were so strong that he felt helpless to resist them.

A shadow moved in the hallway.

'Is that you, Gangai?' he yelled.

There was a pause before Kanakammal appeared hesitantly at the doorway. 'It is me, Master Bryant.'

'Well, you'll do. I'm struggling with this tie and my guests are due shortly. Can you help me, please?'

She stood almost eye to eye with him, which was disconcerting. He was used to bending to every woman he knew. He noticed she wiped her hands nervously on the front of her pale-blue sari.

'I hope you approve of my choice,' he said, realising it was one of the saris he had recently purchased for her. He'd given her sister a bright-green and a deep-red one. Gangai and the butler, as well as the chokra, had all new garments too.

She continued fiddling with his silk tie. 'Yes, sir. I would not wear this sari if I did not like it.'

Jack sighed. He suspected that, as meekly as she presented herself, no one could push her in a direction she didn't want to go.

'Do you know I dreamed of you?'

Kanakammal stood back from him, her face unreadable.

He didn't know why he was telling her this. 'When I was trapped in the tunnel, at my lowest. Exhaustion, pain, fear . . . it was all closing in on me.' Jack turned to the mirror. The knot was perfect. 'I think I was hallucinating, but you came to me in that dream.'

'Did it help, sir?' she asked quietly.

'Yes, it did. The vision urged me on. I found comfort in it.'

He suddenly felt naked for the admission.

'Then it matters not who appeared in the vision. It gave you courage.'

He nodded, frowning. Kanakammal was not yet seventeen, but her grave countenance, combined with her fluent English, lent her a maturity way beyond her years. 'Which missionaries converted your folk?' he asked out of interest.

'A Pentecostal mission, sir. We are Catholic.'

'So you believe in spirits, speaking in tongues and all that mumbo-jumbo?' It came out as an insult, although he hadn't meant it that way. He tried to soften his approach. 'Maybe that's why you're so good at language.'

'And maybe I did visit you in the mine when you were ready to give up, sir.' Her face was blank, the words bland and harmless, and yet the challenge couched within them was unmistakable. 'May I be excused?'

He nodded, confused. 'Of course. Is everything ready for dinner?'

'Yes, sir.' She left, the tinkling of her ankle jewellery sounding her retreat down the hallway.

Jack was waiting for them on the verandah. Once again Ned had been lent the Walker car and it reminded Jack just how thick with the family his friend was. Beside him sat a slim blonde girl with an effervescent smile, who didn't wait for her door to be opened. Ned shrugged at Jack as Bella ran lightly up the steps and flung herself into his arms. 'At last!' she gushed. 'I feel as though I already know you.'

Jack set her back down. 'Dolores, right?' he said.

'What?' she said. 'Oh, no, I'm —' And then she saw his smile and laughed. 'You beast!'

Where Ned was so self-contained, his sister fairly bubbled over with personality. She had sunshine in her voice, her hair, her smile.

'Forgive me. Bella, of course,' he said, taking her hand and bowing theatrically to kiss it. 'It's an honour to meet you.'

'Likewise, Mr Bryant.'

'You make me sound like my father. Call me Jack. Evening, Ned,' he said, slinging his good arm around his beaming friend. 'So you have her at last.'

'Indeed. And isn't she a picture?'

Bella again obliged with a twirl, basking in the admiration.

'I suggest you keep her under lock and key.'

'Oh, I intend to,' Ned warned.

'I thought a nice Pimms might get us started,' Jack said. 'Assuming Miss Bella is permitted?'

'She is!' Bella said. 'I'm allowed to drink Cinzano Rosso. And I've had Campari too!'

'Ah, the ideal aperitif,' Jack remarked, as Gangai arrived with his tray and jug of Pimms, chunks of ice fighting for room with lemon and orange slices, even a sprig of mint and a stick of cinnamon.

'Pretty,' Bella commented with a small clap of joy. 'Perfect for this gorgeous sunset. You surely have the best view in all of KGF, Jack.'

'I'm certainly very happy living here. Ned, have I told you about the property I'm buying?'

Ned nearly spat out his drink. 'What? Are the rumours about you stealing gold true, then?'

Jack wagged a finger, and proceeded to tell him about the annuity and the shop he'd bought and the house he planned to buy. It felt odd to admit to his parents' wealth but his mood was gregarious tonight.

'I can't believe you've never mentioned this previously.'

'It wasn't something worth mentioning. I was, I suppose, the estranged son for all these years.'

'Why?'

'Oh, nothing sinister. I think I just needed to make my own way. And no doubt my father approved of that independence. Anyway, it's not for public consumption,' he said, rubbing his hands. 'That means, young Bella, that when we go into Bangalore, you can help me sign off on the house I plan to buy.'

She gave a soft squeal of delight. 'I love spending other people's money!'

'Don't I know it,' Ned groaned softly. 'How many dresses can a young woman need, Bell?'

'Buy her another one,' Jack joined in.

'Jack, she's got dozens —'

'I insist. She should definitely take one home from here. Bangalore has the best tailors.'

'I can't wait!' Bella cried. 'Thank you, Jack.'

They both looked at Ned. He just shrugged. 'Whatever makes her happy.'

She leant over and kissed her brother.

'Come on. I hope you've brought your appetites because we've cooked up a storm for you.'

'*Nandri*,' Ned said to Kanakammal, hoping his pronunciation was passable. 'Your food is delicious.'

She murmured her appreciation, unsmiling, moving efficiently around the table but lingering by Jack, Ned noticed.

When the gulab jamuns, the highly sweetened local dessert, had been devoured and the dishes cleared away, the three diners sat back with sighs of satisfaction.

'Those were the best dumplings I've had,' Bella admitted.

'Normally they're saved for wedding or festival feasts,' Ned said. 'You're lucky, Jack. You've got yourself a fine cook.'

'Elizabeth,' Bella said, a little too loudly, 'I think your dumplings are delicious.' She sounded entirely patronising, Ned decided with dismay, and gave Jack good reason to chuckle at the innuendo.

Ned saw Kanakammal glance sharply at Jack; he registered her disappointment, felt it keenly on her behalf and watched her withdraw.

'Well?' Bella looked around. 'I thought I was being gracious.'

'In a rather condescending way, actually,' Ned admonished. 'I don't think people like Kanakammal need to be treated like —'

'Like servants?' Bella wondered airily.

'Bell, when did you develop this superior attitude?'

Jack leapt in. 'Oh, come on, Ned. I don't think she was —'

'Just a minute, Jack. Until Bell's twenty-one, I'm still her legal guardian and I'm entitled to guide her in how she carries herself.'

'Ned, are you saying I've let you down?' Bella asked, sounding deeply hurt.

'Not at all. But I'm just wondering how you can talk down to Kanakammal as though she is somehow less than anyone seated at this table.'

Now Bella just looked confused. 'Not less, Ned, but she's a servant. An Indian servant employed to serve Jack and his guests. I thought I was being perfectly gracious in complimenting her.'

'It's not what you said, Bell. It's how you said it.'

'Well, I'm sorry, but my manners are perfectly fit for Madras.'

'That's what I'm afraid of.'

'Oh, come on now, you two,' Jack soothed. 'Elizabeth probably didn't even notice.'

'More like you hardly noticed her,' Ned said.

'Don't start on me. What did I do?'

'It's what you didn't do,' Ned said, flustered now he was on this path. He hadn't meant for it to turn into a confrontation, but ever since Kanakammal's lonely vigil on that hillside Ned had felt she deserved better from Jack. But this was not his concern. 'I'm sorry, Jack. I must be tired or something. Really, it's been a splendid meal. Sorry, old girl, I didn't mean to be churlish.'

'Forgotten,' she said, making the gesture they used to make as children, as though waving away a harsh word. He did like that quality of Bella's to enjoy life and not to think too hard about it. While she might have developed a keen sense of the divide between English and Indian, she hadn't lost what had made her such a charming child.

'I just think she should smile more,' Bella added.

'Pardon?' Ned said.

'That solemn face is quite distracting. She'd be very attractive if she smiled.'

'Come on.' Jack said with finality. 'Coffee on the verandah and then we must let Bella get her beauty sleep.'

33

Jack planned to take the train into Bangalore. He'd had a letter delivered to the Walkers' house telling Bella when he would pick her up; what no one knew, except Kanakammal, who'd been charged with accompanying her sister to deliver the message, was that a second envelope had also been delivered. Jack had also written to Mrs Walker extending a polite offer to include Arabella's escort, should she require one in Ned's absence, in his plans for the day.

He knew Iris would read between those lines.

Iris was in the front garden picking flowers when Kanakammal and her sister arrived. The tall servant had pushed the youngster onto the property, choosing to remain outside the gates. Iris had accepted the letters, then glanced up, shielded her eyes from the sun and looked at the elder sister.

Kanakammal gave nothing away. She took her sister's hand and walked on, pretending not to notice the pretty Anglo-Indian woman.

'Mum!'

'In here,' her mother called from the drawing room, where she was dusting. She allowed no one else to dust her precious Limoges ornaments, a thirtieth wedding anniversary present from her husband. 'What is it?'

'A letter. From Mr Bryant, I think.'

Flora opened the note and scanned it quickly.

'What's he saying?' Iris asked, her heart hammering loudly.

'Well, he's suggesting that we might care to send a chaperone for Bella on her visit to Bangalore.'

Iris's heart skipped a beat. She tried to reply casually. 'Probably a good idea, given the way you lot all talk about him.'

'Oh, Bella's too young for his taste!'

'Well, I suppose Ned is comfortable with it, so why shouldn't we be?'

Flora frowned. 'Still, she's very young . . . Then again, Jack has redeemed himself fully in my eyes. In fact, I feel we must have him over soon.'

'What's your point, Mum?'

'No matter how welcoming we feel towards Jack Bryant these days, others might consider it appropriate if Bella had a chaperone.'

'Whatever you say,' she said airily. 'I'm going to take these flowers to Bella.'

She deliberately disappeared before her mother could speak again. Bella came hurtling out of her room, looking as fresh as the daisies Iris held, ready for her big day. She'd hardly stopped talking about handsome Jack Bryant and Iris suspected she had a full-blown crush. She couldn't blame her.

'He's picking me up at ten. That's in less than half an hour, Iris!'

'Don't look so worried. You're ready, aren't you?'

'I suppose so. Do you think I look all right?'

'You look gorgeous, Bell. That's a beautiful skirt and blouse.'

'Thank you. My dad had them sent over from England.'

Iris let it go. If Bella considered the Grenfells her parents, Ned was just going to have to accept it.

'By the way, Jack's sent a note. He seems to think you may need a chaperone.'

'But why?'

Iris laughed. 'I suppose you can't begin to see why.'

'I'm fine with Jack. I'm looking forward to it.'

I'll bet you are, Iris thought, vaguely irritated. Would this young, impressionable girl from Madras, with her beautiful English-rose skin and perfectly formed teeth, interest Jack?

'It's not that you need protection, Bella. It's just how it looks.'

Flora appeared. 'Ah, Bella, has Iris told you about Mr Bryant's suggestion?'

Bella nodded, somewhat sullenly.

'I actually think it's wise. Iris, dear, there is no one else.'

Iris felt her heart skip again. 'Mum, I was going to help up at the school today,' she protested but not too strongly.

'Oh, please, darling. And you didn't promise them you'd help out today, did you?'

Iris shrugged at Bella. 'Looks as though you're stuck with me.'

Bella brightened, her manners coming to the fore, glad presumably that it was Iris and not Flora Walker accompanying her. That would certainly have put a dampener on the day.

'I'll just get ready,' Iris said and retreated to her bedroom with a sense of triumph. She really didn't understand this feeling. If all Jack asked of her was a single dance in broad daylight, the debt would be settled, she'd have kept her promise and could get on with plans for the wedding. And yet, and yet . . .

She hadn't even accepted Ned's proposal . . . not officially anyway. She intended to, of course, because she loved Ned – had fallen for him long before they'd even met. His letters had helped her through the darkest days in London. It would have been easy to flee home but she didn't want to be seen as having failed. And so she had stuck it out, knowing she could rely on another of his pale-blue envelopes to arrive before too long.

He had sketched her pictures, described life in KGF and made her smile in each letter. It was easy to fall for Ned and his gentle, sweet ways. But where was that breathlessness she'd heard about that came with being in love? She wanted to hear the chorus of angels in her mind each time she looked at Ned. He made her feel like a princess; he adored her in the same way that Rupert and her father did. With Ned, it was easy to feel safe. But why weren't the angels singing?

Ned had shocked her last night. He had come around after supper and drawn her out onto the verandah, saying he had a surprise for her. 'Can't help it. I love your daughter,' he'd said to both parents, then gave Iris a look of something close to a plea. 'Say yes. Make me the happiest man in the world.'

Iris remembered how Ned had reached into his pocket, recalled how she'd held her breath. Surely not! Surely he wasn't going to . . . Yes, he was, all her fears confirmed as he presented her with a small, deep-blue velvet box.

'Be my wife, Iris,' he'd urged, opening the lid to reveal the sapphire that had caught her eye the previous week in Bangalore. It looked awfully small in its box.

'It didn't have diamonds in the shop,' she said in her panic.

Ned had simply smiled and it had hurt her heart to see that smile and how much love was in it. Why hadn't she tumbled into his arms and squealed her own joy? Why?

'I had a diamond set on either side . . . one for each of us.'

'Oh, Ned.' She'd felt as though she were watching this scene unfold in slow motion, its tension making her hold her breath. She'd reached to touch the tiny, exquisite ring but pulled her hand back and placed it self-consciously on her guilty heart. 'I'm overwhelmed,' she'd breathed, genuinely flustered.

Before she knew it, Ned had taken her left hand in his and slipped the ring onto her finger. 'We'll have it sized properly for you, my darling.'

She'd stared at it. The breath she'd been holding had been whisked away.

Ned had kissed her hand, and the ring. 'I love you, Iris. I promise I'll do everything in my power to make you happy.'

She knew that was the truth. She knew Ned would be loyal and constant – a wonderful husband. And yet. From the moment she'd clapped eyes on Jack Bryant he'd made her pulse race. Jack seemed to charge her with an electric current – invisible, tingling, dangerous. He was dangerous and exciting in ways Ned could never be. And it was nothing to do with his rugged looks or powerful stature. It was something darker, more mysterious, like the attraction of two magnets, or two chemicals, that are drawn powerfully together. She could not explain it but she had to have this one final dance with him. She had to be held by him just once more. Memories of him in the hospital . . . those few heartbeats alone with him had felt like an eternity.

In her mind she would have found a way to separate it and justify the dance because she was still officially unattached, but Ned had complicated everything with his declarations and his little velvet box.

'It's beautiful. Thank you,' she had found herself saying, and then worse. 'Of course I'll become engaged to you, Ned. But let's get this sized first or I'll lose it.'

Somewhere in her mind Iris told herself that by not wearing his ring, the engagement wasn't real. Her careful wording gave her a fraction more time. Until Ned's ring was on her finger, Iris would let herself believe she was not promised to anyone.

Her cheeks burned now, recalling that treacherous thought, as she searched through her clothes for her prettiest dress to wear for Jack.

34

Jack Bryant stood framed in the doorway. He wore charcoal trousers, but in the latest Oxford bags fashion Iris had only seen in magazines. With them he wore a pale linen jacket and matching vest, with a white shirt and silver-grey tie. He carried a trilby in his good hand and despite the sling looked so handsome it was hard not to gasp. Bella didn't hold back, of course. She shrieked with happiness as she ran up the hall and carelessly flung her arms around him.

He groaned, amused, and tried to hold her away from his shoulder.

It was a small consolation for Iris that Jack's eyes looked straight over Bella's golden curls to meet her own.

'Come, come, Bella, dear,' Flora said gently.

Bella stood back. 'You look very handsome today, Jack,' she said, unabashed. 'And quite heroic, too, with that swashbuckling sling.'

Iris tried not to let her irritation show.

'And you look like a pretty little flower,' he said.

Flora gave Jack a pained look. 'I hope you can contain all that exuberance, Mr Bryant.'

He gave a short bow. 'Please call me Jack, Mrs Walker. Hello, Iris,' he said pleasantly, and then instantly returned his attention to her mother. 'How's Rupert?'

'We're so pleased with his progress. He's so brave and deter-mined, and following all of Harold's advice and exercises to the letter.'

'I'm glad to hear it. I hope to visit him tomorrow, if that's all right?'

'Of course. And we'd like you to come around for supper soon. Especially as we now have something to celebrate.' Iris glared at her mother but Flora took absolutely no notice. 'Yes, Harold and I are delighted —'

'Have you heard the news, Jack?' Bella broke in. 'Ned and Iris are engaged. Just last night. I do hope I'm going to be a bridesmaid, Iris. But you mustn't put us in salmon pink. I look *ghastly* in that colour.'

Jack gave Iris a cool glance that spoke droves.

'Bella, dear,' Flora warned, 'you really must calm down. Any-way, that's the news. We're all thrilled, as you can imagine.'

'Congratulations,' Jack said to Flora. 'And especially to you, Iris. What a quick decision,' he said cryptically.

'It certainly took me by surprise,' Iris replied carefully.

'Now, Jack, I appreciated your offer for today and I've asked Iris to go along with you both.'

'I hope we haven't interrupted your schedule?' he asked Iris earnestly.

Iris could have slapped his handsome face. 'Oh, not at all. I'm looking forward to it.'

'Very good. Shall we go then, ladies?' Jack offered both elbows crooked and while Bella readily grabbed his good arm, Iris declined, careful not to bump his injured shoulder as he led them down the stairs. 'I'll have them back to you by seven at the latest, Mrs Walker.'

On the train into Bangalore, Jack worked hard to keep the conversation entertaining, never once going near the topic that felt as though it were boring a tunnel through his mind. He regaled the women with humorous tales of life in Penzance, of smugglers and pirates, and merchant ships. And then he turned his attention to the day ahead and outlined his plans.

'I've lined up a special treat for you, Bella.'

'Really?' she said, covering his hand with her gloved one. Iris saw only deliberate flirtation in every soft bat of Bella's eyelashes. She liked Bella but surely she'd been reading too many romantic novels? Jack seemed able to deflect it all with aplomb.

'Yes, indeed. You are to be driven around Bangalore like a fairy princess and at each mysterious stop there will be a clue given to you.'

'A clue? To what?'

'To your treasure.'

Iris tried hard not to purse her lips. How was Bella ever going to accept that the world was not spinning for her if Ned and Jack continued to spoil her like this? She turned to stare out of the window at the dusty brown landscape rolling by, now and then punctuated by a glimpse of a village or a town teeming with people. They'd recently passed by a level crossing where a huge queue of bullock drivers with carts loaded to capacity, men on bicycles, even a car, and lots of people on foot, waited patiently and waved as the train passed. The train driver gave a long whistle and children ran alongside the tracks.

'. . . won't we, Iris?'

'Pardon?' she said.

Jack's greenish gaze impaled her. She'd not given him solid eye contact all morning and now he'd trapped her with it as Bella dug in her bag, looking for something. 'I said, we'll make the best of it, while Bella is gone. While she's on her treasure hunt, you'll have to do the boring stuff with me, Iris. I have a house to inspect.'

'I'm a bit miffed I won't be able to help you choose it, Jack. That was the deal,' Bella said, pouting.

'I know, sweetheart, but it's hardly fun. What you'll be doing is fun, I promise. And we'll be at the other end in Cubbon Park awaiting you.'

There it was! The signal. He'd planned it to perfection, Iris realised, and blushed, rearranging the hem of her pale-blue dress.

Jack smiled disarmingly at her. 'I hope to buy this house, Iris, if it turns out to be suitable.'

Jack's come into an inheritance or something,' Bella explained. 'This is his second purchase. The first is a shop.'

Iris noted Jack's blink of irritation.

'It's an annuity, that's all.'

Iris simply nodded with a soft smile. What a dark horse he was. Who'd have thought he'd have come from a family that could afford endowments?

The train slowed and halted, one of its many pauses that were never explained but just accepted as part of the journey. Outside, Iris saw a small stallholder with people crowded around him. 'Are those guavas being sliced? I haven't had one of those for years.'

Jack suddenly stood up and disappeared, returning minutes later with fresh quartered guavas balanced on one hand.

'Ooh, chillied and salted,' Iris said, salivating. 'What a treat!'

They ate carefully, relishing the stinging bite of the chilli and the salty tang of the fruit. Iris felt Jack's eyes drinking in her every move. She tried not to be self-conscious and turned to Bella.

'You know Ned's hoping to persuade you to stay, don't you?' Iris said, finally, still trying to ignore Jack's stares across the carriage.

Bella's expression turned serious. 'Yes, I know, but, Iris, I have a lovely life in Madras. KGF isn't enough for me. Frankly, I don't know how you can bear to live there. I mean, it's a pretty little place, but, Iris, you were in London!' She hardly drew a breath.

'Besides, I think the Grenfells would curl up and die if I left them. Ned will be fine, especially now he has you. And after the wedding, he'll be thinking about starting his own new family.'

Iris saw Jack shift restlessly and stare out of the window.

'Well, just be sure to tell him soon of your plans, before he gets too carried away,' Iris warned.

Bella nodded. 'I'll come back down for the wedding, I promise.'

Iris wished she'd stop mentioning the wedding. Her guilt was intensifying with each reference.

'Did you bring your ring? Perhaps we could get it sized today?' Bella continued, much to Iris's despair.

'No, I'll leave it to Ned.'

'Oh, Jack, you should see it!' Bella enthused. 'The most perfect little sapphire, and flanked by two diamonds.' She put her joined hands to her heart. 'It's so romantic. A diamond for each of them.'

'Bella, don't be boring,' Iris tried. 'Men aren't interested in wedding talk.'

'It must have cost him all his savings, though, Iris. Ned's not exactly wealthy . . .'

Fortunately they were interrupted by the ticket inspector and the conversation died a natural death until Bangalore drew close and then the talk was all about their day.

Jack was as good as his word. He took Bella in an open carriage first to the Three Aces coffee shop in the middle of South Parade. Strong coffee was served by waiters in highly starched white uniforms with turbans the colours of rich jewels. The clientele was eclectic – one of the reasons Jack loved this place. There were writers, musicians, politicians, diplomats, khaki-clad soldiers, even academics, as well as travellers and locals like themselves.

He ordered dosas for three. Iris was impressed by his love

and knowledge of the Indian food as they tucked into the glorious savoury pancakes, folded over and filled with a soft potato and onion filling, with just the right amount of tart coconut chutney. She sighed as she finished her last mouthful; every bit as good as her mother's.

'On to the ice-cream parlour,' Jack announced.

Bella laughed. 'Have we got room?'

'We'll make room. A short stroll around the outskirts of Cubbon Park and then we'll be ready for our frozen delicacies later this afternoon.'

As they walked, Jack told Bella everything he could about this garden area of the city. He all but ignored Iris and she was beginning to feel every inch the gooseberry. He was very careful in his remarks but Iris was convinced that Bella couldn't completely be blamed for helplessly falling for Jack. Finally, he drew them back to where a beautiful little carriage awaited.

'For you, my lady,' Jack said, helping Bella up into her seat.

'Are you sure you won't come?' Bella implored.

Iris shook her head. 'It's your treat, Bell.'

'Now, pay attention to the clues, Bella,' Jack cautioned. 'Your guide today is a friend of mine. His name is Willie Burgess.'

'Madam,' said the middle-aged man. 'Welcome aboard. I know your brother. He once tried to drink me under the table and lost hideously.'

Jack grinned. 'So did I! Today Willie's taking you to all the landmarks.'

'It's my pleasure, Miss Sinclair,' Willie said. 'I'll have her back to you here in two hours, Jack.'

'We'll be waiting.'

'Have fun,' Iris called as Willie urged the horse forward.

'Bye, Bella. See you soon,' Jack waved.

Bella had looked back and continued waving until she was lost in the throng of South Parade.

Jack gave a huge sigh. 'At last. Another minute and my ears would have bled.'

Iris laughed. It felt dangerous and immediately exciting to be alone with him. 'I thought you did rather well.'

'What you saw this morning isn't the real me.'

'Oh, I don't know. You have a reputation for charming the ladies and you certainly did a fine job on Bella.'

'I'm simply being polite.'

Iris grew serious, as she stopped walking alongside him and turned. 'And I'm Ned's fiancée.' Jack stared back at her. 'I'm sorry, Jack.' She shook her head. 'I don't even know what I'm doing here. I thought I was coming to fulfil a debt but —'

'Forget the debt!' he said, cutting across her words. 'You owe me nothing.'

'Let's just walk, shall we?'

'Yes. Come on, let's walk back through the park.'

They strolled companionably, arm in arm, and for a time it felt curiously pleasant and innocent, no longer awkward.

'Do you love him, Iris?' Jack said suddenly.

Her cheeks began to burn. She shouldn't have hesitated. 'Yes.'

'Enough to spend the rest of your life with him?'

'How can anyone answer that?'

'Is there passion?'

'Jack, don't —'

'Don't what? Speak the truth? At least I'm honest. But you're starting your married life on a lie.'

'Don't say that,' she said, withdrawing her hand from around his arm. 'You have no right. You're his best friend. How can you do this to him?'

Jack stopped now and stared deep into her eyes. 'Why else are you here, Iris, unless you want to be with me?'

She slapped his face. The shock of her instinctive action was so great that she covered her mouth in horror. 'I'm so sorry, Jack. I...I...'

He moved his jaw back and forth. 'I probably deserved that.' He pulled her to a park bench. 'Here, just sit a moment.'

She moved in a daze, allowed herself to be seated. She couldn't believe she'd just done that – and in broad daylight. She turned to him, nearly sickened. 'Jack, I can see my handprint on your cheek.'

'Well, at least I'll have that.'

'Oh, stop it. Please stop. It's livid. You can't walk around like that.'

'I'll wear it as a badge of honour.'

'Bella will see and —'

'I don't care about Bella! I only care about you. Come on.'

'Where are we going?'

'Somewhere to let this mark disappear.'

He hailed a carriage, gave the driver an address and urged him to get them there quickly. It took only minutes before Iris recognised the area sometimes known as Westward Ho.

'That's my old school,' she commented absently, looking back towards the big gates of Bishop Cotton's School for Girls.

Jack paid the fare and took her into the front garden of a beautiful big house.

'Good grief. I used to know the people who lived here. I remember these trestlework monkey tops and the gates. I know this porch!'

'Really?'

'Yes, a lovely couple. He was with the military. Another doctor, I think.'

'Come on in,' he said, holding out a hand. 'I asked the person in charge of the sale to leave the house unlocked, so I could come through.' He led her in.

'Oh, Jack,' she said once inside. 'Look, these lovely terracotta floors. And it's so cool in here.'

'Let me show you, although perhaps you should be showing me through. The drawing room walks through those double doors to a good-sized dining room. Across the hall is another reception room, then a private sitting room,' he said, as they stood in the middle of the hallway admiring the symmetrical chambers that led off it.

The house was just as Iris remembered it. Dark wood panelling and parquet or terracotta floors.

'There are stained-glass windows too, aren't there?'

'Yes, but just in the smaller windows. I rather like the understated elegance.'

'I can smell pipe tobacco.'

Jack pointed to the drawing room and Iris followed his lead. 'I'm sorry to tell you that the doctor died a couple of years ago.'

'That's a shame,' she murmured. French doors led dramatically onto a wide back verandah, which would have surely been considered audacious and indulgent in its time. It suited Jack. She envied him the opportunity and the ability to purchase it. 'So, are you going to buy it?'

'I've bought it,' he said and for the first time she thought Jack Bryant looked vaguely sheepish.

'You're joking.'

'I couldn't wait. It's mine.'

'But what about all this furniture?'

Jack looked unsure. 'Apparently the family doesn't want it.'

Iris looked back at him aghast. 'But there are some lovely pieces – that sofa suite and this rather grand sideboard, more suitable for the dining room perhaps. And that wonderful hall stand.'

'I know. What can I say? There's furniture dotted all over. Do you like the house?'

'Oh, Jack, I love it! Aren't you lucky? I'd give anything to live in such a beautiful house.'

'Anything?' Jack gazed at her and she caught her breath. His face was very serious. 'It can be yours if you choose,' he said softly.

Iris narrowed her eyes and gave him a mock glare. She walked back out into the central hall, moving ahead of him down the worn central rug – a magnificent Indian design that must have been worth a fortune but was now ragged in parts. 'This house has a glorious garden if my memory serves me right,' she said breezily. 'A big jack-fruit tree, I'm sure.'

'Let's go take a look.'

He led her into the private sitting room and through another set of double doors onto the verandah that overlooked a dense, sprawling garden. And there was the jackfruit tree, laden with its large, heavy fruit.

Iris let out a soft squeal of recognition. 'We used to see who could throw the fruit the furthest,' she said, laughing.

'Needs some work,' he admitted, casting an eye over the rambling garden.

'Oh, this will come back so fast,' she said. 'Look at that huge mango tree as well. It's such a gorgeous property. You've done well and I'm envious.'

Jack smiled. 'I'm glad you approve.'

'So what on earth are you going to do with this place?'

'I'm not sure. I bought it as an investment. I know the military would rent it in a blink, so I'm not particularly worried about spending the money, but you know, looking through it today with you, I think I should do something with it for myself. Perhaps you can help me redecorate, make it beautiful again. A place I could call home?'

He was sitting on the low wall of the verandah and in that moment Iris glimpsed how vulnerable Jack Bryant was. He was popular and yet had no close friends, other than Ned. He was arguably one of the most handsome and eligible bachelors in all of south

India, yet he tucked himself away in a quiet community and refused to do anything more meaningful than date girls. In fact, Ned had told her how Jack did most of his carousing in Bangalore, where the wagging tongues of KGF couldn't affect him.

'You're such an island, Jack.'

'My mother used to accuse me of that failing.'

'I don't know that it's a failing. It's just a fact,' she said, drawn helplessly towards him. She touched his cheek. 'I'm so sorry about that. It's looking much better now.'

He covered her hand with his large one, turned it over and softly kissed the palm. Ned had done exactly that just days earlier, yet Jack's action was twice as sensuous, his lips so much softer. His tenderness and this sudden fragility melted her resistance and even though every last drop of good sense screamed at her to step away from him, she moved forward instead, and he was ready for her, already reaching to embrace her. He pulled her between his knees, buried his face between her breasts and clung to her with his one good hand.

She was helpless. Guilty tears fell but still she wouldn't break their bond; she began stroking his thick hair, leaned closer still, until he was moving, sliding upwards to stand, releasing his arm from the sling and then cupping her face in those big hands.

He didn't pause, didn't wait for a look that gave permission. He simply bent and touched his lips to hers very gently. There was nothing hesitant about it. He was in no hurry, but nor did he pause to see if it was all right to continue. He just drew her tighter into his embrace and Iris felt her own passion ignite. From that instant she couldn't have stopped even if she'd wanted to.

They kissed and kissed until she'd lost all sense of time and place. She felt his hands stroking, squeezing, but it was his mouth that was her centre now; his tongue, his breath, his lips making her dizzy, distracted, almost demented with desire.

If Jack hadn't finally broken off, she wasn't sure she could have. Suddenly his mouth was no longer on hers and she felt the loss keenly. Her breath came in shallow gasps and her lips were swollen but she couldn't hear birds, people, the odd horn of a motor vehicle; none of the usual sounds were impacting, other than his voice.

'I can't say I regret that,' he admitted, his voice hoarse. He leaned his forehead against hers. 'But any more and I couldn't be held entirely responsible for my actions.'

Her voice was equally raspy when she could finally respond. 'I hate myself.'

'Don't. It was my fault. All of this was my fault.'

'No, I thought I was strong enough. It seems I'm as weak as every other woman you decide you want.' She let out a half sob that was all frustration.

He pulled her close and held her to his broad chest as if to comfort her grief and anger. She wished Jack would be angry with her but he was being sweet and gentle. It was his tenderness that was undoing her; in fact, she was sure that if he'd been in any way rough, too eager in his passion, she would have found it easy to push him aside. But not this. Not this soft, vulnerable side of him. He kissed her hair, the tops of her ears and then buried his face in her neck.

'I think I fell in love with you before I'd even met you,' he mumbled.

'What? How?'

'Ned showed me a photo of you.' Jack chuckled, cupped her face again and kissed her softly, just briefly. 'You were a child. Perhaps fourteen. A blurry family snap with your arms around your father.'

She smiled. 'I know the one.'

'There was something in that look. Something that caught my attention and wouldn't let go. And when I saw you the first time at the dance, I was lost in your dark eyes, and then I knew I loved you when you told me your secret. Does Ned know yet?'

She shook her head sadly. 'It doesn't seem necessary.'

'Why did you tell me, then?'

'Because you seem to look right into me, Jack.' She turned away but he pulled her back. She shook her head. 'We must stop.'

'Must we?'

'Before it's too late.'

'Too late?' He gave a harsh, mirthless laugh. 'Too late for what? To fall in love? Well, it's already too late for me, Iris.'

'Jack,' she said, her heart filled with guilt and pain, as much as love and desire. 'We can't do this to Ned. We're his closest friends.'

'We could leave. We could go to Bombay, or on to Australia. I hear there's a good life to be lived further east. There's gold mining out there. Or, I'll take you back to Britain. To Penzance. We could —'

'Stop,' she said, tears welling now, as she covered his mouth with her hand to still his words. 'Please. We don't have a future, Jack. What we've done today is unforgivable but it's still not too late for us to rescue this.' She held up her left hand. 'I purposely didn't wear his ring, you know. I told him that until the ring was sized and on my finger, we wouldn't be engaged. So, right now, Jack, our consciences – well, yours at least – can be clear.'

He shook his head. 'You're deluding yourself, Iris. We've both betrayed Ned; we're as guilty this moment as if he were walking in right now to find us naked —'

She hushed him again, as if by covering his mouth she could prevent the guilt from wrapping itself around her. Jack didn't try to finish his sentence. He just looked broken.

'Why does he get you?' he asked.

'Because you can have any woman in KGF, Bangalore . . . hell, the whole of India or the colonies. You'll never lack for women who want you, Jack.'

'I don't want other women.'

'Ned doesn't have the luxury of other women. There's something so fragile about Ned. I suspect it has to do with him losing his parents so tragically and then that whole business of his friend in Rangoon. I'm not sure he's ever told me the whole story, but —'

'One day you must get him to tell it . . . all of it,' Jack replied and there was a cruel edge in his voice suddenly.

She ignored it. 'All I know is that he's somehow . . . somehow damaged from the experience. If I hurt Ned now, it could be his undoing.'

'And so you'll give your life to him . . . to protect him from himself?' Jack asked, aghast.

'It's only you who makes me unsure of myself. I thought I loved Ned. I thought I could be happy with Ned.'

'And now?'

'I still can be – if you stay away from me.'

'I can't do that.'

'Jack, do you really love me?'

'I really love you.' He looked unwaveringly into her eyes. 'I've never admitted that to any woman before.'

She refused to smile. 'Enough that you would stay in India – no, let's say Bangalore – forever and never feel the pull of Britain, or adventuring, again?'

'I —'

'You need to be honest.'

'At this moment my head is filled only with you. But why can't we be together and allow our future to be shaped by events? Why must I commit now to where you want us to live for the rest of our days?'

'Because only then will you understand what true commitment to me really means. It's not just me. It's my family, it's my lifestyle, it's being Anglo-Indian.'

He shook his head unhappily. 'What about my family? My lifestyle? What about being Cornish?'

'Exactly. Ned will make the sacrifice.'

'Ned has nothing to give up.'

'Ned is safe, Jack. Not only will he be a good husband but he truly and completely worships me.'

'Iris, Ned worships everything you represent – it's a bonus that you are beautiful and so easy to love – but what he searches for is stability and family and a place to belong. You offer him that.'

Jack was right but his comments didn't make Ned less suitable in her mind. 'And do you love Ned?'

'He's the brother I never had.'

'Then for the sake of the two people you love best, let me go. I can't be strong without your help.'

Jack stood, struggled to wrench his jacket off and flung it on the ground. He undid his waistcoat, as though needing more air, and then stalked away. She watched him retreat, absorbing every detail of his tall, strong body.

She distracted herself by picking up his jacket, dusting it and holding it close. Jack was leaning against the side of the house, gazing out into the garden. She heard him make a sound – a groan of sorts – like an animal in pain. And then he turned and the wounded look in his expression nearly sent her careening towards him. She squeezed the jacket closer and gritted her teeth, letting his pain roar at her as strongly as if he'd shouted it. But his pain was silent now – a grief-stricken resignation.

She looked down so she wouldn't have to witness his capitulation and noticed a watch on the ground. 'What's this?' She bent and picked it up.

Jack walked over, offered a hand and she placed it into his palm. 'It's my mother's,' he said, his voice hollow.

'It's so beautiful.' Iris stared closer at the tiny blue face, the sparkling diamonds that encrusted its frame and formed a pair of exquisite V-shaped links either side of the face. She touched the clasp, magnificently wrought in silver in the shape of two tiny hands holding each other. 'It's the loveliest watch I've ever seen. Doesn't she miss it?'

Jack shrugged.

'And you carry it around with you?'

'I'm never without it. Try it on.'

She shrank back, torn. 'Oh no, I couldn't,' she said, but her hungry eyes said the opposite.

'Here, just try it. It'd be nice to see it on a woman's slim wrist again.' He undid the delicate clasp and placed the watch around her wrist.

Iris sucked in a breath. The diamonds caught the sun's rays and glittered with a fiery response to their touch. 'Jack, it's divine. How could your mother part with it?'

He looked embarrassed. 'She wanted me to keep something of her close.'

'But it's so precious. I would never let it out of my sight if this were mine.'

'It's with me every moment of each day. It's my family, my Cornwall, my former life.'

'You sound sad.'

He sighed. 'I don't actually look at it that often for that reason. I just dutifully move it from pocket to pocket as required. It's a habit now.'

'Well . . . if you ever want someone to wear it so you can see it on a wrist and admire it from a distance, you only have to ask,' she said archly but undid the clasp and offered the watch back.

'I guess I'll give it to my wife,' he said, holding her stare until she had to look away.

'Come on, Jack. Show me through the rest of the house.' Iris turned, not giving him a chance to respond, returning through the double doors that led into the sitting room. She didn't wait, but heard his footsteps, gritty against the unswept verandah.

At least he was moving, following. The moment of madness had passed. Or so she hoped. But her heart was still pounding with anticipation and her throat felt tight with tension. All it would take was for Jack to touch her and she was sure her skin would sizzle from the heat he was creating around her, deep within her. She fanned herself with her hand and walked on – and realised too late her mistake.

Several large bedrooms led off a T-shaped hallway and she had stepped into one, almost blindly, just trying to keep walking, remain distracted and not think about her breasts suddenly feeling heavy, her nipples aching.

And now Jack blocked the doorway. She would not be able to get by him without touching him, without wanting to touch him! Iris stepped further into the room feeling damned by her own lack of will to walk out but even more so by the huge four-poster bed. Faded curtains were half drawn and through the large windows she saw a camellia bush, more of a tree actually, that gave them secrecy.

Iris felt her cheeks grow hot. She wasn't even sure she was still breathing. She turned suddenly on him. He stood as still as a sculpture, leaning against the doorframe, filling the space, his eyes darker, impaling her with a hard gaze.

Jack pushed off the doorframe, not permitting her to look away from him. She flinched, frightened, yet excited. Oh, she wasn't this sort of girl! It was as though someone else was walking in her body and she was as helpless as a puppet, dancing to the strings of desire that suddenly controlled her.

'Iris,' he said, his voice thick and husky.

'Jack, we mustn't.' The words at least sounded right. They were the correct ones to say, even though it was already far too late for them.

Opportunity, privacy and desire . . . they had come together in perfect synchrony and now the choice was all hers. Jack paused, still not touching her but standing so close she could feel the heat radiating from his body.

It was her choice. He would not make it for her.

Iris chose.

She allowed her face to close the few sparse inches between them and laid her cheek against his chest, and then she was in his strong, all-enveloping embrace . . . and she was lost.

Iris didn't remember him picking her up and laying her on the bed. She didn't even remember Jack undressing her, although later she'd recall the moment where she seemed to step back from her own body, watching him remove his clothes. He was clumsy from his injuries but she refused to help. She simply watched, mesmerised by the sight of him, so overwhelmingly powerful in his naked manliness. There were no curves to Jack, or even the suggestion of round shapes; he was all hard muscle and flat, strong angles.

And as he kissed her, at first so gentle, so tender, tears squeezed out of her eyes to run into her hairline. Bittersweet tears of sadness for Ned. But that sadness was swept away by a primal elation that she was here, in the arms of a man she wanted more than any other.

Both of them were breathing harder, both of them were ready, and when he asked the question and she nodded, he guided himself into her gently and carefully. There was pain, but Iris welcomed it, and her gasp that made him hesitate was one of satisfaction and relief.

Instinctively she urged him closer, and with his kisses deep and demanding now, let herself go completely, following his rhythm, her treacherous fingers tracing every inch of him, committing him to memory, for she knew this was the first and only time she and Jack would ever have this excitement . . . this helpless, hopeless passion that overrode all sensibility and conscience.

They lay within each other's arms, enveloped by a thick silence laced with hesitance, and although Iris would not say deep regret, it was certainly tinged with a ruefulness that she knew she would never shake off. And yet, in a strange twist, she could already feel a jealousy creeping up on her. While she knew she could never choose to have Jack like this again, she already despised every other woman who would feel him inside her, feel his kisses against her skin, feel his hands on her.

It would take a simple yes and she and Jack could be together, but for how long? As heady as this moment remained and as exciting as making love with Jack had been, she knew deep in her heart that Jack was a philanderer. She suspected his adventuring, almost heroic nature that made him so attractive also meant he was not a man who could remain still long enough to be a committed husband. Ned was neither exciting nor dashing but he was solid and trustworthy; he was reliable and she suspected Ned would fall in love only once in his life. And he had chosen her.

It was a terrible decision but she had to make it with a cool head and not get caught up in the fizzing hysteria of passion and desire. She and Jack shared a chemistry. Her body, without her permission, without any help from her mind, was reacting to Jack in a totally instinctive way. Was this her excuse? Were they simply helpless? She thought they were, although Ned would never see it that way . . . or her parents. The image of her father frowning in disappointment and her mother's pursed, angry lips roused Iris into action.

'How much longer have we got?' she asked suddenly as the bubble of passion burst invisibly and silently to release them from its spell.

'Time enough for the dance you promised,' he replied, stroking her breasts.

'Let me dress and I'll fix my lipstick.'

'I hate lipstick.'
'Most men do but we feel naked without it.'
'I'll always prefer you naked.'
And they both smiled sadly at the poignant, accidental joke.

35

Jack took Iris back to Cubbon Park. His watch told him he had twenty more minutes alone with her before Bella rejoined them. He couldn't imagine how he would preserve the façade he had maintained with Bella earlier that day. He dreaded having to face her gushing ways and her embarrassing efforts to flirt with him again.

The octagonal bandstand came into view, its cast-iron lacework at its prettiest in this afternoon light. Plenty of strollers and music lovers had gathered. Some were seated on the chairs around the stage, others stood by to hear one or two songs, and dancers twirled elegantly to music being provided by one of the military bands. As they drew closer, the music changed from an upbeat tempo to a gentle waltz.

He found a smile. 'They're playing our tune.'

'My mother's favourite,' Iris admitted.

'I know. Rupert and I sang this to keep our spirits up when they were at their lowest. It kept him conscious. I could almost say it saved our lives.'

'That's touching and fitting, then, for our farewell dance.'

'You know it doesn't have to be farewell, Iris.'

'It must be, Jack.'

'Just dance with me.' He led her onto the dance area and drew her close, their bodies melting into each other again with a deep recognition.

'Are you sure you can . . . with your shoulder?'

'After what we just did?'

Iris blushed instantly, and he knew it was unfair to bait her. She didn't deserve that.

His voice softened. 'I could bear any pain if it means I can hold you.'

Iris smiled sadly. 'Do you recognise anyone here?' she asked nervously.

Jack cast a careless glance around. 'No. Nor do I care.'

They danced and within moments he was oblivious to the people sharing the tune with them – it was just Iris, himself and the music. Closer and closer he pulled her, their steps shortening until they were barely moving. Other couples danced around them as they put their cheeks together and became lost in each other once again.

———

Bella Sinclair was sitting in the carriage clutching a handful of written clues, each one given to her at individual stops of their tour around the city.

'It's a dress, Willie! He's going to give me a dress!'

'Aye. I guess you've worked it out, Miss Bella.'

'I've had a wonderful afternoon, Willie, thank you. It's a beautiful city.'

'I said I'd wait with you. They shouldn't be long. We made good time and we're a few minutes early.'

'I can hear music,' she exclaimed, as he helped her down from the carriage.

'The Royal Air Force might be rehearsing for tonight's music presentation. People will even be dancing.'

'Dancing! How lovely. Oh, I must see.'

'I can't let you go alone, Miss Bella.'

'Then come with me, Willie. We can't miss Jack and Iris. They'll be coming down this pathway anyway, won't they?'

'I suppose.' He tethered his horse, gave it a nosebag.

She patted the horse goodbye. 'Let's hurry, Willie. I want to see the dancers, and I love this tune – so sad and romantic.' She began to hum to the Irving Berlin hit as she sped closer to the bandstand.

Willie was hurrying to catch up with Bella when she suddenly stopped so abruptly that he nearly collided with her back.

'Miss Bella? Are you all right?'

She was silent, rooted to the spot, looking shocked. Willie searched for whatever her gaze had locked onto. He shouldn't have been surprised but he felt for the young woman, who had gushed excitedly about Bryant, and whose lip was trembling now to see him in the arms of the other woman.

'Ah, lass. Perhaps we should have waited with Horace,' was all he could say.

Jack reluctantly pulled away from Iris, ignoring the disapproving glances of the older people.

She was struggling too, he could see it in her eyes. 'We'd better go,' she said.

'We still have a few minutes,' he said, desperate to kiss again and rekindle the memory of the last couple of hours.

She didn't resist, instead melting against him as he led her from the bandstand, perhaps equally desperate for a final moment of intimacy.

'Iris, I —'

'Jack Bryant? Is that you?'

Both their heads whipped around guiltily. Jack took a moment to recognise the man before him. 'It is you, you old rogue.'

'Henry! Bloody hell! Where did you spring from?' He shook Henry's hand.

'You obviously didn't get my letter. Ah, well, that's Indian post for you. I would have got word to you anyway through the mine. I only arrived this morning, so don't feel bad,' Henry said. He raised his hat. 'Forgive us,' he said to Iris. 'My very rude friend is not introducing us. I'm Henry Berry,' he said, giving a short bow.

Jack faltered, but it couldn't be avoided. He had to say her name. 'I'm sorry. Er, Henry, this is Miss Iris Walker from Kolar Gold Fields.'

'Pleased to meet you,' she said, allowing Henry to gently take her hand. 'Are you enjoying the music?'

'My word, yes. I love this spot. I see you two were enjoying it too.'

Jack felt Iris stiffen beside him. 'Iris is recently returned from London and was determined I dance this hit tune with her. Henry, do you remember Edward Sinclair? Iris is the daughter of the doctor you met with Ned. Harold Walker.'

'Oh, right. Yes, I recall him.'

'Edward Sinclair is my fiancé,' Iris said flatly and Jack could tell she was determined to do her own damage control.

'Oh,' Henry faltered. 'Oh, right. Top show. Er, congratulations,' he said.

Jack didn't think Iris had helped their cause, but it was too late now. He sighed inwardly as she continued, the additional and unnecessary information only deepening the air of guilt around them. 'I'm chaperoning Ned's sister, Arabella, as Jack promised to show her around Bangalore.'

'Right,' Henry repeated, obviously embarrassed.

'So how long are you in town for?' Jack said, trying to steer the conversation away.

Henry brightened. 'I'm going to be based here for a brief spell. But I'll be doing short hops into Madras. You're still enjoying life in KGF – work going well?'

Jack nodded. 'Senior engineer,' he replied.

'I wouldn't doubt that for a second, Jack,' Henry replied, smiling nervously at Iris. 'Anyway, I'm at the club for now. I expect to be seeing you regularly, old chap.'

'Any developments with Eugenie Ross?'

Henry blushed immediately and his nervous tic reappeared. 'I'm deeply aggrieved to say she married some roughhouse Australian mining magnate and they're disgustingly happy, horrendously wealthy and living in Melbourne, I believe, with two young children to boot.' He gave a sound of feigned despair. 'I don't even have a budgie to welcome me home.'

Jack had to laugh. 'I'm sorry, Henry.'

'Don't be. Eugenie and I write often. We're dear friends, to tell the truth, and that's almost as good.'

'Jack?' came a sullen voice.

They all looked around.

'Bella!' Iris exclaimed. 'Oh, I'm sorry. Are we late?'

'I guess you were both distracted.'

Jack heard anger in her voice. 'Bella, this is a good friend of mine, Mr Henry Berry.'

Henry looked instantly mesmerised. 'Enchanted,' he said, taking her hand and bowing over it. 'I didn't know Cubbon Park attracted angels.'

Jack groaned but at least Henry's comment won a smile from the near-scowling Bella.

'I hear you're visiting?' Henry continued.

'From Madras, yes,' she replied, regaining some composure and remembering her manners.

'Well, well, Miss Sinclair. I shall be in Madras in the next few weeks. May I take you out for afternoon tea, perhaps a picnic at the lake? I'll have a car and driver at my disposal. All chaperones are welcome,' he said, darting a glance at Iris.

'That would be lovely, Mr Berry. It appears I might be returning sooner than I'd planned,' she said and Jack heard the unmistakeable barb in it. 'My stepfather is Dr Arthur Grenfell, married to Amelia . . . Millie. We live in Georgetown and our family would be glad to receive you.'

'Excellent! It's a date, Miss Sinclair,' he said, even daring to kiss her gloved hand. 'Well, if you'll all excuse me,' he said, no doubt sensing the tension as he tipped his hat to the ladies. 'I'll continue my walk. Stay in touch, Jack. Telephone the club.'

They murmured farewells and watched Henry disappear around the next path.

'Everything go smoothly, Willie?' Jack asked.

'I think I showed Miss Bella everything she needed to see, and no doubt a few sights she didn't,' he answered. It was said with levity but Jack's heart sank.

'Right. Time for your treasure to be revealed,' he said, loading on the false brightness.

Bella's mouth twisted. 'Jack, if you don't mind, I'm not feeling terribly well. Could we please go home?'

'Home? Bella, there are three amazing ice-cream flavours awaiting you at the Lakeland Milk Bar . . . and I'm sure you've guessed that my tailor wants to measure you up for a beautiful dress.'

Her sour look refused to budge. 'Perhaps the dosa has upset me. I do think it's best to return home. I had a lovely morning, though,' she said, adding a not very sincere, 'thank you so much.'

There was nothing for it but to return to the station and take the two o'clock train home, the journey mostly silent. There was so much Jack wanted to say to Iris but he maintained the frigid quiet in their carriage and even in the horse and cart taxi he hailed at the station to drop the ladies back at Oorgaum. After he helped Bella down from the wagon, she barely paused to whisper a hurried farewell before she was running into the Walker house.

'She knows,' Iris said, alighting the carriage.

'What does she know?' Jack asked, angered now by Bella's childish behaviour. 'At worst she saw us dancing.'

'Yes, cheek to cheek.'

'So what?' Jack said and paid the driver. He waved the man away. 'It's her word against ours. Say nothing, Iris. Don't give her accusations room to breathe. Treat them with contempt. You're the adult. Act like it.'

Iris nodded. 'I'm surprised. It sounds as though you actually care what others think.'

'Of course I care! Listen, Iris, if you choose me, it's because you love me. But I'm not prepared to rub Ned's face in anything or make trouble for him if you don't. Not like this.'

'What about Henry?'

'Henry's a man of the world,' he said, as though that answered a wealth of questions. 'Stop worrying. We did nothing.'

'Jack! How can you say that?' she said, distraught, but turning her back on her parents' house in case her mother was watching. 'I can see taking my virginity was meaningless to you.' Her face was pale with anger.

Jack ached to reach out to her but knew he couldn't. 'I mean, what we shared privately remains private,' he said in a firm, low voice. 'I will never forget our time together at the house. Never!'

Iris fought back tears.

He took her hand politely and bent to kiss it, saying in a low voice, 'Make a choice, Iris. Don't think about others, or how it will look. Make a selfish choice. It's the rest of your life. And it's no good living a lie.' He gave her one final hard look. 'And know that I will never love another woman as I love you.'

He turned and left her at the gate.

———

Iris knocked on the door of Bella's room but there was no response. She opened the door. 'Bella?'

'Go away.'

She walked inside and closed the door. Bella was lying on her bed, staring through her mosquito net to the ceiling. 'What is this all about?' Iris inquired.

'As if you have to ask.'

'I do, because I want to understand.'

'Why are you acting so innocently, Iris?'

It was time to be firm. 'I really don't know what you're talking about, young lady.'

'I'm talking about you and Jack, behind my back, but worse, behind Ned's back.'

Iris felt her alarm take wing like a flock of birds rising as one. But she kept an outward control, feigning confusion. She had to. This was too dangerous. She wasn't ready to lose Ned. 'What are these delusions?'

'Iris, did you think I didn't see you dancing cheek to cheek with Jack?'

Iris laughed scornfully, despite the fear crawling up her spine. 'Cheek to cheek? You are delusional. Poor Bella. While killing time waiting for you I agreed to a single waltz with Mr Bryant, that's all.'

'Oh, *Mr Bryant*, is it? Well, it looked a lot less formal from where I was standing.' Bella was all but shouting.

'Girls, girls! What's all this noise?' Flora exclaimed, rushing into the room.

'Sorry, Mum. I think Bella's upset stomach is more of an upset head if you ask me,' Iris said. 'She's got it into her mind that Jack Bryant and I are lovers.'

Her mother's shocked expression stunned both women. 'Bella! I hope you can back up such a wicked, wicked accusation.'

Bella looked less certain of herself, Iris was pleased to see.

'Well,' she hesitated. 'I know what I saw,' she said, ripping aside the mosquito net and swinging her legs down from the bed. 'Iris and Jack were dancing as though *they* were engaged.'

Iris turned away from Bella's pointing finger to her mother with a scathing look of disdain. 'Yes, we were *dancing*. Since when was that a sin? Mum, Bella might have seen me sharing a waltz at the bandstand, in the open air, in the middle of the afternoon, with dozens of onlookers, but that doesn't make us lovers! Her claim is as ridiculous as it is hurtful and this is plain mischief-making.'

'What?' Bella screamed. 'Why would I?'

'Listen to me, you spoilt little girl!' Iris said. 'You've acted half your age since you met Jack. Your flirtations with him today were sickening – and not just to me. I can assure you he was very uncomfortable with your juvenile behaviour. But everything about today was for your benefit, Bella, and your actions are unforgivable. The sooner you go back to Madras, the better for everyone, especially Ned, if this is how you reward all his love.'

Iris stomped from the room and into her own, breathing rapidly, hardly daring to believe what she'd just said, what she'd just done. It was only when she'd closed the door that she permitted herself the tears of shame that freely came and streamed down her face to cleanse her skin of Jack's soft kisses.

36

Ned returned early the following evening to find his sister's belongings packed in her trunk and a pall of tension hanging over the household. Bella was first to see him striding up the drive and was out of the door, running down the garden path before Iris could even leave the sitting room where she'd been watching for him.

He looked so happy, as if he didn't have a care in the world. It was probably Iris's mind playing tricks, too, but he also looked taller, even broader. After all her soul-searching, it only took this single glimpse of Ned to settle at least one aspect of her anxiety very swiftly. She did love him. Of this she now had no doubt, yet she'd been doubting that love since Jack's lips had found hers. The dark truth was that she loved Jack too.

She wished she could split herself in half and devote one half to each man. Then she would feel whole.

Ned's love was safe, reliable, adoring; Jack's would always be passionate, stormy and probably dangerous. She wanted the solid 'rock' Ned offered, but she also loved Jack's crashing seas.

Jack had told her to choose. And she knew he meant it. Neither man would wait – both too proud. And both injured in their own ways. She didn't fully understand Jack's hurt but she sensed something had gone wrong at home. Why else would he be in the colonies earning what he could as a miner, when there was clearly money in the family?

If she closed her eyes, she could instantly recreate the sensations of Jack touching her, kissing her, moving inside her. Iris had to stop doing that for suddenly the notion of losing Ned – and it was a very real possibility – seemed unthinkable. Ned believed he was the luckiest man alive to have her in his life, whereas Jack believed it was his right to go after anyone he wanted . . . and he'd chosen her. Would his burning passion cool now that he'd stolen her virginity from Ned? Jack had ruthlessly come after her and he had won – would he now move on to the next conquest? If she believed Ned – and all the other talk around KGF – then Jack would not stay long at her side. Was she prepared to risk Ned's love? To break his heart? Was Jack worth the sacrifice?

She watched Bella's theatrics, shattering Ned's good mood as she crumpled into his arms, sobbing. She could hate Bella in that moment and yet Iris had come to terms with the youngster's savagery over the last day and night. Bella was hurting – Iris understood that.

Iris heard their servant open the door and welcome Ned back and then she heard Ned speaking softly to Bella, urging her to give him some private time.

'Hello, Ned, dear,' she heard her mother say. 'I'm so sorry about all this. Iris is waiting for you in the sitting room. I've ordered some tea.'

She heard his steps crossing the hallway and then he paused at the door.

'Iris?' he said, softly.

'I'm here, Ned,' she answered, close to tears herself. How could she have done this to him? Suddenly she wanted everything back to how it had been. Now her heart was torn over two men, but it was bleeding only for Ned – for the pain she was causing him, for the irrevocable damage she had inflicted on their relationship, for the hurt she knew would be in that sad face of his. She had to make it right with him somehow. Jack would survive. So would she. Ned was the fragile one. They had to protect Ned.

He stepped inside. 'Hello,' he said, warily. 'I guess you know what I've been hearing.'

'Yes. Bella's been making accusations. She's made sure both my parents think me some sort of tart.'

She watched him flinch at the harsh word.

'Bella's talking about returning to Madras.'

Iris stood, unsure of whether to kiss him, suddenly too guilty to move. 'I think she should, Ned. She's being quite poisonous here. She must be bored or homesick for the Grenfells because nothing we can do makes her happy.'

'But she's only been here a few days,' he appealed, still standing a long way from her. The divide felt so wide. She had to bridge the gap if there was to be any future for her and Ned. And suddenly their future felt important.

'I know, I know. But she's unhappy and taking out her frustration on us.'

'Can I hear it from you?'

She didn't need him to explain what he was asking.

'Are you asking me if Jack and I are suddenly lovers?'

'That's not at all what I'm asking. I want to hear your perspective, that's all.'

'Did you know when Rupert and Jack were in hospital that I visited them both? I dropped by to thank Jack.'

Ned nodded.

'I recall saying something like I don't know how I can ever repay you for saving my brother's life. Jack was dosed with morphine, but he made some silly remark that he would exact the payment of a single waltz. It was a light-hearted attempt to save our whole family from this overwhelming feeling of being hopelessly in his debt.'

'So you repaid the family debt?' Ned sounded cynical. And she didn't like it. Not from him. Not from her romantic, idealistic Edward, who thought the very sun shone from her.

'Yes,' she said, tiredly. 'Except you make it sound so ugly . . . just like your sister. Firstly, Ned, my mother made me tag along that day to make sure Bella was properly chaperoned. Do you honestly believe with that in mind I'd let my family down in the way Bella is suggesting?' Iris felt sickened by her own ingenuity. She hated herself but pressed on. 'Jack took a day out of his life to treat Bella and she threw it right back in his face.'

Ned ran a hand through his sandy hair but it flopped straight back into the same position. She noticed he'd started growing a moustache; perhaps to offset the boyish looks he still possessed. It tweaked at her heartstrings.

'Don't you see, Ned? It's Bella who believes herself in love with Jack. She was flirting outrageously with him. Frankly, she made me blush.'

Ned turned now to gaze out of the window, sighing. 'She's still so young and impressionable. I should have guessed Jack's presence would be like touching a lit taper to dry kindling.' His voice sounded resigned. He was blaming himself. Iris had never felt so wretched and still she pushed on with her story.

'But she saw us sharing a dance.' Iris fixed him with a stare; this was where she needed to be her most convincing. 'One-thirty in the afternoon, Ned, people everywhere. When a particular tune came on and I happened to remark that it was Mum's favourite, Jack naturally and politely asked me if I'd like to dance. I made some offhand response that I did owe him a dance . . . and that's what Bella saw. Now she's contrived some cock and bull story because she's a jealous little girl who probably felt slighted. I'm sorry, Ned, that you have to hear this. I know you wanted us all to be one big happy family but Bella's been indulged for years and she expects everyone to spoil her. Have you heard the way she talks to the servants?'

This last comment seemed to register.

She breathed deeply, took a few tentative steps forward and softened her tone. 'Look, the truth is, I think Bella has some growing-up to do. But this accusation of hers is damaging.'

'Bell is not a liar, Iris,' Ned said, quietly.

She hadn't expected that. 'So I am?'

'I didn't say that. But something's really upsetting her if she's clinging to this story after all that you've told me. I can't explain it.'

'Me either. But, Ned, with the greatest of respect, this is the first you've seen her in a very long time.'

'Bella and I have shared plenty over the years. I think I do know my sister. A leopard doesn't change its spots. Remember that,' he said. Ned was giving her a clear warning.

'But it's my reputation and Jack's that are being damaged.'

A smile ghosted across his face and she sensed a fresh gust of cynicism. 'Oh, I think Jack's shoulders are broad enough. Besides, he's used to it.'

'Well, I don't have broad shoulders, Ned Sinclair, and I refuse to accept that sort of tarnish even once.' She was breathing hard now. The anger was not contrived but the guilt was heavy.

Ned looked resigned. 'We won't argue any more about this, Iris. It's ugly, as you say, and one person's word against another's. I have no desire for us to be at loggerheads. I'll speak with Bella; if she's still unhappy, she can go home. Perhaps we can bring her back for the wedding . . . if there is to be one.'

Iris's bent head whipped up to glare at him. 'What's that supposed to mean?'

'Simply this, Iris. Wear my ring. Prove you've chosen me. And if you haven't, then stop dithering and make a decision. There's nothing more I can do. I love you. I've told you that every way

I can and I've proved it every day since your arrival. I'm no hero, Iris; I'm just an ordinary fellow. Not especially handsome, not tall, not strapping, not wealthy. I'm also not stupid, or especially patient. Make a decision!'

How his words stung her. So filled with accusation. Ned knew, but he was giving her a way out while keeping his own pride intact.

He turned on his heel and left the room. She didn't try to stop him.

She heard sister and brother talking in the hall, then footsteps and new voices. People were on the move. Iris dried her tears and knew she had to be strong now. She walked into the hallway.

'Goodbye, Bella,' she said, as Joseph carried the young woman's trunk outside. 'I'm so sorry your trip has ended like this.' She saw gratitude in Ned's expression; at least he appeared impressed by her graciousness, which was probably more than he could say for his sister.

'I don't like being called a liar, Iris,' Bella sniffed, as Flora wrung her hands but remained uncharacteristically silent.

'There's been a misunderstanding, that's all. But I'm sorry again that you're upset enough to leave.'

'Don't apologise to me. It's my brother who needs the apology.'

She left without looking back. Iris didn't have enough scathing words in her repertoire to hurl silently at the spoilt youngster's back. Bella hadn't said a word to Flora; not even a humble thank you for the hospitality.

Ned paused, throwing a glance of apology at Flora before addressing Iris. 'I'm taking Bell back to my house. I think it's best. And she does want to go home. So I'll travel into Bangalore with her and hunt down someone who is going to Madras. I don't like the idea of her travelling so far alone.'

Iris nodded, not trusting herself to say anything.

And then he too was gone, leaving behind his ultimatum for

her to wrestle with. It was identical to Jack's and she felt hollow. The decision was already made. It had been made on the verandah in the deserted house in Bangalore but she had not been strong enough to resist Jack. It wasn't that she was now satisfied – not even close. But she couldn't bear for her family to think any less of her and she refused to let Ned go.

She must let Jack go instead. She wouldn't have to say anything. He'd know her decision by the way she would now avoid him. It was the only way – to avoid all contact, banish any treacherous thoughts the moment they bubbled up in her mind. Rub her skin clean of his caresses and never, ever wear that pale-blue dress again for fear of being reminded of him undoing its buttons one by one and pulling it over her head.

———

Jack brooded. He had swapped to the night shift in a deliberate move to avoid facing anyone by day; Gangai could tell callers the master was sleeping. Sleep! That was a joke. He tried but it eluded him. He would close the shutters, draw the curtains and stare into the darkness at the ceiling. The house had become silent by day for him and if not for the ticking of the big mantelpiece clock, he would hardly know anyone else was alive around him.

It was Namathevi's job to wind the clock each day at the same time and he listened out for her jingling arrival. Like her sister, she wore gold anklets with little charms. She had a sunny smile and a sweet singing voice but none of the dramatic presence of her sister.

Elizabeth was unhappy with him; he could tell, but he didn't care. She didn't like his unshaven, slovenly look, she clearly didn't appreciate his new shifts or the fact that he hardly touched her food. But she said nothing. Her soulful grey eyes did all the talking for her.

His bedroom used to be the domain of only Gangai but there

was a woman's touch about it now. Fresh flowers found their way in and were changed every few days. Darning and repairs were mysteriously taken away and returned, and he noticed the dhobi was now calling each couple of days for laundry, rather than once a week. She perfumed his room with sandalwood oil and while it could well be to make his room smell less of sweat, alcohol and his hair tonic, he was convinced Elizabeth used the very precious fragrance to bring him relief. The local Hindus ground up sandalwood bark with paste to smear on a devotee's forehead at their temples as a means of controlling anxiety.

It was vaguely touching that in among her disapproval she was also worried for his health. He wondered whether she knew the reason for his sour mood. Somehow he thought Elizabeth saw and understood everything.

All the good feeling surrounding the purchase of the house, even the news that his motorbike would be delivered this week, had been devoured by his despair over Iris. He hadn't been near her house in a fortnight, vaguely glad that his and Ned's shifts were not on the same cycle again, although it meant he was completely in the dark. He clung to the hope that she would somehow communicate with him, even by letter. But the silence was damning.

He had not seduced Iris, or forced himself upon her. She had given herself up to him freely. If not for Ned, he knew Iris would be his. But as each day passed with no sign from her, he felt bleaker.

He couldn't lie here any longer, his mind filled with the same black thoughts. He got up. It was far too early, given that he'd only returned from work a few hours before, but perhaps he could snatch a nap a little later. Right now he was wide awake and too angry to even doze. He threw open the shutters, squinting at the sharp morning light, and noticed a bowl of fresh potpourri. He couldn't decide whether he was irritated by Elizabeth's invasion or touched by it.

He went down the hallway in search of Gangai and some tea. In the kitchen he found Elizabeth, cross-legged on the floor with a granite slab before her. On it were little piles of ingredients; he could smell garlic, onion, ginger. She was making a green paste; probably coriander. She was rolling a second chunk of much smoother granite across the first, the rhythmic movement very quickly turning the herb into a fragrant pulp.

She looked up, startled. Jack rarely came into the kitchen. He'd stolen up on her and stood at the doorway, half undressed, unshaven and bleary-eyed.

'I'm looking for Gangai.'

'He took Namathevi to the market, sir. We did not expect you to be awake so early.'

'No, neither did I.'

She unfurled herself gracefully; Jack compared it to a sinewy snake. Her fingers glistened from the gloss of coriander juices but her gold sari was immaculate.

'Can I fetch you some tea, sir? Perhaps some breakfast?'

'Yes, oats, thank you. I'll go and wash up.'

She regarded him sombrely, unblinking, until he turned and walked back down the hall, feeling somehow like a scolded child for appearing so dishevelled and grumpy.

He felt better for the shower and shave – the first in three days. It was nearing midday but was still cool enough on the west-facing front verandah. He welcomed this time of year. November brought cooler days and much drier weeks after the monsoon months that led up to September, when it would rain most days.

Elizabeth appeared with his porridge and pot of tea. She'd chopped up finger bananas onto the oats and drizzled it with golden syrup.

'I made you a fresh dosa as well. You aren't eating enough.'

He gave her a wry smile. 'Are you my mother, now?'

'If you collapse and die from starvation, I shall have no employer.'

The smell of the dosa was seductive. He cut into it, enjoying the crispy crack of the pancake as he plunged deeper into a velvety potato filling. The explosion of taste as the spicy tang of the coconut chutney hit his tongue felt like he was returning from the dead.

He'd had several days of living on gin and snatching snacks, leaving most meals untouched since his return from Bangalore.

'I'm surprised you keep returning for more rejection, Elizabeth.'

'My food will win over your will, sir.'

He laughed. 'It certainly makes porridge seem very dull.'

She flashed a brief, hesitant smile.

'I've bought a house in Bangalore. Do you think you would come and cook for me there?'

'Are you leaving KGF, sir?' She sounded disappointed.

He sighed. 'I don't know. I think . . . well, circumstances will dictate . . .' He knew he wasn't making sense. 'I'm not sure. I may even leave India.'

'Back to England?'

'To Cornwall,' he said, and the words rolled tenderly from his tongue. 'I miss her.'

'Do you mean this place you speak of, or a woman, sir?'

He glanced at her, his laden fork halfway to his mouth. 'You don't miss much, do you?'

'I pay attention.'

'Do you have any suitors, Elizabeth?' She frowned at him. 'Are you promised to a man? That's how you do it here, don't you?'

'Not our family, sir. Families may approach my parents but the decision remains mine.'

Jack raised his freshly poured cup of tea. 'I'm glad for you. I admire that. Always troubles me that you people marry for reasons other than love.'

'Plenty of Westerners marry simply for convenience and

money. At least Hindu families put a lot of thought into how the two families being brought together will work. Money is part but not all. I watch white women here every day, sir, who would marry happily for status alone.'

'You're right. Me, I could only marry for love.'

'And what if she is not yours to love?'

Jack threw his cup down on the tray. It broke, tea spilled into his dosa and his fork hit the verandah. 'Who are you to question me like that?'

She flinched but she stood her ground, away from him – as far as possible from him, in fact – but still towering above him as he sat in his cane chair suffused with fury.

'I am no one, sir.'

'That's right. No one!' He stood. 'What gives you the right?'

'I suppose the same right that allows you to make observations about my life, sir.'

'You are my servant!'

'But not your slave,' she corrected, her eyes the colour of a rain cloud. 'I work for you. I am happy to do this. But you British think you are so much better than us, so much cleverer, yet I speak your language with ease, while you cannot pronounce my name.'

'What do you want from me?' he roared suddenly. 'I always feel you're expecting something.'

She shook her head, eyes lowered, silent.

'Say it! As your employer, I demand you say it, whatever it is. Whatever is it that's burning in those accusing eyes of yours?'

She looked up now and the rain clouds had turned into a storm but her voice was still calm.

'She will not make you happy. And you will not make her happy. You are too similar, too greedy, too used to getting your own way. You need someone who will always give and so does she, but you are both takers.'

Jack was silent, mostly out of astonishment. Her words overrode his anger, cutting through his pain and his determination to have Iris for himself, to where there was still rational thought, and there they resonated, echoing their truth. He wanted to dismiss it. Wanted to pick up his tray and fling it at her. Instead he clenched and unclenched his fists, hating her for seeing through him and knowing him so well.

'And you think Ned Sinclair can offer her all that she needs?'

'It is not my place to comment.'

'Really? Why stop now? Answer me. Is Ned Sinclair the answer to her dreams?'

'He is your best friend, sir. Search your own heart.'

'Get out of my sight. In fact, get out of my house!'

Her anklets told him she had gone.

Perhaps she had found her sister and told her what had occurred because later Gangai returned alone with the groceries. Someone was riding up the hill but Jack was still too angry to be bothered about it.

'I'm sorry to have kept you, sir.'

Jack nodded absently. 'Did you hear I've got rid of our cook?'

'Yes, sir.'

'Don't look at me like that, Gangai. You can find me someone else.'

'Yes, sir.'

Before more could be said, their visitor arrived; it was Ned on the bicycle and Jack sighed inwardly. 'Can I talk to you a moment, Jack? Privately.'

Jack didn't want to presume as to what this was about. It had been days since he'd last seen Ned; in fact, the last time was over a Pimms on this very verandah with his brattish sister in tow. But by the set of Ned's mouth, it didn't take much to guess what was on his mind. He would let Ned lead this conversation. 'All right, come up and we'll get some coffee organised. I'm on night shift, so —'

'I won't stay. Don't worry about the coffee, Gangai,' Ned said, awkwardly. 'Just wanted a quick word.'

'All right.' He gestured to Ned to join him on the verandah. 'What's this all about?'

'Oh, I'm sure you can guess,' Ned began, balancing his bike against the stairs but not actually climbing beyond the second. He leaned against the banister. 'Bella's gone.'

'Gone?'

'I put her on the evening train almost a week ago, back to Madras.'

'I'm sorry to hear that.'

'She and Iris have fallen out.'

Jack cleared his throat. 'That's a pity but women – especially pretty young women – will always bitch, Ned.'

Ned ignored the comment. 'Do you know why?'

'I can't imagine.'

His friend eyed him dubiously. 'It was over you.'

'Me?' He tried to sound incredulous.

'Don't. Please don't. Everyone seems to think I'm clueless, or blind, or dim.'

'Ned, listen —'

'No, Jack, it's time for you to listen. I loved you, Jack, and looked up to you. You've been my one true friend and once I would have trusted you with my life. But I don't trust you with my future wife. I want you to stay away from Iris.'

Jack's mood boiled over. 'Whatever poison your bubble-brained sister has been telling you is —'

'Likely the truth,' Ned interrupted, coolly. 'I have no proof and I won't call Iris a liar, but if life's taught me anything, it's that there's rarely smoke without fire, Jack, and I can see the flames of passion burning brightly in you. They have since you met my fiancée.'

It was no use pretending to anyone any longer, least of all himself.

'I didn't see a ring on her finger, Ned. Are you sure you're not jumping the gun here?'

'And I see you don't deny it.'

'I'm not accountable to you or anyone. Why does everyone think they can tell me how to lead my life?'

'Everyone? I'm not giving you advice on how to run your life; I'm simply asking you to stay away from Iris.'

'Why? Nervous the best man can't win?' Jack hated himself for hurting Ned.

'The contrary actually.' Ned looked back at Jack sadly. 'Terrified that the best man will win. You don't need her, Jack. You just think you do. If you really love her, leave her be.'

He swung a leg over the bike.

'A word of warning,' Jack said coldly, stung by the barb of truth in Ned's words. 'Why don't you and Iris start being honest with each other?'

'What's that supposed to mean?'

'I know things about Iris you don't,' he said cryptically and watched Ned's mouth narrow. 'And you and I share a secret that would give Iris a whole new opinion —'

'Don't you dare.'

'Don't ever dare me, Ned.'

'I'm warning you. That stays buried.'

'Or what? You'll kill me in a rage?'

'Shut your mouth, Jack!'

'I'm not scared of you, Sinclair. I don't know where you get off thinking you have a claim. She won't even put your cheap ring on. Why don't you ask her why, Ned? You can go on pretending that it's too big, or you can face the truth that Iris isn't sure whether she wants to be with you – or with someone who'd lavish the world on her. You don't have a world to lavish. You have nothing.'

Ned swallowed, seemed to take a moment to compose himself.

'I'm not a man of means. But my love for her —'

'Oh, get off your single tune, Ned! Love isn't enough!' Jack roared. 'Look at Iris. Do you really think living in a company bungalow is going to be enough for her? Wearing homemade dresses and giving you a brood of kids and playing the Jaldi Five on a Monday afternoon to win twenty rupees to pay the dhobi?'

Ned looked murderous but Jack didn't care. Everything was being laid bare now. He also didn't care if Iris suffered for this – why *shouldn't* she suffer the same pain he was going through? She should have contacted him.

Ned's voice was winter itself. 'It was enough for her until you turned on the charm.'

'She sought me out, Ned. From the moment we danced at Oorgaum Hall, she was always going to seek me out. She visited me in the hospital alone – did you know that?'

'She told me.'

'Did she tell you how she touched me? How she laid her hand on my chest as though she was trying to feel my heart beating? It was like electricity running through me. Iris and I are connected in a way you and she could never be. Never! Accept that you have a rival for her affections and act like a man! Win her, Ned. Win her fair and square. No more threats, no more ultimatums or pathetically hoping I'll walk away just because you've asked me to. Don't just assume your right to marry her, you weak bastard. *Earn* it.'

Ned shook his head in disbelief. Their friendship lay in ruins. He unleashed his own despair. 'I didn't carry her brother up from the bowels of the earth and save his life; I don't have money to splash around and impress her with; I don't have your presence, Jack, or your arrogance with the ladies to make her even step away from your fabulous glow. But I do know this, *I'll* be there many years from now, still faithful, still loving her, still giving her everything I can. You? Who knows. Riding your motorbike across India, having affairs left, right and centre when you get bored of her and her family, breaking her heart, dying of alcohol poisoning. Take your pick. It's all on the cards.'

'Well, at least you're fighting back.'

'How did it come to this?' Ned asked, breathing hard, looking wounded. 'We were best friends. Why did it have to change? You can have anyone you want – your own servant would lay down her life for you, let alone every single girl panting for you, including my own sister.'

'But it's Iris I want.'

'That's right. You want her like you want a motorbike, or a piece of property. I've earned her, Jack. Years of loving her from a distance.'

'It's not enough. Until she chooses you, you have as much right to woo her as any man does, but no more.'

'Then I'll make her choose me,' Ned said with finality.

'That's the spirit, Ned.'

'And if she does choose me?'

'I'll accept it.'

'And go nowhere near her again?'

'You have my word.'

Ned held out his hand. 'Shake on it. By week's end, at the Nundydroog dance, you'll have your answer.'

'That soon? Such confidence! And if I win her?' Jack asked, as he reached for Ned's hand. 'You have no guarantee of your success.'

'I'll leave KGF for good,' Ned said without hesitation.

Jack shook Ned's hand and they both realised in that instant that their friendship had breathed its last. Jack didn't feel proud of backing Ned into this corner. He was closer now to having Iris as his wife than he'd ever thought possible since they'd exchanged frigid goodbyes at her garden gate – and yet he felt no triumph as he watched Ned cycle away down the hill and out of his life.

37

Jack's motorbike, known as a Fanny B, arrived a couple of days later and, in spite of his morose mood, he couldn't help grinning alongside Gangai and the butler, who were waggling their heads with appreciation.

'Very, very nice, sir,' the butler said, his grubby dhoti reminding Jack that both he and the new gardener should have more than a couple of loincloths to rotate.

'You will look most prosperous riding around KGF on your beautiful new machine, sir,' Gangai added.

Jack nodded. Beautiful was certainly the word. Its engine drove a two-speed gearbox with an aluminium case, painted a shiny bright red. It was the first of its kind to have foot-boards with toe guards. He'd have loved to share this moment with Ned but he had no one who really cared. He missed Elizabeth's quiet presence terribly. The food had been wretched since she'd left and chores were being neglected. Gangai did his best, but little jobs like winding the clock, oiling the timber, airing the house, beating the carpets and even feeding the chickens regularly were overlooked.

Jack was surprised to find he missed the fresh flowers and the scent of sandalwood, too. He often thought he heard the soft tinkle of bracelets or anklets and he'd look up, expecting Elizabeth, but it was his imagination. The smell of roasting spices or freshly ground herbs was definitely lacking in the house; even the tea was tepid again.

He understood now how much he'd taken for granted the smooth running of the household under Elizabeth's quiet, firm hand, and although it was hard to admit it, he would re-employ her in a blink if she would return. But he suspected she was far too proud and he knew hell would freeze over before he lowered himself to beg her to come back.

'Are you going to take it out for a spin, as they say?' Gangai asked, his dark eyes dancing with excitement.

'Of course!' Jack said.

He ignored the leather helmet but pulled on the goggles. His new toy started with a purr and he revved the engine deliberately to see his onlookers' collective grin grow wider. The audience had increased with the butler's three sons and the chokra. The four boys ran alongside him as he gently set off but they were soon standing in a cloud of dust as he roared down the hill, making a tremendous racket that gave him his first good reason to laugh out loud in weeks.

He drew level with the officers' bungalows at Marikuppam, before swinging left past the Top Reef's mine superintendent's house and onto the main street that led into Funnell's Hill. Men raised their hands, waving from the verandah of the mines hospital, which was about where Jack kicked down a gear and hit a decent speed as he passed the turnoff to Robertsonpet. He took a grim pleasure in making as much noise as he could as he charged past the electric department's compound and the Walker house as he entered Oorgaum.

Towards the club a couple of men fresh from an early round of golf had likely heard him coming for more than a mile and had strolled out to see what the noise was all about. But he didn't slow until he'd passed Bullens Shop, frightening the women doing their groceries. It was fast enough for him to create a satisfying screech as he hurtled around the Five Lights junction. He didn't pause, simply swung around and went back over the same path until he was pulling up over the gravel of his own driveway to the applause of his audience.

The exhilaration of the ride had blown away the cobwebs. Jack showed up for work feeling and looking the best he had for several days, which was reassuring for his boss, who had begun to wonder whether making Jack the youngest senior engineer they'd had at KGF had been the best idea.

Jack threw himself into his work with vigour – it was a busy week with some visiting executives from head office in Britain. The days passed with his mind occupied and then too tired to fret about Ned. He had been given the role of guide.

And so Jack had shown the two men first through his section, enjoying their awe at the size of the two dynamos that generated the power to work the motors that turned the great winding drum to lower and raise the men or ore. Jack made sure the men had scrubbed the black-and-white tiled floor and cleaned down every inch of the generators so that their black paint shone like a pair of well-polished boots. The Victorian-style buildings erected in KGF for the Taylor mining operation were among some of the finest he'd seen. The tall, red-brick buildings with gothic-style windows and soaring ceilings brought comments from his guests that made him feel proud.

He introduced them to various key people including the Punjabi guardsmen and the Anglo-Indian 'banksman', who took note of every cage of men going up or down, but especially of the quartz being sped along the tracks to the mills. He walked them through the crushers, where enormous hammers smashed the rock into smaller chunks. Here Jack couldn't talk, for the noise was so loud. The visitors simply watched in shocked amazement and then continued following Jack through the various chambers that each had their own processes to extract the gold from its ore.

This area was strictly off-limits to Indian workers and was

essentially run by Anglo-Indian men. Their journey drew to a close at the concentrate plant, where gold was finally viewed landing onto 'James' tables that rhythmically shook the now-released niblets of gold from all the other stone and dust. The table had a rippled surface and small holes that, when shaken, permitted the heavy gold to slip through, while the debris skimmed across the top and was taken away.

The visit ended in the smelting room, where furnaces melted the raw product, and liquid gold was poured into steel moulds that would cool and form the ingots to be stamped and transported out of KGF.

It took Jack almost three hours playing host but he was given a very solid pat on the back the next day. For Jack it was nothing more than a diversion; he cared about his work, took pride in it, but Iris was rarely far from his thoughts.

His shoulder was feeling better; another week or two and he reckoned he would be as good as new. He spent one afternoon organising work to begin at the shop in KGF; the remodelling on the house at the back would start first. He'd made the initial overtures on this project, which pleased him immensely, and by the time he was taking a smoke on the verandah that night, he felt calm – not exactly at peace with himself, but looking forward to the Saturday night dance. He didn't have a formal invitation and certainly no partner. Jack was going along simply because he knew the Walkers would be there. He had to see Iris. It had been nearly four weeks since their day in Bangalore.

He'd ensured his new tuxedo was ready, his shirt was laundered and pressed, and his dress shoes were polished so highly he could see his own reflection in them. Gangai had done well but had not been so successful in finding a replacement cook.

'What do you mean there's no one?' Jack asked, irritated when he realised Gangai had been forced to prepare his evening meal again.

'I have tried, sir. There is no one suitable at the moment but I will have a cook for you by next week, sir. That I promise.'

Jack knew Gangai's cooking was woeful. 'Give it to your family, Gangai. I'll head down to the club this evening, I think.'

He rode down to the club, more quietly this time, and noticed the Walker household was fully lit with voices, women's giggles and the odd bark of a man's laugh, drifting from within. He rode by slowly on his bike, finally pausing in the shadows on the other side of the street, imagining Ned among them and feeling instantly dislocated from the lives most others were leading in KGF. The truly active members of the community were the Anglo-Indians and he wasn't integrated into their lives – he rarely attended their gatherings and quietly envied Ned his ease with the various members of mining life. Despite Ned's quiet manner, he was a well-liked and respected member of the community, as popular with the Brits as he was with the local Indians and very much part of the fabric of Anglo-Indian life.

Ned ruffled no one's feathers and had an enviable knack for getting the locals to do his bidding without ever making it sound like an order. It was the quality Jack perhaps most admired about his old friend and yet he couldn't match it. He thought about the way he had treated Elizabeth. She had deserved better, but as with all the women in his life, he'd shown that unenviable tendency to shatter a relationship through his self-destructive ways. He knew she was one of the few people in his life who wanted to take care of him, despite his seeming determination to make himself impossible to like.

Ned had suggested that the girl's attachment went deeper. Jack didn't think so. Her expression had been one long look of disapproval when she'd been at his house. He remembered how Ned had stood up for her at the dinner party, and Jack realised that Ned was right – he probably had offended her regularly with his offhand manner. And still she had tried to care for him. She'd been judge-mental, but a small voice reminded him that nothing she'd said was misguided.

It looked like a dinner party at the Walkers' – perhaps Ger-aldine had introduced her new beau to the family, or more likely Rupert had finally emerged from his room and his fiancée had been invited to meet Iris. Jack felt badly that he hadn't seen Rupert since hospital and he doubted now that he'd ever be welcome near the Walker family again. It didn't matter. His isolation kept him strong and independent, or so he told himself.

He revved gently and took off in the dark, only turning the headlight back on when he had cleared the Walker property.

On Saturday morning Iris was going through a trunk and discov-ered an evening dress she had forgotten all about. She'd packed it carefully in a satin pillowcase and now it tumbled out in all its pale-pink glory. The scooped neckline and short sleeves had been all the rage last summer in London and she had spent many evenings escaping her loneliness by using the dressmaking skills she'd inher-ited from her mother.

Iris's excellent memory allowed her to copy dresses she'd seen in salon windows or patterns she'd glimpsed in her employer's magazines. With little else to spend her paltry wages on, she'd bought fabric and never turned down an old silk dress or scarf thrown carelessly her way by her employer bestowing a rare favour. As a result, Iris had created a small but superb selection of outfits in the latest styles.

This dress would probably cause a stir at the dance because it was so daring. The young women in KGF were still wearing cotton lace tea dresses, nothing nearly so slinky as this. The narrow line and loose hang of the dress suited Iris's boyish figure. She recalled the hours of beading involved in the exquisite shimmering design. But really it was the colour and rich silk that spoke the loudest; she'd made the dress from a stunning Chinese silk dressing-gown she'd been given. She'd never worn the dress, too frightened that her employer would see its magnificent reinvention and demand it back.

Iris scoured the trunk for its accompanying scarf and found the smoky grey gauze, a long piece of near-transparent silk she would drape loosely around her neck and let trail down her back. She'd have to borrow her mother's long strand of pearls and matching earrings to complete the look.

As if on cue, Flora Walker arrived. 'Iris, dear, I've promised your brother some dhal and pepperwater with rice and I've run out of asafoetida. Everyone's deserted me today.' There was a plea in her expression as much as her voice.

'All right, I'll go, if you'll hang this out to air,' she said, lifting the dress out of the trunk.

'Don't tell me you're wearing that! It looks like a slip.'

'Mum, in London, this is the height of fashion.'

'Well, London can keep it. You'll look naked.'

'I'll look dazzling.'

Flora smiled and her accompanying sigh said, *Of course you will*. But that poignant moment was ruined by her awkward pause. Iris watched her mother's mouth twitch with determination and knew something important was about to erupt.

'Iris, please don't drag this out any longer. Have you made a decision yet?'

'I promised Ned an answer by tonight. But, Mum, don't push me. I have to be sure in my own mind, not just because you and Dad – and everyone else, it seems – love Ned to bits.'

'To have someone love you as much as he does is rare, my girl. Don't squander it.'

'I know. But it's not as simple as it was for you. You married Dad when you were sixteen and he was the first man you ever kissed.'

'I'm not sure I like the sound of this. I hope none of Bella's accusation is true.'

'Stop. I'm just trying to explain that it's more complicated now. We don't have to marry the first person who asks us, simply because our parents approve. I have to be sure I can spend the rest of my life with Ned. Now, let me go and get that asafoetida before I change my mind.'

'You'll have to try the petty shop in Marikuppam. Spencer's is out of it.'

'Well, you'll have to lend me your string of pearls tonight, then.'

'All right. Just get going, please.'

It was a lovely morning anyway and Iris could almost smell Christmas in the air it was so deliciously cool. She wondered whether Jack Bryant might ride down the road again. She'd seen him last night; he couldn't have known she'd been in the garden, talking quietly with Jim about her marriage decision.

'That's a motorbike,' Jim had said, looking through the branches of the tamarind tree to the headlights shining in the distance.

Iris's belly had twisted. There was only one person she knew who threatened to have a motorbike in KGF. Sure enough, they had watched Jack slow down and then pause. Jack had stared towards the house.

'Nice bike,' Jim had whispered. He was the only one who didn't seem to judge Jack. 'Look at him pining for you, Iris,' he'd teased.

And she'd pinched him in the darkness.

As she rode now to the petty shop, she recalled the spike of guilty longing she'd felt. She'd not forgotten his heated embrace, that amazing moment of triumph when they'd enjoyed the full intimacy of each other's passion. Whenever she tormented herself with these recollections she could taste Jack, but with each passing day the madness of that day trickled away, replaced by a more recent memory of how it felt to risk losing Ned.

Ned had called by yesterday before his afternoon shift. He hadn't stayed, simply inquired as to whether she would be going to the Nundydroog dance.

She'd wanted to kiss him but something in his manner had forbidden it. She'd said she was planning to go with the family. He said his shift finished at ten p.m. but he'd see her afterwards and hoped she would give him her decision. Iris recalled how she'd nodded dumbly, and then he'd gone and she'd got involved in preparations for a dinner party with her siblings and their families to introduce her to Rupert's long-time girlfriend and likely the woman he would marry. Iris had liked Jennifer immediately – although Rupert was now officially an invalid, the lovely young woman had not changed her affections towards him.

Jack's arrival had stirred up her emotions again. There was no denying her attraction to him but his love felt too big, too deep, too intense.

After he'd gone yesterday she had realised she'd been holding her breath and had to let it out silently. Jim had grinned at her in the dark. 'What's it going to be, sis?'

'Never you mind,' she had scolded, but she thought now as she rode laboriously up the hill that she did know. She just needed a simple sign that her decision was the right one.

Iris was surprised to see Jack's servant in the petty shop. She couldn't recall her name. She was tidying some shelves and Iris had to assume that her family owned the store.

Iris was the only customer so it became uncomfortably necessary to acknowledge the young woman's presence, now that she'd turned and was looking gravely at her.

'Er, hello. We met during the accident,' she began.

'Hello, Miss Walker. I remember.'

Iris felt embarrassed that the tall woman had recalled her name and spoke such fluent English. She hesitated.

'Can I help you with something?'

'I . . . I thought you were working for Mr Bryant.'

'I was.'

Her gaze was unnervingly direct. Those striking pale eyes seemed to look through her, searching her.

'Er, I'm s-sorry,' Iris stammered, momentarily lost for words.

'Are you looking for something particular?' she asked, her irritating calm making Iris feel even more awkward.

'Yes,' she said, steadying her thoughts. 'Asafoetida.'

The woman nodded. 'I have some.' Iris followed, realising she had been standing in the tiny stationery section.

On her first brief meeting with this woman Iris had felt ungainly and somehow inadequate beneath her gaze and nothing had changed.

'Here,' the girl said. 'It is the highest quality.'

Iris looked at the pale powder that was a crucial addition for digestive purposes when eating lentils or vegetables. 'Thank you. I'll take a small scoop, please.'

Iris followed the woman to the counter, watched her elegant movements, heard her gold bracelets jangling pleasantly as she ladled the spice into a small packet and sealed it carefully.

'Do you miss him?'

The grey eyes flashed. 'Who, madam?'

'Your employer, Mr Bryant?'

'Perhaps he misses me.'

Iris was taken aback. 'Why should he?' The words were out of her mouth before she could bite them back.

'Why do you think I should miss him?'

'I . . . I was simply making conversation, er . . .'

The woman nodded. 'My name is Kanakammal, Miss Walker. That will be two annas.'

Iris paid, still trying to formulate a sharp retort. As Kanakammal handed her the packet, Iris bristled. 'Well, I doubt I'll need to remember your name, young lady, because I'll have no reason to ever come back here. In future, please don't address me. We have nothing to say to each other.'

Kanakammal obliged her with a nod and it suddenly occurred to Iris that the girl knew about her and Jack . . . and disapproved.

Rattled, Iris sped back down the main road, not even braking as she hit the top of Funnell's Hill, hoping the wind would cool her blushing, angry cheeks. By the time she got home she was feeling nauseous. Flora was soon by her side with a soothing damp flannel.

'What's this all about?' her mother asked.

'Nerves, probably.'

'Whatever for?'

'Well, can you blame me when I have such a big decision to make?'

Flora touched her cheek. 'My girl, it's not a hard one. Search your heart. It will give you the answer immediately. But if you want my advice, Iris Sinclair has a very nice ring to it.'

————————

Jack arrived late to the dance. It was more crowded than he'd anticipated and he was convinced the entire Anglo-Indian community had turned out for this one. He soon realised why. Jeffrey Matthews and his Big Band was playing tonight and Jack knew the music would be good. The sound was polished even when the band was tuning up.

He parked his bike beneath a tree and it instantly drew a herd of young men, whistling and ogling the machine.

'Can we sit on it?' one of the youths asked.

Jack nodded. 'But don't scratch it or I'll come and see your dad.'

The lad grinned and his mates crowded round as he wasted no more time in climbing on the leather seat and making fake revving noises.

Jack slipped the keys into the pocket of his tux and entered the hall. He knew dozens of eyes regarded him; some suspiciously, others longingly, some jealously. He was used to it, and although he scanned the room he was taking no particular notice of anyone; he was searching for one person alone.

He saw her before she saw him.

She looked ravishing in a simple dress that hid her petite, slim figure but accentuated her smooth, creamy-coloured throat and that graceful line of her neck. He recalled how it felt to kiss that neck, to feel the pulse at her throat against his lips.

Jack's breath caught as she turned and saw him. He watched her working to keep her expression even but he could already feel the tension building between them.

She was distracted by some late arrivals moving around the room, saying their greetings to friends. Jack glanced at his watch. It was just a few minutes to nine. Ned had three hours and those couple of minutes to pull off a miracle; he'd sounded confident at the beginning of the week that by a second past midnight on Saturday he would have won her hand. Jack doubted it so much that in the spirit of fairness he'd given Ned the grace of this week to do his utmost. But now it was Saturday night, the deadline fast approaching, and Jack was not going to be patient or sporting any longer.

He would have Iris . . . if she would have him. Neither Ned, nor the Walkers, and certainly not his Indian servant, would keep them apart.

'Do you want to scribble something on my dance card, Jack?' someone said.

'You'll have to forgive me, Sheila. My shoulder's still incredibly painful. Don't be fooled by me in this jacket. It took several burly men and a lot of painkillers to get me into it.'

'Really?'

'No dancing for me tonight,' he said gently, surprising himself that he'd taken the time to be so decent about it.

'Next time, then?'

'I'll be at the front of the queue.'

She giggled and moved away to find another dance partner. Jack genuinely felt a bit sorry. One dance wouldn't have killed him.

He checked his watch again. Four minutes to nine. He shook his head. Why didn't he just march up there and either ask her to dance or be even more bold and ask her if she'd like to go for a walk? That would set the tongues wagging.

But no, he wasn't going to do that. He saw another fellow turn down Sheila Hall and it pricked his conscience. He recalled what Elizabeth had said about him being a taker. He didn't want to believe she was right. Damn the girl! He strode across the hall and found Sheila again.

'I've changed my mind, Sheila,' he said in front of the pockmarked face of Melvin Fernandes who'd been churlish enough to turn down Sheila as well. Melvin was running to fat and should hurry up and find himself one of these nice Anglo-Indian girls because soon they'd be the ones turning him down. Jack focused all his sparkling attention on trembling Sheila, who looked as though she might just curtsey . . . or faint. 'You look far too pretty for me to miss out on a twirl around the floor with you.' He held out a hand and she took it, half disbelieving. 'Come on. I like this tune,' he urged.

In moments he had her spinning around the dance floor, the biggest smile on her face as she turned every now and then to find her friends and giggle hysterically. Jack took it all in his stride. Sheila was a good dancer too; he appreciated that.

'Sheila, you can do a lot better than Melvin Fernandes. Don't let me see you asking men to dance again. Make them come to you.'

She blushed. 'Well, I like this tune too and those boys never dance with anyone and I thought Mel might be desperate.'

'Desperate, eh? Is that why you asked me?' Jack grinned.

'Oh no! No. You were a bet.'

'A bet?'

'Well, a dare actually, but we had money on it.'

Now he genuinely laughed. 'Excellent! You'll be able to claim that now, won't you?' He winked and ended the tune on a flourish, spinning her and leaning her back. To really impress her friends, he leaned over and kissed Sheila's hand.

Walking across the floor again, he glanced at Iris, who gave him an arch look and then turned back to her family. Jack took a position near the door to get some air and to keep an eye on his bike. It also gave him a wonderful vantage point from which to enjoy staring at Iris.

He'd give her until nine, by which time the slower dances would begin and he promised himself he'd ask her to join him on the dance floor.

He had only thirty-one seconds to wait.

The band leader began tapping the microphone. 'Ladies and gentlemen, can I have your attention, please?'

Much of the talking settled down, people clinked their glasses with a fork and the murmuring died down.

'Now, if I may ask, where is that beautiful Iris Walker, newly returned from London and back into the bosom of her family and KGF, where she belongs?'

A cheer went up and the Walker family all looked at each other, bemused.

'Aha, there she is. Stand up, young lady, if you please?'

Iris stood, clearly embarrassed, looking around and wondering what this was all about. Jack straightened, his eyes narrowing.

'Now, Iris, I have a very special message for you.'

Iris shook her head, confused. Jack sucked in a breath, looking around the room. Was Ned here? He'd heard the poor sod was working.

'Ladies and gentlemen, on my mark, can I ask you to start counting down nice and loudly from ten? Everybody . . . and ten!'

Obediently, the entire hall of people began chanting. Iris was laughing, looking at her family, who were joining in but didn't seem any the wiser. What on earth was this all about?

'. . . four . . . three . . . two . . . one!'

And as they said 'One!' in unison, all the lights in the hall, and in Marikuppam, and all the lights over the whole of KGF dipped. The world went dark momentarily and then flashed back on to full brightness.

People laughed, applauded and cheered, excitedly asking each other what it meant.

'Settle down, settle down, everyone,' the grinning band leader said. 'That was arranged by Ned Sinclair, whom many of you know is the new manager for the electricity department and the sweetheart of Iris Walker.' Jack's breath caught. 'Iris, Ned asked me to tell you that he's sorry he couldn't be here tonight, but that was him dipping all the lights of KGF to you, because you shine brighter than all the stars in the sky for him.'

A gasp went up from the women in the hall and many of the men smirked, impressed by Sinclair's clever piece of romancing.

'He says the nine o'clock wink was his way of telling you he loves you with all his heart, and if you agree to marry him tonight, he plans to give KGF the nine o'clock wink every single night, so the whole community knows how much he loves you every day for the rest of his life.'

Jack watched the entire hall erupt. The Walker family was on its feet, Iris was fighting back happy tears in the middle of them, people were clapping and whistling and there wasn't a dry-eyed girl in the house; their glowing expressions attesting that Iris Walker was one lucky girl to have such a romantic man chasing her.

Jack felt his jaw beginning to grind so loudly that it was reverberating through his head, louder than the applause that was echoing around the hall. From beneath the well-wishers, Iris extricated herself, laughing and crying, but her gaze searched for Jack and found him staring back at her.

She walked over to him, smiling and receiving congratulatory kisses. Finally, she was standing before him, near the door. He pulled her out onto the step for just a moment of privacy, unsure of what to say, because he could see from her sad, dimpled smile that her mind was made up.

'I'm sorry, Jack.'

The words were hopelessly inadequate for what he was feeling. 'Why does his love mean more?' he demanded.

'Because you're stronger,' she said. 'He needs me. You don't. I came to the dance tonight wretched with indecision, but then I watched you dancing with Sheila, making her laugh, making her blush, and I realised you will never want for a woman.' She shook her head. 'I fear all Ned has is me.'

'So you feel sorry for him?'

'No, that's not what I mean. What I'm trying to say is that because Ned needs me, he'll always be there for me. I want children, Jack, and I want to be near my family. This is where I fit. Most importantly, Ned loves my family. It's the Anglo-Indian way to stick close. I just know that wouldn't suit you. It would drive you away.'

'You don't know that —'

'I do.' She held up her hand and Jack saw the sapphire on her finger. 'I'm engaged to Ned, now. I'm going to marry him. I do love him and nearly losing him because of my madness with you, and his declaration tonight, made me realise just how much. Let us be, Jack. Keep our secret because I'm asking you to and because I need you to be a gentleman about it. Walk away from me and don't make it any harder. I can let you go but only if you help me.'

He began to protest but she wouldn't let him speak.

'Stay away from me, Jack, I beg you. If you love me, just let me go.'

It felt as though this conversation had stretched over a lifetime of pain and yet she had whispered these words in a torrent. A few of her peers were now pestering Iris to see her ring, and were actually pushing Jack back as they clustered to kiss her.

He stood for a moment longer, lost for words as the full weight of realisation sank in that Ned's stunningly romantic gesture had won through.

Jack turned on his heel and strode away.

38

It didn't take long for Jack to get himself spectacularly drunk. He didn't care what the poison was, so long as it was high-percentage alcohol and it dulled his senses quickly. He finished a quarter bottle of Scotch neat and chased that up with what was left of the gin and a glass or two of white rum.

The cocktail worked and within an hour of screeching back into his drive Jack was lurching about the house, banging into things and shooshing himself, unaware that only Gangai was present, watching silently and unhappily from the shadows, prepared to intervene only should the master hurt himself.

Jack noticed the time through his haze of blurred thoughts. It was just past midnight and he began to laugh; quietly at first and then it gathered momentum until the laugh took on a more crazy quality of a man possessed.

He stood suddenly from the armchair in the drawing room where he had most recently collapsed, alarming Gangai. He staggered out into the hallway, onto the porch, finally reaching into his pockets on the verandah and finding what he wanted. With a whoop of triumph he lurched, almost fell down the stairs, and then disappeared momentarily from Gangai's sight. A minute or two later the sound of the motorbike purred into life as Jack sped off, oblivious to Gangai waving his arms and shouting. He was on a mission now.

Gangai watched until he saw the tail-light of the bike disappear as Jack swept left and made for Funnell's Hill.

In the Walker house it was all smiles and congratulations. Ned had heard, long before he actually knocked off his shift, that his party trick – forever to be known as the nine o'clock wink – had won him the heart of Iris Walker.

She had flung herself into his arms when she'd seen him walking up their driveway. She was still in her gorgeous party frock – he had never seen her look more beautiful than now, in the dark, just the moonlight hitting her smile as she showered him with kisses. There was a frantic quality to her affection as though she needed to remind herself that this was real.

He didn't care what was driving her thoughts. All he could do was drink in the sight of her and marvel that she looked happy, that she appeared to be in love, that she was wearing his ring. He banished all doubt because there could be no room for it any more. Iris had accepted him. And whatever had occurred that day in Bangalore, he would never know and didn't want to know, for Iris was in his arms, wearing his ring, whispering his name.

Nothing else mattered.

On the verandah was a large, smiling family who loved him too. Even Rupert had hopped out from his room on the single crutch he was learning to wield with his remaining arm to join the celebrations.

'Well, I think it's official,' Walker said on the verandah. 'I do believe tonight's dance has now changed into an engagement party. Congratulations to our darling Iris, and to her splendid husband-to-be, Edward Sinclair.'

The family clapped and cheered. Ned didn't even blush; he was too happy, too charged with emotion to feel embarrassed.

As they all trooped in, Walker calling for celebratory drinks and hot snacks, Ned held Iris back momentarily.

'I heard Jack came.'

She nodded.

'And how was he?'

'Calm. He accepted it,' she said.

'He did say he would accept your decision.'

'You spoke to him?'

'I did. We agreed the choice was entirely yours.'

'You spoke to him and you're not angry? What did he say?'

'What I expected. That he didn't think I could give you the kind of life you deserve. And he's probably right in this.'

'Oh, Ned —'

'But while he can give you more material things, Iris, I know emotionally, spiritually, physically . . . no one will ever love and support you as I will.'

'I know, Ned, I know. The decision wasn't hard.'

Ned didn't have the heart to tell her that her words confirmed she'd been in two minds. Instead he smiled, relieved and happy. 'I'm glad. And I hope the "wink" was romantic enough for you.'

The dimples deepened in her cheeks as she smiled, and he told himself that her love for him was obvious. 'Very theatrical!' she admitted, slapping his arm lightly. 'All the girls are hugely jealous.' Iris's features suddenly twisted. She gulped. 'Oh Ned, excuse me,' and she rushed to lean into the bushes and retched.

'Iris? Are you all right?' he asked, worried, taking her by the shoulders.

She sighed, dragged a shaking hand across her forehead. 'I'm so sorry. Give me your handkerchief.' He did so and she dabbed her mouth and wiped her face.

'What's wrong?'

She shook her head. 'That's the second time. I could be coming down with something.'

'Have you got fever? Shall we speak to your father?'

'No, no. Please. Come on. They're in a party mood. Let's not let them down. I'm fine now. It's passed. You know, I think it's just nerves getting to me. I haven't enjoyed the last month.'

'I know, my darling. I was very distant from you but —'

'Sh!' She hushed him, her fingers to his lips. 'Let's not talk about it.'

'Forgive me?'

In answer she pulled him close and hugged him. 'Let's not wait, Ned.'

'What do you mean?'

'I mean for the wedding. I don't want a long, drawn-out engagement. Tonight we're engaged. Let's get married at Christmas.'

'That's barely four weeks away!' Ned warned, taken aback by her urgency and yet privately thrilled. 'Iris, I'll marry you tomorrow but I'm thinking of you, your family. Brides always need so long, don't they?'

'Not this one. Marry me next month before the festivities begin, and then we can have our Christmas celebrations and go to the big Boxing Day picnic as Mr and Mrs Sinclair.'

He kissed her linked hands. 'If that's what you want, all right. I'll go see about St Michael's for that date. I'm sure there isn't a queue for it!'

They laughed.

'Come on, you two lovebirds,' Jim interrupted. 'Dad's found some ghastly old bottle of sparkling wine he's about to pop. He wants everyone to toast you.'

Jack weaved an unsteady path up the Walkers' driveway and he barely noticed his bike fall over as he tried to kick out the stand but failed.

The lights were on in every room. And through a window he could see Ned, standing next to Iris. They looked so happy. The family was gathered and everyone had glasses in their hands.

'To Iris and Ned!' Harold Walker declared.

'Iris and Ned!' his family repeated loudly and raised their glasses.

Jack paused, swaying on his feet. He watched them ceremoniously take a sip from their glasses, and then Iris and Ned followed suit, smiling doe-eyed at each other. The bile rose in his throat. Jack was in his shirtsleeves, the tuxedo long ago discarded. But he was still in his fashionably cut dress pants, one side of his shirt tail dangling outside of his trousers and his bow tie predictably flapping either side of his neck when he'd tried to take it off but only succeeded in loosening it all.

He yelled at the window. 'Ned Sinclair!'

It was impossible not to hear it and the whole family paused after their toast. Ned looked down and then excused himself.

Jack waited, feeling slightly more sober; sober enough to realise that he was very, very drunk.

Ned appeared on the porch. 'Hello, Jack.'

'Ah, the victor arrives.'

Iris walked out, too, and Jack couldn't be sure but he thought Ned told her to stay where she was. He walked down the stairs towards Jack.

'You're drunk.'

'Cheers!' Jack called to him and then belched.

'You shouldn't be here, Jack.'

'Hello, Iris, you betrayer! Be careful, Ned, she's a temptress, that one. There's treachery in her heart.'

'Careful, Jack. You're speaking about my fiancée and I'd ask you to show some respect.'

'Respec'?' Jack slurred. 'What do either of you know about that when you both lie . . .' He swallowed back another belch. '. . . to each other?' He looked up. More of the family had gathered. 'You should all hear this. Hey, Iris! Did Ned ever tell you about a man called Brent, who buggered his friend and in retri . . . retri . . .' He couldn't find the right word. 'Anyway, Brent's dead, Iris. Convenient, eh?'

'Shut up, Jack,' Ned said in a low growl.

Jack looked at his old friend. He swayed on his feet, loathing himself for being so weakened by a woman.

'You gave your word,' Ned urged in an undertone. 'We let her choose. She chose me, now go away. Go back to Cornwall and buy yourself a wife with all your father's money.'

No one saw it coming. Even Jack was surprised, staring at his fist, mystified as to why Ned was suddenly on the ground bleeding. Iris screamed and there was a lot of shouting before Jim, some servants and Iris, perhaps even a sister or two, were wrestling him back.

Walker appeared, looking grave. 'I think you've said your piece, Jack. Go home and sober up.'

'Go, Jack,' Jim muttered beneath his breath. 'It's over.'

Jack stared at Ned clutching his jaw, his head cradled in Iris's lap. She was weeping and Ned was bleeding all over her pretty dress. Iris looked at him, her eyes full of pleading.

'Go away, Jack, and leave our family be.'

'Iris,' he began, regretting his anger, his drunkenness, the fact that he had not only lost Iris to Ned but lost his friendship also . . . the only one he'd ever had.

But Iris looked away and it was her father who spoke again. 'I must see to Ned's jaw. Jim, show Jack to the gate, please. Help him with his bike. That shoulder of his is not fully healed and he won't be riding that machine home. He can send someone to pick it up in the morning.'

All the family began to move, helping Ned to his feet and ushering each other inside.

All Jack could do was watch through a blurred gaze once again. 'I didn't mean to hurt —'

'But you did. Come on, Jack. You really aren't welcome here,' Jim said kindly but firmly.

Jack shook off Jim's hands. 'Don't touch me.'

Jim stood back, his hands in the air now. 'All right, all right. But you need to leave.'

Jack struggled to pick up his bike.

'I don't think you should be riding —'

'And I don't give a fuck what you think!' Jack snarled. He managed to get his leg over the seat and his machine started with the first kick. He gave Jim a dazed glare for good measure, and then once again rode off into the black night, his headlamp casting only a soft glow.

Almost all the houses were in darkness now so Jack had no means to guide his path, but instead of taking it carefully he continued to increase his speed. He almost made it home but then he reached the corner that would lead him up the hill.

The bike began to skid as Jack's judgement was seriously compromised. It continued to slide, on its side, Jack beneath it until it came to rest in a ditch.

Gangai had seen him coming at speed; Jack had roared past him, oblivious. The sudden squeal of tyres and the sound of a crash filled the air. Long before Gangai reached Jack, the crickets that had fallen silent began their chirruping once again.

———

When Jack regained consciousness, he could barely open his eyes and he had no idea where he was. He moved his head slightly, and whether it was the pain in his neck that prompted it or the hang-over, everything that was in his belly came up.

Someone was with him, he realised, and was quick enough to anticipate the eruption. Afterwards his face was wiped down with a wet flannel, which was then placed on his forehead to cool him. He ached. His head throbbed, his side was on fire and his shoulder felt as though he'd re-dislocated the socket.

If he was ever a man close to tears, it was now, as last night's events came back to him vividly. He tried to say something but it came out as more of a croak than any discernible words. He tried to sit up and the pain hit.

He came back to his senses a while later, realising he had blacked out.

'It is wise not to move,' said a voice he recognised but in his confusion couldn't place.

'Where?' he managed.

'Home.'

He swallowed and noted his throat was near parched. 'Who is this?'

'It is Kanakammal, sir. Gangai insisted I come. I can leave if you wish?'

'No! Stay.'

She said nothing.

Hours, perhaps a whole day, went by as he passed in and out of sleep, hardly moving but all the time aware of her comforting presence. She remained silent; still as a painting until he needed her help with sipping some water or wiping his lips.

She'd kept the room darkened so he had no idea of time but at some point – he thought it must be the following day – he felt more lucid.

'How long have I . . . ?'

'It is Monday afternoon now.'

Nearly two days. Work.

She seemed to read his thoughts. 'Dr Walker has spoken to your boss. They've said for you to take a couple of weeks – you're owed them anyway.'

'Walker?'

'We had to call someone.'

'How bad is it?'

'It is the bang on your head. Concussion. You've scraped your side and it needs re-dressing regularly.'

'My arm.'

'Just the old wound.'

Jack nodded, hating himself, hating the world and especially hating Kanakammal for finding it within herself to forgive him when he didn't deserve such grace. He plunged into a dark mood as the days stretched long and the nights even longer.

Kanakammal had taken to dozing in the chair across the room. She would disappear for periods and delicious cooking smells wafted into his room. Although Jack found it hard to admit, he was aware that if not for Kanakammal's presence, he would not be healing so fast.

Walker sent in a doctor to check on him daily and the young medico pronounced him on the mend. Lots of rest, plenty of water, some sun on his back and some light exercise was recommended. After a week Jack was back on his feet. He spoke little but did as he was asked in order to achieve a full recovery. He spent an hour at his desk each day and managed to get work underway at his shop and house. He'd decided it was to be a general store and he would call it 'Funnell's' because of its position at the top of the hill.

He had found a way to blank his mind. He tried not to think about what his colleagues would make of his drunken behaviour and subsequent accident – and he shut out any private thoughts of Ned and Iris. If either threatened to enter his mind, he distracted himself, playing solitaire or doing odd jobs. He did anything and everything to give himself time to distance himself fully from that bleak Saturday night, but especially to erase the memory of him moving inside Iris, kissing Iris, wanting Iris.

But of course he couldn't fully shield himself from the community. Harold Walker paid a house visit when his young doctor was rushed to an accident. Walker was businesslike with Jack; the only words exchanged revolved around Jack's injuries.

'I think you're well enough to head back to work full time, Jack. You can certainly fulfil your role at the engine house.'

'Thank you,' Jack replied.

'Well, good day. I won't need to see you again,' Harold said and turned to leave.

Jack followed him out onto the verandah, his arm back in a sling for safe measure. 'Dr Walker?'

The old man turned.

'I'd like to apologise for my behaviour.'

'I think it's best for everyone if we don't refer to that night again. Our family wishes to forget it.'

'I'm sure, but you see, I can't, and so I'd like you to know that I do regret my ugly behaviour.' He gave a small bleak smile. 'In fact, I can honestly say I regret ever meeting your daughter, sir. She has created a dark hole in my heart.' He hadn't meant to say that much but it was said now.

Walker regarded him as a scientist might a specimen. 'Jack. Not so long ago you saved my beloved son's life and our family owed you a debt of thanks that I'm sure we've fallen hopelessly short of. But I don't believe our family – least of all, my daughter – should feel obliged to keep showing our gratitude. What's done is done. Your actions were heroic and you both lived to tell the tale.'

Jack nodded.

'Now my daughter is marrying Edward Sinclair shortly. Very shortly, in fact. They've decided on a brief engagement, which is a pity because it denies my wife lavishing her daughter with the build-up to a wedding that they should both enjoy. Still, the decision is made and they will marry in a couple of weeks. And I feel sure this bright young couple have been forced into it. The reason I'm telling you this, Jack, is because you only have to look at them to see their devotion to one another. I want you to stay away from our family wedding and create no more problems for Iris and Ned. Is that clear?'

Jack couldn't help himself. Hackles rising, he asked, 'Or what?'

'Or you will deal with me, sir! I don't know what you were hoping to achieve by raking back over that old case involving Mr Brent from Rangoon. But it was clear to all that you feel Ned has something to answer for. I don't want to know. Frankly, it's in the past and nothing dredged up now will give the man his life back. But you can bet your last rupee that if you insist on drawing attention to that case, then I will have something to add to it.'

'Oh, yes and what's that?'

'Perhaps you forget that Sabu has served me for a good many years, Jack. He was with us when the first of our children were born and I hope he'll still be with us when we welcome our first grandchild. Whatever passed between you and Sabu is your business . . . but it is also mine, because it happened in my house and Sabu owes his loyalties to me. I know he lied for you. I know all about your visit to our house even though you told the police otherwise. I have chosen to stay silent all these years because I couldn't see the point in muddying the waters of a case the police considered so cut and dried, and because Ned was cleared of all suspicion. But I will indeed muddy the waters and I shall use your name to do it if you intend making trouble for that fine young man.' Walker's voice dropped to a hoarse, angry whisper and his face had turned a deep scarlet. 'Leave my Iris and her husband-to-be well alone, Jack Bryant.'

He turned, got into his car and drove away without so much as a glance back at Jack, who stood frozen on the verandah, all his aches overshadowed by his deep fury.

39

Burying his emotional turmoil, Jack returned to work at Top Reef, and for the next week he went about his work with diligence and an expertise that the mine executive noted in reports to head office. Everyone had agreed that his appointment had been a risk. Jack needed them all to believe that the risk had paid off.

But while his work by day settled into a routine, his nights were filled with bleakness, alternating between dark rage and mind-numbing despair.

Through it all, Kanakammal was his constant companion. Mostly silent, she moved like a ghost around the house, staying awake to keep an eye on him. She cooked meals he picked at, made pots of tea or coffee that he left to go cold, and tidied behind him when he would finally cast off his clothes and clamber between the fresh sheets she'd laundered and returned to his bed. The flowers were back in his room, so was the sweet-smelling sandalwood oil, although he never did find its source.

Jack had not glimpsed Ned or Iris, keeping his movements to Marikuppam, with the odd journey to check on progress of work at the store. He did all his drinking at home . . . alone.

On the twelfth of December, Christmas decorations began appearing all over KGF. Each mine erected a huge tree with massive lights and while Jack ensured his team did their part in decorating Top Reef's tree for all the families who belonged to that mine, it was Kanakammal who made sure the Bryant house, despite its pall of gloom inside, looked just as festive from outside as the next.

Days crept by, carols were sung, the various mines started gearing up for their Christmas parties – the highlight of the KGF year. Jack dreaded the festivity and as each sunset threw its glow across the town, he counted another day closer to the wedding.

On the day Walker had told him Iris and Ned were to be married, Jack's resolve faltered. It didn't help that he had the next two days off work and thus far too much time and opportunity to think about the happy couple. He could even watch them tie the knot, if he gave his self-destructive tendencies free rein.

He hadn't been drinking as hard and was certain Kanakammal had threatened Gangai with something worse than death because the man was not replenishing his alcohol stocks with any speed.

'Gangai! Did you get me any more gin?'

'I . . . I will tomorrow, sir.'

'No, you'll do it now. Go down to Robertsonpet and fetch me a bottle of gin and one of Scotch and don't come back with any excuses.' He pulled out a wad of notes. 'Here. If there's change, it's yours for a bottle of arrack.'

Gangai smiled and sped off on a bicycle. Kanakammal appeared not long afterwards with a plate of onion bhajis.

'Shall I bring your dinner early tonight, Mr Bryant?'

'I think I'll go for a walk first.'

'You should walk up the hill, sir, if you haven't before. It is a marvellous view from the top.'

Jack smiled inwardly. He had to admire her for trying. Like Gangai, she'd been watching him all day, waiting for any sign that he was going to change the steady course he'd been on. And she knew the moment had come and was probably hoping to divert him from going anywhere near St Michael's Church this afternoon.

'I shan't be long,' he said mildly, inhaling hard on his cigarette.

She watched him as he blew out the smoke and he tried not to squirm beneath her scrutiny.

'I see through you, Elizabeth. I know what you're doing . . . and you can't save me from myself, I'm afraid. No one can.' Jack dropped the cigarette and crushed it beneath his boot.

He looked up at her again. 'Why aren't you married yet?' When she didn't answer he shook his head. 'The men of this region must be mad to let a woman like you go begging.'

'I do not beg for any man, sir.'

He gave a rueful laugh. 'Yes, I think I know that. But I meant it as a compliment. You're really quite extraordinary and Ned's right. I've taken you for granted. So let me say now, before I'm too drunk, that I'm glad you came back. I'm glad you're here.'

'I am glad too, sir. I don't enjoy serving in my father's shop.'

'Why's that?'

'People talk down to me. The half-breeds especially. To them I'll always be a servant.'

Jack chuckled at her insulting term. 'Don't care for the Anglo-Indian women?'

'I don't care for anyone who thinks they are better than me. My blood is red, just like theirs. They began blood storage at the hospital nine months ago. My father was one of the first to queue and donate his blood. I was next in line. I'm sure no one cares when their precious son or daughter needs it and then they'll happily take blood from an Indian.' Her voice remained low and controlled, but he sensed her anger.

'And so you don't want to work in a shop again?'

'Perhaps I'll own my own shop, sir. Then no one can talk down to me.'

'Good for you.'

'I will prepare your meal.' She disappeared.

Jack tried to put his hands behind his head but his shoulder

gave a sharp protest and he was reminded of the time on the verandah in Bangalore, when Iris had found a way to take all the pain
away.

Iris.

She would be married today. She would sleep in Ned's bed
tonight. He gritted his teeth at the thought. He imagined all the
family hurtling around, organising the decorations for the church,
the wedding reception – no doubt at Oorgaum Hall. Where would
Ned take Iris for their honeymoon? What could he afford for her?

Jack would have taken her up to Srinagar, the summer capi-
tal of Kashmir that Henry had told him about; onto one of those
majestic houseboats, once the domain of maharajahs, and on the
idyllic crystal calm of Dal Lake. With their curtains drawn about
their boat, he would have made love to her, slowly, tenderly. The
image in his mind felt so real he almost groaned when it was shaken
loose by the sound of a bell ringing in the distance. Bells only rang
on a Saturday to proclaim a wedding.

He stood, unsure what to do, but he left the front garden of his
house and he walked . . . down the hill, in the direction of the main
road of KGF that led him into Oorgaum.

———

Iris stood in her underwear before the mirror, laughing. Her mother
stood behind her with a small pot.

'I can't believe you're going to do this,' she said.

'My mother and grandmother did this for me,' Flora replied.
'It's tradition. And I've been saving this beautiful powder from
England that your father brought me for this very occasion. April
Violets, Iris.' She laughed. 'I know that sounds like a contradic-
tion but it's the prettiest of perfumes and it suits you. How are you
feeling?'

Iris smiled. 'I'm fine.'

'But I've heard you sickening.'

'I promise you it's just nerves.'

'Rushing into this marriage has left you overwrought.'

Iris shrugged. 'I just want to be sure there will be no more confrontations with Jack.'

'That man has no right!'

'Don't, Mum. It's the past.'

'Let's hope he's got the message, then,' Flora said.

'Let's begin the ritual,' Iris said.

Her mother took a couple of steps back, pinched a generous amount of talcum powder from her pot and gently tossed it towards Iris so that it cascaded down her back, some of it fluttering and catching against her skin. She repeated the action, walking slowly around Iris until her whole body from her neck down was lightly dusted.

'Now I feel like a loaf of bread,' she said.

'Well, you don't smell like one. And your skin will be silky and fragrant for your husband tonight.'

Iris blushed. 'You're not going to have that conversation with me, are you?'

'If you want me to.'

'I think Ned and I can work it out.'

Her mother touched her cheek affectionately. 'You're such a beautiful child. You've made a very good decision in marrying Ned. He will never stop loving you, Iris, and that's worth more than all the money or status in the world. If you have a man who cherishes you, you are rich.'

'I know, Mum.'

Her mother smiled, gave her daughter a lingering look. Then she snapped out of her thoughts. 'Right, now the perfume. Don't tell your father but I ordered some to go with the talc. It cost a fortune, my girl!' She watched her mother dig beneath some items in a top drawer of her dresser and pull out a tiny box. Inside was an even smaller bottle. Using the stopper, her mother dabbed the exquisite scent on her daughter's pulse points.

'There. You smell divine.'

'Oh, it's just beautiful, Mum. Thank you.'

'And it's yours,' Flora said, pressing the tiny vial into Iris's hand. 'That's your bridal perfume. We'll have to find something else for your sisters.'

Iris kissed her mother. 'Thank you for doing all this at such short notice.'

Flora hugged her. 'We just want to see you happy.'

'I am.'

'It's time for the dress.'

The next fifteen minutes was spent in near silence as Flora and Iris set to, doing up all the hooks and eyes of her tight-fitting pearl and crystal bodice that flared out into a princess-like frothy skirt. Iris groaned inwardly as the final hooks locked into place, feeling the satin cutting into her waist.

Flora was lost in a moment of admiration, flicking off invisible lint and stray threads. 'Now, darling, you're not due your period, are you?'

'No, Mum,' Iris said hurriedly.

Flora beamed. 'Good, that solves a headache for tonight, although I'm looking forward to my grandchild just as soon as you can make one.'

Iris could only stare at her mother, lost for words. It didn't seem to bother Flora, who stood back and admired her daughter, entirely preoccupied.

'I'm going to need help with the veil. I'm too short.'

On cue there was a knock at the door. It was her two sisters. 'We're ready,' Geraldine said. 'And so are your two flowergirls.'

'Oh, come in, come in. Let me see,' Iris said and they all

bustled in with squeals of delight as they saw the stunning bride. 'But you all look as pretty as pictures. I'm glad those pale-pink dresses worked; they're lovely.'

'The flowers are downstairs,' one of her tiny cousins remarked. 'My bunch matches my halo.'

Everyone laughed. 'Bouquet, darling,' her aunt corrected but she permitted her niece to consider her circlet a halo.

In another house the males in the wedding party had been ready for hours.

'Looking good, Rupe,' Ned said.

'Well, for someone with only one arm and a crutch, I reckon I'm a pretty ordinary-looking best man,' he commented.

Ned admired Rupert hugely. He had decided to make the best of life and to use his dry humour to deflect his sadness. Ned often wondered whether he would have had the same courage. It seemed fitting that without Jack in his life – his first choice as best man – Rupert Walker had taken on that role.

'Have you invited him?' Rupert asked.

Ned didn't need clarification. 'No. But I fully expect he'll turn up.'

'He's mad.'

'Mad for your sister, yes. Which is why I suspect she wants to get the wedding over quickly. The sooner he accepts she's mine, the sooner we can all get on with our lives.'

'It's a shame. You were such good friends.'

'We were. And now we're just as good at being enemies.'

'Perhaps you'll find a way to —'

Ned shook his head as he straightened his black bow tie.

'Well, it's not your problem any more. Come on. It's time we got to the church. You're going to have to practise taking the ring from me because . . .'

'No need to explain,' Ned said at the helpless look on Rupert's face. 'We'll work it out.'

When Jack arrived at the Anglican church, he saw lots of familiar people in their Sunday best crowding in through the double doors. He doubted whether the speed of this wedding had allowed Bella sufficient time to get over her spite and return for the ceremony. That would hurt Ned, but not even his precious sister would get in the way of him marrying Iris and shutting Jack out for keeps.

He hung back in the open gardens of the rectory nearby, standing beneath a jackfruit tree. He'd convinced himself that until he saw Iris in her wedding dress, he couldn't fully believe she was lost to him. He needed to see the bride for himself. Once he did, he had promised himself he would let her go for good.

The first wedding party arrived. It was Ned and the Walker brothers. Jack grimaced, stepped back further into the shadows. Ned was clearly bursting with anticipation and pride, accepting slaps on the back and handshakes as he entered the church. Jack should have been alongside his friend, helping him to celebrate his big day. No sister, no best friend. Ned had sacrificed a lot. But then, Ned had the ultimate prize – Iris – and everything else paled in her wake.

Next to arrive was Flora and her two sisters, the bridesmaids hot on their heels, in one of the mine manager's cars. The Walker girls, two small flowergirls, and an even smaller pageboy in shorts and a dinky bow tie, frothed and bubbled from the car but waited outside the church, smoothing down their dresses, and shooshing the little ones as they clutched their tiny hands.

Jack had stepped inside the reception hall for a moment on his way. It was wildly decorated with pink and silver streamers, with a few horseshoes – for luck, presumably – painted and stuck up everywhere too. Anglo-Indian weddings were usually generous, boisterous affairs, and this one was shaping up to be no different. There would be far too much food, drinks flowing freely and great music playing late into the night, long after the happy couple had retired to loud applause.

The smell of food enveloped Oorgaum Hall as a small army of servants cooked up a storm. Spotted by one of the people setting up the tables, Jack had slunk off, feeling every inch the unwelcome outsider. There was nothing new about that.

He was dragged from his thoughts by the arrival of Harold Walker's car. Walker was driving and at the back, in a froth of white, sat Iris. Jack's heart pounded at the sight of her. As she alighted from the car – a picture of beauty in her wedding gown – his breathing turned ragged. He thought he would be strong enough to survive this moment and not feel bereft, but his courage failed him.

He wanted to yell out to her. He wanted to strike out at someone for the unfairness of her marrying a man that he knew in his heart she didn't love enough.

Jack reminded himself that Iris had given herself to him first.

'Second-hand goods, Ned,' he sneered. But it only made him feel worse, and in that moment he hated himself more deeply than ever before. He would always be the invisible thorn in their lives.

He watched the bridesmaids clamour around to billow out the bride's skirt, fuss with her flowers and straighten her train. And in that moment, as she turned, he saw her clearly.

Not even her veil could keep out his searching gaze, and through it he saw his dark-haired beauty. She was radiating a glow of such happiness it hurt his heart more deeply than any of her words had. Her dimples were deep in her cheeks for her smile was so wide, and he could tell she was trying not to cry from her joy, although her chin trembled slightly when her father proudly offered his elbow for her to take the walk down the aisle.

Jack heard the processional music give way to the first strains of 'Here Comes the Bride'.

Just before they set off in time with the music, Jack watched Harold Walker pat his daughter's hand that was crooked around his elbow, and then he leaned down and kissed the top of her head. Moments later the shadows of the church consumed Iris and she was gone.

A sob escaped Jack but he knew it was over now. He didn't wait for the service or the hysterical casting of rice and rose petals at the married couple. Instead, he ran. Ran like a man possessed, back up Funnell's Hill, all the way to Marikuppam, where he knew two fresh bottles of solace awaited to help him drown out the sound of the victorious wedding march in his mind.

Despite the speed at which they'd had to pull the wedding together, the reception had been a brilliant party, the likes of which KGF hadn't seen in years. The Walker women and friends had put on a spread fit for royalty, with gold leaf glinting from the tops of the platters piled high with the traditionally festive biryani rice and its waves of colours – pale orange and yellow layered with white. A variety of delicious meat and vegetable curries were on offer, and a magnificent spread of roasted meats and accoutrements were laid out for those who preferred Western fare.

By the time they got around to cutting the four layers of rich fruit cake with its dense covering of marzipan and equally thick coating of bright white icing, most guests were groaning from over-indulgence and begging for a chance to move around the French chalked dance floor to work off some of the feast.

Ned had never been the focus of anyone's attention before. The notion struck him as he looked down the rows of tables from his privileged position on the bridal table and marvelled at his life.

He was one of the two most important people in KGF this day. Sitting next to him was his new wife, arguably the most beautiful young woman in KGF . . . or indeed India! He had taken possession of a new, large house that he could now raise a family in for as long as he remained in his new position of manager of the electrical department. And he was still so young. Ned looked around him. People were raising their glasses, smiling, toasting him. He gazed at Iris and she looked radiant, a little weary perhaps from all the celebrations and the wedding dance that seemed to go on forever, stretching over not one but so many tunes.

Perhaps it was time? He felt a tremor of excitement that soon they would be alone. He wondered whether Iris was nervous. Ned wasn't a virgin – Jack had seen to that, dragging him into Bangalore to meet women, even paying for him the first time.

'Let's get that monkey off your back,' Jack had laughed.

While Ned didn't exactly feel easy around women, he believed he would be a tender, loving guide for Iris and she would never regret giving him the gift of her virginity.

'Shall we go?' he whispered to her, suddenly fired with desire.

Iris turned, smiling, and nodded. 'You know my family's been into the house, don't you?'

'I fully expect Rupert had supervised an applepie bed for us.'

She giggled. 'No, I forbid him to ruin our special night.'

'Come on, then, Mrs Sinclair. I can't wait to get that beautiful gown off you.' He stood, offering Iris his arm, and within a blink it seemed the entire hall had noticed their move and an eruption of cheers went up.

'You know they'll make us run through the good-luck tunnel, don't you?'

'I'd be disappointed if they didn't,' he replied, kissing her cheek.

And so, to the sounds of wild applause and whistling, their

heads being touched for luck, Ned and Iris made their way through the arch of linked hands, laughed at the fresh avalanche of pearly white grains of dry rice and dried rose petals and survived yet another round of congratulatory kisses and hugs.

Waving to her parents, they were finally permitted to flee. They did so on foot, Iris believing there was something of a fairy-tale quality to run down the drive, across the main road towards the electricity department and to the back of the property where her new house awaited her.

Ned opened the door and turned to her. 'Let's do this properly, shall we?' He picked her up amidst soft squeals and giggles, and as he carried her over the threshold of their new home he buried his face in her neck and kissed it.

'I love you, Iris. Thank you for marrying me.'

'Oh, Ned,' she began and then dissolved into tears. 'Don't thank me.'

'I want to. I want you to know you've made me the happiest man in the world. And nothing's ever going to come between us. I love you more than life itself. I know that sounds dramatic but this is a very dramatic moment for me.'

'I'm sorry Bella wasn't here to share this day.'

'Bella and Jack. Perhaps one day we can repair the damage but for now I have you and that's all that matters to me . . . you and our children.'

She swallowed hard, making a gulping sound that was half sob, half despair.

'Now, don't cry on our first proper night together. I want it to be perfect for you . . . no tears, just happiness.'

'Perhaps we'll make a baby tonight, Ned,' she said hesitantly.

He was the one who felt choked now. 'Nothing in the world would make me happier.'

They barely noticed the lavender strewn over the floor that

released its fragrance as they crushed it underfoot; they hardly realised it mingled with the scent of fresh rose petals scattered over their bed of new white linen – a gift from Rupert – or the roomful of flowers in vases with humorous notes attached to each one . . . everything from directions for how to undress a woman to sketches offering advice on the birds and the bees. More of Rupert's dry wit.

Ned had eyes only for Iris, and when she was finally released from her glorious prison of a gown and stood before him in her silk and lace underwear, he felt suddenly too frightened to shatter the stillness of the moment.

Despite her pretty new underwear, Iris felt naked with guilt. Ned hadn't moved. He was staring at her, staring into her. She prayed that he would never guess the truth of what lay behind the skin he was admiring so intently.

Jack remained a bruise on her heart. She didn't hold out the same high hope that Ned had for the possibility of building bridges with Jack.

Frankly, she'd prefer it if Jack would simply leave KGF and make it easier on everyone. Right now, his presence was a constant threat. She begged herself to stop thinking about Jack, to let herself go, so she could finally enjoy Ned and his affections.

Ned was gentle and generous, taking his time, making sure Iris's pleasures were entirely in tandem with his. But when that nerve-tingling explosion erupted deep within him and seemed to come from his toes, he felt as though it would go on forever.

He wished it would. He wished it could.

It had never felt this amazing before. But then, he'd never made love to a woman he truly loved before. And he realised, as he lay in a tangle of their intertwined limbs, that the romantic books he'd read were right. Love was the difference.

'I've never been happier,' he whispered.

'I'm glad,' she replied, her voice muffled by her face snuggled deep into his neck.

'Was it . . . was it all right?'

'It was exactly how I'd imagined it would be, Ned,' she said, stirring and raising herself onto an elbow. 'It was wonderful.'

He smiled. 'I didn't want to hurt you.'

'You didn't.'

'In that case, let's do it again,' he said, winning a spate of giggles from his wife.

He hoped the laughter would never end.

———————

Jack cleared a throat that was choking with emotion. 'Just leave it there and fetch me some more ice and a fresh glass,' he ordered.

Gangai looked troubled as he set the second bottle down and went off to do his master's bidding, returning with a small bowl of ice and a crystal glass.

'You can leave for the night, Gangai. I won't need you any longer.'

'Yes, sir,' the man said, unsure.

'Go and enjoy your arrack, while I drink my poison.'

He'd ignored Kanakammal's food and made a main course of Scotch on the rocks; dessert was gin with a bare dash of tonic and plenty of lemon. Getting drunk was the easy part, but it didn't do its job of blanking his mind. His irrational, freefalling thoughts were now well and truly out of control. Images of Iris lying naked with Ned were so vivid, he felt he was going mad with fury and jealousy.

He began to rant, moving around his sitting room. He didn't remember even moving inside off the verandah, and now everything seemed to be in his way. He heard china and glass smashing and realised it was him, blundering into the small side table where the servant had put his food. Damn the food, he thought. 'Gangai!'

He'd forgotten that the manservant had gone but he didn't care that Kanakammal was the one who answered his roar. He smiled crookedly; she was the only one brave enough to confront him in this mood.

'I need a glass!' he bellowed.

'You shouldn't drink any more, sir.'

'Get me a glass, woman!'

She turned and left the room, returning briskly with a fresh glass and a broom with rags to clean up the mess. He sat down heavily and poured himself a new slug of the gin.

'Leave that!' he said, waving an unsteady hand at the upended food and broken crockery.

'No,' she said evenly. 'Or you'll walk through it.'

She elegantly arranged her sari in order to kneel down and then set to cleaning up his mess. Jack admired the curves of her body that he could see quite clearly now that her loose sari was stretched over her haunches. Her long arms moved gracefully, deliberately.

'You disapprove of me, don't you?'

She stood in that sinuous way of hers. 'My opinion is not important.'

'But I want to hear it,' he demanded.

'The last time I gave it, you banished me.'

'I won't do that again. I missed you too much,' he said, the alcohol dropping his guard. 'Tell me what you think.'

She turned and regarded him. 'This is only a short escape from your troubles. Tomorrow morning, they'll still be there and she'll still be married to Mr Sinclair.'

'I know,' he said sadly. She seemed to understand everything about him.

'Is getting married so important to you?'

He laughed, waved the bottle at her. 'No, but every man needs a wife.'

'Then choose someone else.'

'I want Iris.'

'I think you're too used to getting what you want.'

Jack stood unsteadily, a bottle in one hand, a half-empty glass in another and threw his arms out wide. Gin flew from the glass and hit the wall. He didn't notice. 'Who, then? Who will have me?'

She looked down. 'It is my understanding that most of the single women in KGF would welcome your attention, sir.'

'And how would you know that?'

'People talk in our shop. They think we are stupid because we're Indian.'

'Well, you're far from stupid. In fact, I'd go so far as to say you're the most intelligent and irritatingly wise woman I know. And you're a mere girl! Now me, I'm a drunk, a lecher, apparently. I'm no good and soon any girl who took me on would see that.'

Kanakammal raised her face to him and even through his intoxication he felt the burn of that icy glance, like frostbite. It wounded him to feel her disdain. At least in his own home he shouldn't have to put up with scorn, but there was something else lurking in her look that he couldn't read.

'You're no good to anyone when you're like this,' she said, surprising him with her daring.

'I'll drink to that,' he said and tipped what remained in the gin bottle down his throat, not even bothering with the glass. 'You know, we're a good pair, me and you.'

She just stood there staring at him as he pointed the empty bottle at her. 'No one's good enough for you.' He belched. 'And I'm not good enough for anyone.' Jack laughed at his clever words. 'We should get married. At least I'd eat well!'

She remained still. Not even her bracelets jangled.

He nodded, pleased with himself. 'Yes, that's it. We'll get married. I'll show Iris Walker and her snivelling, murderous husband. I don't need either of them.' He looked up in a pleased blur. 'What's your name again?'

'Kanakammal.'

He tried to pronounce it and failed miserably. 'Nope, I just can't say it. So Elizabeth it will have to be. Elizabeth Bryant – it has a good ring to it. Come on, get your coat.'

She put down the broom. 'Let me help you into bed.'

Jack waggled a finger. 'Ah, no, you vixen. That comes later. We're going to see your father now.'

'You are not —'

'Don't tell me what I'm capable or not capable of doing. Do I repulse you?'

He wasn't sure if she understood the word but she certainly got the meaning of his question. She shook her head.

'Well, I should! I repulse myself.'

'I refuse to marry you,' she said firmly.

'Aha, you see. Even my own servant, when offered all of this, all of my worldly goods . . . even she can't bear to marry me.'

'I refuse to marry you now, in this state. Tomorrow morning, if you still remember, you can ask me again.'

She didn't wait for his reply. She left him swaying in his sitting room, unsure of what just occurred.

Jack woke to the sound of parakeets squabbling in the tree outside his window. He expected to feel sick with a huge headache but after hauling himself from his bed and standing beneath a cold shower, he was surprised to find he was pulling up reasonably well. It didn't make sense, he thought, as he slicked back his hair.

He was wearing grey Oxford bags and a plain white shirt,

open-necked. He looked thoroughly normal but inside he felt as though he were teetering on the edge of a precipice. He didn't know how to make this despair go away.

He could hear his father's voice urging him. Pull yourself together, John! You're a Bryant, man! Act like you belong to this family. Get on with your life. Get yourself a good woman, someone who loves *you* this time.

He heard the soft tinkle of jewellery and swung around to see Kanakammal with a tray.

'I brought you coffee, sir.'

'Er, good, thank you, although I thought I'd be needing a lot more of it to sober up. How much did I drink last night?'

She took a breath. 'Not as much as you think.'

He frowned.

'I threw most of it away. And whatever remained was watered down as the night went on.'

'You what?'

'Forgive me. I didn't want to watch you get sick, sir. You haven't been well and you are not a happy man. Gin can only make you feel worse.'

He looked at her in astonishment. 'You threw my gin away . . . when?'

'When you visited the bathroom, sir. I also hid the Scotch. You only drank enough to get a little drunk. Your sorrows did the rest.'

He regarded her now with a mixture of admiration and disbelief. 'I'm sorry about last night. I'm sorry for some of the things I said.'

'You always say bad things when you drink.'

He let it pass. 'Listen, I seem to recall discussing marriage with you.'

She looked down. 'I didn't think you would remember.'

'I'm afraid because of your clever trick I remember everything.'

'It doesn't matter,' she said. 'I'm leaving today, sir.'

'Leaving?'

'I cannot live like this any longer. You frighten me. Your devotion to Mrs Sinclair is destructive, and I am the one who suffers your rage. You send Gangai home but I must stay here, in this house, not knowing if you're going to kill me or kill yourself. I cannot risk Namathevi.' She swallowed. 'Forgive me. I am your servant but I have decided I will work for my father and I hope you can find someone else to cook —'

'I don't want anyone else here,' he said, his tone sullen.

'Then you must eat Gangai's food or learn to cook.'

'I want you here and you cooking and you looking after me.'

She actually smiled. 'That sounds like marriage to me. I am sorry the women in your life keep denying you, Mr Bryant. Don't let your coffee go cold. I am packed. I am leaving now. Goodbye, sir.' She turned.

'Kenkakamal! Wait!'

And she laughed. Her laugh was pure and infectious. Having never heard it, or seen anything close to joy touch her eyes since she'd come to work with him, its warmth touched him deeply.

'I'm sorry. I really can't say it. My tongue gets twisted.'

'I am pleased that you finally tried.'

'Don't leave me.'

'Why?'

'Look,' he began, half shocked, half bemused with what he was leading up to. He ran a hand through his hair, confused. 'I don't think I can love any other woman in the way she should be loved. How I feel ... felt ... no, still feel about Iris is not something I have control over.'

'You don't have to explain —'

He held up a hand and she fell silent.

Jack continued, his voice hoarse from the night before as much as the difficulty of what he was revealing. Saying it aloud seemed to help get it all into some perspective. 'I can't control my feelings for her in the same way that I can't control my heartbeat. It's something my body just does. But I can control my own behaviour and I think yesterday, seeing her so happy at the church, well, I think *I'm* the one with the problem. Iris has made her decision and got past whatever feelings she had for me. And so it's time I took control of my behaviour and kept my feelings to myself.' He gave a long sigh. 'The thing is, Kenkamal,' and he refused to look at her now in case she was readying to explode into laughter again, 'I do want a home, not just a house, and perhaps until there's a Mrs Bryant, that's not going to happen for me. I need to prove myself here. And remaining a bachelor is only going to lead me further down the path of irresponsibility rather than the more stable lifestyle my employers, my parents even, would admire.' He stopped talking and stared at her. He really had shocked himself that he was standing here, with this question on his lips, but it did seem right. Whatever invisible force had brought him to this point was urging him on.

She blinked, unsure of what was expected of her. He could see in her expression that she was running back over what he'd just said to see whether a question had been asked that she was required to answer.

'What I'm saying, K—' He sighed. 'What I'm trying to say is, why don't we marry? I'm not in love with you, you surely can't be in love with me, but I don't want you to leave and I already know you hate working in your father's shop. If I wrote this all down on a piece of paper, it would make perfect sense. It is a very convenient marriage, you could say.'

'Convenient,' she repeated.

'Yes, you know, it works out well for all parties involved.'

'I know what convenient means, sir. I'm just not sure I want to be associated with a marriage like that.'

'Would you prefer to marry an Indian? Is that it?'

'I would prefer for the man I marry to love me.'

He scratched his head, embarrassed. 'Well, I suppose I do love you, Elizabeth. I just don't love you in the way I love Iris.'

'How exactly do you love me, sir?'

He weighed up her question. 'I love your mind and the way it works. I love your grace and the way you move. I love your food. I love the way you care for me. I love the sound of your bangles and anklets, and I missed them sorely when you were not here. I love the way that when you're in the house everything seems in balance. I love your saris. I'd rather like to see your hair unplaited and falling around your shoulders, and above all, I love your eyes and the way they see through me. Now, don't you think I love enough about you that marrying me won't be such a hardship for you?'

'What would people think?' she whispered.

'Do you care?'

She stood for a few moments in silence and then finally shook her head, lifting her eyes to him. He smiled at the way they blazed in defiance.

'Neither do I.'

'We would have to speak with my father.'

He nodded.

'Will I still be your servant?'

He laughed. 'Absolutely not! You will be Mrs Elizabeth Bryant. I'm afraid I just can't get to grips with your name.'

'I am not wearing clothes like the half-breeds.'

'I would be sad if you did. You are glorious in your saris and I will buy you one in every colour.'

'I do not fit the society you move in, sir.'

'I do not expect you to. Nothing will change. We shall live here, as we have, no doubt fighting as we do. But you will be my wife and you will have status that no one can take from you.'

'I can tell Gangai what to do?'

'Don't you do that already?'

She gave a tentative smile and again he was struck by how the warmth touched her eyes and made them thaw.

'I will need to bring my sisters and a brother to live here.'

'Fine. Er, how many of them?'

'Namathevi, her twin brother and the next sister down.'

'Children.'

'Yes. They need training.'

'No problem. So long as they live out the back and don't fiddle with my gramophone.'

'You don't have one, sir.'

'I'm getting one. Don't call me sir. You will have to learn to call me Jack.'

'But you can't say Kanakammal?'

'I mangle it and you deserve better. But the name I am giving you is very, very loved where I come from. It is a compliment. Do we have an arrangement, Elizabeth?'

'Yes.' He saw no hesitation.

'Then let's go see your father and we shall be married immediately.'

She laughed and it was a deep, throaty laugh, nothing at all like Iris's.

———————

Later, alone with her father in the back of the shop after Jack had left for his shift, Kanakammal embraced her father.

'I could hardly refuse him, but why?' Chinathambi asked, this time in Tamil.

She smiled sadly to herself. 'Would you believe me if I told you I love him.'

He stared at her, astonished. 'Truly?'

'From the first moment I saw him.'

'But you never spoke of this.'

'It was not my place to. He has been my employer – until now, nothing more.'

'And does he love you?'

'In his own way, yes.'

'Is it enough for you?'

'I will make it enough. I want to be his wife, no one else's.'

'Marrying an Englishman will have its problems.'

'I am prepared for it.'

'He has said he will provide for all of us. He is generous.'

'He is. We are lucky.'

'I would never ask this of you.'

'I know . . . and you didn't. Be assured I make this decision freely. I love him, Father. I could not be with another man now.'

'Be certain before I tell your mother and all the wailing begins.' She grinned and he touched her cheek. 'You are my favourite, you know that. I want you to be happy.'

'It's not because he's English but because he's Jack. I want to be with him. I shall be Elizabeth Bryant.'

His smile when he took her arm was halfway between sorrow and bemusement. 'Come. We shall close for today. We have wedding arrangements to make.'

The wedding a fortnight later was tiny at Jack's behest and, given that it was a mixed marriage, it was easier to keep it small. Their vows were taken, their marriage blessed quietly with no fanfare at the local Catholic chapel after the Sunday service when the KGF community had disappeared inside their homes for traditional family gatherings.

It's not that Jack wanted secrecy particularly but he wanted no fuss, and Kanakammal was equally determined to keep their wedding as private as possible. Nevertheless, lots of Indians filed into the church. Jack had no best man, pulling the pair of thick gold rings from his waistcoat pocket himself and placing them on the open bible.

His bride, magnificent in a beaded and silver-threaded pure white sari, made her vows in a firm, clear voice.

Later, in the back garden of his house, far away from prying eyes, Kanakammal's family and friends gathered for some traditional Tamil blessings of the house and couple. As her family and most of the people attending were converted Catholics, there were fewer rituals than Jack had anticipated. But the food was glorious, cooked by her mother, Kanchana, and a host of aunties.

Later still, when the festivities were done and Jack was finally alone with his new wife, he reached into his pocket and withdrew his mother's watch. He'd been feeling its presence more keenly this day than any other and it was fitting that he give his precious keepsake to Elizabeth. As he had taken his vows he had realised that she had become a lifebuoy in his ocean of discontent. She would rescue him. She would bring balance and stability. And he suspected that she would love him in a way he could not love her. He felt sorry for both of them that Iris stood between them; but Elizabeth was going into this entirely open-eyed. He would do his utmost to provide for her.

He was sitting on the bed. 'Come here.' He patted the eiderdown.

She moved shyly and joined him.

'You were very beautiful today.'

'Thank you. I felt like a goddess with all that attention.'

'You looked like one.'

'Thank you for making my family and friends feel welcome.'

'I did nothing. They did everything.'

'You permitted them into your home.'

'Our home.'

She smiled. 'Can I get you anything?'

'No. But I want to give you this. Consider it my wedding gift. It is the most precious item I own, not because of its value but because of what it means to me.'

She stared at the exquisite wristwatch in his palm.

'It's fine if you don't care to wear it. I know it doesn't really suit what —'

'I will wear it proudly because of who gave it to me and what it means to him. Is this your mother's?'

'Yes.'

'It is so elegant.'

Jack clasped it around her and the black wristband looked incongruous alongside her gold bangles; they challenged the glint of the diamonds in the lamplight of their bedroom.

She looked at him. 'I have nothing to give you.'

He gave her a wicked grin. 'Then I'll just have to take what I please,' he said, reaching for her, and revelled in the clean, pure laugh of his wife as she fell into his arms.

40

Iris stroked Ned's hair as she placed his breakfast of two fresh eggs, fried with a small piece of bacon, in front of him.

'You know we can afford an ayah,' he said.

'I know,' she replied and kissed his head. 'I just enjoy cooking for you at the moment,' she added dreamily. 'I'm not in any hurry to have other people in our house.'

'I wish it was ours,' he said, poking the yolks with his fork.

'Hmm,' she said, sitting down beside him. 'I always save the yolks for last.'

He took a sip of his tea. 'Listen, you said you want to work at the school and there may be a position coming up. I know it's important to you, so why don't you at least start looking for someone who can help out around here?'

'I promise.' She picked up her own cup and sipped. 'I hate it when you leave.'

'Exactly. If you had an ayah, you'd have company. Anyway,' he said, suddenly looking earnest, 'are you happy, Iris?'

She laughed softly. 'Of course I am. Whatever makes you question that?'

'I just want to be sure. I'm sorry we didn't go on a proper honeymoon but I'm working on that. You did say you'd like to get back to Ooty, didn't you?'

She nodded.

'Well, I was thinking of taking you up there in a couple of weeks when I can have a few days off.'

She leaned forward and kissed him. 'Perfect. More time alone.'

He gave her a lustful look, which made her laugh again. 'I do have something to tell you,' he said, carefully.

'Oh? You sound hesitant.'

'No, not really. I'm just not sure what you'll make of it. Frankly, I'm delighted.'

He paused.

'What?' she urged.

'It's Jack Bryant.'

Ned watched her swallow the tea carefully and then silently put down her cup. She licked her lips. 'Yes?'

'He got married a couple of weeks ago.'

She stared at him as though he had suddenly started speaking in Arabic.

'Married? An Anglo-Indian?' she said in a small voice. 'I don't believe it.'

'No,' he replied, relieved that the news he'd sat on for a fort-night was finally shared. 'She's not from your mob.' It was said with affection.

'But there are no single English women in KGF.'

'I seem to recall that her family's from Tumkur originally.'

Now Iris looked at him as though he were joking. 'That's a dusty village from what I hear! You must be mistaken. Ned, tell me who it is.'

'It's Kanakammal,' he said flatly.

She stared, then blinked a couple of times. 'You're telling me Jack Bryant has married his servant?'

'Well, she's officially Mrs Elizabeth Bryant now.'

'That witch!'

'Iris, please . . .'

'Oh, Ned, come on. He's married a villager. She's probably cast some sort of spell on him. This is ridiculous. It's just plain —'

'Stop it,' he cautioned. She bit back whatever she was about to say. 'Kanakammal looked very happy.'

'Of course she's going to look happy!'

Ned put down his cutlery and stood. 'What Jack Bryant does is his business. And just for the record, I think you're being very ungracious towards his new wife. I believe she loves him. And she seems to understand him. Perhaps he loves her back, Iris. But the marriage is done and I don't particularly wish to discuss it any longer.'

'I've spoken to her, Ned, and she was rude to me. She's obviously been hatching a plan to ensnare him because she has a very high opinion of herself and —'

'Well, whatever the story is, it's none of our business. I'll see you tonight.' He gave her a perfunctory kiss, disappointed and angered that the mention of Jack could have them bickering almost instantly.

Iris ran after him. 'Ned, wait!'

'No. I don't want to discuss another word about Jack,' he glowered.

'It's not about Jack. It's about us.'

'Us?'

'Don't be angry. I, too, have something to share.'

He blinked. 'All right, I'm sorry. Tell me.'

She took a deep breath and then smiled. 'We're having a baby, Ned.'

He wasn't sure he'd heard right. His expression must have explained that.

'Yes. A baby Sinclair.'

Ned strode back to her, looking at her belly instinctively and then into her eyes. 'So soon?'

'I come from fertile stock.'

'But you're sure?'

She nodded smugly and he grinned.

'A baby,' he murmured. 'My son!'

'Our baby, and quite possibly a daughter.'

Ned kissed her, his sour mood gone, excitement sparking around him. 'I'm going to scream it from the rooftops.'

She grabbed him. 'Don't you dare! We have to wait. Besides, Mum and Dad must know first.'

He kissed her again and hugged her. 'I love you, Iris. I'm sorry I growled at you earlier. This is the best news you could give me.'

She laughed. 'Now go to work. And concentrate.'

He blew her a kiss and walked next door, doing a skip and a hop, knowing she was watching.

Iris turned, still smiling, leaned against the door, her heart hammering. She placed a hand on her belly.

'Forgive me, my darling,' she whispered to her child, and then the familiar sensation of nausea hit and she lunged for the bathroom.

Fate threw both women together that day. Kanakammal was on her way to the civil hospital, having just got word that one of her younger sisters had broken a wrist after falling from a mango tree. She knew her mother would need help with the baby and tried to catch them up on their walk to Robertsonpet.

Iris had decided to visit one of their second cousins, in the Mines' Hospital for a brief stay. It also meant a chance to see her father. More than anything, it was a welcome distraction for her mind.

Jack's sudden marriage offended her at some deep level she couldn't quite place. She knew she had no right to be fretting over it but she simply couldn't imagine that after all Jack's declarations to her he would simply turn around and marry an Indian girl . . . his own ayah!

Not glimpsing him these last seven weeks had made it easier to cope with her situation and her own confusion about the deception she was now living. There was even a moment when she'd been able to persuade herself that the afternoon in Bangalore hadn't really happened, and that she and Ned had been the ones 'as busy as rabbits', to coin a favourite saying of her father's.

She loved being married to Ned, and turning the electric department's house into their home. Her parents had bought them a suite of furniture, and given her plenty of other bits and pieces too. Family and friends had all been generous with their marriage gifts and they were well set up for a young couple.

Ned's affection was overwhelming and his love was infectious. She believed that her feelings for Jack would pale over time and she was furious with herself that this news of him had so derailed her. She shouldn't be upset – but she was! Was it jealousy? Was it the speed of him moving on from his apparent undying love for her? Was it her pregnancy? Her body's chemistry out of kilter? Or was it his choice of bride?

Oh, it made her mad enough to scream, but instead she grabbed a parasol, determined to keep her skin pale and unblemished, and stomped up the hill. She'd just passed the new shop when she saw a familiar figure. She was unmistakable. Tall, with a long, graceful stride, looking striking in a violet and silver sari against the predominantly dusty-brown and olive-green backdrop.

The closer Iris drew towards her, the more she felt her blood rising, firing her jealousies and her anger. She couldn't ignore her, as the woman was now staring at her.

'Good morning, Mrs Sinclair,' Kanakammal said, infuriating Iris even further that she didn't even have the high ground of making the decision whether to acknowledge her or not.

She made an effort, though. 'I'm sorry. I don't recall your name . . .' she began.

'I use the name Elizabeth now. It is easier for my husband.'

It felt like a slap in the face, hard and stinging, yet there was nothing in her tone or her expression to suggest she was punishing Iris.

Iris gave a short laugh. 'So it's true then – you have married Jack Bryant?' she asked, taking in the beautiful jewellery Kanakammal was wearing: dozens of pure gold bracelets, three large diamonds set sumptuously into a thick gold band on her marriage finger, and an exquisite gold chain, heavy with sovereigns, that sat perfectly across her dark skin. Her height suited the bold jewellery. And then Iris saw the watch. Jack's mother's watch! The one that meant so much to him. The watch she adored. The one he had playfully tempted her with. Iris felt the bile rise in her throat and she forced herself to find composure; she must not let herself break down in front of this woman.

'It is true,' she replied calmly.

'Is this your idea of a joke . . . of some sort of revenge against me?' Iris hated herself for sounding so breathless and squeaky.

'No, Mrs Sinclair. I would not joke about marrying someone. And I would not marry for any other reason than love.'

'You're his servant!'

'I am his wife. We were married in a church, before God, just like you.'

'He couldn't have the woman he wanted, so he married the next woman he saw! That's the pathetic truth of it.'

'I'm sorry that our marriage hurts you.'

'Hurts me? How dare you, you wretch. It doesn't *hurt* me . . . it offends me. It makes a mockery of marriage. He can't even pronounce your name! I see you're wearing his mother's watch but you should know that he offered it to me first.' She sounded ugly but it was too late to take it back.

Kanakammal's calm expression hadn't faltered. 'I shall go, Mrs Sinclair. I do not wish to see you so upset.'

'Don't you dare turn away from me! Remember your place!' It was as though she were possessed by a demon, who was speaking for her, because Iris had never talked down to the locals. She was acting far worse than Bella ever could.

Kanakammal turned back and fixed her with a stare that made Iris quail. 'My place is beside my husband, Mr Jack Bryant. Yours is not. You had your chance. You must let him go now and get on with your own marriage. You have a good man and he deserves all your love.'

The green-eyed demon that had Iris in its control lifted her arm in preparation to strike but Kanakammal was faster. She caught Iris's arm easily enough. She was taller, stronger, with a simmering white rage now that Iris could feel through the young woman's grip.

Iris wrenched free, embarrassed and humiliated, and furious with herself for showing such weakness. What if it got back to Ned?

'That was wrong of me,' she said, trying to regain some composure.

'Yes, it was.'

'I have nothing more to say to you. I think you are a conniving young woman and if it's money you're after, you should think again. Jack is not so stupid. What's more, you've committed yourselves to being outcasts. Tell Jack not to come running back to me and Ned when it all goes horribly wrong. We want nothing to do with you or him.'

'I will tell him and I will remember your warning,' she said politely. 'Good morning, Mrs Sinclair.' And she left Iris standing alone, fuming and filled with self-loathing.

Jack's life had become uncharacteristically calm. Days stretched into weeks. His marriage, so swift and surprising, acted like a cleansing blade, cutting away the cancer that had been eating at him. His wife made no demands of him. He came and went as he pleased – enjoying nights at the club, playing snooker, and taking off for a day or two to meet Henry when he was around and to spend some time in Bangalore.

Elizabeth continued working in the kitchen with her sisters, teaching them how to shop for food, how to prepare the spices, how to cook and serve meals. The youngsters were wholly responsible for presenting the main meal of the day, depending on Jack's shifts, and while they took their responsibilities very seriously, it was a source of much laughter between the married couple.

'You frighten them,' he said, 'standing there so stern.'

'I will make these girls good housekeepers.'

'Oh, I know you will. But I think we should let the boy work with Gangai. Merry —'

'Marimuthu.'

'He should be part of a man's world.'

'I shall ask him to give my little brother some jobs.'

Jack looked pleased. 'Why won't you sit down and eat with me?'

'I like to watch you eat.'

'From the doorway. It feels very odd.'

'Still, my place is to take care of you.'

'Elizabeth, you do that very well. I don't see you as a servant any longer.'

'But I think some others might see me in that way still.'

'Who? Which others? Has someone said something?'

'No. They don't need to. But I don't mind for myself. I am worried you might one day feel sorry you agreed to this marriage.'

He stopped eating, stood up and crossed the room. He took her hands. 'What is this about?'

She shook her head slightly, wouldn't answer him.

'Firstly, I didn't *agree* to marry you. I asked you to marry me and you accepted. More importantly, I don't care what anyone else thinks. I feel content.'

'I only care what you think. I know you warned me you could never love me, but —'

'That's not what I said, Elizabeth. I was honest that my heart belonged to another, but you don't have to question my commitment to you.' He held up her chin. 'You're not unhappy, are you?'

She shook her head again. 'I am not unhappy at all.'

'Well, then, no long face. Are the young ones asleep?'

'Yes.'

'Then come to bed and we'll make some of our own.'

She smiled, then frowned at the sound of someone coming up their front drive. Jack heard it too, and began rebuttoning his shirt. Elizabeth opened the door.

'Hello, Kanakammal.'

'Mr Sinclair, sir. Please come in.'

'I'm sorry to call so late. I won't come in, thank you. Is your husband in?'

'Yes. I'll get him for you.'

Jack froze momentarily on hearing Ned's voice and then tucked his shirt swiftly into his trousers, noticing that his wife looked fearful.

Jack walked out onto the verandah. 'Ned,' he said, sounding stiff and formal. 'I didn't expect to see you at my door again.'

'Jack,' Ned replied, equally awkward. 'I'm sorry for disturbing you.'

An uncomfortable pause stretched between them and it was Jack who surprised himself by deciding to be gracious. The last few calm, sober weeks had taught him that it wasn't Ned he hated so much as himself. He had created the mess by deliberately pursuing Iris, knowing the rift it would cause. And he missed Ned. Looking at Ned's worried face now, he told himself that he could be the one who made it possible for them not to be enemies. He imagined his wife, silently urging him from behind.

'What's going on? Is Iris . . .?'

'Iris is fine, thank you. Three months' pregnant and just fine.'

Jack swallowed, glad of the shadows. 'So, why are you here?'

'I need to speak with you privately.'

Jack glanced back to where Elizabeth stood in the doorway. 'Coffee?' If Ned was reaching out, then he would permit a civil relationship at the very least. She disappeared, not needing to be asked. 'Sit down,' Jack offered, pointing.

'Thanks.' Ned rubbed a hand through his hair. He looked uncharacteristically dishevelled.

'I didn't imagine you and I would ever talk again.'

Ned's expression was one of injury. 'It's a great pity what has occurred between us.'

'I realise now that my argument was never actually with you, Ned.'

Ned gave a sad smile. 'But mine was with you.'

'Then what the hell are you doing here? To gloat about a pregnancy?'

'Don't be ridiculous!' Ned shifted nervously. 'There is no one else I can talk to about this, Jack.'

'About what?'

'The letter from the chief of police in Bangalore. Surely you got one?'

Jack felt a chill crawl through him. 'No, but Elizabeth probably hasn't picked up the post. Did it arrive today?'

'Yes. You won't mistake it.' He gave a small, helpless laugh. 'Brent's wife is demanding the case be reopened.'

'What? Why? After all this time?'

'Well, Harold informs me she's been pressing for this for years with little success. But now she's got herself an Indian lawyer from Delhi who's hungry for fame and fortune and has quite a reputation for taking on the establishment. She's in Bangalore right now, kicking up a stink. She says she has new evidence.' He began to tremble.

'You were exonerated and there will be no new evidence.'

Kanakammal arrived with pots and cups on a tray. 'It needs to draw,' she warned, glancing at Ned. 'Perhaps a brandy?'

Jack nodded, grateful. Nothing was said between the men as Ned stood and stared out across the hills of KGF and Jack paced, thinking through this new shocking turn of events.

She reappeared with the drinks. 'Goodnight, Mr Sinclair.'

He swung around. 'Thank you, Kanakammal. I'm sorry, I haven't congratulated either of you on your marriage.'

Jack hoped Ned couldn't see him sneer in the shadows.

'Thank you,' she replied.

'Don't wait up,' Jack said to her as she disappeared again.

'You're a fortunate man, Jack.'

'You think so?' The words were spoken dryly as he handed Ned a glass.

Ned knocked back the brandy in one gulp and then groaned. Jack couldn't help but feel sorry for him. Despite all the anger he'd directed at Ned during his rages, none of his pain was Ned's fault. His gripe was with Iris; his disappointment was with himself. Ned had acted nobly throughout. 'You have to stay calm. Panicking won't help.'

'Calm? I killed a man, Jack. And you want me to stay calm as they reopen the case and go hunting for clues?'

'There are no clues. They will have no fresh evidence. If you're backed into a corner and someone can place you in that room, you can always say he made a pass at you, perhaps even touched you improperly, and that you brushed him aside and left. They have absolutely no witnesses to attest that you were in the room at the time of death.'

'They have something, Jack, or we wouldn't be summoned. I have a wife . . . a child on the way,' Ned groaned, sitting down heavily and covering his head with his hands.

'If you listen to me, they'll both be safe.'

'I listened to you before.' His voice was muffled, distraught.

'Well, no one else is running to save you. All you've got is me.'

'Jack the hero, eh?'

'What have you told your family?'

'Nothing! Iris knows nothing.'

'Perhaps she should know.'

'Not now.'

'Ned, she's stronger than you think. You can't keep this from her.'

'I've mentioned it to her parents.'

'What possessed you to do that?'

'Because I may need their support. I've only told them the case might re-emerge and I may need to go into Bangalore.'

'Harold knows I was at the house that evening, even though Sabu denied it.'

Ned looked shocked.

'He's not going to say anything so don't panic.'

'So what do I do?'

'Well, don't go rushing off to Bangalore until we're formally summoned. This letter sounds like just a courtesy, and that's probably all it will ever be.'

'We can't be sure of that. We have to get our stories right.'

'The story doesn't change, Ned. That's the point. Do not embellish, do not take anything away from what we've already said.'

Ned sighed. Drained his coffee. 'I'll go. Thanks for listening. I'm on mornings for the next two weeks if you think of anything else.'

Jack didn't go directly to bed. Instead, he found himself riding up the long driveway to the club, and although he wasn't appropriately dressed, the bearers permitted him to use the phones after he'd explained it was an emergency. He was put through to the Bangalore Club and had Henry Berry called to the phone.

'What's the matter, Jack? Not like you to make calls in the dead of night.'

Jack explained, fringing around the truth. 'I was the one at the club who found Brent. He died in my arms. Everyone thinks he must've tripped and hit his head. He only said a few words so I was no help at all but unfortunately it did involve me in the case.'

'So you want me to find out what they know?'

'Well, I don't want to make a trip into Bangalore unnecessarily. It will mean time off work and grumpy wives.' He tried to sound as offhand as possible. 'I mean, it's got so little to do with us. I wish I'd never even raised the alarm.'

'All right, old chap. I'll see what I can find out. I'll call you in a few days.'

'Thanks, Henry.'

'Don't mention it. Talk soon.'

Jack hung up. He rode home, slowing as he passed by the store that he believed could be open for business within the month. He had an idea about it that he wanted to talk over with Elizabeth. He felt sure she would like his plan. He wished this whole business of Brent hadn't erupted. Just when he thought he had managed to get his life into some order, life itself got in the way.

He knew she would be waiting. She never slept until he was by her side, even on the worst shifts when he'd arrive home in the early hours and slide in next to her, exhausted, she would be more awake than he was. Whichever of the benevolent gods had sent him Elizabeth, he knew he should thank them each day of his life, for she was an angel in their midst.

41

Henry tapped the phone. 'Are you there, Jack? Jack? Damn it, he's dropped out! Jack?'

'I'm here, Henry,' Jack said, forcing out the words through his shock. He quickly gathered his wits and composed himself. 'As I thought, of little consequence. Anyway, I guess we'll just have to wait and hear. Thanks again, Henry.'

'Not a problem at all. I suppose you'll be here for the inquiry, will you?'

'Yes, I suppose. I promise to call.'

'You do that. It's my turn. Dinner at the Bombay Duck, I think.'

'You're on. See you then.'

Jack hung up. His lips felt numb and his face clammy. He needed to tell Ned, but first he needed a drink.

Several whiskies later, he had the courage to speak with Ned. It was nearing two. He might just be able to catch Ned coming off his shift. He rode his bike to the electricity department and waited outside, trying not to think about the information Henry had just passed on. The implications were grave.

If he could find a way to set things right, get them both out of this trouble that was deepening around them, then he was going to change his life for good.

And the first thing he was going to do was to start a family with Kanakammal. He smiled to himself. He could say her name in his mind when he didn't think too hard on it. Yes, he would take her into Bangalore and show her their house there; he would buy her more jewellery, and lead her through the shop he hoped she would agree to run for him. The more he involved her in his life, the less he would think about Iris.

He wanted to set up another shop now, in Robertsonpet, perhaps another at Nundydroog. Jack could already envisage a chain of stores, perhaps with soda bars that could become meeting places serving good food, great coffee and, of course, ice-cream and cakes. It was a nice daydream and he wanted to make it a reality. But first they had to get past the ghost of Brent, who had returned to haunt them.

If he were granted this one last escape, he would put Iris behind him once and for all. He made this pledge silently, casting it out, begging for his vow to be heard.

Ned walked out of the electrical compound and Jack felt his throat close; how was he going to tell Ned? And more importantly, how was he going to protect him?

'Jack?'

'We need to talk,' he said, revving the engine. 'Hop on.'

'Iris will be —'

'This is important.'

Ned could see he meant it. 'Well, I can't be too long. Take me up to the petty shop, then I can buy something for her and say I wanted to treat her.'

'Sounds like she keeps you on a short leash.'

'I keep myself on one.'

Jack gunned the engine. Later, after Ned had chosen some Rowntree's Table Jellies and a small tin of cocoa to take home, they walked down to the railway line. It was a quiet spot.

'I've found out what we need to know, and it does complicate things.'

'Tell me.'

Jack took a breath and outlined what had been twisting in his gut since he'd heard the news. 'It seems the zealous lawyer and his very determined client have got a witness who confirms we were at the club together, looking for Brent.'

'What?' Ned's face blanched.

'Breathe, Ned, breathe.'

'That can't be.'

'I'm afraid it can. It was my oversight not to get that particular palm greased. Damn it!' He banged a fist into his hand. 'Stupid, stupid!'

Ned looked glazed. 'Who is it?'

'The man called Ramesh.'

'Ramesh?'

'The bearer I spoke to as we arrived. Damn him! And damn that woman's lawyer for even finding him.'

Ned looked distraught. 'But can they trust his memory?'

'Well, we could deny it, but they'd then have to ask themselves why he would lie. No, we need something to discredit his memory. I'll have to think about it. For now we hold our nerve.'

'What? And hope it goes away?'

'Ned, it's an old, old case. Think about it. The police don't want to get involved in a fresh inquiry . . . that suggests they didn't do their job properly in the first place. We don't want it rearing its ugly head so we're not going to be in a hurry to help. That leaves Brent's widow and her highly paid lawyer out on a limb and all the pressure on them to come up with a watertight case, which I suspect they don't have. For now we don't overreact. Let others take the lead.'

'I don't know what game you're playing.'

'It's an old favourite. It's called Saving Ned Sinclair's Arse. Just carry on normally.'

'Is that it?'

'Unless you want yourself torn to shreds by your wife. I know how possessive those Anglo-Indians can be.'

Ned shook his head wearily. 'Leave her alone.'

'I have.'

As Jack watched Ned slouch down the hill he wasn't convinced about his state of mind, and whether he could cope with this latest news. He really didn't want to, but maybe he'd have to speak with Iris.

———————

Kanakammal was waiting inside for him, quiet as always. If she had questions, she kept them to herself.

He kissed her hello. 'Let me take you to see the shop. It's nearly ready.'

'I have some news,' she said, surprising him with the urgency in her voice.

'Tell me,' he said, sitting down and pulling her next to him.

'I am having our child.'

Jack was speechless. 'A baby?' he finally said. She nodded and Jack sprang up. 'A baby!'

Kanakammal laughed her throaty laugh. 'It can happen.'

Jack grabbed her hands and pulled her back to her feet. He kissed her. 'That's the best news I think I've ever received.'

'Yes?'

'Yes!' he yelled. 'Yes! A son, perhaps. A new generation of Bryants. He has to be named Howel, after an old Cornish king.'

'It could be a girl. We could call her Muthulakshmi,' and then she burst out laughing at the look on his face. 'An English name is good but she will need an Indian name too.'

'That's fine, so long as we can baptise them with good Cornish names.' He grinned. 'You clever girl.'

'You helped.'

He kissed her again and it was deep and loving. 'Thank you for our child. It's a sign.'

'Of what?'

'That my life is blessed by you.'

She smiled but there was something in her eyes that flashed concern. It was gone quickly but he'd seen it.

'What is it?'

She shook her head, pretending she didn't understand.

'Something's wrong.'

'It is nothing.'

'Please tell me.'

'I just had an odd feeling that you would have to leave me.'

'Don't be ridiculous. You're stuck with me now. We have everything to look forward to.'

Kanakammal nodded, but Jack noticed a slightly haunted expression that wasn't fully disguised by her smile.

42

Iris said she'd send the newly employed chokra down with a tiffin for his lunch and then stood with her hands on her hips, head cocked as she regarded her husband.

'You didn't hear a word I just said, did you, Ned?'

'What?' he asked, absently.

'I suppose I should be grateful that you're at least shaving again. What's got into you?'

'How do you mean?'

'You're so distracted, distant. Have I done something wrong?'

He did up the last button of his work shirt and reached for her. He knew he was acting vacant but he was worried. It was all he could do right now to get through each anxious day. 'Don't be silly.'

'You're acting awfully strange, Ned.'

'I'm sorry. I've got a lot on my mind.'

'Like what?'

'Everything. Being in charge of the electrical department isn't a walk in the park, Iris. I have a lot of responsibility now and the company wants its pound of flesh.'

'I understand, but you're not eating, you hardly talk any more and recently it's as if you're not even paying attention to what's going on around you.'

'I'm sorry, I'm sorry,' he said, planting a kiss on her cheek. 'I'm busy, that's all. I've got villagers trying to steal electricity and it's getting out of hand. What began as one or two is now a small organised mob of wily shopkeepers.'

'Well, don't bring those problems home. You work long enough hours as it is. When you're here, I want you here for me. You can't ignore your new baby as you're ignoring me.'

'I'm not ignoring you!'

'You are. You don't even come to bed with me any more. How do you imagine that makes me feel? I'll tell you . . . unattractive, unwanted, certainly unloved.'

'Oh, Iris, please don't talk like that.' He tried to kiss her pouting mouth but she pulled her head away.

'No, think about it, Ned. I want more for us. You don't take me dancing, we never did get on that honeymoon you promised, I need some new shoes but —'

'Money doesn't grow on trees,' he began, as Jack's caution that Iris's needs would outgrow what Ned could provide began to echo.

'Don't patronise me. I know what we can and can't afford. You remind me often enough.'

'Perhaps you married the wrong man, then.' He'd wanted it to come out lightly, as a jest, but the ever tightening anxiety in his chest forced it out like a challenge.

She stepped back as if slapped. 'What's that supposed to mean?'

He'd said it; he couldn't backtrack now. 'Well, clearly I'm not providing all that you need.'

'Clearly you're not even trying,' she said. 'Most of what I need won't cost you anything.'

'I don't want to fight with you, Iris.'

'You can't just ignore me because you don't want to talk about it.'

'Talk about what?' he said, his voice raised now.

'Whatever's going on in that head of yours. What's worrying you so much?'

He needed to throw her off the scent. 'Well, perhaps I'm not enough for you. Perhaps *Jack Bryant* would have been a better provider.'

It made her cry and he felt like a bully. He had no right to question her loyalty. Iris had been nothing but a loving and devoted wife since they'd married.

'I'm sorry,' he tried.

'Go to work, Ned. Just go away.'

He didn't linger, storming out as though he were the victim of their angry words. And it did nothing to help his fragile state of mind. Suddenly the world that had seemed so bright felt dark and crowded and bleak again. This was how he'd felt in Rangoon; and all that horror was reaching for him again, wanting to suck him back into its maw. It had taken his parents, it had taken his friend and, although he felt Bella was now safe, it seemed as though it hadn't completely finished with him. Brent's malevolent shadow hovered above him, wanting to guide him behind bars.

If he was found to be Brent's murderer, what would that do to Iris, to the Walker family, to their unborn child? He would rot in jail knowing his son or daughter was growing up with a murderer for a father, doing his time at the prison in Sheshadri Road. He gave a harsh, mirthless laugh as he walked down the short path to work, realising he would have come full circle, for the Bangalore prison was just a hundred yards from his first abode in the city.

He didn't want to die in an Indian jail; he'd rather end his life on his own terms. He shook his mind free of his unhappy thoughts and turned into the compound, hoping the shift would keep him so busy he'd have no time to think.

Jack was back on nights but he'd found out that Ned was on days. He'd caught up briefly with Ned the previous afternoon and was shocked by his hollow, unshaven appearance. Ned had been distracted and nervous, saying several times that he would rather kill himself than do time in an Indian jail. It was ridiculous. Jack firmly believed there'd be no case to answer and the only reason the police were sending out letters was to appease the angry widow.

All she had was a servant's memory from almost seven years ago at the Bangalore Club. Jack didn't think that would be enough to convince the authorities to formally reopen a case. And even if it was, it would then be Ned's word against Ramesh's. Jack would fare better but only if Ned held his nerve.

But Ned was threatening to unravel, and that's why Jack needed to call in help. Jack was damned if he'd go down as an accomplice to murder. As much as he wanted to save Ned a jail sentence, self-interest drove him too.

He sped down to Oorgaum, skirting the back of the Sinclair property, and hiding his motorbike beneath a low shrub. Ned's company house sat alone in its own small but private grounds. Nevertheless, he jumped the low fence and approached by the back door, scattering chickens and terrifying a chokra boy feeding them.

'Is the madam in?' he said.

The boy seemed to understand. He pointed towards what Jack assumed was the kitchen area. The door was open. Jack heard soft music from a radio and the sound of sweeping, a woman's voice humming softly.

'Hello?' he called and then stepped inside.

Iris appeared, tucking back a curl of hair from her flushed face and wearing an old house frock with an apron on top. She looked more lovely than he could possibly have imagined.

'J-Jack!'

'I'm sorry to call unannounced,' he said, not elaborating.

She put down her broom, hurriedly pulled off her apron and tried to straighten her hair. It didn't matter to him. She looked beautiful.

'What are you doing here?' She glanced behind her. 'Why did you come to the back?'

'I need to speak with you privately.'

'Jack, I —'

'It's about Ned.'

'Ned?'

'I'm worried about him.'

She shocked him by crumpling into tears that had clearly been close to the surface. He crossed the kitchen in two short strides and reached for her.

'I'm sorry. I didn't mean to —'

'It's not you,' she wept. 'It's . . .' but couldn't finish.

Jack had promised himself he would keep a safe distance from Iris but here she was dissolving into his arms. He was holding her and soothing her with meaningless words, his face bent so close he could smell the sandalwood in her shampoo.

'Oh, Jack, he's acting so strangely. But he won't talk to me – I don't know what's wrong but he's so unhappy.'

He led her into what looked to be their small sitting room. It was dark and cool and he sat her down on a sofa, carefully lowering himself next to her.

'I know,' Jack said.

'How do you know? Are you two talking again?'

'I wouldn't say we've buried the hatchet, but we are talking. And while I couldn't call us friends, we're not enemies.'

'I'm glad,' she said, resting a hand on his, but Jack pulled away as if burned. She acted as though she didn't notice. 'Because he doesn't have anyone else.'

He cleared his throat and stood up, fearful of what their closeness might provoke. He backed away to the mantelpiece, creating distance between them. It was so hard to look at her, even harder to have her touch him like that and not be able to respond instinctively.

He gave a small cough to steady himself, buy some time as she stared at him. 'Iris, you need to be very understanding of Ned right now. He's got a lot on his mind.'

'But *what*? If he can tell you, then why can't he tell me?'

Jack sighed. 'Ned needs to tell you himself. I'm just here to ask you to support him, be strong for him. Don't let his demons get the better of him.'

'Demons?' Her lips thinned. 'Please tell me, Jack, what you know.'

'It's not my business to tell —'

'Well, you made it your business by coming here. You can't just give me some cryptic message when I don't know what I'm up against. Is he in some sort of trouble?'

'No, no, but this goes back to before he met you, Iris. I don't know how much he's told you about his time in Rangoon but he probably should – it will explain a lot.'

'I know he lost his parents and stowed away with his sister.'

'Yes, well, it's a bit more complicated than that.'

'So tell me.'

Jack sighed, began to pace. He felt Iris's gaze roaming over him. The electricity was there between them and the tension in the room had nothing to do with Ned's predicament. He had promised his wife he could be trusted. If he was ever going to live up to his father's hopes, being a faithful husband was surely a first step.

He took a breath and began. 'There was a man called Brent – a doctor, apparently – at the orphanage. Turns out Brent had a taste for children.' He watched Iris's expression change. 'Ned fled the orphanage to get Bella away from there. To cut a long story short, Brent ran into Ned again in Bangalore, and as it happens, Brent died that same night.'

Iris gasped. 'And they blamed him?'

'He was exonerated. I was the one who actually found Brent dead.' There was the lie. And now he'd given it to Iris and it sounded so convincing, he could believe it himself. 'He'd died as a result of an accident. The post-mortem confirmed the head wound. Of course they had questions for both of us – me finding the body and raising the alarm and Ned being one of the last people he spoke to, in your parents' house.'

'So . . . so why are you telling me this? What has this got to do with Ned now?'

'There's talk that they might reopen the case. Brent's widow is determined that the coroner's decision of accidental death needs more scrutiny, but she's clutching at straws.'

'And this is what's upsetting Ned?'

'Yes. And it's reopened a Pandora's box. All the fear and grief he escaped in Rangoon has returned to haunt him because he hated Brent, and perhaps that's what the widow is using to try and prove some sort of foul play on Ned's part.' He noted Iris's baffled expression. 'I know, it's ridiculous, but it's still upsetting him badly. We all handle emotional turmoil in different ways. You and your family gave Ned a whole new life. KGF has treated him well. He was in a real mess when he arrived in Madras.'

Jack wasn't ready for it when Iris stood up and rushed to hug him. 'Jack, no matter what you think, you are a good friend to Ned. I'm sorry for all that happened between us.' She pulled back to look up at him. 'I really am.'

He smiled, unable to tell her that this was the hardest situation he'd ever been in. As much as he admired and needed Elizabeth, just a touch from Iris threatened to undo all his promises.

She was still talking hesitantly. 'In fact, there's something I should share with —'

But Jack interrupted, needing to stop any further intimacy. 'I'm not sorry about what happened between us, Iris,' he said sadly.

'I accept your decision. But this,' he said, easing her hands from around him, 'only makes it harder.'

Ned's thoughts were fractured, but he needed to make amends.

'You off already?' one of his fellow workers asked.

'I thought I'd take tiffin at home with my wife.'

'Is that what newlyweds call it these days?'

Ned felt his colour rise but he knew he needed to laugh, needed to stop being so intense about all that had gone wrong in his life.

He walked out of the double-storey building. Originally the familiar red brick of all the mine buildings, the electricity department had recently been whitewashed. It was now starkly visible from almost anywhere around Oorgaum. The house, however, had escaped the whitewashing and remained quietly grey in its local stone and matching walled garden. He loved the tall trees surrounding the property, giving it a feeling of such privacy, although the red-tiled roof could be glimpsed between the branches.

He had been feeling suddenly out of his depth again, as he had all those years ago in Rangoon. The familiar insidious thought that everyone he loved ultimately abandoned him had come back to haunt him. Even Bella had deserted him now, preferring her adopted parents and her lifestyle in Madras. The voice in the back of his mind taunted him further. And now Iris is already tired of you. Do you hear the weariness in her voice? And by the way, can you count? Are you sure that baby is yours?

He banished his vile thoughts, forcing himself to focus on Iris. She was mere yards away. He would apologise for his behaviour this morning and she would instantly forgive him. He mustn't doubt Iris. She had chosen him. She would not desert him. There was happiness now in his life. And once this police formality was done with, he would take her away somewhere. A real honeymoon.

They would make love beneath the stars, and pick a name for their child and plan for the future.

He had nothing to worry about. Nothing!

Ned let himself in through the front door but didn't call out. He wanted to surprise her.

———————

Iris clutched Jack again, burying her head in his chest. 'Thank you for coming today. I needed this more than you could know –'

She felt Jack freeze and her words died in her throat when she looked around and saw Ned framed by the doorway.

'Ned,' she said in a choked voice. 'It's not what you think!'

Jack sighed. His arms weren't even around Iris but he knew Ned was only seeing what he wanted to.

Ned's gaunt face looked suddenly wraith-like. There was no anger, only a sort of deeply injured and sad acceptance. 'I thought I'd spend my break with you,' he said to Iris, his voice hollow. 'But it seems you've got all you've ever needed.'

'Ned, no!' she said, moving towards him.

But Ned was already gone. Jack heard the door slam and Iris let out a choked sob and slid down the wall to the floor. Jack picked her up, cradling her in his arms, and looked around for somewhere soft to lay her down. She couldn't talk for weeping. Jack took her into one of the bedrooms to make her comfortable. It was small, sparsely furnished. Quite unlike his own home. They really didn't have much.

Love is enough, Ned had once said to him, long before Iris had returned from London, and Jack knew Ned believed this. Jack didn't.

He laid Iris, still sobbing, onto the bed before covering her with a shawl hanging nearby. He then went in search of the chokra. He gave him terse instructions and tossed him a couple of annas. '*Jaldi!*' he urged.

Jack sat on the back step, waiting, and half an hour or so later,

Kanakammal arrived. He gave her a sheepish shrug and explained as best he could.

'Ned and I are involved in an old police case. It is nothing for you to worry about but Ned is fearful this is going to ruin his marriage, his life.' His wife didn't seem interested in detail. Her expression told him all she wanted was the truth as to why Jack found himself here at this house, alone with Iris. 'I needed Iris's help.' He pushed back a lock of hair. 'But it seems my presence here has created an even bigger mess.' He was still shocked by what had happened. 'Iris was crying, I was consoling her and Ned walked in at that moment. It looked guilty but it was totally innocent.' He took her hand. 'You trust me, don't you?'

She looked at him gravely. 'You are my husband.'

'Elizabeth, I promise you, I came here to help Ned, not to see Iris. If I intended to spend time with Iris in the way Ned believes, I would not visit her in her husband's house, next door to his work-place, in broad daylight in KGF with servants around and the back door wide open.'

She nodded. 'I know.'

'So you trust me?'

'I am here,' she replied, somehow making the obvious sound so reasonable.

'Stay with her.'

'Mrs Sinclair will not like it. She despises me.'

'What? She doesn't even know you.'

'She knows who I married.'

'You're imagining it.'

'I'm not imagining her warning me not to cross her threshold.'

'What?' He stared at her and she didn't flinch. He looked torn. 'Just, please, keep an eye out here. Her parents are in Kolar, that's why I sent for you – but they'll be back soon enough. I have to see Ned, explain everything.'

'For you and Mr Sinclair, then, I'll stay.'

'Thank you.' Jack kissed her cheek. 'I'll be back.'

He ran after Ned but he was too late. At the electrical department, he was told Ned had already gone.

'Where?'

'Somewhere beyond Bangarapet. The villagers there are stealing electricity. Ned has gone to see for himself.'

'All right. I'll see him later,' Jack said hopelessly, wondering whether Ned would ever talk to him again.

He returned to the Sinclair household and found Kanakammal standing outside. 'Ned's left KGF for the afternoon. Back late afternoon probably. What's happening?'

'As soon as she stirred I came out here. She's stopped crying. She's been throwing things around so I think now she is angry.'

'Good. That's better than despairing.' He glanced at his watch. 'I've got to get ready for work. Can you stay just a bit longer?'

'I'll leave when one of her family arrives.'

'You're an angel,' Jack said over his shoulder, already jogging to retrieve his bike.

Jack never reached the Walkers. On the way he was hailed by the man from the post office.

'Mr Bryant, sir?'

Jack slowed. 'Something for me?'

'Yes, sir, a telegram. I was coming most directly to your house.'

'Lucky you found me, then.' Jack grinned, although telegrams were invariably bad news.

He held his breath as he opened the envelope; perhaps this was the summons they'd been dreading. But the news it contained was far worse than he'd imagined.

Jack dearest, your darling father passed away yesterday.
Heart attack. His final words were of you. We miss you,
now more than ever. Your loving mother.

He crushed the telegram in his fist and let out a howl of anguish that echoed across the goldfields.

43

When Kanakammal arrived home she sensed that something was wrong. There was a silence blanketing the house, which even from outside felt suffocating. Gangai came hurrying down the side of the house, his finger to his lips.

They spoke Tamil rapidly.

'Is he drinking?'

'Anything he can find. I have sent your sisters and brothers to my family around the corner.'

She nodded. 'Thank you.'

'I think he is weeping.'

Kanakammal hadn't expected that. She kept her shock to herself, though, betraying nothing to Gangai as she squeezed his wringing hands in thanks and nodded.

She found Jack slouched on the floor in the corner of the front room. He was still clutching a ragged piece of paper in his hand. He had never looked more handsome to her, dishevelled as he was. Around him were bottles of all description. She knew her husband hadn't taken alcohol in weeks and everything had benefited – his health, his home life, his work.

Work! She glanced at the clock. He was due on shift in a few hours. One look at him and she knew he wouldn't be making it.

'Elizabeth,' he murmured. His eyes were reddened and his face looked ghostly from sorrow.

'I'm here,' she said softly. 'What can I do to help?'

'He's gone.'

'Who's gone, Jack?'

'I never got a chance to say goodbye. I never got a chance to thank him. I never told him that I loved him.'

She tiptoed over and crouched by him. 'Who have you lost?' she asked, stroking his hair, his back, realising this was grief, not anger.

'My father,' he answered flatly. 'Fifty-four. Too young. I should have written more often. I wanted him to know about us, about our child; he shouldn't have died not knowing that the Bryant name continued. I didn't —'

'Shh,' she said, holding him, but Jack waved her comfort aside.

'No! I'm no good. Everything about my life is one big regret.'

Kanakammal forbade herself to take that personally. 'I will let you grieve. I am not far away.' She stood, noting for the first time how heavy she felt. Her belly was still as flat and tight as a drum, but within herself she felt the subtle changes; a ripeness deep inside, a tenderness at her breasts.

'I shall send a message to Top Reef with Gangai.'

'No!'

'You cannot go to work.'

'Don't tell me what I can and can't do.'

She sighed and left him. There was no point in talking to him when he was like this, although something made her turn at the doorway and voice one final warning. 'I will make some coffee. You need to sober up if you plan to go on shift.'

'Leave me!' he commanded and she did.

At some point he left the house. She didn't hear him go but Gangai came running in to inform her that he'd taken the motorbike.

'Was he dressed for work?'

Gangai shook his head.

'Did he say where he was going?'

'Andersonpet.'

She sighed. There was only one reason her husband would go into Andersonpet and that was to pay a visit to the local hooch house, where he could drink the colourless, odourless, vile arrack that was the ruin of many a villager.

———————

When Jack finally returned, his trousers were torn, his leg was bleeding and there was a strange fire in his eyes Kanakammal had never seen before. She kept her distance; knew from experience that although he would never strike her, his mood gave him a dangerous tongue and prompted the most irrational behaviour.

'Can I get you anything?' she said, as he threw off his clothes. She glanced at his leg now that he was naked, and saw the long, deep cut.

'I need to sober up,' he said, waggling a finger at her.

She busied herself making coffee and frying some chappattis. With a belly full of food, he might just drift off to sleep. But he came to her table, hair wet, shaved – despite the nicks from his razor – and dressed for work. His eyes were roaming, though, as though he couldn't focus. They were ringed in red and she could hear his laboured breathing.

'I made you breakfast,' she tried.

'Just black coffee.' He slurred his words slightly.

Disappointment knifed through her. But she poured him a cup of steaming coffee and eased herself down quietly in the chair opposite. She spoke to him in Tamil.

He frowned. 'What's that?'

'It was easier to say it in my language. I can say it better.'

'What?'

'How sorry I am for you.'

He shrugged. 'We all die.'

She realised his armour was back on.

'It is right to grieve.'

'My father wouldn't want me to waste time grieving over him.' He was speaking slowly as though concentrating hard on his words. 'I remember when our dog died. I was seven. I cried all night and my father got angry with me. She was his pup and he loved that dog but he said her life was over and there was no point in making a big fuss. She'd known she was loved, she didn't need all the wailing afterwards.'

'That is good advice,' she said carefully.

'Yes, old Rosie knew she was loved. But did my father know that he was loved? I didn't show it.'

'He knew.'

'How, damn it?' Jack groaned, smashing his fist on the table. 'How could he know?'

'Your sorrow tells me you loved him. He would have known.'

Jack shook his head hopelessly. 'I was a useless son. So useless, in fact, that my mother has likely already buried my father. It obviously didn't seem worth waiting for me.'

'Drink your coffee. Perhaps your mother felt it was best not to bring you home simply to bury him.'

He drained the cup, ignoring her idea.

Kanakammal poured him another.

'Any news from the Sinclairs? Iris?' he demanded.

She was surprised he could remember. 'Once Mrs Walker arrived, I left.'

'Damn Ned, and his jealousy.' He stood suddenly, steadied himself at the table. She stood too.

'Don't fuss, woman. I'm going to work.'

'Is that wise? You are grieving. And Ned?'

'Ned's a fool, my father is dead. I can't help either,' he said, sounding savage. He strode into the hall and reached for his work cap. He pulled it on and, with one final haunted look, he was gone.

Kanakammal rushed out to the verandah but he was already heading down the road. She stared out across the hilly scape to Top Reef. She could see its big fly-wheel and the skeleton of its winding equipment, lonely against the darkening sky. As she watched her husband walk away from her, she placed a hand on her belly. It was early days, yet she could have sworn she heard crying. Kanakammal was convinced she was giving her husband a son and she cried with her son now, for the father and for the husband who was walking away from them.

44

It was an extremely large office with a clock sombrely ticking away the hours from the dark timber shelves lining three of the walls. Awards, cups, books and ornaments littered those shelves, as well as formal photos of the man who was seated behind the huge leather inlaid desk in the middle of the room. Around the walls hung pictures of former chief inspectors. He looked forward to the day when someone else behind this desk would glance up and see him frowning down.

But right now Chief Inspector Dravid, of the Indian Police in Bangalore, regarded Margaret Brent as he stirred jaggery into his tea. The tea was still frothy from where his aide had poured it from a height, cooling it slightly.

'The Indian way,' the chief inspector said.

'How quaint,' Mrs Brent said, somewhat waspishly, he thought, but then it suited her thin lips and those dead-looking eyes that glanced around his office with a constant glare of disapproval. She fanned herself endlessly, even though he'd politely turned the ceiling fan up a notch.

'How do you breathe in here, Chief Inspector?' she grumbled. 'It's airless.'

'I am used to it,' he replied calmly, continuing to stir, knowing it was annoying her. He didn't like this English woman. She had come from Rangoon to discredit his police force. Dr Brent's death had been unusual; odd rather than suspicious, and as far as he was concerned, it was death by accident.

He'd already had two conversations with her. During the first – by phone – he had asked her most politely why she continued to pursue this case. And while she had given a brief explanation of wanting to establish the truth, he had worked out for himself that Brent's death had essentially signed the death warrant of the orphanage and his wife's future in Rangoon.

During the second conversation, in Bangalore, details of Edward Sinclair's very short stay in the orphanage had emerged. 'Have you fully explored that, Inspector, as I insisted?' she had pressed.

'Chief Inspector, madam,' he had corrected politely. 'Yes, Mr Sinclair told us about the connection but they had only spoken briefly at the Walker house, not at the club.'

'The man who found him was Sinclair's friend. Does that not strike you as fishy, Chief Inspector?'

'No, Mrs Brent. It struck our police officer as the coincidence it was. It is mentioned in his notes. I know you have repeatedly asked us to find motive, Mrs Brent, but once again I have to assure you that there was no sign of forced entry, no sign of a struggle, no unexplained fingerprints, there were not even the usual accoutrements of murder; no weapon, no blood, no guilty party the police were able to establish.'

She had been furnished with a full report and he'd hoped that would be enough. But now she was back, this time brandishing details of a previously unknown witness. Dravid thought the witness a particularly unreliable one, one who would certainly be discredited against the word of an Englishman.

With a long sigh Dravid had agreed to have this third and, he hoped, final meeting to try to explain to her why it was best to let the dead lie in peace . . . and take their secrets to their grave.

———

Ned's mood was bleak and he had made this journey on the pretext of it being essential but the truth of it was he needed distraction. To see Iris standing in the arms of Jack Bryant had sickened him initially but very quickly that had given way to a dark, cold fury.

He stared at the mess of wires and grimaced. He looked at his colleague, a much older Anglo-Indian man called Verne, who'd driven up from Bangalore to meet him. Together they'd converged on this point not far from the town, in a field, where canny village folk had decided to divert some of the power that electrified Bangalore before it reached KGF.

Ned stood at the top of the ladder they'd carried in together.

'I can remember the teams of people who used to move through the city each evening with their kerosene; filling lamps, trimming wicks and lighting up the place,' the older man sighed. 'And now we take instant light for granted.'

Ned was in no mood for reminiscing. 'But too many people, like these jokers,' he said, pointing to the jumble of wires, 'have no idea how electricity works or how dangerous it is.'

'If we dismantle it here, it will be back in no time somewhere else.'

'Yes, I agree.' Ned looked around, glad to have something to occupy his mind. He hated Jack, but in that moment of seeing them together, he hated Iris more. She was carrying Ned's child, their marriage barely three months old, yet she was back in Jack's arms again.

Barely three months. The words haunted him. The whispers in his mind had been repeating themselves since he jumped behind the wheel of the car. They jeered at his faith, mocked his belief that Iris could be pregnant so fast to him.

He closed his eyes momentarily to chase away the demons. 'I've been giving it some thought, though,' he said to Verne. 'What if we change the voltage coming through from the power stations, convert it into a level none of the villagers can make use of, and then convert it back once it's arrived at the destination?'

The old man scratched his head, then looked at Ned with a slow smile spreading across his face. 'That's so simple. I'm surprised we took so long to come up with it.'

Ned should have felt elated at his triumph – it was a damn good idea – but all he felt was a sense of hollowness, as though nothing would ever be worth smiling about again. He managed to feign just the right tone of responsibility. 'Simplicity is the key. Whatever it costs, I think we have to do something. Lives are at stake.'

'Agreed. All right. Can you make a report? I don't think anyone else should steal your thunder.'

'I could but I'd prefer if you did. It might sound better than me blowing my own trumpet.' Ned knew his reasoning sounded far too modest.

'Fine, but your name goes on the report and you get all the credit.'

'I don't need credit.'

'But it's important, son. And we need youngsters like you coming through with clever innovations.'

Ned nodded sombrely.

'Are you all right?' Verne asked.

Ned sighed. 'A little preoccupied with how dangerous this is. Let's get it all unravelled, shall we?'

His colleague stepped back. 'No, I don't think that's our job.'

'Well, someone has to.'

'I won't touch that. And you shouldn't either. I know you understand it but it's still too dangerous. Look at the tangle. You'd have no idea what's live. We should bring a team down and talk it through before anyone touches it.'

'A team of electricians? I'm an electrician, Verne. Fully qualified, fully capable of working this out.'

'It's nearing dusk, Ned. This is a job for another day . . . unless you want to die, fiddling around with high voltage in the dark.'

Who would miss me anyway? Ned thought miserably. Verne was waiting, looking up to where Ned was standing. 'Look, I can't leave here with this on my conscience. A child could be killed here tomorrow, when I could have done something about it today. Please go and get my equipment from the van. I'll just see if I can't at least make it safer until we can bring a team back.'

This seemed to appease Verne. He ambled off grumbling about medals not being handed over for courage in the workplace.

Ned watched him walk slowly away through the tamarind trees, his thoughts rapidly returning to his own problems that suddenly felt so insurmountable. Brent's ghost was back from the dead and Ned couldn't see his way out of the situation, not even with Jack's creative mind at work. And whereas before, Jack had done all the lying for him, he wouldn't get so lucky a second time. If the police interviewed him again, he would crumble, he just knew it, and end up telling them the truth.

From start to finish he wanted it told, *needed* it told. And even though he would be branded a murderer, he would at least be sent down as the man who took a serial child molester and killer off the streets. Cold comfort, perhaps, but Ned believed in truth, which is why seeing Iris in Jack's arms again was the last straw. How could they do that to him? Had they been meeting behind his back all this time? Was he the laughing stock of KGF? Iris had been in an awful hurry to get married.

The only constant was his job. His work had given him a life. Now it could take it. Verne's warning had suddenly showed him a way out of this mess . . . He hated where his thoughts were going but he couldn't seem to stop them..

If he lost his life while on a shift, Iris would be taken care of. She'd get a pension from the mine plus other benefits. She and the baby would be all right – and they'd never have to go through the mess of a trial or see him jailed for murder. And if Jack was the man Iris truly wanted, at least this way she could have him guilt-free.

He stared at the jumble of wires and likened his thoughts to them . . . irrational, out of control, no longer safe.

Verne had paused to chat with one of the villagers before he collected Ned's bag of tools. He was just entering the tamarind grove on the return journey when he heard a muted bang in the distance.

The sound was familiar. And it terrified him. He dropped Ned's tools and yelled over his shoulder, screaming at the villager to fetch help. He began running, praying he wasn't too late.

Verne arrived in the clearing, panting hard, and let out a groan of despair to see the young electrician sprawled forlornly on his back, the ladder also fallen away and the telltale spit and crackle of electricity sparking between some wires overhead.

Verne cast a prayer to the wind that the young man had simply fallen; a broken bone or two that would mend within a couple of months. But as he grabbed the youngster's arms, dragging him away from where wires could fall and reach them, he could see young Sinclair's eyes were glassy and staring, his mouth open, tongue lolling deep inside his cheek.

Unaware of his tears of frustration, Verne pumped Ned's chest, hoping against hope he could resuscitate him using this modern method they had all been taught for emergencies. From the corner of his eye, though, he could see that both of Ned's hands and part of his arms were burned; a sure sign that electricity had slammed into his body.

Still Verne kept the chest compression going, recalling now with renewed fear that Sinclair had only recently married.

The villager came speeding to the scene, halting abruptly and keeping his silence as he watched Verne doing his best to force Ned Sinclair back to life.

Finally, after ten more long minutes had passed and Verne was flagging, the villager crouched beside the older man and risked touching his shoulder lightly.

'Too late for the young master, sir,' he said, the whites of his eyes wide and bright around his chocolate-coloured irises. 'God has him now.'

'So, Mrs Brent,' Dravid began, sipping his cooled tea. 'Did your lawyer explain our position?'

'He did, Chief Inspector, but I am not to be diverted from this path. I assure you that while my husband was a heavy man he was not a clumsy one.'

The senior policeman put his cup down and held up his palms. 'Accidents happen to us all, madam,' and then before she could launch into the tirade he could see was simmering, he held up a finger. 'You see, Mrs Brent, forgive me, but I fail to understand what you've hoped to achieve with all the years of questions. Let me summarise your position. Seven years ago now your husband died in Bangalore. Not only the military but also a civil doctor confirmed that the depression in his skull was most likely due to a fall, during which he hit his head, suffered a serious contusion, subsequent concussion and internal bleeding, and death resulted.'

'I know what the reports say, Chief Inspector.'

He understood she considered herself superior to him and that she was probably used to ordering around hapless little Burmese. India was changing – all of Asia was changing. One day soon the likes of Mrs Brent would be 'out on their ear', he thought, enjoying the quaint English phrase.

'But, madam, what do you want to achieve here?'

'Chief Inspector, we have a witness that places Edward Sinclair at the Bangalore Club on the night of my husband's death. Now, that contravenes his statement, which surely demands that you question him again.'

'Indeed. Mr Sinclair also has a witness that says he was at the home of Dr Harold Walker at the time of your husband's death. The only person near your husband was a Mr John Bryant, known as Jack.'

'A friend of Ned Sinclair's!'

'Well, madam, they had only met for the first time that week. And all those Englishmen who frequent the Bangalore Club are pretty friendly. You could probably cite half the members at the time who might have known Sinclair or Walker or Bryant, or your husband for that matter.'

'So you have no intention of helping me?'

'Please, Mrs Brent. This is what I am doing. I have no doubt your lawyer from Delhi is charging quite handsomely for his time. And I suspect he is the only person who will benefit from reopening the case. The witness you cite will most likely be discredited.' Again he held up a hand to stop her bluster. 'Sinclair's original witness will be considered more reliable than someone found years later relying on an old memory of someone in the dark who might have been Edward Sinclair. Mr Ramesh's description matches half the young Brits in Bangalore. What's more, Sinclair has no motive.'

'I'm telling you they had words. That boy was sullen and defiant. He walked right out of the orphanage, kidnapped his sister and then stowed away on a ship to India.'

Dravid smiled gently. 'The way you tell it, Mrs Brent, it does sound damning. But Mr Sinclair was eighteen at the time, his sister was his kin and came willingly.'

'I don't agree.'

'Nothing you're doing will bring your husband back, even should you be successful.'

'If I'm successful, Chief Inspector, then I shall sue Dr Walker, Dr Grenfell, Edward Sinclair, Jack Bryant, the shipping line who carried the Sinclairs, the Bangalore Club for its negligence, the police force for its shoddy work and anyone else I think is complicit in my husband's death.'

He sighed. Here was the truth of it. Margaret Brent was seeking damages. 'I see.'

'I will clear his name,' she pressed.

Dravid gave a flicker of a smile as the woman gave him the perfect opening. 'I'm afraid that might not be possible.'

'What?'

'Please,' he said, then made her fume by pausing to sip his tea. 'There is something I should explain.'

'I doubt there's anything that can change my mind.'

He smiled wryly. 'Mrs Brent, when your husband died in Bangalore it was necessary to look into his life to be sure that he had no enemies. You see, while you feel we made a cursory decision that it was death by accident, I must inform you that intensive police work was conducted at the time. You may recall a visit or two from our colleagues in Rangoon?'

'What of it?'

'Well, in the process of those inquiries some details came to light that involved Dr Brent . . .' He paused.

'Yes?' she said irritably.

'Why don't you read the report for yourself? I'll give you a few moments.' He turned around the manila folder that was open on his desk and pushed it forward before standing and taking his tea to the window. When he returned, Margaret Brent had developed a grey pallor.

'Can I get you something, Mrs Brent?' he asked politely.

'Water, please,' she croaked.

He obliged. 'Better?'

She nodded and he noticed a tremor in her hand as she placed the glass down.

'As you can see, I don't think it would be wise for you to pursue your inquiries. I don't believe there is any worthwhile new information relating to his death, but there is other information that will almost certainly be exposed relating to his life. Rangoon Police have several former students of the orphanage who would be willing to testify,' he added.

'Where did you get this?' she asked, her voice pleasingly small and shocked.

'Our police work is not so shoddy, madam. But I would like to assure you that what's in that file stays in that file, if you would like me to keep it that way. I see no reason to besmirch your husband's name. I would far prefer to keep the Brent name synonymous with the good work you have personally overseen regarding Rangoon's orphans.' He made sure his voice sounded very reasonable, with a soft note of encouragement.

'Yes, yes, of course,' she said, sounding suddenly bewildered.

'Shall I close this file, Mrs Brent? Put it away for good?'

'Please do that, Chief Inspector.' She even gave him a begrudging half-smile. 'You've been very sensitive of my position.'

He shrugged magnanimously. 'Let me have one of my drivers deliver you back to your hotel.' He held out a hand, enjoying the way his twenty-four-carat gold ring on his small finger glinted beneath the desk light.

She shook his hand and thanked him.

Dravid asked his aide to send in his secretary on his way out. 'Tell him I have two telegrams to send to Kolar Gold Fields.'

45

Jack arrived at the engine room half an hour before he was due on his shift that would see him working through the night until around two in the morning. He'd had to leave the house; he couldn't bear to see the look of disapproval but mostly disappointment in his wife's eyes.

He knew he'd let her down by being alone with Iris. He had nothing to answer for, yet he felt so empty. He'd let Ned down again but his real sorrow was for the loss of his father.

At least he hadn't drunk too much today. No doubt his wife imagined he'd gone into the toddy house, but he'd found himself at the Andersonpet Beer House, sitting in the shade alone, no one aware of the problems churning in his mind. He had drunk beer but it had been slow enough and watery enough that most of it had passed through already.

Yes, he felt a bit 'furry around the edge' but he was fine. He needed to set aside the news from Cornwall for now. He had a nine-hour shift to get through. Jack caught himself yawning as he pulled on his overalls, and so did one of his team.

'You all right, Jack?'

'Big day,' he replied, making light of it. 'My wife's pregnant. We've had people around celebrating.'

'Hope you didn't celebrate too hard?' It sounded like an admonishment.

Jack's irritation flared. This fellow was around the same age but Jack was his boss. 'You worry about your work, Robert, and I'll take care of mine.' He slammed his locker shut. 'And don't ever question my ability to do my job again.'

Withering beneath Jack's grim stare, the man nodded nervously, and turned away. So did Jack, to hide his desire to yawn again. He took a long drink of water to refresh himself and then sat at the small desk to briefly work out which men would be assigned which tasks for the shift.

Ten minutes later, stretching to clear the cobwebs in his mind, Jack walked across to the platform where he would take charge of winding. He could work alone raising and lowering the men before changing over the cages to the bigger ones that would carry the quartz trolleys up, filled with ore. These were routine tasks he knew backwards. It's not that it didn't require him to think, but much of what this particular job involved was intuitive. His hands, his mind knew what to do; his eyes and ears took their own cues, without him having to worry about checking and double-checking. Jack knew he could rely on himself to perform his duties instinctively.

'Hello, Don,' he said to the man just wrapping up his shift. 'Everything calm tonight?'

'Smooth as silk, Jack. The banksman is changing over now. You've got Marty on tonight.'

Jack yawned, covered it with another stretch. 'Good. Marty's reliable,' Jack said, referring to the man who would keep an eye on all of the cages going up and down, whether they carried men or ore. He would signal to Jack when to lower, when to raise, using a system of bells.

Jack stepped up onto the platform and instinctively his gaze moved to the two enormous black dials in front of him that told him the depth of the cages.

'Right, Jack. I'm off.'

'See you, Don.' He lifted his hand in a wave and turned back to his dials. He'd love to have caught forty winks but the team was already dribbling in. Damn them all for being so prompt this evening, he thought, uncharitably. Jack took one last walk around before he knew the bell would signal. He stretched once again, feeling a satisfying click in his spine, then splashed his face with the cool water nearby and felt immediately better for it.

As he walked past an open window Jack could smell cut grass; everyone wanted their lawns manicured during the festive season. In the distance he could hear men's voices. The next shift of workers was gathering, mainly Indians on this night, but he imagined their conversations were the same as any group of blokes; debts, wages, family.

He yawned as he relieved himself in the ablutions block. Burrell, one of the older men, noticed, but clearly knew better than to shoot his mouth off.

'Jack,' he acknowledged.

Jack washed his hands. 'How are you, Stan?'

'Fine, fine. Have you seen they've put the mine's Christmas tree up?'

'Have they?'

'The lights were supposed to light up all over the town.'

They walked out of the block together, the noise of the ore trolleys rattling up the tracks drowning out other sounds.

Jack had to shout. 'What's the hold-up? You have to tie Ned Sinclair's hands normally to stop him throwing the switch beforehand.'

Burrell shrugged. 'There's some commotion going on at the electrical department. I saw a crowd of people outside the Walker household.'

Jack frowned. 'What?'

'I thought I saw your mate's wife being helped inside.'

'Helped?'

'Oh, well, you know. It was dark but I thought it was her. Anyway, come on, the siren's about to go.'

Jack nodded, disturbed, his anxiety for Iris, for Ned and his own grief reawakened.

————

As Jack was stepping back onto his platform, awaiting the siren that would signal the changeover and the bell for him to begin winding, Iris was being given a sedative.

'Two cachets of Veronal should do it,' her father explained as he tipped the white crystallised powder into the mug of milk that her mother had warmed. He stirred it briskly. 'Now, get it all down her.'

'Do we have to drug her? What about the baby?' Flora asked, wiping at the silent, helpless tears streaming down her face.

'Flora, she's near hysterical. She must be still. I'm thinking of that baby and trying to keep our grandchild safe. This will bring Iris some rest quickly.'

After collecting herself, Flora entered her daughter's bedroom where Rupert and Geraldine struggled to calm the sobs of their younger sister.

'Please, darling,' Rupert was soothing Iris. 'I'll hold you, I promise. I won't let you go.'

The last time Flora had seen Iris she'd been screaming, so these chest-heaving sobs were a marked improvement. But it wasn't just Iris; they were all in shock. Fortunately, she had been with her daughter when the news had come through. She thought about that terrible hour or two now as though she were watching it play again, as though it were happening right before her.

That silent, brooding woman who'd married Jack Bryant had sent the chokra to fetch Flora. Flora had been confused enough by

Mrs Bryant – of all people – being at her daughter's house, but to be summoned by her because her daughter needed looking after was even more mystifying. But right enough, Iris had seemed agitated, mumbling about Ned seeing her with Jack. Oh, Flora couldn't make head nor tail of it.

There had to be some misunderstanding but she couldn't make sense of Iris's frantic ramblings. Then, just as she'd settled Iris into a shower, there had been a knock at the door.

When Flora opened the door she had been confronted by two grim-looking men she recognised from her son-in-law's workplace.

'Hello, Bernie, Ron,' she'd said, frowning. 'Ned's at work.'

The men looked at each other and she sensed the tension immediately.

'What's going on?' she asked, her hand instantly to her chest, peering around to see if Iris was out yet. She could still hear the water flowing. 'Has something happened?'

Bernie looked down. 'Flora, can we come in?'

She opened the door wider. 'Tell me, before my pregnant daughter comes out. She's upset enough today.'

Bernie shook his head. 'We should tell her to her face —'

'Don't you dare, Bernie Molloy! I went to school with your father! Show some respect for your elders. Now, my daughter's had enough upset for today. What do you think I'm doing here? Sucking eggs?' It was an old Anglo-Indian saying. Both men had heard their own mothers say it many times. And Flora Walker was not one to trifle with. They shook their heads in unison. 'Don't upset Iris,' she warned.

It was Ron who found the courage after a deep breath. 'I don't think we can avoid that, Mrs Walker.'

Flora felt the colour drain from her face and was suddenly feeling backwards for a chair. They helped her, sitting her down in the small front room.

Steeled by his companion, Bernie continued. 'There's been an accident, Mrs Walker. It's . . . it's Ned.'

She stared at them blankly. How bad was it? She didn't want to ask, didn't want to know; she was frightened for Iris and what this would do to her.

Into that terrible silence came a small voice. 'Mum? Ron, what are you doing here? I . . . I'm sorry. I was . . .'

Bernie cleared his throat and Flora forced herself to be resolute; her daughter needed her. Ned was obviously going to need care, and all the family would help. She rallied her courage, crossed the floor and took her daughter's hand.

'Iris, my love, you have to be brave, darling. There's been an accident.'

'Ned?' Iris asked, searching the men's faces for information.

They both nodded.

'How bad?' she croaked.

Ron looked up, his eyes helplessly watering. 'Iris, I'm sorry, he's dead.'

Flora heard the final word but it seemed to take an age to register. It hung between the four of them like a disease; sinister, unwelcome, final. None of them wanted to claim it. She certainly needed to run the word over and over in her mind to make sense of it in connection with the young, vital Edward Sinclair, the father of her unborn grandchild.

'Dead?' she heard Iris groan. 'Are you sure?'

It was a mad question. They'd hardly be here otherwise.

But Iris was not yet ready to accept it. 'How?' Flora saw her daughter shake her head as though what she'd been told was impossible. 'I mean, he left here a few hours ago, perfectly healthy. What do you mean *dead*?' Suddenly Iris was running across the floor and beating Ron's chest with her fists. 'What do you mean *dead*?' she screamed again.

Flora reached for her daughter but she wouldn't be consoled, couldn't be quietened. Over the noise and beyond the shock, she found her wits. 'Bernie, go fetch my husband from the hospital now. Be quick! We have to think of the baby.'

And then she had wrapped her small arms stoutly around her child and held her so firmly that all Iris could do was weep, screaming intermittently that the news was wrong. But her mother refused to let go. Three generations of her family sat on the sofa in that lonely, frigid house and she was going to make sure all of them came through this safely.

And now she ignored her daughter's cries and protests again, gently but firmly getting the warmed milk down her throat. It was soothing on its own but her fatigue from all the anxiety combined with the fast working barbiturate had her sleeping sooner than Flora had imagined.

Rupert sighed in relief, his face pinched and weary.

Geraldine was crying and excused herself.

It was only now that Flora allowed herself to cry. She turned into her husband's arms. 'Harold, what are we going to do?'

He stroked her neck. 'We're going to stay strong as a family and we're going to help Iris come through this.'

'Have you found out any more?' she said, stepping back a little from his embrace, digging in her sleeve for her hanky.

'An accident, not far out of Bowringpet.' He gave a rueful sigh. 'Ned was trying to fix a dangerous site.'

She stifled a sob at the horrible irony.

'He'd been warned to leave it. I don't know what was in his head; he was such a cautious young man. It was obviously a terrible tragedy, no one's fault.'

'Who knows?' Rupert asked. 'Has anyone told Jack Bryant?'

His father shook his head. 'No one knows. And I've asked it kept that way for now until Iris wakes up at least. '

'And Christmas is just days away,' Flora bleated.

Harold hugged his wife. 'Our only concern now is Iris and the safe delivery of her baby. She'll be stronger then, and with a child to look after she'll have every reason to look forward, even if it won't seem like that to her just now.'

'We might as well move her stuff back home. They won't let her stay here,' Rupert said and shrugged at his mother's glare at his insensitivity. 'She can't hear me, Mum, and it needs to be said. Let's save her the trauma and start packing things up now. I can handle that – I'm no good for much else.'

'Don't say that, son,' his mother said.

'You're right, Rupert. She'll have to leave,' Harold followed up. 'I'll leave that with you, then. She's best at home with us anyway.'

They heard the sirens from the various mines signalling the next shift and it seemed to break the spell in the room. Harold and Rupert left Flora, who was settling herself into a chair so she could sit and watch her daughter sleep and be there for when she woke to the realisation that it had not been a nightmare; Edward Sinclair was dead.

———————

The siren sounded above the loud groan of the engines. Their noise was so constant that the engineering team had learned to live around its endless accompaniment and talked, unconcerned, above it. But Jack worked alone, gloves on, deep in his thoughts, checking dials, levers, preparing for the process that would raise the cages of fatigued, dust-encrusted men from the afternoon shift, and replace them with clean men, lowering them for their long haul through the night in the belly of the earth.

Marty gave the signal, the bell shook, jangling above Jack's head. Not needing to look at the lever, his eye on the big dial, Jack heard the engine sigh, and the hauling began.

He heard the whine of the engine as it responded to his controls and he watched the great wheel rotating. The generators groaned a bit louder than usual as he coaxed the engine and the black cables, strung taut, wound effortlessly and the first cage-load of men arrived back at the surface.

'Are they double loading or something?' Burrell commented as he walked behind Jack.

'What?'

'She's complaining tonight,' he said, referring to the engine.

'That's her way, Stan. They wouldn't dare add a single person more to the cage than instructed, not without asking first. No, we're all good here.'

Burrell walked away as another groan sounded. Robert heard it too.

'Ominous,' he remarked, as he passed.

Burrell shrugged. 'Bryant knows what he's doing and he knows that engine better than any of us.'

Robert gave the older man an arch look that defied Burrell's sentiment.

'Go about your business, Robert,' Burrell suggested. He strolled back to Jack. 'Need any help?'

Jack glanced around. 'What is this, the third degree? First bloody Robert Powell and now you?'

'You look a bit tired, Jack, and your eyes are bloodshot.'

'Stan, I'm going to let that pass but I'm resenting all this scrutiny from my own people.' He lowered the lever and the winder responded, reversing its direction. 'Powell's always looking to undermine me when he can. He's never got over my promotion and you know it.'

'I know. I think the accident at William's Shaft has made us all a bit nervous.'

'That was a rock burst, Stan. Nothing to do with engineering.'

'Yeah, you're right. Sorry.'

'Me too. I'm probably a bit touchy tonight. Best left to myself.'

'All right, Jack. I'm going out to check the pumps.'

'Good. Don't forget we also need to check the ore chutes are clear. Or we'll get blamed again. And Stan?'

He turned.

'Get Powell out of my sight, will you? He can check the leats are clear on the levels.'

'Will do.'

As Burrell left, Jack stifled another yawn and shook his head to try to clear the blurriness in his mind. Somewhere he registered that he must be in shock over his father's death, because right now all he felt was numb. He couldn't think about it, not yet. He sensed his brain blanking and shying away from the fact of his father's death . . . Work! That was the thing. His work was something he knew how to do.

He waited for the hand signal from the man below. The cage emptied and a new complement of Indian workers trooped in. The cage itself was approximately twenty feet tall and carried its human cargo in two layers, up to thirteen men in each layer.

Jack checked the dial. All steady. It would take roughly three minutes to lower the men. He waited for Marty to make his notation of how many the next cage contained. All was ready.

The banksman gave the signal and the bell above him told Jack it was time to lower. He was already thinking about the bigger cages that would be changed over shortly to begin the all-night hauling of the quartz to the surface. There'd been some repairs to the ore cages and he was looking forward to a problem-free shift.

Jack checked the dial. The men were already at three thousand feet. That seemed to have happened faster than his instincts told him. He shook his head, moved his jaw from side to side in an effort to rouse himself. The coffee wasn't working its expected magic. He needed to stay alert. He called to a tiny Indian man nearby. Babu was never far away, instantly recognisable in his baggy black trousers and deep charcoal shirt, sleeves rolled back to his elbows.

Babu grinned, his thick moustache widening, always pleased to be called upon. 'Yes, sir, Master Bryant?'

'Get me a water, will you? I'm very thirsty.'

He nodded and hurried away. Jack wished all his men could be as enthusiastic as little Babu, who seemed to consider it the height of privilege to be the engineer's sidekick.

He was back in a blink. 'Here, sir.'

Jack took the enamel mug and drained it loudly. 'I needed that,' he said with a sigh, his gaze on the dial.

Was it his imagination or was the cage descending faster? The men were at seven thousand feet. Jack refocused his attention on the dial. Perhaps he should slow it. He eased back on the lever, felt the response immediately, heard it too.

He blinked hard, feeling suddenly and overwhelmingly weary. Once the men were lowered, though, he told himself, everything became easy, almost monotonous, and he could hand over to one of his team. He would join Burrell on the checks, remind the man who was boss here.

His mind wandered to Ned and how he could set the record straight with his friend. And naturally his thoughts drifted to Iris and the news that something odd was going on at their house. Come to think of it, the nine o'clock wink that irritated Jack no end hadn't occurred tonight. That certainly was strange.

There was a sickening crunch as all the machinery sputtered. A jarring shudder ran through the great wheel. Jack felt it through the levers, through his gloves. In that split second he felt like he'd been catapulted back years in time to a wintry morning in Penzance. He held his breath as shock ripped through him; he glanced out at the wheel and it was intact, cables still shivering from whatever the impact was.

He had the presence of mind to hit the brakes and shut down the engines to an idle. Jack's mind felt blurry. He was expecting shattered machinery but everything was intact as far as he could tell.

Burrell came hurtling into the winding room yelling and Jack could hear Marty screaming from the shaft's entrance. The bell was jangling overhead and a telephone was clanging angrily nearby.

But it was Babu who was pointing, his eyes wide with fright, moustache twitching as he urged his boss. 'The dial, Master Bryant, sir. The dial.' He kept jabbing a thin finger at the depth dial.

Jack's eyes flashed upwards, his gaze dragged fearfully to the dial that told him much too clearly that the men had been lowered to a depth of nine thousand feet.

Nine thousand.

Too deep!

Men were trapped in cages that were firmly locked from the outside, having been lowered to the floor of the shaft where deep pools of water naturally gathered.

'They're drowning!' Burrell howled, leaping onto the platform. 'The pumps are compromised, remember?'

'What?' Jack said, befuddled and slow.

'Raise them!' Powell screamed, newly arrived, white as a sheet with fright.

Around him was a familiar sound of pandemonium and Jack uncharacteristically stood back in a daze of shock. Powell pushed him aside and took control of the winding machine, instantly throwing the lift machinery into reverse, dragging the cage out of the water. But it had been over three minutes.

The siren sounded – a different tone this time – the one every woman in KGF dreaded hearing.

And then Burrell was at his side. 'Get out of here, Jack!' he growled. 'Go and sober up somewhere.'

'Sober?' Jack repeated, sounding confused.

'I smelled it on you earlier. I was a fucking fool. Now they'll blame you!'

'What do you mean?'

'Get out!' Burrell hustled him from the engine room.

Jack wanted to fight back but all the fight had suddenly gone out of him; he could already hear the shrieks and screams. He knew what came next.

He wasn't given a chance to think. Burrell bundled him into one of the mine's vans and gave orders to an Indian to take Master Bryant back to his house. Jack wanted to say something but nothing was coming out of his mouth.

All he could see was his father's face, gloomily shaking his head in disappointment at his son. In the back of the van Jack finally broke. He crumpled in on himself and drew deep, silent, heaving breaths as his emotional dams burst and his sorrows erupted for the men who had surely perished on his watch, for Ned and Iris, for Kanakammal, for the shame of what his child would now grow up knowing about him, and ultimately . . . and always . . . for the father he had never managed to live up to.

Kanakammal heard the long siren and her heart skipped a beat. She should hurry up the hill, to join the other wives and mothers, sisters and aunts, who would be panicking, trying to get to the mine shaft quickly, as though by physically being closer, they could save their men.

But somehow she knew she was not required this time. Jack was not below the earth. He was here, being brought home in a van, waving away help and tumbling out of the passenger seat. She could see he was in deep shock.

She steeled herself for what was to come, and waited for him to mount the steps to the verandah. He fell into her arms and wept like a child. There was nothing to do except hold him until this wave of desolation passed.

She couldn't tell him about Ned; she had trouble enough believing it herself. She'd gone to her father's shop and found the Sinclairs' chokra boy. He'd been dismissed by Mr Rupert Walker and told he'd no longer be required. Mr Walker had paid him and given him some extra money, and let slip that the master and madam were not coming back to their house. That was all the boy knew. Kanakammal had walked down the main street to find out more. She passed one of the orderlies from the hospital.

'A man was killed today. A terrible accident. He was electrocuted,' her friend had said in Tamil, wide-eyed.

'Do you know who?'

'He was married to Dr Walker's daughter.' She waggled her head. 'Poor Dr Walker.'

Kanakammal stared at her friend. It wasn't her fault that she had stated the facts so baldly; she couldn't know that Kanakammal knew Ned Sinclair personally.

The pain and shock had caught in her throat and she'd had to excuse herself. She'd run all the way back home and then stood in the middle of the back garden, hugging herself, as if she were cold. Monkeys running up and down in the trees called down, hoping she might throw some fruit scraps to them, but Kanakammal was heedless to their pleas.

No, she would not be telling Jack the news of Ned just yet. For now it seemed he had enough agony to deal with.

'I don't understand,' he groaned, as they separated and walked into the house. 'I did everything right.'

Almost immediately, they heard a car pull up outside. Kanakammal stood and craned her neck. 'It's the mine people,' she said, feeling a rising anxiety. She went to the door and let the men in. Even though she still had no idea what had happened, it was obvious it was traumatic. Both men were from Britain; a Scot she had met once before in passing with Jack, and an Englishman she didn't know. She pointed to the front room and hovered at the door when they'd gone inside.

'Jack,' the Scot said. 'How are you, lad?'

Jack stood. He appeared sober but his eyes still looked dazed.

'I'm devastated, Mr Mackenzie. I . . . I would have stayed and helped but Stan Burrell —'

'Did the right thing in sending you home,' the other man said.

'Mr Johns, I don't know what to say or think. It wasn't my fault.'

Johns nodded but Kanakammal sensed it was just a way of shutting Jack up. He wasn't agreeing; he was simply humouring him. She walked into the room and stood beside Jack.

'This is my wife, Elizabeth.'

'Your wife?' Johns said, unable to mask his surprise. Then he checked himself, giving a half-hearted bow to her.

Mackenzie was far more polite. 'Mrs Bryant.'

'Perhaps your wife,' Johns said, adding a slight emphasis on the last word, 'could make some tea?'

She knew he was trying to get rid of her. She also knew he assumed she didn't understand English. 'Do you take it with milk or lemon, Mr Johns?' she said.

He threw her an acid glance. 'It doesn't really matter, Mrs Bryant. We'd like to talk to your husband alone.'

Jack stared at the men. He felt as if his thoughts were trying to stay afloat in a stormy sea but were losing the fight. There was such a sense of drowning; his sorrows combined with his anxiety and conspired with a weighty fatigue to drag him deeper.

Johns was fairly new to KGF; recently out from head office and full of eagerness and stiff-upper-lip briskness. In any other circumstances Jack would have slung the man out on his ear – senior or not – for the way Johns had sneered at his wife. But this was no ordinary night and he had looked at Elizabeth and given a small nod. She went without another word, although she threw a glance of encouragement back at him before she disappeared.

'You have a beautiful wife, Jack,' Mackenzie said.

'Thank you, sir.'

Mackenzie was the executive engineer at the mines and liked by everyone.

'All right, Bryant. There's no way we can sweeten this for you so I'm going to tell you exactly what we're up against,' Johns said, taking a seat without being asked.

Jack gestured to Mack. He was terrified; there would be no good news.

'We have seventeen confirmed dead.'

Jack leaned forward, his head in his hands, and began to deep breathe. It was either that or throw up.

'We have another two who are likely brain dead.' Johns continued without mercy. 'You not only lowered them to the maximum depth, Bryant, but straight into ten feet of water in a locked cage. All thirteen men in that bottom layer perished.'

'Mack,' Jack appealed, his voice tight with shock. His breathing had taken on a shallow rasp. 'I don't know what happened. Everything was normal.'

'Not everything, Bryant,' Johns said viciously, before his colleague could respond. 'There's talk you showed up for your shift *under the weather*, as they say.'

Jack looked up now. Mack was eyeing him with genuine sympathy but Johns' eyes were burning with intensity.

'What does that mean?' Jack asked.

'Several of the men saw you yawning. One is prepared to go on record that you'd been drinking.'

'Find me a miner who doesn't drink in this town, Mr Johns.' It was not the right approach.

'But you are not a miner, Mr Bryant. You are the senior engineer at Top Reef mine. The mine took a risk with you and it seems that faith was misplaced.'

Jack stood, his hands balled into fists. He hoped he didn't sway.

'Sit down, Jack,' Mack said softly but firmly. Jack obeyed. 'The fact is it doesn't matter what the reasons are. We're now concerned for your safety.'

Jack frowned.

'Yes, and the company is responsible for it,' Johns added, looking sour. 'These deaths come hot on the heels of the dreadful business at William's Shaft. A lot of Indians died down there and now another load at Top Reef. There's a bad mood brewing, Bryant. The local workers are constantly griping about safety and equipment, but this is going to make them militant. This time only Indians died.'

Mack got to the real point. 'The thing is, Jack, if they get wind that one of the Brits wasn't on his game, they aren't going to be reasonable. Hell, lad, they'll tear you limb from limb.'

Jack looked between the two men. 'Are you serious?'

'Deadly,' Johns said. 'You're not safe.'

'But I didn't —'

'It doesn't matter, Jack,' Mack said softly. 'They want to blame someone. They'll blame the man operating the winder. I can't tell you how ugly the mood is. We don't have long.'

'What are you suggesting?'

Johns impaled him with a hard look. 'We get you out tonight – immediately.'

'Out? Where?'

'I'll drive you to Bangalore. From there we'll arrange passage home for —'

'Wait. Leave India? No, I —'

'Mr Bryant. The company is not asking you, it is telling you. It's in your contract. There are no ifs and buts. The company has the right – and particularly in these circumstances to safeguard your life – to remove you from India, back to your place of origin.'

Mack moved to sit next to Jack, put an arm around his shoulder. 'Mr Johns is right. It's written into all our contracts. Any sign of trouble and they send us back.'

Jack shook his head. 'The Indian workers —'

This time Mack interrupted him. 'Times are changing, lad. India's changing. These aren't the meek village folk of ten years back. The push for independence from the Crown is gaining momentum. Have you heard about this fellow Ghandi?'

Jack shook his head, his mind spinning too hard with the notion of leaving KGF to worry about politics.

'Right now, if there is any way that the Indians can strike back at the British they will. These two accidents in such a short time could be a catalyst for a much bigger uprising. I'm not saying getting you out can stop the inevitable, but —'

Johns cut across Mack's words. 'The company does not want your blood on its hands, Mr Bryant. Do you understand? It wants no further responsibility for you. It will see you back to Britain and it will not require your services again . . . anywhere. Now, you have ten minutes to grab a few things. Time is of the essence.'

Jack felt his world collapsing in on itself. They were serious. He would be gone tonight. They believed he had killed those men through negligence. A voice at the back of his mind, sounding a lot like Stan Burrell, agreed. Kanakammal had begged him not to go to work; she'd known, and deep down so had he, that too much had happened today, and too much liquor had been consumed. Seventeen men dead on his watch, in his cage, dead because he had failed to pay attention to the depth dial. The depth dial – the lynchpin of a winder's existence! He should have listened to Elizabeth.

His voice was forlorn and desperate when it came. 'My wife . . .'

Johns shook his head. 'Just you, Bryant. You can send for your wife. She is safe. She's Indian.' Perhaps he tried not to smirk but Jack saw it all the same.

Mack must have caught it too. 'Come on, Jack. Let's move. Grab some clothes, shaving gear . . . just throw a few things into a suitcase and I'll get you to Bangalore. Do you know anyone there?'

Jack rubbed his face, dismayed, confused. 'Yes, yes. Henry Berry. He works for the government.'

'Good. He can get you on a ship home.' He bundled Jack towards the bedroom, where Kanakammal had been listening.

'Elizabeth,' Jack began.

'Just go,' she said. 'Be safe first. Mr Mackenzie is protecting you. The people won't listen to reason tonight.' She stood up and started gathering Jack's belongings together into a leather holdall.

Mackenzie stood by awkwardly. 'We'll send the rest, I promise. Just take what you need for a journey.'

Within a few minutes Kanakammal had him packed.

'Come with me,' Jack said. His offer sounded hollow and meaningless. They both knew it was impossible.

'I cannot,' she said.

'Then I'll come back for you when this has blown over.'

She nodded, eyes lowered.

Mack grabbed the holdall and Jack's arm. 'Let's go.'

It was Johns who sounded the alarm. 'I hear them. Hurry!'

Sure enough, they could hear the angry murmur of excited voices like a wave, coming down the hill.

'Jack,' Kanakammal began, so many things still needing to be said.

He broke free of Mack's grip and grabbed her, hugging her hard. 'I'm sorry,' he whispered. 'I'm so sorry.' His eyes were watery.

'I know,' she said, and kissed him softly. '*Naan wooni nasikiran.*'

Jack didn't need any translation. 'I love you too, Kanakammal,' he said, surprising himself, because he meant it with all his heart. A pain stabbed in his chest as he realised they might never see each other again.

Kanakammal knew it too.

'Then no distance will change that,' she said in English, and she gave him a pure sweet smile that felt like the sun warming his cold, fearful heart.

The first lamps of the mob appeared on the hillside.

Johns was already in the car. 'Mr Bryant, I cannot protect you a moment longer!'

'In the car, Jack,' Mack ordered. He turned to Kanakammal. 'I'm sorry. We'll get word to you.'

She nodded at him and then at Jack, her hand absently held against her belly.

And then they were gone, Mack gunning the engine, lights switched off so they could make their getaway, stealing away in the darkness that felt as black as Jack's heart.

Minutes later, still stunned and unable to say much, Jack noticed they were driving into Oorgaum. He leaned forward to tap Mack's shoulder.

'I need to let Ned Sinclair know I'm going,' he said.

Johns didn't slow.

'Mack, please, you've got to let me say goodbye. Ned is —'

Johns turned. 'Edward Sinclair is —' but he didn't finish because Mack gave him an intimidating glare that said plenty.

'The Sinclairs aren't at home, Jack,' Mack said gently.

Jack hadn't missed the glare or the tension that had flared at the mention of Ned's name. Something was badly wrong – he knew it.

'Then I'll speak to the Walkers!' He reached for the handle, opened the car door and tumbled out, rolling once in the dust. The car hadn't been travelling fast so he was on his feet by the time Johns had braked to a halt and running towards Harold's house, which seemed to have every light blazing, despite the hour.

He looked behind him as he banged on the door. Mack was walking up the gravel drive slowly, a pained look on his face that Jack could just make out in the glow cast out from the house. Johns reversed to idle the car outside the Walkers' gate. The Christmas lights were not switched on and there was an eerie silence surrounding a house that looked to be wide awake.

He banged solidly again and the door was pulled open before he'd finished. 'Sabu.'

'Mr Bryant, sir. This is not a happy time for calling.'

Jack frowned. 'Is Ned here?'

Harold Walker emerged from the depths of the house and to Jack's eyes it seemed as though the man had aged a decade.

'Dr Walker!' Jack called.

Rupert followed behind on his crutches.

'Jack,' Walker said and shook his head. 'Please go away.'

'What's going on? Something's wrong and no one's telling me. Is it the baby? Is Iris . . .'

'It's not Iris, Jack,' Rupert answered.

Mack arrived, looking apologetic.

'There's been an accident at Top Reef,' Jack explained, not wanting Mack to elaborate for him. 'I have to leave KGF tonight, it seems. Have you been called to the mine yet, Dr Walker?'

Harold Walker shook his head. 'There's scant need for doctors up there, but the morgue will be busy.' His voice was gritty.

Jack felt his throat close so tight he could barely swallow. 'Seventeen dead,' he said, baldly. 'I am being held responsible, although —'

'Frankly, Jack, I don't care,' Walker said. 'I've got rather more on my mind tonight.'

Jack felt Mack's hand on his arm. He shook it free, frowning. 'Rupert, what's going on?'

Rupert looked to Mack. 'Why hasn't anyone told him?'

'Told me what?' Jack roared, barging into the house. 'Iris!'

They tried to restrain him but it was like trying to hold back a Cornish storm on a winter's night. 'Iris!' he yelled again.

Flora came running. 'You stay away from her, Jack Bryant!'

Mack had his burly arms around Jack but it was Flora who stopped him in his tracks. She was so small, but fierce in defence of her daughter.

'I just want to talk to her.' She blocked his path.

'You can't. She is sedated, unconscious,' Walker explained, taking charge at last. He sighed. 'Jack, I'm sorry you have to learn this now, on top of everything, but there was another accident today involving Ned.'

Jack tried to say something but nothing came out other than a soft moan.

'He's dead, Jack,' Rupert said, glancing at his father.

Jack heard the word, understood its meaning, but somehow couldn't grasp how it applied to Ned. He looked around at Mack, but Mack's expression was as haunted as everyone else's.

'He was electrocuted,' Walker continued. 'His body's in the morgue too.'

Jack's head was spinning. Too much death. 'Iris . . .'

'She knows. That's why we've sedated her,' Rupert added unnecessarily.

'I want to see her,' Jack began.

'No!' both Flora and Harold said together.

Rupert stepped closer, put a hand on Jack's shoulder. 'We've only just got her calm, old chap. You can't imagine the state she's in and we're all thinking of the baby. Please, Jack.'

'But —'

'We have to leave now, Jack,' Mack said, pulling his arm.

'No! I won't leave her this way.'

Flora's mouth thinned, her eyes flaring with anger. 'If you can leave your wife, Jack, you can leave our daughter. She's with her family. We'll get her through this.'

Mack pulled again on his arm. 'Johns won't wait much longer. We don't want a scene with security. There's been enough tragedy for one day.'

'Jack, just go. I promise I'll tell Iris you came.' Rupert eyed him intently.

Jack nodded helplessly, control swirling helplessly away from him as he allowed himself to be led back to the car. As they drove away from the Walker property, Jack looked around, craning his head for one last glimpse, but the family had already closed their door and their ranks.

In the back of the car, silent, helpless tears rolled down Jack's cheeks . . . he was no longer sure who he was grieving for.

They were already approaching Five Lights. Oorgaum and the people he cared about were behind him. He absently recognised the hockey pitch moving past as a dark smudge. Johns finally turned on the lights and instantly hit the accelerator, the car gathering speed until Jack could see the tall tower of lights and the five-road intersection coming towards them. In a moment they would be past even the outskirts of Kolar Gold Fields. The life he'd known would be behind him . . . for good.

The journey into Bangalore was mostly silent. Mack had warned him not to remain in the south.

'Heed the warning, lad. The company wants you out of India. If you come back under your own steam, just remember you'll be alone with no protection from Taylor & Sons. Have a spell back at home and give yourself some time to think.'

'What about clearing my name? I don't want people thinking I ran away during the night because I accepted guilt.'

'It's irrelevant. Negligent or not, you were at the controls of the engine. You'd obviously consumed liquor tonight. You're damned either way,' said Johns.

Jack had to stop himself from reaching around Johns' throat and choking him.

'My wife is having a child,' Jack said in a monotone.

Mack sighed. 'Ah, lad, I'm sorry about that. Once the dust settles, the mine can file its report, Taylor & Sons can exonerate you and then you can hold your head high. You can probably be back in a year.' He was being generous. They both knew in their hearts there was unlikely to be any exoneration.

Over the journey Jack had run the scenario through his mind repeatedly and no matter which way he looked at it, he was the operator in charge of lowering the men. Unless the dial could be shown to be faulty – a notion he was clinging to – then he would be roundly blamed for drowning the Indian workers. Unforgivable for any winder, especially an experienced one who knew the dangers. Burrell was checking the pumps – there was maintenance to be done. Stupid, stupid, stupid! He had been distracted by the events of the day.

Jack felt glad that his father was dead and would not have to see Jack return to Cornwall with this burden hanging over him.

'From hero to villain, eh, Bryant?' Johns said, pulling into the driveway of the Bangalore Club. 'Let's hope your friend is still awake.'

Kanakammal stood alone on the back stoop. From her high vantage she had a great view of dawn breaking over KGF. Any moment now and Jack's cockerel would start his crowing to herald the sunrise. The sky was still smudgy with dark clouds, although there was now a golden-pink luminous quality to the east. A new day was almost upon KGF but few would welcome it this morning.

Here he comes, she thought, as the cockerel sprang onto the fence post to tune up. He arched his back, raised his beak and began his first call of the morning to proclaim his territory. He was young and handsome and brash; his harem adored him. He was like Jack!

Jack would be in Bangalore by now. And then he would need to find a ship with a spare berth. She suspected he would be on a train to Bombay and on the sea back to his own country perhaps even before Christmas.

As dawn stole boldly across the sky, Kanakammal reached up and undid the magnificent gold chain of sovereigns Jack had given her and laid it in the veil of her sari on the ground. One by one she pulled off the dozens of gold bracelets he had also presented – for he knew that Indians showed their wealth by the gold they wore and he wanted her people to know that she had married a prosperous man. She removed her earrings and they landed on the veil alongside the other jewellery. Finally she took off the watch Jack had given her, but this did not join the gold. She placed this aside.

She left her wedding ring on – though Jack was lost to her, he was still her husband and she would never take another. Her anklets that amused him so much she had already removed and surreptitiously packed with his clothes. She hoped when he found them he would know she had sent something special of herself to be with him.

Finally, with the jewellery bundled and tied, never to be worn again, Kanakammal stared at the sunrise – at new beginnings – and permitted herself the indulgence of tears. She wept for her lost love and for the child who would never know his father.

46

Henry Berry stared at the broken man in front of him. He'd heard the full and terrible story, taken charge of Jack and booked him into the club.

They sat in Jack's room, a decanter of brandy between them, with glasses of the deep golden liquid still untouched at their sides. Jack's face was covered by his hands as he leaned his elbows on his knees. He looked so distraught, Henry was at a loss. How could so much trauma and hurt and despair surround one man?

He plumped for practicality. 'Taylors will cover all costs for getting you home, old chap. I've got the club making some calls now. It's late but under the circumstances I think we can raise someone in Bombay to check all sailings. I think the *Naldera* might be open. Nice and familiar for you.' He paused, watched his friend, and knew what he was thinking. 'You have to go, Jack. You can't stay.'

'How can anyone find me in Bangalore, Henry? They're villagers!'

'It's not the point. You signed the contract. They're not singling you out. The company wants you gone as per the rules. Don't raise its ire by disobeying, especially if you want to come back to India some time.'

Now Jack raised his head and regarded him.

'You and I both know I'm not coming back, if I leave now.'

'Don't say that. You don't know that.'

'The dials must have given a false reading. I . . . I don't under-stand how else . . .'

'Jack, they have to establish that.'

'I can't defend myself!'

Henry spoke in a freshly soothing tone. 'The machinery will tell its own tale.'

'The dials were compromised. I'll stake my life on it.'

'You don't have to. Taylors will look to prove it.'

Jack gave a mirthless laugh. 'You trust the company, Henry? The company only cares about its name, its reputation. It's hardly going to admit to faulty machinery. Far easier to blame human error and let one man take the whole rap.'

'Well, Jack, right now you are the company and so in pro-tecting you, they do protect the name. Please heed sound advice. You're not seeing things clearly right now and who can blame you. Truly, Jack, what you're enduring is more than any man should have to bear. Give yourself permission to grieve, and to take some time to recover. Sailing back to Britain is the right decision, the only decision.' He sighed. 'Look, I was going to Madras but I'll travel back to Bombay with you. I'll get us on the first train tomor-row morning.'

Jack growled like a wounded animal.

'Don't fight it.'

'I received word today that my father has died. Perhaps it's right I go back and pay my respects, take care of my mother.'

Henry's tic twitched. On top of everything! 'Jack, I'm so sorry.'

'I know. Before you turn in, Henry, I need you to ask you to take care of some things for me.'

'Of course. What sort of things?'

'Property, mainly.'

'Are you sure you can think clearly?'

'There's not really that much to think about but it has to be done. My father taught me long ago that emotion must never get in the way of business. It's one way I can honour him, I suppose.'

Henry thought it was a rather twisted logic but who was he to judge? 'Consider it done,' he said kindly. 'Are you sure you don't want to leave this until you get home, have a chance to think everything through? After all, you might come back, you might –'

'I'm not coming back, Henry. I saw it in my wife's eyes. She knew it too. I think India's been trying to get rid of me since I arrived.'

'Don't be ridiculous, old chap.'

Jack shook his head. 'Too much has happened.'

'But what about your family in KGF?'

'I don't know. I must provide for them. Elizabeth is strong. Stronger than me, than all of us put together. She has family too. I'll make sure she is well looked after, just in case.'

'In case of what?'

'I don't know what the future holds. All I know is that I want to make sure my business here is neatly tied up.'

'Just a moment. I'll get my notebook. We'd better do this properly.'

The next morning Jack Bryant climbed aboard a train bound for Bombay with his good friend, Henry Berry. Three days after his arrival, the *Naldera* did indeed call into Bombay on her way back to London and Henry was able to secure Jack a stateroom.

It took Jack just under four lonely weeks on board, where he kept himself to himself, attended none of the social events, and spent his evenings after a quiet dinner on the most isolated spot of the top deck that he could find, coming to terms with his new life.

Before long, the other passengers stopped trying to find out more about the tall, good-looking gentleman with the west-country accent and respected his obvious need to be left alone. Jack was glad he'd greased the palm of the purser and a few of the bearers on board to surreptitiously pass the word around that he was grieving over two close deaths.

He lost himself in regret for a while. Now, looking back on the last few tumultuous months, he could blame only himself. His desire for Iris had led both her and Ned towards his friend's death. If Jack had only kept his distance from Iris, he was now convinced Ned would still be alive. Perhaps he might not have married Elizabeth . . . and now he had shattered her life too. She had never asked anything of him. Now she carried his child. He wondered whether it would be a son. He hoped so. He intended to make sure that the boy would be able to hold his head high, despite his father's abandonment.

Did he hate himself? Yes.

Would he come back for his wife and boy? He doubted it. There was no future for him in KGF and there was definitely no life for a black woman and her half-caste son in Cornwall. They could have perhaps lived together in Bangalore but the temptation of Iris so near and widowed would be too strong. He knew he would be helpless where she was concerned and he could only imagine her family's reaction if he reappeared in her life. No, Iris had always belonged to Ned and it had taken Ned's death to make Jack realise that he and Iris would never be together.

They could live elsewhere in India – perhaps Madras or Bombay – but tearing Elizabeth away from the family she adored was more cruel than deserting her. Indian families stuck close. Elizabeth felt a strong calling to help raise her siblings and to take care of her parents. It was her role as eldest. Besides, in all honesty he had no desire to live again in India. Now that he was on a ship, back on the seas that he loved so much, he was vaguely excited to be going home.

Jack missed Cornwall.

It seemed Cornwall had missed Jack, too. His welcome to Pendeen was akin to the Prodigal Son. His mother and a small entourage awaited him on the platform when his train from London finally drew into Penzance.

He'd been inhaling the salty air for hours, having hugged the coast on the long journey west. The sight of Cornwall's aquamarine water, her rugged cliffs and green hills filled him with unexpected joy. He didn't mean to allow himself this sense of elation but the countryside alone had begun to lift his spirits.

To see his mother, her lips trembling with emotion to have her precious boy returned just when she most needed his presence and comfort, was the real catalyst to his recovery, though.

'Look at you, my darling. So tanned and strong!'

Jack smiled. 'When did you get frail enough to be in a wheel-chair?' he replied, frowning at the nurse standing nearby in the group of well-wishers.

'Just a precaution, darling. I haven't been too well . . .'

He hugged her again. 'Well, you have nothing to worry about now. I'm home and I'm not going anywhere.'

And he'd held her hand in the back seat of his father's new motor car as they were driven back to the house, which had been renovated and extended to include a whole new wing with its own suite of rooms.

When she had given Jack the tour, walking comfortably arm in arm with her son, Elizabeth Bryant had smiled, her eyebrow arched slightly. 'Do you approve?'

'It's magnificent, but why all the renovations?'

'It's for you.'

'Me?'

'Your father hoped that when you came home you would feel comfortable enough to remain with us. He said we had some ground to make up as a family.'

'He said that?' Jack asked, almost breathless.

She nodded, smiling. 'He loved you. He just didn't know how to say it. This is his way of showing you. I'm so sad he never got to see you again, see your pleasure.'

'Well, I'm here now.'

'Did you come home for us, Jack?'

He tensed beside her.

'No, darling, don't answer that. I'm just grateful the seas brought my son back to me. And I'm sure it's playing on your mind but as I told you in a letter, you were exonerated with regard to the mine disaster.' She raised a hand as if to say *enough*, even though Jack hadn't opened his mouth to speak, and continued as though he had objected. 'It was categorically proved not only that you observed all the right protocols, acting swiftly and decisively, but that you were something of a hero on the rescue mission.' She blinked at him as though he should make no attempt to deny her firmly spoken words.

'I didn't feel like one,' he grumbled in token defiance.

She shook her head. 'Your father was always such a complex fellow. He considered himself a modest man – of course this house and his possessions shouted the opposite,' she sighed, 'but he decided not to make a big thing of the letter from the mine or the visits we had from the people of the whole region who apologised for even privately thinking you may have been to blame.'

Jack looked at her askance. 'They apologised?' he repeated, his expression incredulous.

'Unreservedly. Billy's family was first to queue up,' she said, only a hint of sarcasm permitted to escape. 'Actually, I tell a lie. The first person to offer her deepest regret for how you were treated was Mrs Shand, who much as I adore her seems to hold every living young man responsible for the death of her son. Forgive me, I know that sounds cruel. Darling Jack, you look a picture of shock. Your father was wrong not to tell you. He said it wouldn't have made any difference to you.'

Jack had to agree. 'It wouldn't have while I was in India but now I'm home I think it means everything to me.'

'Hold your head high, son. That was your father's dying wish. He made me promise I would tell you that.'

He said nothing, emotion clogging his throat, but he kissed the top of her head in thanks.

'Come on. I'm cold. Mrs Shand has a fire lit and she's serving tea and crumpets.'

He shook his head, bemused by the sudden familiarity of his old life, and realising just how much he had missed it.

Later, slouched before the fire, the wind beating against the window panes, the Cornish night closing in on Pendeen, he stared into the flames and searched his heart for the guilt he should feel. He came up wanting. Curiously, it was that alone that pricked at his conscience.

'Did you mean what you said, Jack?' his mother asked, searching his eyes. 'Are you home to stay? Will you take over the reins now?'

Jack sat up and fixed his mother with a deep gaze. 'Mother, wild horses couldn't drag me away from Cornwall. Yes, I am home for keeps and I will take over the business and finally make my father proud.'

She sat back, satisfied, before reaching for a small bell on the table beside her. She jangled it, and just for a second, he was thrown back to his last traumatic night in KGF, when bells had announced a tragedy in the making.

A pretty young woman appeared in the sitting room in answer to his mother's summons, mercifully dragging his attention back to the present. Apparently her name was Gloria, but she'd rather daringly introduced herself as Glory.

'That's what everyone calls me,' she'd said, and Jack was sure she'd stopped just short of winking at him.

Gloria Payne was a newly qualified nurse from Redruth who had been hired to care for Mrs Bryant's daily needs. It wasn't that Mrs Bryant needed complex medical help; she was simply emotionally fragile after the death of her husband.

Gloria's role was to help Elizabeth Bryant through this period, make sure a sleeping draught was delivered each evening, be at her side for her walks and run a few errands. It didn't bother her that she wasn't really using her nursing training. In fact, Gloria was delighted to swap her parents' tiny family home in Knox Street for the very grand house in Pendeen, with all the status of looking after the highly respected Mrs Bryant.

But now life had taken a fresh turn, and she could barely contain her excitement. The return home of the fabulously handsome son she'd heard so much about could only make her job more enjoyable.

Gloria Bryant. She liked the way that rolled off the tongue. It was a dashing name, she thought, as she smiled at Jack now. She loved the way he stood at her arrival, his looming presence making her catch her breath.

'Hello, Glory,' he said, his smile broad and sparkling in his bronzed face.

Her knees felt weak. 'Evening, Mr Bryant,' she said, with her most dazzling smile.

'Have you come to take Mother for a nap?'

'A nice bath and to help her dress for supper. Mrs Shand's got a feast prepared for you, Mr Bryant.'

Jack grinned at his mother and she sighed. 'It's so nice to have a man around the house to feed again.'

'Listen, Glory. Call me Jack, otherwise you'll make me feel like my father and we can never replace him, now, can we ?'

'I'll come back for the tray and crockery,' Glory said to him, as she held the door open for Mrs Bryant. There was a definite glint in her eye and she wanted him to see it.

Jack didn't tell his mother that he'd named a young Indian woman in her honour. In fact, it never passed his lips that he had married that Indian girl, or that somewhere across the oceans a child of his was growing inside her.

And as the weeks lengthened into months Cornwall began to feel familiar again, especially the joy of the biting winds on his cheeks, the delicious savoury comfort of eating warm pasties overlooking the view of implacable St Michael's Mount. These were the delights of home, he realised, the small things that suddenly felt important when you'd been denied them.

There were moments when he thought he missed the colours of India – from the jewel-bright saris on the girls to the array of strange and wonderful fruits and vegetables . . . and the pure dove-grey of his wife's arresting eyes. Yes, he missed those colours but he didn't pine for them. That he had to admit.

Jack found he had dozens of ideas about how he could broaden the scope of his father's operation, not the least of which was property – he would start with pubs and inns, investments he was sure would flourish through good times and bad.

Only in very rare honest moments could Jack admit to himself that he revelled in playing the young squire. People looked up to him and although it was still early days, older men – men who used to ruffle his hair as a boy – were now making appointments to call on him. Yes, all in all, Jack had slipped back into Cornish life with ease, driving his father's new car, even planning to set up a townhouse in London and another in the north, perhaps Manchester, for his business trips.

His life in India and the events that had unfolded there began to feel far removed, so very distant and dream-like. The memory of a dusty road and that pretty English-style community that had sprawled either side of it felt like a fantasy, especially now he was back striding across the familiar cliffs of St Just, his new terrier, Conan, gambolling alongside.

This life was real. This was the life he had chosen. And it was, he realised now, the one he had always wanted.

He could hate himself for being so hard-hearted but Jack was used to that feeling of self-loathing. It felt like a comfy old coat, familiar and instantly recognisable and, above all, safe. Safe because when he opened up his heart to someone, invariably it resulted in pain.

Iris was the finest example. She was someone he equated only with pain; her memory still prompted a dull ache when he permitted himself to think of her. The gut-wrenching despair of Ned's death never left, of course. They had parted on such bad terms, had never resolved the issues between them. And Ned died not knowing that the Brent case had been dropped. Henry had taken delight in sending on a telegram attesting to the closure of the case but it felt like a hollow victory. Jack chose to believe it was that case, more than Ned's suspicions about Iris, that had pushed him into the abyss of anxiety that led to him taking that stupid risk with his life.

And Elizabeth – damn it – he couldn't even put together the first few syllables of her real name any longer . . . she was all about pain. So loyal, so trusting, so long-suffering. His guilt over her nagged like an old wound, so he banished it by not allowing himself to dwell on her or his child, due in just a month.

In truth, he had twice tried to write but screwed up the page both times, asking himself what was the point? What could he say to her that didn't sound like a betrayal? It was easier never to mention the Elizabeth Bryant who lived in India; easier, in the end, to pretend to himself that she had never existed.

47

September 1927

Henry loved the south; it was so much cooler than Bombay, where he was posted again full time, and where he was now setting up a proper home for his new bride, Mrs Arabella Berry. Henry's promotion had seen him leap-frog another two levels and he was something of a power-broker in the city for the British Government now. His promotion meant annual trips home to London and a far larger expenses account for his housing, servants, entertainment . . . how could Miss Sinclair have turned him down? Henry liked to tell himself that Bella had married him because he was irresistible, but even when those nasty little internal demons whispered that he was deluding himself, he would gaze at his beautiful young wife, bask in her gloriously sunny smile and remind himself that it didn't matter why – it only mattered that she had. He would keep her busy with the round of important social engagements, not to mention the palatial new house and the retinue of servants under her command. The gowns, the jewellery, the travel and status – he knew they would keep Bella happy . . . and that made Henry happy.

In fact, he was looking forward to writing to his old friend, Jack Bryant, and bringing him up to speed. He was sure it would prompt a big smile from Jack to know that Henry, despite all his moans and groans to the contrary, had found the girl of his dreams.

But before he could write that letter there was some business he needed to finalise. He hadn't been in a position to carry out all of

Jack's requests until now, almost eight months later, when he was back in Bangalore.

He'd spoken to the lawyers and done all that he could, but he was relieved he was finally here in KGF to finish things.

The driver pulled the car in now to the small petty shop run by a man called Chinathambi. He kept the engine idling as Henry, dapper in a white linen suit, emerged, squinting into the sun. He straightened his glasses and walked into the shadows of the shop.

'Hello, sir,' chorused two children.

Henry grinned. 'Well, hello,' he replied, impressed. 'Is this . . . er,' he consulted his notes, 'Chin-a-thumbee's shop, please?'

They giggled at his pronunciation. 'Daddy,' they yelled together and an older man appeared at the back.

'Sorry, sir, sorry. I was just taking a delivery of rice.'

'No problem at all. What a charming pair. Are they your grandchildren?'

Chinathambi laughed. 'They are my children, sir.'

'Good grief, man. Congratulations!'

'I have many, sir. They will look after me in my old age.'

'I believe I'm looking for one of your children, actually. A daughter. She uses the name Elizabeth Bryant, perhaps?'

'Ah, this is Kanakammal.'

'Indeed. Very pretty name. Where might I find, er, Mrs Bryant? I've been asked to contact her by her husband, Jack Bryant.'

The man nodded. 'She will be at the market, now, sir.'

'Oh, right. Well, I could wait, I suppose.'

'She will not mind being interrupted.'

'All right. We shall go to the market. How will I know her?'

'I will send her little brother, Marimuthu, with you. He loves cars, sir,' Chinathambi said, wobbling his head with pride, as he pushed forward a young lad no more than eight years old.

'Excellent. Let's go then, Master M.'

His father briefly gave instructions to the boy and then he clambered into the car's back seat, eyes wide with delight.

It didn't take long to reach Andersonpet; Henry was impressed by how developed it was all this way out in the sticks. He'd visited KGF once or twice before he'd met Jack but curiously never since.

The boy pointed for the driver to turn. 'Here, sir. The market.'

'Jolly good. So, shall we take a walk together?' The streets teemed with people, animals, carts and stalls. 'Good gracious!' Henry added, as they alighted. 'All this food and these lovely smells make me hungry.'

The boy grinned. 'I shall find Kanakammal, sir, if you'll buy me a ladu,' he said, rubbing his belly.

Henry laughed. 'I shall buy you two, young man.'

Marimuthu grabbed Henry's hand. 'Come, sir.'

Henry followed, mesmerised by the market's assault on all his senses. His work, his position and now his status had him moving around in the clean atmosphere of a car, with a driver always on call, taking him from the office to his home. It was a novelty to be amongst Indian people again as they went about their daily marketing.

He moved aside as a bullock meandered through the crowd. It had right of way wherever it chose to go. Small, rangy dogs ran in and around the feet of people, scouting for food scraps.

People were calling out their wares, others asking prices, touching and smelling the goods. The colours were alarmingly bright, saris doing battle with fruit to be the brightest. Nobody batted an eyelid to see a shortish, bespectacled white man being led by a young lad through the throng of stalls selling pots, pans, household goods, past the knife sharpener, shoe repairer, basket weaver and hardware stall, moving quickly towards the fresh market.

Here the fragrance of flowers lured him. Henry paused to admire the garland-makers, little girls who sat cross-legged by their mothers or aunts, surrounded by huge baskets of orchids and bougainvilleas and many blooms Henry couldn't even name. The colours were spectacular; deep reds and creamy whites clashing magnificently with the orangey saffrons and sunny yellows. He strolled beneath the garlands that were hanging up, already prepared and ready for sale, their fragrance enveloping him.

'How much, Master M?' he asked.

The boy grinned and spoke to the vendor.

'She says for you, two rupees, sir.'

'Twice as much for me, eh?' he joked.

Henry didn't mind. Two rupees was a trifle. 'Please ask her to pick me a beautiful one,' he said and handed over the money.

The vendor offered to place it around Henry's neck. 'No, no, thank you. This is not for me.'

They moved on into the vegetable stalls.

'What is that?' Henry said, in awe, pointing to a ridiculously long, dark-green tubular vegetable.

'A bean, sir.'

'It's got to be two feet!'

'Very nice with dhal,' Marimuthu assured.

'And these?' he said, pointing to a pyramid of ugly-looking pumpkin-like vegetables, with knobbles and gnarled shapes.

'Gourds, I think you say.'

Henry was impressed. 'Your English is excellent. I think we should make that three la-doos for you, whatever they are!'

'They are sweets, sir. Come. I will show you.'

He led Henry to various stalls laden with items vaguely resembling biscuits and perhaps fudges, but there was nothing that struck him as being appetising in the way that a tiny cake, a beautiful piece of coconut ice or a toffee, might strike an Englishman. In fact, to Henry, these sweets looked downright unappealing in their bright, vulgar colours, but he could see the youngster was all but salivating.

'Show me,' Henry said.

'There, sir,' Marimuthu said, standing on tiptoe and pointing, his face only just clearing the stall's counter. 'Ladus!'

Henry regarded the smallish, golden orbs, the size of golf balls. 'I see. And what are these made from?'

'I don't know.' Marimuthu laughed. He said something to the vendor that Henry didn't understand but the vendor replied happily enough. Marimuthu looked back at Henry. 'Rice, cashew nut, lots of sugar, ghee, cardamon spice . . . I can't remember the rest.'

'It sounds perfectly horrible, but let's have three, shall we?'

Marimuthu nodded gleefully and ordered his sweets, which were duly wrapped in a small square of newspaper and handed to him as Henry offered a rupee, wondering if it were enough. He was given a handful of change, which he promptly gave to the boy.

'Enjoy,' he said. 'Now, let's find your sister.'

'Come, sir. I think she will be with the spices.'

Henry followed, although the smell of spice on the air hit him well before Marimuthu led him into the darker covered area where the spices were sold. Here, men ran around with little carts laden with sacks of bright-coloured powders and brown- or grey-green seeds. The smell was delicious yet overpowering and Henry instantly began to sneeze. In fact, he couldn't stop sneezing as pepper and chilli, saffron and cinnamon assaulted him, setting off a loud attack.

When Marimuthu pointed excitedly and began dragging him towards a tall figure with her back to him, Henry was digging in his pocket for his handkerchief. A woman with a long dark single plait down her back turned and fixed her pale, arresting gaze upon him. Henry felt suspended in motion, his sneeze instantly stopped.

He realised his mouth was open. And then he exploded into a sneeze, which set Marimuthu laughing. He spoke quickly to his sister. She frowned and then beckoned, gesturing for Henry to

follow. They emerged from the side of the market and she pointed
to a water trough. Henry used it to splash some water on his face,
being careful not to get any in his mouth. Brother and sister waited
patiently as he wiped his face with his handkerchief and composed
himself.

Finally, he sighed, took a deep breath and held out his hand.
'Mrs Elizabeth Bryant?'

She nodded, no smile.

'I am Henry Berry, a friend of your husband's. I brought this
garland for you.'

She regarded him gravely but said nothing.

'Please, do accept the small gift,' he pressed, feeling awkward
with it hanging from his hand.

'Thank you,' she said, quietly, taking the garland but not wearing it.

Henry hurried on, trying not to blink beneath that austere
gaze. 'Er, well, I have some important business to discuss with you,
Mrs Bryant . . . If I may . . . Jack, that is, your husband, asked me to
conduct these formalities on his behalf.'

She didn't say anything at first and it was only now that Henry
noticed she was heavily pregnant.

'Um, Mrs Bryant, I have a car. Perhaps we can take you home?
I . . . I don't have terribly long in KGF and I wonder whether . . .'

She handed her basket of goods to her brother. 'Thank you,'
was all she said again before leading him back roughly the way they
had come.

Marimuthu saw them to the car. Here, she hesitated. It was
clear she hadn't ridden in one before, but watching her brother's
enthusiasm, she followed suit.

'Comfy?' Henry asked, getting in.

'I am,' she said, perhaps a little self-conscious as she stared out
of the window at the villagers.

'We'll have you home in no time. Where shall we head? Perhaps you could tell my driver.'

She directed him and before long Henry recognised KGF. Kanakammal pointed up the hill and they finally pulled into the driveway of a gracious bungalow that stood alone at the peak.

'This is my husband's house. Once the baby is born, I will move. I suppose he will want to sell it,' she said calmly. She didn't wait for the driver to open the door but was out of the car quickly, despite her size, and up onto the verandah to welcome Henry in.

Inside, it was scrupulously clean and neat. It smelled of sandalwood and linseed oil. He was led into a sitting room where a clock was the only sound, ticking away the minutes somewhat ominously, Henry thought. The furnishings were all thoroughly English, even down to the lace runners on the tables and antimacassars on the armchairs.

'Would you like some tea, Mr Berry?'

'That would be delightful, actually,' Henry said, suddenly parched.

She nodded and disappeared, after giving orders to Marimuthu to go back to their father's shop.

'Er, wait, Master M,' Henry said, when he realised the boy was leaving, clutching his precious sweets. 'Thank you for your excellent navigation.' He gave the lad three rupees. He knew it was a fortune to the boy but he liked him, liked the family.

The boy's eyes lit up, his glance searching for his sister in fear that she'd make him return it. He stuffed the money into his shirt pocket. 'Thank you, Mr Berry.'

Henry was left alone to glance around the room that he could swear still smelled of Jack's cigarettes. Kanakammal returned not long after with a tray and all the accoutrements for an English tea.

Henry had been standing by the mantelpiece, admiring two grainy photos of Jack. In one he looked rather solemn but dapper in his suit; in the other he was grinning in shirtsleeves with an arm carelessly thrown over the shoulder of a man Henry recognised as Edward Sinclair.

'Ah, Ned Sinclair. I feel almost responsible for their meeting. Jack and I were at my club when Harold Walker brought a newly arrived Ned from Rangoon. Um, you probably don't know but I married his sister, Arabella, earlier this year?'

'I hope you are very happy.'

He twitched. 'Thank you. We are very happy.'

She nodded, said nothing.

'I was very sorry to hear of Ned's death, of course. And Bella is taking a long time to get over his loss.'

He watched her turn the pot of tea three times. Perhaps Jack taught her that old superstition. 'It was a terrible day for all of us. He died on the day my husband left, the day of the terrible accident at Top Reef . . . and the telegram from England.'

'So I heard. Jack told me, still in shock himself, although he and I haven't spoken since he left.'

'I have not heard from my husband, Mr Berry, and I am unable to write to him because I do not know where he is.'

Henry felt a twist of sadness in his gut for this beautiful woman.

'I see. Perhaps I can give you his address?'

'It has been a long time. He knows where to reach me if he wishes to,' she said and he knew it was an admonishment, even though the words were not said unkindly.

It sat between them that Jack obviously had no intention of contacting her directly.

'When is your baby due, Mrs Bryant?'

'Nine days. It will be a son and you can tell his father that I will name him Charles Edward Bryant and I will keep his father's image and memory strong in his mind.'

Henry swallowed. What a sad situation. 'Er, I shall do that for you.'

'Milk and sugar, Mr Berry?'

'Just milk, please. Mrs Bryant, I owe you an apology. Jack gave me instructions the night before he left Bangalore and on the morning of his departure we visited a lawyer together to finalise his assets and business dealings in India.'

'It seems then he knew he would not return,' she said evenly.

'I cannot say, Mrs Bryant. Jack was very distraught at that time. His thoughts were certainly with you and the child. I'm sure he'll appreciate the names you've chosen.'

She nodded, and waited for him to continue.

'Anyway, down to business,' he said, brightly, covering his embarrassment on behalf of Jack. Henry opened the wallet of paperwork he had brought with him. 'It's really quite simple, Mrs Bryant. Jack has left all his money and all his assets in India to you and your child.'

When she said nothing, Henry took a nervous sip from his deliciously strong tea, and continued. 'Um, let me give you a quick rundown of what that entails. There is this house, of course. There is a very large and beautiful home in Bangalore that is worth a fortune. He bought very well a year ago. There is a property in KGF – it says here it's located at Funnell's Hill. I hope that means something because I am not familiar with it.'

'Yes, I know where that is.'

'Good. Well, this property comprises a shop that has been fitted out and fully refurbished, as I understand it?' He scanned his notes. 'It's ready to open its doors once stocked. Behind it is a small three-bedroomed house with a garden and some outbuildings. The house has been fitted with a newly attached kitchen and bathroom. So that property is complete and could be sold or rented.'

Again, she remained silent.

'And then, of course, there's the money.' Henry cleared his throat. 'It's a sizeable sum, Mrs Bryant. I've written down the amount and it is in a bank in Bangalore. I can have that sent to you as you choose.' He handed her a piece of paper.

Kanakammal took it and read the figure but showed no reaction. Henry wondered whether she fully understood what he had just told her. She was now a very wealthy woman.

'Thank you, Mr Berry.'

'Please call me Henry. I'm sure if we'd met when Jack was here, we'd have been good friends.'

She gave him a small smile and it made a dazzling difference to her countenance.

'I have no need for such money or property.'

Henry smiled benignly, sipped his tea. 'Oh, well, nevertheless, it is all yours to do with as you choose.'

'May I ask for you to help me as you have helped my husband?'

'Of course. I will be delighted to assist in any way that I can.'

'Thank you, Henry. I would like you to sell this house,' she said, looking around.

'Really? But where will you live?'

'My child and I will live in the house behind the shop. I think I will open my own store.'

'Mrs Bryant, is this a little hasty? Perhaps you need some time?'

She shook her head. 'I do not want to remain here. I shall move as soon as the baby is born. You may start whatever preparations you need to make to sell this house. Jack always said the mining company would pay a top price for it.'

Ah, Henry thought, so Mrs Bryant is thinking clearly. 'All right, I shall make an approach to Taylor & Sons. And shall I deposit the proceeds into the bank account that has been opened in your name?'

'No. The proceeds will be used to build a new school in KGF for the local children. I also wish for each family of the men who died in the accident that sent my husband away from me to be given a sum of money. I will leave it to you to work it out. I do not want that money to be traced back to me in any way, but I do not want the mine to take any glory from it either. The families must know that Mr Jack Bryant gave them this money, not out of guilt, but out of care.'

Henry was astonished. Momentarily lost for words, all he could do was nod.

'Will you take care of this for me?'

'Yes,' he finally spluttered. 'I'm sure I can arrange this.'

'Then I am very grateful. There is one last task.'

'Yes?'

'The house in Bangalore you mentioned.'

He dreaded what was coming next. Jack had been so proud of this house. 'Please don't say I have to sell it,' he said, surprising himself.

She smiled again and it touched his heart. 'No. But again I have no wish or need for it in my life. And my son is well provided for.'

'Well, you don't have to decide now —'

'I know exactly what I wish to do with it.'

'Ah,' he said, not entirely surprised any more.

'I want you to sign it over to Mrs Iris Sinclair. Ned's widow.'

It was too much for him. 'Surely not. I mean —'

'I insist. Although I don't wish Jack to know, I think my husband would be very happy that she is living there.'

'I don't understand.'

'It's . . . complicated, as they say,' she said, folding her hands neatly across her swollen belly. 'Perhaps you know that my husband was in love with this woman?'

Henry's tic spasmed and he began to make a blathering sound.

'Please don't be upset. I have always known this. With her

husband dead, she has nowhere to live of her own, very little means other than Mr Sinclair's pension, I imagine. I have more than I need.'

'How do you know all of this?'

She smiled again. 'I take an interest in her because of what she meant to Jack. But I must do so from a distance because she despises me.'

Henry rocked back in his chair. 'And you want to give this woman part of your fortune?'

'Jack loved her. He should have looked after her.'

Henry couldn't fathom it. Was this young woman some sort of apparition? She certainly showed none of the traits he was used to in the women he knew. His own wife would probably need to have a lie-down once she heard this news, especially as he knew Bella had no time at all for Iris Sinclair. In fact, Bella had told him Iris was almost certainly having an affair with Jack Bryant when she was engaged to Ned.

He shook his head. 'I suppose I can't persuade you against this.'

'She has a new baby and she's living with her parents. I see her from a distance and she never looks happy. I think there are too many bad memories for her here – she lost everything that was meaningful to her in the space of a day and night. I have no need for a big house in Bangalore but perhaps Mrs Sinclair might thrive there. She was born and raised in Bangalore, as I understand it.'

'And I suppose I'm not permitted to tell her where this gift has come from?'

Kanakammal flashed him a steely glare. 'She is never to know that I have given this house. Tell her whatever you want, but my name is not to be mentioned.'

He nodded, resigned, took off his glasses, polished them, and put them back on again. 'All right, if these are your instructions.'

'They are. One more thing.'

'Yes?'

Kanakammal rose, left the room and quickly returned with something in a handkerchief. The linen was monogrammed with Jack's initials. She handed it to him. 'Please also give her this.'

Henry opened the handkerchief to reveal a beautiful woman's wristwatch. 'Surely he gave this to you?'

She smiled. 'I do not wear jewellery any more, Mr Berry. I have no need for it. She will cherish it. But please tell her it is a gift from Jack.'

He shook his head in disbelief.

'I will carry out your instructions to the letter, but with your permission I will inform Jack of these details.'

'You said it was my money and property to do with as I please?'

'It is.'

'Then my husband need not be informed of my decisions, other than the naming of our son.'

He nodded. She was absolutely right. 'As you wish. Then I had better see Iris Sinclair immediately and inform her of this gift.'

'Thank you.' She smiled, a flash of wickedness in it that caught him off guard. 'The money in the bank, of course, I shall keep.' And after a brief pause, she laughed deeply and Henry delighted in her amusement. She'd understood everything, particularly that she was now a very rich woman.

48

Iris Sinclair sat across from the government man from Bombay. She frowned slightly, wondering whether he was showing signs of possessing a small tic; catching herself staring she was glad to be distracted momentarily by the servant who delivered her sleeping child back into her arms.

'All clean?' Iris said.

'Yes, madam,' the young woman said and disappeared.

Iris glanced shyly at Henry as she settled the dozing infant with its shock of thick dark hair into the crook of her elbow.

He was in a better position to admire her; the first time they'd met it had been so brief and she had appeared distracted, embarrassed even, and now he knew why. He hadn't fully believed Bella's claim that Jack and Iris were lovers, but the irresistible Kanakammal had confirmed it. She'd been so matter-of-fact, too; Henry was still in awe of her composure and her incredible generosity of spirit. He stared at the other woman in Jack's life: Iris, painfully thin, exquisitely fragile and hauntingly beautiful with it.

Her sadness seemed to seep through her, from the tentative smile to the deep sorrow in her large, dark eyes. 'My parents have been so good to me, to hire some extra help for the baby.'

'He or she?' Henry politely inquired.

'She. I've called her Lily.'

'Iris and Lily ... a tiny bouquet,' Henry said, pleased with himself.

Iris indulged him with a courteous smile and he cleared his throat. 'So, Mr Berry —'

'Henry, please.'

'Henry,' she nodded. 'Let me organise some refreshment for you. It's so rare that I have a visitor.'

'Oh, I can't believe that,' he said, sounding jolly.

But her expression remained pensive and she bit her lip. 'What I should have said is that I rarely accept visitors. I just can't bring myself to make small talk, I'm afraid.' She shook her head. 'Forgive me. Tea or coffee, or perhaps you'd prefer a small sherry?'

'Tea would be lovely,' he replied, wishing his tic would settle and hoping he could manage to drink another cup of tea.

'Sabu,' she said, turning to the door.

'I will organise it, madam,' said the tall Indian who had been standing sentry by the door.

'Thank you. And could you close the door, please?' Iris smiled conspiratorially at Henry. 'My mother uses Sabu as a spy. She'll be desperate to know why you're here, you see, but this way it remains between us.'

He smiled. 'If you don't normally receive visitors, why did you agree to see me, may I ask?'

'Because you mentioned Jack.'

'Ah, even the wretched man's *name* opens women's doors,' Henry said, then wished he hadn't. Iris's expression only became more maudlin. 'I'm sorry,' he said softly.

She shook her head lightly. 'So, is Jack all right, Henry?' She sounded fearful.

'Yes, yes, absolutely; from what I hear, he's fine.'

'We never did get to say goodbye, you see.'

'I know. But as I understand it, he did try to see you.'

'Yes. It was a traumatic time for all of us. I know my family had my best interests at heart, although I'm not sure I've fully forgiven them for not permitting him to say goodbye.'

'I'm sure it was a terrible time for everyone.'

'Jack has never written since, never made any contact, so this is a surprise.'

'He left quite bereft.'

She stared at him. 'So why are you here?'

He reached into his briefcase and withdrew a small sheaf of papers. 'Do you recall the house in Bangalore that Jack bought last year?'

'Yes, I remember it very well,' she replied calmly, but he noticed her blush.

Henry sighed. This felt wrong but he couldn't go against Kanakammal's wishes. 'Jack wants you to have the house. These are the deeds.'

She regarded him for half a minute, unmoving, but it felt like an eternity to Henry. 'May I just check that I've understood you correctly? You're telling me that Jack Bryant has asked for his house in Bangalore to be given to me?'

Henry was a poor liar. 'Well, er, he knew that your husband's passing would have made life difficult for you and the baby.'

Iris shook her head and Henry hated seeing her eyes beginning to water. 'But, why would he do this?'

'Surely because he cares about you?'

She looked suddenly broken. 'It's a glorious house, Henry; I think he wanted it to be a home, hear the sounds of a family in it. It was like his secret but he chose me to share it. We felt very close that day . . .'

'I understand.'

'Ned's sister never did,' she said sadly.

'Iris, there's something I should tell you. Do you remember I told Bella Sinclair that I'd pay her a visit in Madras?'

'I do.'

'Well, I should tell you that Arabella Sinclair is now Mrs Henry Berry.'

'What? Really? Good grief, Henry. You've taken my breath away.'

He laughed. 'I can hardly believe it myself, sometimes. She is a lovely young woman and has fitted into Bombay life with surprising ease.'

'I'd like to see her again some time.'

'She has matured a lot in a year, Iris. And she was devastated by the loss of her brother. I think she would benefit from knowing she had a sister-in-law and larger family down here who cared about her.'

'We do. Of course we do.'

'Then I must bring you up to Bombay some time for a stay with us. Bring Lily. Bella would love it.'

Iris smiled and nodded. 'That would please Ned,' she said, her eyes misting over at the mention of his name. 'Forgive me. It's all still fresh.'

'Again, please don't apologise on my account.'

Sabu arrived with the tray. 'I'll do it, Sabu,' Iris said.

The man moved his head from side to side and left silently, closing the door again.

Henry straightened as she leaned across to pour his tea. 'So, may I take it you are happy to accept this gift?'

She pushed his cup and saucer forward, frowning. 'Why doesn't Jack sell it and keep the proceeds?'

'His father was a wealthy man. From what I can gather he won't be short of a penny. And this is what he wanted, even then.'

'You mean he's planned this gift since last year?'

'It seems so,' he said carefully.

'And what about her?'

'Her?'

'The grasping Indian wife,' Iris said, sudden bitterness lacing her tone.

Henry was stunned. 'Er, do you mean Mrs Bryant?'

'I hate her being called that,' Iris said.

'Why?'

'I always thought Jack married her out of spite.'

'Spite?'

She seemed to regret airing this thought, fiddling with her hair. 'Jack fell out with Ned over our engagement.'

'That's a pity.'

'Jack found it hard to accept my decision to marry Ned.'

'He is not a man to accept failure.'

'No,' she said, suddenly staring into space. 'I wish we'd had a chance to talk before he left.'

'Do you not think he loved his wife?' Henry wondered, trying to keep his tone generous.

'Loved? She was his servant! He married her in a blink.'

'Do you resent Mrs Bryant?'

'Yes, I resent her. But the sad truth is, I am desperately envious of her, Henry, because, you see, I have been lying to myself, lying to my family . . . and worse than either, I lied to Ned. I loved my husband, Henry, but I'm horrified to admit to you – and you only – that even now it's Jack I dream about. It's his face I see before I fall asleep at night and his name that comes to mind when I'm feeling sorry for myself. It should be Ned's. But I loved Jack in a dangerous way,' she said, so baldly, so unexpectedly, that Henry's glasses slipped forward in his haste to stop her telling him any more.

'I . . . er . . . I don't think you should say any —'

'I must. It's time I was honest! All this grieving . . . it's really about guilt. I'm guilty of the worst sort of treachery and I've hated myself, Henry. Until you walked in, I haven't had anyone I could talk to. My family wouldn't understand.'

'Please, Iris. I'm really not —'

But she cut him off again, alarming him by suddenly standing. The baby squirmed but didn't wake. She kissed her forehead.

'Poor, darling Lily. Do you know why I named her that?'

Henry didn't want to know but felt certain she was going to tell him. He shook his head silently, fearful of what was coming.

'Because Jack loved lily of the valley, the emblem of a tin-mining town called Helston, not far from Penzance where he came from. It was his mother's favourite flower. He told me that on our afternoon in Bangalore.'

Henry swallowed hard. He sensed where this was going.

Iris had a fire in her eyes now, and it blazed with memory and a guilty joy. 'You see, Henry, Lily is not Ned's child.' Henry's throat closed with fear and deep regret. 'She is the product of that afternoon with Jack in Bangalore. I make it sound dirty but it wasn't. It was pure and very wonderful. We were in love but we knew it was wrong.'

'Did Ned know?'

'Perhaps about Jack and myself, I can't be sure, but not about our baby.' Her face sagged. 'At least, I don't believe so ... I hope not, for his sake.'

'So Bella was telling the truth.'

Iris nodded. 'She was. I lied to her, to Ned, to my family and to myself. I suspected I was pregnant as I was formally engaged. My body had a serious reaction and I was sickening constantly. I knew I had to marry Ned quickly.'

Henry's face must have expressed his horror. 'Does Jack know?' 'No!'

'But why didn't you tell him?'

Iris began to pace, swaying with each step to keep the baby peaceful. 'I don't know.' She shook her head, a combination of anger and regret in her expression. 'I . . . there were so many people involved. I was frightened. Ned – oh, poor Ned,' she wept, clutching Lily closer. 'He was such a lovely man. He loved me so much, Henry, so much that I just couldn't hurt him. He was so excited about the baby. And I knew Jack was too dangerous to love. I couldn't trust that he'd stay.'

'And he didn't,' Henry said softly, almost to himself. 'He left two of you, pregnant and alone.'

'Perhaps you will tell him,' she said, pulling a hanky from a pocket. She sniffed. 'He should know about her,' she said, staring lovingly at Lily. 'I know he's not coming back. If he wanted me with him, he could have written, or found a way to get a message to me. Despite all I once said to the contrary, I would have gone, run to his arms in Cornwall, but . . .' She looked at him, wearily. 'Just tell him about Lily, that's all.'

'I'll write to him as soon as possible, I promise. And you'll take the house?'

'Yes, I'll accept Jack's house on his daughter's behalf. She will have somewhere beautiful to grow up in and to remember her father by. It will force me to be honest about Lily with my family too. Bangalore will be good for us. I can get a job as a schoolteacher – perhaps at my old school across the road.'

'I'm glad,' he said, relief flooding through him.

'I'm very grateful for your understanding.'

'Oh, there is one more thing,' he said, praying he could do this next bit without adding to the whole sorry tale of lies. 'I was asked to give this to you as well. Perhaps it is something Lily can wear when she's older.' He held out the watch.

Iris gave a soft gasp. 'I thought he gave it to his servant.'

He hated the way Iris denigrated Kanakammal. Henry didn't dare speak for a few seconds. He shook his head, then shrugged to cover his embarrassment. 'Perhaps his wife wore it for a while.

Anyway, it is a gift to you.'

She took it and he nearly sighed with final relief that his part in this was complete.

'I shall caretake it for Lily. It makes me feel very special to know that he remembered and wants me to have this.'

Henry stood, eager to be gone. 'Well, I should be going. I'm at the Bangalore Club for another couple of days if you have any questions, but I think everything is in order now. I'm deeply sorry again about your husband.'

She smiled sadly. 'Thank you. Everywhere I turn is a constant reminder that he's not here and not coming back.'

He wasn't sure whether she meant Ned or Jack . . . perhaps she didn't know either. Henry gave a small bow. There really was nothing more to say. Iris saw him to the door and waved as he climbed into his waiting car.

He had never been so relieved to see his driver. 'Get me out of here, George.'

And as they passed a busy junction where five roads connected and then drew level with a large neem tree on the left, he saw Jack's wife standing beneath its branches, a radiant ivory sari draped gracefully over her bulging belly. As he saw her, her name came to him in perfect rhythm. *Kanakammal*. She was tracing a finger on the bark of the tree.

'Stop, please,' he said.

Henry got out of the car and walked up the slight incline to her. 'It's done,' he said.

She nodded. 'I am glad.'

'Are you sure there is nothing else I can tell Jack?'

She paused, considering his request. 'Please tell my husband that his son and I will pray for his happiness every day. And that I heard him say my true name the night that he left . . . and that it gave me joy to hear him speak it.'

And then she turned and walked away in her bare feet, heading down the road to KGF.

Henry felt momentarily lost. He glanced towards the tree and noticed the initials *JB* carved into the bark. It was an old marking, perhaps when Jack had first arrived in KGF and made his decision to stay. Nearby was another set of initials – *ES* – and Henry felt a spike of sorrow.

He swung around to watch Kanakammal again, hoping she might pause, or even turn to say more, but she never looked back.

49

Gloria watched Jack as he sat alone at the bottom of the walled garden reading the letter she had picked up from the post office that morning. It had arrived by special delivery and was obviously important.

She'd held it up to the sunlight, trying to see what she could make out, but no luck. The neat handwriting on the back told her it was from a man called Henry Berry, postmarked Bombay. She'd read about Bombay once in a magazine but she had no desire to see exotic places where coloured people lived and wild beasts roamed the streets. No, she was happy to stay in Cornwall and find herself a good husband.

She glanced back towards Mrs Bryant's dressing room, waiting for her mistress to emerge, but quickly returned her gaze to the son and sighed as she stared at his thick dark hair. What wouldn't she give to run her fingers through it? His face was hidden but she knew it well enough in her dreams.

There was tension in the hunch of his shoulders and she had watched him read the letter more than once, poring over its pages.

'Gloria, dear?' Mrs Bryant's voice startled her. 'Have you seen my son anywhere?'

'He is in the garden. He's had a letter from India,' she said carefully.

'Oh?'

559

'Yes.'

'Good. I was hoping I hadn't missed him,' Elizabeth said, pulling on a single strand of pearls.

'Do you think he'll ever go back?' Gloria said, watching Jack from the corner of her eye. He seemed to be staring into space.

'To India? Over my dead body! No, I have my son back with me now and everyone here knows he's been exonerated from any fault in the Levant disaster. Cornwall is where he will remain. There's nothing in India for him.'

'Do you want me to fetch him for you, Mrs Bryant?'

'Thank you, dear.'

Gloria couldn't get down the two flights of stairs and into the side garden quickly enough, having to stop herself running by the time she was out of the double doors and onto the small patio. She slowed down, smoothed her clothes and took a deep breath.

She sauntered along the winding path that would take her beneath the magnificent rose arbour and down to the bench beneath the apple tree. But when it came into view, it was empty. Jack was just closing the back gate and standing on the other side.

'I'm sorry to disturb you, Mr Bryant,' she said.

Jack swung around wearing a faraway expression.

She nodded towards the envelope. 'I hope it wasn't bad news.'

'A friend writing with all the latest gossip, that's all.'

'Do you miss it?' she asked shyly.

'Sometimes.' He hesitated but then shook his head. 'Did you want me for something?'

'Mrs Bryant sent me. She wonders if you'd come and see her?'

'Certainly,' he said.

She took her chance. It was rare that she had any time alone with him. 'I don't mean to speak out of turn, Mr Bryant, but you've made her very happy by coming home. I think we're all very pleased to have you here.'

'That's kind of you, Glory. You must remember to call me Jack.'

She grinned. 'You should get yourself out a bit . . . Jack, if you don't mind me saying so.'

'Out?'

'You know, dancing, or perhaps to a show. I think you could do with some cheering up.'

She tried not to squirm as his hard gaze regarded her silently in the late-afternoon sunshine. Summer was ended and the leaves were just turning. It was still mild enough to sit outside in his rolled-up shirtsleeves. She noticed the tan on his thick arms had long ago faded and she hoped his memories of India would fade equally quickly.

'Maybe you can help cheer me?' he said suddenly.

She felt her pulse quicken, wanted to respond eagerly, but he'd already turned his back on her and she couldn't tell whether he was simply teasing.

'Come on, Conan,' he said softly to the small dog, and over his shoulder he murmured, 'Tell Mother I'll be up shortly.'

Before Gloria could say another word, he strode away.

———————

Jack didn't want Gloria's company and he couldn't face his mother immediately. The letter had unsettled him, stirring buried emotions. He had thought he'd locked India and his time there safely away, not to be glimpsed again. But Henry's succinct prose had reopened the past and Jack had to confront it again.

He hadn't meant to walk this far but he found himself sitting on the clifftop down the lane from Pendeen church. It had become a place of keen significance for him and he frequently came to this same spot where he'd last spoken to his father, as if by being here he could hang onto Charles Bryant, feel close to him.

Jack read the letter again and it still seemed unreal that he was now the father of two children. A daughter to Iris, whom she had called Lily. Henry wrote that Iris wanted Jack to know she had named the child for him.

Henry didn't dwell on Iris, which gladdened Jack because he knew that she'd been right; their affair had been doomed from the outset. He could see that now. Thinking about Iris could still ignite his desire, but did he truly love her? With the benefit of hindsight and distance, he suspected that passion, perhaps even lust, had been confused for love. A vague sense of shame niggled, but if he could ignore the guilt for long enough, he would leave it behind, just as he'd left behind the women whose lives he had irrevocably changed in India. Iris would never be without suitors, and once her grief was set aside she would be open to their approaches. Henry assured that while Ned's widow appeared thin, she was also looking forward to a new future in Bangalore.

Jack's feelings towards his daughter were quite different. In fact, his heart lurched at the news of Lily and he made a solemn private promise that he would support her and ensure a good education, whatever she needed. Jack even wistfully imagined them meeting one day; he could picture her arriving off a ship in Southampton, dark and beautiful like her mother. He suspected he would fall instantly in love with his daughter, and it would be a real love.

But if his heart had skipped a beat at the news of Lily, it seemed to break at the knowledge that he now had a son. Henry, back in Bombay, had received word that Kanakammal had given Jack a fine, strong son, as she'd promised. She had called the boy Charles after his Cornish grandfather. Jack wept as he read Henry's precisely looped handwriting once again:

> *When we met she gave me the impression that she will do all in her power to ensure that your son knows you. She hopes you will meet him one day but until then will keep your*

*memory alive for him. No distance will prevent him growing
up honouring you as you honour your own father.*

Jack crushed the letter in his fist. His wife was showing him
that she forgave him all the sorrows he had brought upon her and
that she had kept the very best of him – his son. The Bryant line
lived on through this boy and he kept chewing at the notion that he
must bring this child to Cornwall so that he might know the land of
the Bryant men that had gone before him.

Jack was struck by the painful irony that his son and his father
not only shared the same name but managed to prompt identical
anguish in him. Would young Charles love him? It was a question
that had always gnawed at Jack regarding his father. More importantly, would Jack live up to the honour that Kanakammal spoke
of? He would try to. Kanakammal was making it possible for
him to start developing a relationship with his son. She asked for
nothing more from Jack, but would she let him take Charles away?
No mother gave up her son willingly. Jack didn't care. He wanted
his boy at his side more than anything else he'd ever wanted in his
life. And it wasn't just a wistful dream that he could ease his son
into the family business empire that Jack had such big plans for.
The notion felt real and attainable. Perhaps he could, at last, do
something right in raising a son properly; something that the elder
Charles would approve of. Imagining his father as finally proud of
him brought fresh tears to Jack's eyes, but it was a good feeling, an
exciting one, that lifted his spirits and banished the heaviness that
he'd carried in his heart this last year.

Jack looked out to sea as the soft summer breeze dried the
tears on his cheeks, and the emerald water and cloudless sky made
him momentarily dream of sailing again to an exotic land where, in
fields of gold, his past and his future awaited him.

Author's note

The story of my two grandfathers – one a Cornish miner, the other a Scot who lost his mother when the family was in Rangoon, and who both ended up in Kolar Gold Fields in the 1920s – has been buried in our family's history for long enough that no one else but a writer growing up within its ranks would see its fascinating potential. My maternal grandfather did marry a wonderful Anglo-Indian called May Iris, the daughter of a doctor, and they had seven children and remained happily married until he died suddenly aged forty-two. James Patton is my Ned in this tale; he did flee Burma, did become an electrician and was the manager of the KGF electric department at his death. Meanwhile, my paternal grandfather, John Richards, known as Jack, did ride motorbikes, did own property and most certainly did marry his beautiful Indian servant – I'm sure much to the shock of his peers. She gave him three sons. Her name was Kanakammal – but he called her Elizabeth for ease.

I am the only blood granddaughter of this quartet. Both my grandfathers died long before I was born but I did enjoy an especially happy and loving relationship with my granny (May), who migrated to England where I was born. I met Kanakammal when I was teenager in 1973 and fell in love with her for the short time we were together in India. She died a few months later.

To my knowledge my grandfathers barely knew each other in

life – neither did my grandmothers – but why on earth would I ruin a good story with the truth!

This is a work of fiction so I haven't aimed for historical accuracy at every turn, even though I borrow ruthlessly from real times and events. Thus I have taken liberties with dates and facts and even crafted a non-existent shaft in KGF. Any discrepancy a well-informed reader might spot is likely deliberate, and if accidental, is my own fault and not that of my brilliant team of generous and willing helpers around the world.

I wanted this novel to read with pace and ease, so I have consciously avoided trying to recreate the language, dialects or manner of speaking of the time in which this story is set. My aim for this tale is purely to entertain. I do hope it does just that. Thank you for reading it.

Acknowledgements

Where to begin to thank a small army of people who have been instrumental in getting this project from idea to reality?

I guess it begins with one of Australia's most beloved storytellers. Bryce Courtenay convinced me ten years ago to write a book and set me on a new career path. *Fields of Gold* is my sixteenth novel and it's the one I've always wanted to write. Thank you, Bryce, for insisting I finally write it and also to Bob Sessions at Penguin for becoming such a strong supporter of this project and for giving me the wonderful Ali Watts as my editor. Ali, you are pure joy to work with. Thanks also to Belinda Byrne for your brilliant, hard work to help me to get the very best out of this story. Of course, all my new Penguin friends deserve big hurrahs – Gabrielle, Peg, Peter, Lou, Sally, Dan, Mary – thanks all for the support and highly professional way in which you do everything.

So many people I now realise have been involved in helping me to garner the research material I needed. Ian McIntosh must take pole position here, having read so many books on every subject from life in the times of the Raj to endless ship manifestos during the 1920s . . . and for taking me to India to retrace the footsteps of my grandparents as well as to meet the family I barely knew I had in Bangalore. Thanks also to Nicole Lenoir Jourdan and all at India Tourism for their brilliant support in making Bangalore, KGF and Tumkur so accessible to us for the book's research; to the fantastic

VisitBritain team in helping me to get across to Cornwall and to have four days exploring that magnificent coastline. And in Penzance, my sincere thanks to Pete Joseph, curator of the Trevithick Society, who selflessly gave his time and knowledge to me on everything from the St Just region history to where the best pasties are cooked in Penzance. In Cornwall, Carol Heathcote from the Chacewater Society was relentless in her determination to help me find my grandfather's place of birth and baptism.

Malcolm Longstaff, thank you, for your seemingly endless historical knowledge of passenger ships, and thanks to the wonderfully calm Kristin Stammer for your timely help.

Draft readers – Pip Klimentou, Sonya Caddy, Judy Downs, thank you! And to the enthusiastic booksellers in Australia who have no objection to me writing across genres and cheerfully help readers to find me all over their stores.

My gratitude to the sprawling family who gave me the bones of this story at the outset, and finally to my own trio, Ian, Will and Jack . . . love and thanks for your endless patience and support that allows me to disappear for hours to write my stories.